I0614681

Readers love the Wolf Winter series by TA Moore

Dog Days

"Wow. *Dog Days* turned out to be even more than I expected… Trust me when I say you won't regret reading this… not if you love twists, turns, and horror."

—Rainbow Book Reviews

"I really enjoyed *Dog Days* and I am really hoping there is more to come."

—Joyfully Jay

"I was completely sucked into this story right from the beginning. I couldn't put the book down. I was completely fascinated with the lore and how the world is set up and the background for each character."

—Molly Lolly Reviews

Stone the Crows

"…it's a stunner at every level and element. Horror, urban fantasy, and romance. There is nothing this author and book doesn't excel at."

—Scattered Thoughts and Rogue Words

"It's well written with strong characters, good pacing, compelling plot and realistic world building."

—The Novel Approach

By TA Moore

Every Other Weekend
Ghostwriter of Christmas Past
Liar, Liar
Take the Edge Off

BLOOD AND BONE
Dead Man Stalking

DIGGING UP BONES
Bone to Pick
Skin and Bone

ISLAND CLASSIFIEDS
Wanted – Bad Boyfriend

LOST AND FOUND
Prodigal

PLENTY, CALIFORNIA
Swipe
Bone to Pick
Skin and Bone

WOLF WINTER
Dog Days
Stone the Crows
Wolf at the Door

Published by DSP Publications
Collared

Published by Dreamspinner Press
www.dreamspinnerpress.com

TA MOORE

WOLF AT THE DOOR

DREAMSPINNER PRESS

Published by
DREAMSPINNER PRESS

5032 Capital Circle SW, Suite 2, PMB# 279, Tallahassee, FL 32305-7886 USA
www.dreamspinnerpress.com

Trade Paperback ISBN: 978-1-64405-719-3
Digital ISBN: 978-1-64405-718-6
Library of Congress Control Number: 2020940946
Trade Paperback published October 2020
v. 1.0

Printed in the United States of America

To the Five, who always believed in me. To my mum, who always gets the first copy. To Elizabeth North and Lynn West, who gave this series a chance.

Prologue

For the first time in generations, the Numitor came down from his high perch, crossed the dark waters of the loch, and walked into town. He arrived on four feet, drenched and with ice heavy in his thick ruff, but shrugged his skin back on and padded naked through the empty streets.

A courtesy he remembered, although to whom had slipped away from him.

Wolves wore the years lightly enough. The Numitor might be old, his hair run to gray and most who'd loved him in the ground, but he was strong and straight. Every full moon he led the hunt, and only a few of his wolves could keep pace with him. But if age couldn't claim her tithe from his flesh and bones, she'd take her due from his memory.

She'd give him fifty years, a hundred even, but after that, she had first pick. It had seemed like nothing at first—a first kiss whose face was worn down to the scruff of ginger stubble and the *idea* of love, a brawl he could remember every detail of except it floated unmoored in the "when," a promise he'd made to someone important enough it was ingrained in his bones even when the idea of them was a ghost—but what was gone was gone forever.

Now, when he looked back over his long, bloody life, it was like an old house someone had started to shut up for the night. Some rooms were lost, bricked off, and others were only lit by a few fairy lights of sweet memories. And every time one of his old friends died or some touchstone wore to nothing under the passage of years, another light went out.

Frost crusted on the thick fur that layered his body even as a human and pinched his toes and the tips of his ears as he walked through the abandoned brick boxes of Lochwinnoch. Most people had left early, locked their doors and drawn their curtains behind them. For a few days after the town was all but abandoned, it still lit up at night, clockwork precise as the old lamplighters, until the wind tore up the electricity pylons. Some villagers had left it until the last moment—the priest, old farmers in their crofts—as though they thought the old gray stones of this place somehow belonged to them.

The Numitor had sent the Wild to the wolves to show them their error. Broken doors and slaughtered herds, supplies that rotted overnight or sprouted like they'd been planted and seen the year through to harvest.

He'd no desire to kill them. The people of Lochwinnoch had been tolerable enough over the decades, insular and incurious about their neighbors and the sullen, wild children who came over the lake to have figures and letters drummed into their heads no matter how much they snarled about it.

They were wolves, but they were men too. A wolf had its fangs and its speed, but a man had the brain between his ears and what he put into it. The Numitor had no room in his space for a fool who wouldn't keep both honed.

Tolerable or not, there was no place for them here but in the ground. The Wolf Age had begun, and there was no place for men but as prey.

Most of them had realized that on their own. They'd left their houses open to the elements, once-scrubbed hallways full of snow and the things they held precious left to crack and ruin in the cold. Better the things than the people. For now, anyhow.

As for the ones who'd stayed, the Numitor had come to deal with them himself. Some things you didn't delegate.

The old gray walls of the church were limned with ice. It dripped down from the snow-tipped spire and clotted around the windows and the high peak of the door. The Numitor's skin stuck to the black iron gate, the metal hinges frost-cracked and broken, as he pushed it open and walked up to the door.

It was unlocked. Not that it would have stopped him if it weren't.

Candles burned on every surface—thick yellow wax dripped in long trails down the altar and walls, and cast unsteady, gray shadows over the walls and windows.

The priest was still there, seated in black robes and a heavy parka on one of the old oak benches. A black fisherman's hat was pulled down low over his ears, and white tufts of hair stuck out under it. The head was in his lap, loosely cradled in his arms. It had been severed roughly at the neck, the skin torn in ragged strips and the pink-stained vertebra cracked.

Blood puddled around the old man's boots, dark red and curdled with the cold as it sank into the stones. It was still fresh, the salt and metal tang of it sharp as it rose off the cold stone.

The bittersweet nostalgia that had dogged the Numitor's heels like weeds from the lake withered under a raw-meat flash of anger. He had no real desire to murder an old priest tonight, but that someone had dared to snatch his kill from between his teeth made him growl. The sound echoed off the high bare walls.

"So, whose balls dropped?" the Numitor asked. He walked into the church, and his feet left wet prints on the stone as he paced from flag to flag. The air smelled of blood and hot wax, cut with a bitter undertone of some spiced incense that itched the throat. He coughed and spat to clear it. "Or was it your fangs? You here to challenge the old wolf?"

Somewhere in the building, something scraped, metal on metal. The Numitor turned toward the noise and took a step forward. His heel came down in the puddle of blood, unexpected warmth between his toes, and then he heard the heavy rasp of labored breathing outside.

More than one. Had he grown old enough to miss such an obvious trap, he wondered, but then he felt the evergreen tug of the Wild in his bones. He took a deep breath of it—a cold so clean it burned—and let it ripple through the church. For a moment, haphazard old trees, trunks glued together with moss and frost, took the place of the walls. The eerie blue of a sky untouched by smog shone overhead, and a stag's raw head, antlers glassy with ice, was strung from the branches. Misshapen shadows moved through the trees, snouts wreathed with the wet steam of their breath.

In the Wild they stank of rot, greasy sweet like old pork in the back of the Numitor's throat, and a hint of that sweet, pickled incense. He let the woods and the trees slip away from him, burst like bubbles on the hard-edged stone of this world, and he could almost taste the smoky burn of perfume on his tongue and something like….

Sickness. The nicotine and sour smell of a sick room, of curdled ulcers and the hopeless sweat of someone who didn't think they'd get better. The stink of it reached down the Numitor's throat and stoked the heady flush of anger. Another scent cut through that fetid stink, though—a familiar one.

He pulled the wolf up until it pressed hot and itchy against the underside of his skin, the fangs and ache behind the bones of his skull.

"Jack," he said. He should have known. What other wolf would walk the Wild to come and challenge him here? Now, at the end of things. The reek of them… there were strange things in the Wild these days. Old things. Maybe they'd killed something foul and rolled in it. "Gregor. Which of you is it, boy? Who's come home?"

It shouldn't have been an easy choice. He'd tried to love them both, and he would mourn the fallen, but he knew which son would take something of who the wolves were now through the long wolf age.

The wolf split through his skin. He let the thick, dense hair bristle over his shoulders and crawl down to his knuckles, the sharp nails on the ends of his fingers split to let claws through, but no further. The wolf pushed at the back of his throat, but he scruffed it back. He wanted to say goodbye to his last son.

It was the first time he'd been challenged and not wanted to win. He'd kill his child—again—if he had to. The wolves needed a strong leader, but if Jack, or Gregor, put their teeth in his throat, he'd not curse them for it.

Age had already closed up the windows and boarded the doors of his life. Maybe it was time for him to turn off the lights and leave before winter.

"DON'T KEEP me waiting," he said, the wolf's rasp trapped under his tongue. "Come and give an old man a hug before you try to kill him."

Someone stepped halfway out of the shadows behind the altar. A raw scalp shone red in the candlelight, black charred strings of flesh stuck to it, and a bloodshot eye peered at him from under a scar-wrinkled, stitched-open eyelid.

"If you insist," she rasped, the inside of her mouth bright and blister raw. "Take him."

The windows smashed, shards of stained glass bright as they rained down into the church. Splinters of it caught in the dead priest's coat and lay in bright flakes on the puddle of his blood. The Numitor instinctively turned his head away, one hand raised to shield his eyes, and felt the needle pricks of it against his skin.

"Old wolf," something slurred, the words wet as though it had to chew them out, "Old man. Easy prey."

The Numitor dropped his hand. Threads of blood dribbled down his palm and dripped onto the stone. Three raw-boned things—all broken bones and twisted flesh—jumped down into the church. Bones poked out of them at strange angles, broken and taped back together with straps of muscle, and hair sprouted in mangy lines and patches of matted, tawny fur. Inked lines pulled out of true over humps of muscle that bulged at shoulder and hip, sutured lines pulled tight enough to tear and peel. Broken, ragged bone stuck out of their mouths, between and behind small human teeth, and the insides of their mouths were bloody red bags of skin.

He had seen monsters before. When he was young, the Wild had still spread across the world, thin in places, pulled taut over worked stone and mathematics that merchants brought back from the East, but deep as a lake in others. Things had lived in those places, monsters that no human had seen and lived to spread stories about and that wolves were smart enough to hold their tongue on.

Even centuries back, things like this in a town they'd burned. Twisted bones and monstrous stories had been blamed on the plague, and after some thought, the survivors of the neighboring towns had chosen to believe it.

But he'd never seen the ink he'd worked into his sons' skins strained over the leathered hide of a thing.

The Numitor let the wolf have him. The huge gray dire wolf, built with the shoulders and jaws to take down an Irish elk, to fight off a bear, snarled and lunged for the monster that wore his son.

Or had *been* his son.

CHAPTER ONE—JACK

THE BLADE hurt least the first time it went under Jack's skin. In the moment, as the old bitch sliced him from hip to hip and unzipped him like a coat, he hadn't thought that was true, not as she pinched the flap of his flesh between bony fingers and peeled it off his bones, the raw crackle of torn fibers lost under the raw scrape of his screams.

Then it grew back.

Soft skin, raw nerve endings, virgin flesh.

Then the old bitch started again, and it hurt more this time. And the next. The next....

Jack startled out of the memory. The back of his throat felt caked, thick with the taste of his own pain, and a snarl tried to find fangs to twist over. His heart hammered against his breastbone, alarmed at the phantom threat of pain, and he reached out blindly for Danny.

He was there, curled against Jack's side under a tangle of blankets. Jack gripped his forearm for a moment—warm skin and muscle under a scratchy Aran sleeve—and then rolled away from him. He sat up, the stink of his own sweat with him, and caught the jet-black glitter of eyes in the dark on the other side of the car.

Wolf eyes saw better in the dark, but even skin-side Jack wasn't human. It took a second for his eyes to adjust, but once they did, he picked out the silhouette of the little god sitting cross-legged on one of the crates. If Jack had been a god, even a minor one, he'd have picked a better body to steal than Nick Blake's. Even the heavy wool coat he wore didn't add enough bulk to his scrawny frame, and he had the face of a ferret behind that nose.

Maybe a bird. Definitely not a wolf.

Yet Gregor loved him. Jack still wasn't sure what put him on his heels more, that his brother *could* love or that he loved someone that had been—mostly—human at one point.

"You should sleep," Jack said. His voice sounded rough as it squeezed out of his throat, and it still tasted of blood. He wiped his mouth on the back of his hand and was glad it was dark. He didn't need to see if his dreams had clawed his throat raw again.

Nick smiled wryly and shoved his hand through his crest of dark hair. It had gotten darker since they jumped the train in Girvan, a stain that spread down the strands like reverse aging.

"That's what he says," he said. Jack glanced automatically at Gregor, his brother's body sprawled out as though, even in sleep, he was too arrogant to worry about anything. In disagreement, Nick clicked his tongue behind his teeth and, when Jack looked back at him, tapped his finger against his forehead. "The bird. He wants to roost."

"But you want to watch me sleep?"

When Nick smiled, Jack could see the old bitch from Girvan in his face. It was in the slightly crooked cant of his mouth, the long crease of a dimple that slashed from cheek to nearly his jaw. The family resemblance wasn't strong, but it was there. Sometimes Jack wasn't sure what bothered him more, when he saw Nick's god or when he saw his grandmother.

"You aren't sleeping," Nick pointed out.

Jack grimaced and pushed himself up off the floor in one smooth movement. He wanted to turn his skin and run on four legs, track the slow crawl of the train through the white countryside. Life was always easier in the wolf's heart, the chaff of regret and doubt shed like a baby tooth. Except he didn't trust Danny to Nick's care, not after the old bitch had collared and leashed Danny, bound him into a dog's skin against his will when even Jack—the Numitor's own get—hadn't known that could be done.

The prophets had known. It turned out that the prophets knew a lot of things wolves didn't—a fact that made Jack even more uneasy than the current company.

"What did your gran tell you about us?" Jack asked.

Nick shifted. "Nothing," he said. "Before Girvan, I thought she was dead. I hadn't spoken to her since I was taken into care."

For a second the horror of the ruined old wolf with the knife and Nick's smile on her face was cut through with contempt. Every wolf in the Old Man's territory knew to stay under the radar of the authorities. They went to school enough not to raise alarm in their neighbors, and when they had to go into town, they behaved themselves… more or less.

None of the Scottish wolves cared that much for humans, but only a fool ignored that they could be dangerous if they had the numbers. A fool or a prophet, he supposed.

"She never talked of the wolves before that? Of the prophets? Her plans?"

The bird-bead glitter went out of Nick's eyes, and he looked simply human again as he hunched down into his coat. He pulled the cuffs down over his hands.

"Nothing useful," he said. "Children's stories, about the Wolf Winter and the wolves who'd come down over the Wall."

"Is that why you can't sleep?" Jack asked. "You think we're going to kill you?"

Nick glanced past him, into the shadows. His eyes flickered as though whatever he could see had moved. "Wolves weren't the only monsters in her stories."

Something cold tickled the back of Jack's neck, a thread from his T-shirt, a rough tag, or a single ragged nail. Jack tried to ignore the itch. He couldn't stomach it for long and snarled in frustration to himself as he spun around to see what Nick saw behind him. Nothing. Even when he tugged at the Wild, the smell of cold heather sharp in his nose, there was nothing there, just a faint stink of old meat and old milk that clung to the tarred oak walls.

The smell hadn't been there before. After a few days in the car, doors pulled shut against the sporadic inspections of the armed escorts, Jack knew what every corner and board smelled like. The faded stink of human sweat, fresh—or it had been yesterday—blood from the man who'd tried to catch a ride on the train and went under the wheels instead.

Nothing like milk.

"What was it?" he asked.

"Nothing," Nick said. His eyes still looked human, unusually dark but without the obsidian glitter of an animal. There was something sad in the set of his mouth, and there wasn't anything of his grandmother in that. "An old grudge."

Jack shook himself. He was a wolf. The strangest thing he'd ever met was himself, but the Wolf Winter had brought more than snow and blood out of the Wild. Maybe the prophets knew what. Nick's grandmother had certainly known how to open the way across… even if they had stopped anything at the threshold.

It had been an insult originally, the prophets. The wolves only sent the dregs of their kind to parlay prayers, the caitiffs and the degenerates, to show what they thought of the gods. In hindsight that might also have been a mistake. The prophets knew more than they told in the catechism or read in the auguries, and they hadn't shared all of it with the wolves.

At least—Jack thought grimly of Job's claim that the Old Man had full knowledge of all this—he hoped they hadn't told.

"Go to sleep," Jack ordered roughly, as though there wouldn't be anything there if Nick didn't get to see it. "We'll reach Irvine tomorrow, and there's no more free ride after that. We walk."

It was the god who laughed, a caw of scratchy amusement as Nick tilted his head to the side. "You'll walk."

It wasn't the Wild. Jack knew the Wild—the smell and taste of it. Whatever it was that flickered around Nick was something… else. Something that smelled like the charred bones and long dead of the bonefires on the beach.

Whatever it was wiped Nick away and let the bird out. The coat dropped in a heavy puddle to the crate below. An empty sleeve dangled limply over the edge, and a black crow-like bird mantled a thick ruff of feathers. A black eye glittered at him down the pickax length of bone-white beak, old words carved like scrimshaw along the smooth plates, as it turned its head to watch him.

It was only the human gods the wolves had issue with, the ones that had made them and used them and then shat on their long service. The gods of fur and feather—the coursers and feasts of their masters—they were neutral too. In theory. As the first wolf in centuries to come snout to… beak… with one? Jack felt no kinship with it. There was something essentially alien behind that bone-carved beak.

Maybe that was because it was a bird. And at least it didn't look like the old bitch.

He curled his lip in mute warning he wasn't roadkill for its breakfast and then went back to his nest of blankets and lover. Jack wrapped himself around Danny, who turned sleepily into him with a yawned "What?" and an arm curled over Jack's hip.

"Nothing," Jack said. He tangled his fingers through Danny's hair, grown out in messy curls after his days being leashed, and brushed a kiss over his forehead. "Don't worry about it."

Danny grunted something skeptical but let himself slide back into his dreams. The soft huff of his breath was warm against Jack's throat, a metronome to count down until dawn. He'd told the bird to get some sleep, but Jack had no intention of taking his own advice. Not until he had to.

Wolves didn't dream like men did, or—Jack absently stroked Danny's hair—like dogs, but Jack didn't want to dream at all. He already knew what the Wild wanted to show him, but he didn't feel like doing what it wanted right now.

In Durham—with Danny back in his bed and Gregor at his back instead of his heels for once—he'd plotted a hero's return to the Scottish Pack. Whatever the wolves thought about where Jack put his cock, the Wild had chosen him. Even the Old Man would respect that. Then the old bitch had carved the pride out of him, and the Wild had let her.

Without the Wild's seal of approval, Jack was just another exile, come to beg for scraps.

Jack laughed a dry choke of noise, as he rolled away from Danny and stared up into the dark at the ceiling. The rattle of wheels over frozen tracks vibrated through his bones and hummed between the plates of his skull. He ran his hand up under his shirt and spread his fingers over hard muscle and healed, naked skin. No, not just another exile. One who had taken the time away to double down on what made him unwelcome. Not only had he refused to fuck one of the women in the Pack, he'd taken a dog as his mate. He didn't even have proof of his rank anymore.

What else could the Wild show him to make it worse?

IT WAS barely dawn when the train groaned sullenly to a halt a few miles away from Glengarnock. Ten miles from home. The sun hung low and pale in the sky, as if the cold had sapped its energy to climb any higher, and the brakemen grumbled to themselves as they stumbled off the train. Propane tanks were slung over their shoulders as they shuffled along the tracks with flamethrowers to unseal the wheels. Steam spluttered and poured from under the train as though it were a much older model.

Soldiers in gray-and-white winter gear ignored them as they spread out along the tracks. They kept their guns trained on the white wasteland that spread out from the tracks. Nobody talked much. Their patience for small talk had been worn down to nothing by the time they stopped briefly near Girvan.

They'd had to use them twice yesterday, once to warn off a pack of scruffy dogs who slunk up out of the bushes. They'd probably been pampered pets once—some of them still had grubby, once-glittery collars around their necks and one had the rags of a bandanna—but hunger and grime had replaced domestication. At some point between abandonment and the tracks, they'd slipped into the Wild, and the passage had rubbed the bred-in differences down and brought out something more essentially… dog. They were still tame, though, somewhere down under the gnaw of empty bellies, and the angry voices and crack of bullets made them scatter.

The man who burst out of a house along the tracks—flushed red with fever and duct-taped into a quilt as a makeshift coat—hadn't been so wise. He'd put his faith in the envelope of cash he tried to shove into the engineer's hand for passage. When he wouldn't take no for an answer, the soldiers shot him in the foot and dragged him away from the tracks. They left him in a puddle of red-stained snow, his curses futile as they bounced off the train.

The wolves' catechism predicted that "*no man would have mercy on another*" during the Wolf Winter, that men would set to killing each other without the wolves even setting fang to the task. It was hard to say if that was prophecy or just prediction.

"The train's probably full of supplies," Danny muttered as he shifted his balance on the frost-covered coupling underfoot. They were squeezed in between two cars, pressed shoulder to shoulder as they waited for their chance to make a break for the houses behind the iced-over fence. "There must be bunkers up here for rich people—politicians, businessmen, the Queen—to ride out the disaster."

Jack grunted as he shrugged his pack onto his back. He unfolded the strap so it lay comfortably over his shoulder.

"It will be a long wait," he said. "Three more years of winter, and then the gods will have found their home."

The mention of the gods made Danny grimace. He started to push his glasses up the bridge of his nose and fumbled as he remembered they were gone. The prophets hadn't planned to let him be human again, so they hadn't bothered to keep them. Even after the Wild's intervention and the prophet's monsters, Danny clung to his skepticism like a miser to his gold.

He always knew wolves were real—the Sannock Dead he'd seen, like moonlight, storm wrack, and rot on the beach by the bonefires—but gods? He wasn't ready to believe in them yet, not until he saw one with his own eyes.

And without his glasses, Jack thought wryly, they'd have to be quite close.

"Ma always said don't borrow money or trouble," Danny murmured. He leaned against Jack to steal warmth from him, and his breath smoked around his lips. "Add gods to the list. Worry about it when—if—we have to."

Fair enough, Jack supposed. The gods could wait. Although it did feel strange to hear those words in Danny's mouth. The future had been all Danny ever thought about when they were teenagers. It was why he'd left to chase the future he'd set his mind on among the humans.

Maybe the future was more appealing when you thought you could do something about it.

Snow crunched under heavy boots on the rails outside. Jack stiffened and pressed himself back against the cold side of the carriage, his shoulders damp as the sheath of ice melted enough to soak into his shirt. Adrenaline scraped under his skin, twitched in his heels, and he exhaled slow mist into the air.

He *could* change. The idea sunk into his brain, and he couldn't deny its appeal. Wolves had kept themselves from humanity for centuries. The last time they'd trusted a man with their true nature had been when they still served Rome, and he'd exiled them over the Wall for it. What difference would it make now, though? The age of men was almost over, his da's authority was fractured or gone, and Jack had already been banished once.

The temptation swelled inside him and then washed away as the soldier stepped into view. A balaclava was pulled down over his head, the gray fabric crusted with ice around mouth and nose where his breath had frozen, and heavy, black-lensed goggles hid his eyes. He carried the black semiautomatic rifle with the butt tucked into his armpit, gloved finger flat against the trigger. The smell of gun oil and sour anger washed off him like BO as he paused in front of Jack to scan the scrub on the other side of the fence for any signs of life.

As a young wolf, Jack had been charged by a stag he'd brought to bay. It had smashed his ribs and broken his jaw when it trampled him. His ribs popped as they broke, a hollow sound as his side caved in, and he hadn't known whose fear he could smell—his or the stag's. It tumbled him ears over tail on the hard stone, and by the time it finally made a break for the tree line, he'd not known where his feet were to get them under him. Da had stood back and watched so Jack would learn the lesson. Just because something was prey didn't mean it was weak.

A bullet wouldn't kill Jack, but it had taxed his wolf to keep him alive under the old bitch's knife. Then he'd dragged it into the icy Irish sea—fur frozen in spikes—to drag a half-dead dog back to shore. With the prophets to defang and a showdown with his da on the table, it wasn't the time to test the limits of his recovery. He'd still heal, but it would take longer than usual.

Danny folded his arm over his mouth to hide the evidence of his breath and pressed back into the narrow threshold of the door.

The soldier stood for a moment, then rasped a rough "All clear" into his radio and trudged back up toward the front of the train. Jack listened for a moment as the crunch of snow and huff of tired breathing retreated, then he reached over and tapped Danny's elbow.

"Now?" Danny mouthed as he shifted his weight forward.

Jack shook his head and leaned in to steal a kiss from cold lips. He buried his fingers in the matted curls at the back of Danny's neck and pulled the long, lean body into his. For a second, he could taste the disapproval on Danny's mouth, and then it softened into something else. They hadn't been apart since Girvan. The back of Jack's neck crawled every time Danny was out of his sight for more than a minute. They hadn't fucked either, too cold or too tired or too bloated with nightmares.

His cock had been the one thing the old bitch hadn't cut off, for all her threats, but it felt like she had somehow. Jack had never lain down with Danny and not gotten hard.

The tug of tempted heat in his balls was welcome testimony that everything down there was intact. Badly timed as gunfire cracked suddenly in the background, but welcome.

Although, a small voice in the back of his head murmured greasily, in some ways it would have been… simpler.

Jack told himself he didn't know what that meant, and he ignored it. He roughly shoved Danny away and flashed him a hard, sharp-edged smile.

"Now," he said.

Chapter Two—Jack

DANNY, MOUTH tender and cheeks flushed from the kiss, the cold, or both, stared at him in confusion for a moment. He'd catch up. He always did. Jack spun on the balls of his feet and jumped off the train. The snow around it had been pressed down under the soldier's feet, compacted into a hard, slick-frozen crust of ice. Jack's boots slid when they hit it and nearly went out from under him. He spared a second's remorse for his decision not to shift—a wolf's feet were made for the snow—and caught his balance.

"Hey!" someone yelled. Surprise and alarm cracked in their voice, no authority. One of the brakemen, then, not the soldiers. "What the hell…! There was someone on the train! Fuck. Fuck me. Lieutenant!"

Jack bolted for the fence, and some instinct made him glance to the right. They'd made no agreement about when to break for the fence before they split up, but it didn't matter. They still made the break from the train at the same time, almost in step as they ran through the snow.

Except Gregor was alone, and Danny was at Jack's heels.

Or the other way around. Long legs and a coursing dog's turn of speed, even in human form, sent Danny past Jack at a sprint. Snow kicked up from his feet in grubby arcs of white and off-white. It sprayed into Jack's face, wet and musty with an aftertaste of smoke and oil from the trains.

"Stop!" a man barked behind them. "Stop right there and put your hands up."

Danny hunched his shoulders up and head down, as if that would help. They'd go for the center of mass, the biggest, steadiest spot on a moving target.

Gunfire stuttered across the ground in front of him. The bullets churned up the snow and threw up chunks of hard, gray concrete.

"Fuck," Danny spat as he zagged away from the line cut through the snow in front of him. The cultured vowels he'd picked up down south had slipped and let the Scottish out. "I thought I'd at least get home before someone tried to kill me."

Jack barked out a laugh. The air was cold as ice water as it hit his lungs.

"If you don't stop…," the man barked. Jack glanced around and saw the soldiers running awkwardly toward him. Heavy boots and thick thermal gear kept them warm enough to function but made them lumber through the knee-deep snow. The man at the front jerked his gun up to his shoulder as he stopped. "We will fire."

Nick swooped on him from above. The huge, black bird dropped out of the sky and onto the soldier's head. He dug his claws into the balaclava and jabbed down with that thick, bone-cracker beak. The Wild—or something like it—caught between the blue-black feathers of his wings as he flapped to keep his balance.

The soldier yelled in surprise and swatted at his head with one hand. The gun swung loose from the other as he tried to drag the bird off his head.

Despite his distrust of Nick and what went on behind those bird-black eyes, Jack laughed. Ahead of him, Danny reached the fence. He jumped up, grabbed the top of it to haul himself up, and kicked with his heavy boots at the frozen metal struts. Chunks of ice and snow dislodged as he scrambled up. A gunshot zipped past Jack's ear and hit the metal post inches from Danny's knee. The post rattled with the impact, and the sheath of ice cracked from top to bottom.

The sharp stink of fear punched through the cold air. Danny gasped out a curse and jumped off the fence. He landed clumsily on the other side, on his hands and knees in the snow, and then scrambled back to his feet.

Jack turned to flash a growl at the soldiers, a flash of white human teeth and a throaty roll of something not human at all in his throat. The Wild was weak here, buried deep under the worked-iron-and-rail skin of the world, but for a second, it flickered green and sharp in his nose. Somewhere, not quite here, he caught the stiff creak of long-frozen trees and the distant thread of a wolf's howl in the wind.

One of the men shuddered and stepped back. His gun sagged between slack fingers and he looked around nervously, as though it would help to have something solid to blame the chill at the back of his neck on. The other soldier, balaclava gone and tracks of blood over his forehead, didn't have the same vestigial awareness of… something. He set his jaw, tight under a few weeks of salt-and-pepper stubble, and tightened his finger on the trigger.

The magazine exploded off the gun in a spray of broken bits and unfired bullets that flew over the snow-packed station. Splinters of metal tore up the soldier's sleeves and shredded his face with small, razor burn cuts. Drops of blood welled and dripped down his face.

"Son of a bitch," the man yelled in shock as he flung the deconstructed gun away from him, trigger guard twisted and the innards of the rifle exposed. "What the hell is going on here?"

Jack laughed. He turned and ran at the fence. One smooth leap got his hands on the top of it, and he swung himself up and over. He landed in a crouch on the snow and then toppled head over ass as the crust gave way under him and spilled him down the bank in a miniature avalanche.

The Wild giveth, and Winter taketh, he supposed as he sat up and shook chunks of ice and grass out of his hair.

"Show-off," Danny accused as he offered a hand.

Jack grabbed it even though he could have gotten to his feet on his own. He kept a grip on cold fingers as he dragged Danny away from the tracks and along the high-walled gardens that backed onto it. Halfhearted gunfire chased them, stuttered across the ground and bounced off the trees behind the same way they'd chased off the dogs. Even though he knew it was stupid, Jack found himself vaguely offended. He was a wolf, and definitely more of a threat than a feral mongrel who used to feed from a dish and wore boots when it went for a walk.

He ignored the brief urge to prove that to the soldiers and instead thumped ice-locked garage doors and rattled padlocks on the way past until they finally fell through a broken blue gate into someone's abandoned garden.

"Leave it!" one of the soldiers ordered behind them. "Crazy bastards didn't have anything with them, and they'll freeze soon enough. Get back to work. We need to get moving again."

Danny swore breathlessly and bent over, hands braced on his thighs. Steam wreathed his face as he panted, the smell of spent adrenaline thick and musty on his skin.

"All that time I was gone," he muttered as he wiped his sleeve over his mouth. "Not one person tried to kill me."

Jack laughed and grabbed Danny's jacket to drag him up into a quick, cold kiss.

"I always knew the south was fucking boring," he growled against Danny's mouth and tasted the reluctant tilt of a smile. For the first time in days, he felt like himself again.

HE SHOULD have known it wouldn't last.

"Fuck," Nick muttered, and his voice slid thickly Glaswegian as all those practiced vowels deserted him. He turned and pressed the back of his hand to his mouth as he gagged. The hunch of his shoulders tried to conjure disgust, but Jack would smell the sharp nutty sweetness of hunger off his skin. "Are those…?"

"Dogs," Danny said flatly. "They're all dogs."

The soldiers on the train wouldn't have trouble with any feral packs for a few miles from the look of it. The streets of Glengarnock were full of dead dogs. They'd been slaughtered in the streets, blood spray left to dry on the churned-up snow and the gray walls of abandoned houses. Skinned carcasses were hung from street signs and splayed out over cars.

"Your grandma left us a message," Jack said, the words rough as he dragged them up out of a dry throat. "Or maybe it was a packed lunch for her darlin' boy?"

Gregor glared at him, green eyes cold behind frost-flecked lashes. Whatever fragile ceasefire they'd cobbled together since Durham, it was still tainted by years of resentment and competition. If it came to a choice between Jack and the bird, Jack wouldn't win.

Not that Jack would pick Gregor over Danny, if it came to that, but that was different. Danny had been Jack's since the first time he saw him, and Danny wasn't a carrion god in a bony man's skin.

The crack of Nick's laugh, more tension in it that humor, broke the silence. "If it was for me, she'd have left the eyes."

Danny made a wet sound in the back of his throat. "That's disgusting."

Nick hunched his shoulders up to his ears and grimaced. His voice was dry as bones as he admitted, "I know."

The body of something that, in life, had been a mastiff of some sort was lying curled neatly in the middle of the road. As though it was asleep. Jack walked over and crouched down, cold jeans pulled tight over his knees.

"Careful," Gregor said as Jack reached out of the dog.

It should have been ridiculous, but after the last few months, Jack supposed Gregor had a point. Every wolf pup in the Scottish Pack had been raised with the Wolf Winter as the bloody golden ring at the end of their long exile. Hadrian had sent the wolves he found in his legions up over his Wall, and Fenrir would lead them back down again. It had always sounded simple enough, but now the Wolf Winter was here, nothing had gone as Jack expected. Nothing that had come out of a prophet's mouth could be trusted as fact, and even a dead dog couldn't entirely be taken at face value anymore.

Jack touched the dog. It was solid. That's why they hadn't smelled the charnel house on the way into the town. The flesh and muscle were frozen solid and furred with a light coat of hoarfrost. The warmth of Jack's fingers left wet, red prints on the shoulder of the corpse.

It had been a quick death. At least the animal's throat was slit from ear to ear before they skinned it. The skin was gone, the canines and guts.

And the eyes.

"Sacrifice?" Gregor suggested as he crouched down next to Jack. Other than his hands, the backs still riddled with slow-to-fade thick white scars, he was Jack's mirror image. For a while there'd been differences between them that Jack had relished and resented in equal measure, the side effect of too much time spent as a wolf. They'd faded since the prophets had cut Gregor's wolf out of him, reset him to the template they'd both been cut from. Identical twins, always a bit interchangeable. "Whatever she wants, it'll have a price."

"What's a dog worth?" Jack asked.

Gregor shrugged. "To the gods, who knows? To me? Nothing," he said. There was a thread of cruelty in his smile as he glanced over Jack's shoulder at Danny. It was an unexpected courtesy that he dropped his voice. "To you? We'll find out when we face the Old Man."

That made Jack flinch. Sometimes he forgot that no one, not even Danny, knew him as well as Gregor. Understood him, hardly ever, but they'd shared a womb and grown up cheek by jowl. They'd never been able to read each other's minds, but they didn't need to when their thoughts were written on the same page with the same pen.

Yet somehow a neutral thought always turned shitty when the other read it aloud.

"Go to hell," Jack said quietly.

Gregor smiled sourly. He scratched at the scars where they clotted between his knuckles.

"I've been there," he said.

Something dark flitted through Gregor's eyes as he said that, shadows under the green. Jack looked away before he had to acknowledge the familiarity. So, they'd both suffered. That wouldn't change anything. One day he might have to kill Gregor—he'd known that since he was a pup, a fact of life like the moon or the cuff of his dad's hand—and he couldn't let sympathy make him hesitate.

Not when he knew Gregor wouldn't.

"I hoped the Sannock Dead's prison would hold her longer," Jack said instead as he pushed himself to his feet. The warmth of his body near the dog had been enough to thaw the outer layer of frost. He could smell the stink of the raw meat. "It held them long enough."

"Wolves are better," Gregor said. "Otherwise it would have been our prison, while the Sannock Living walked abroad and told their children horror stories of us. Who else would do this?"

It was a good question. There were plenty who'd have seen their absence as an opportunity and who wouldn't be thrilled to see the pup princes back to stake their claim.

They would have tried to kill them, though. Maybe from ambush with the weaker wolves as backup, as though the twins were prey, but honest enough in its way. It would have come down to the simple question of who lived and who didn't. Not… this. *Cats* played games, and toothless prophets.

"People do terrible things," Nick said. He'd turned back around, but his chin was tilted up so he could stare fixedly at the horizon instead of the carnage. His hands were shoved into the pockets of his coat, and he shivered under it as he nervously shifted his weight from foot to foot. "I was a pathologist. My gran's a wicked old woman, but she wasn't the only monster in the world, even before the… the Wild… cracked open."

Jack glanced around skeptically at the slaughterhouse explosion of what had once been a quiet main street. He'd seen humans who liked to kill. Like any other animal that had a sickness, Da either had them chased off or put down if they came onto his lands. Glengarnock didn't seem the sort of place such a thing could go unnoticed until it exploded like this at the first opportunity.

"He's right," Danny said in a stiff, distant voice. He used the side of his boot to scrape bloodstained snow up over a nearby corpse. "People can be worse than any wolf, but it doesn't matter anyhow."

Gregor curled his lip. "After what the bitch did to Nick? To Jack?" he rasped. The old growl wasn't there, the wolf's hackles behind human words, but he made do. "I know you're a dog, but even a cur'll bite a hand raised to it eventually."

"Jesus, Gregor," Nick blurted in surprise, the divinity offended right out of him. His eyes were dark and indignant as he dropped them down from the skyline to glare. "That was—"

Danny interrupted him with a harsh laugh. "Thicken your skin, Dr. Blake," he said. "If you want to run with the wolves, you'll hear worse than that out of them. And it doesn't matter who did this, Gregor, because it doesn't change anything. If Rose dragged her mangy hide out of the Wild or a madman with a butcher's knife decided to play dogcatcher, we'll still need to get over the loch to tell the Numitor the prophets have turned on him… if they were ever for him. And we'll never get there if we stand here all day, playing *Columbo* over a dead dog."

"Who?" Gregor asked blankly.

Danny rolled his eyes and stalked away. He picked his way through the corpses, careful of where he stepped, but he couldn't avoid the bloody snow. It caked his boots in heavy, stained clumps and soaked the lower legs of his jeans.

"Sometimes I wish I'd left you back in Durham," Jack said flatly. "Danny's right."

"No surprise you think so," Gregor said, contrary out of habit as he stood up and brushed the snow off his knees. "That dog's nearly been the death of you already, and you didn't even learn anything."

"I learned I'm not a prophet," Jack snapped. He could still taste the sour bite of the prophets' brew as they poured it into him, feel the burn of shackles that pinned him out in human form like a sacrificial goat. The stink of the prophets' monsters, only enough of them left to suffer, still woke him gagging at nights. Children's stories and myths. That was what the Wolf Winter had always been, but somehow he'd expected the advantage to belong to the wolves. "I learned my catechism, I hated the gods, but I never talked to the prophets or went to their rituals. None of us did. That's how they managed to betray us with nobody any the wiser. Maybe Da will know what this means. Or not. Either way, a dead prophet can't plot anything."

There was a pause, and then Gregor smiled at him—a hard, humorless slant of his mouth. He inclined his head slightly. "That, little brother, is one thing we can agree on."

"Go fuck yourself," Jack told him.

Gregor laugh was a bark of amusement that disturbed a handful of crows from the rooftops. They flew away, shadows cruciform and gray on the snow, and Jack hoped it was coincidence they were headed for the loch. He looked at Nick, whose attention clung to the tails of the birds until they disappeared behind the tree line.

If his face could be trusted, he hoped the same thing. But it couldn't, so that didn't help.

Jack shook himself. He missed… the wolf who'd come down from the Wall, he supposed. Back then, he'd been sure of his place in the world, sure of his da even after exile, and he'd never woken up with the taste of fear and his own blood in the back of his throat.

He'd trade a lot to have the wolf back.

"Start walking, Gregor," he said grimly. "The prophets won't kill themselves."

"You don't know that," Gregor said. There were knives in his voice. "They're supposed to be able to see the future. Maybe they'll take the easy way out."

Jack hoped not. Maybe if he killed enough prophets, he'd find the certainty they'd carved out of him. He gave the dogs one last hard look, in case there was a chance Da would know a cause for the butchery, and loped down the street after Danny.

Behind him he heard Gregor question Nick, "*Columbo*?"

CHAPTER THREE—DANNY

DANNY CLENCHED his jaw, the ache in his teeth from the cold a new constant as he struggled through the knee-deep snow that drifted across the road to Lochwinnoch. His jeans were crusted with slush and the wet denim chafed against his cold skin. His breath had frozen against the collar of his coat, a thin skin of frost where he tucked his chin down behind the zipper.

It only took a couple of hours to walk to Lochwinnoch from Glengarnock. It had taken Danny less when he'd left home with a backpack and an acceptance offer to the university, even with how many times he stopped and *almost* went back. A wolf could have done it quicker than that, even on two feet.

They'd already been on the road for half a day, slowed down by the wet resistance of the snow and the ice-needled wind that pinched ears and worked its way through every zipper and seam. It pushed them back until they had to lean into it like mimes to make any progress. Danny tried not to think about the Hunt in Durham, when he'd caught the Wild like a tailwind as he ran. This was just weather. If the Wild didn't want them back on the Old Man's territory, then Jack or Gregor would have said something.

Instead they took point, grimly silent as they broke a path through the snow for those not lucky enough to be wolves. All Danny could see without looking up was their sodden jeans and old, ruined boots as they kicked the fresh-fallen snow out of the way. Their uncomplaining stamina made him feel guilty for the sluggish weariness that dragged at him.

He could feel the dog's restlessness in his bones. If he shifted, he could cut across country and move faster. The cold wouldn't bother him as much, and the dog didn't need glasses.

Danny grimaced at the reminder and rubbed the bridge of his nose.

He'd gotten his first pair of glasses when he was eleven, old enough to realize his ma couldn't deny he was a dog, but she wouldn't accept any other defect in him. The fact he couldn't see farther than the end of his arms, the way he sneezed the spring away, and his habit of being too tall to go unnoticed all had to be character flaws. Something he could overcome if he worked hard enough.

He hadn't blamed her, not much, anyhow. She'd wanted him to live, to thrive, and that was how she thought she could make it happen. But he wanted to see, so he bunked off school and went to the optician.

The sharp edges of the world had amazed him. His ability to land a punch in the right region impressed his ma enough she'd let him keep them. For a while, in Leeds, he tried contacts, but they'd never felt right. The glasses always had, the weight of them on his nose the evidence he didn't belong up here.

Now they were gone, and Danny still didn't belong.

He *refused* to belong. Even if sometimes—when Jack pulled him into a kiss or slung a lazy arm over his shoulders—he wanted to. It was easier that way. If you didn't want something to start with, no one could take it away from you.

He went to push his glasses up his nose again and huffed out a misty sigh of exasperation when he poked his eyebrow. At least there was nothing along this road he'd miss out on seeing. Even before he lost his glasses, Winter had blurred the edges of the world. It was long stretches of white and the pencil scrawl of bare trees that lined the road. They stood out black against all the white, stripped down to the bark. Ice coated the branches and hung down in long, glittering spears. The trees groaned and creaked under the weight, and occasionally one of the icicles would break free and drop down to break into brittle sprays of needles against the ground.

Abandoned cars lined the road. A few of them—left behind in the first days of winter—had pulled in crookedly to the verge and locked the doors behind them. Others had been left where they stopped, ice crusted up around their tires and doors left open, so snow filled the inside.

Danny paused for a second next to an old green Ford. There was someone inside, propped up in the driver's seat. Danny pulled his sleeve down over his hand and scrubbed it over the window to dislodge snow and a layer of loose ice.

There was a woman inside, wrapped in a heavy parka and a tartan wool blanket. Faded red hair was clipped up top of her head and her eyes, glazed gray with death and ice, stared blankly forward. Danny wanted to say they'd been blue.

"Do you know her?" Nick asked. He'd struggled even more than Danny since they left the train. The long black coat he refused to abandon was matted with snow from hem to knees, and the cold pinched the end of his nose white. He still sounded sympathetic, in the slightly distant way that people who dealt with death—pathologists, funeral directors, very bad doctors—tended to approach grief. Danny supposed that carrion gods would have the same polite remove.

"Maybe," Danny said. She looked about the right age to have been one of the Lochwinnoch kids he'd practiced his humanity on back then—his friends. It was Scotland. A lot of the girls had been redheads thanks to nature or a bottle. He hadn't bothered to keep in touch with them when he left. It hadn't even occurred to him. But with Nick's attention still on him, that didn't feel like something he could admit. So, he lied. "Heather, I think. I went to school with her."

"She didn't suffer," Nick said. The obvious lie gave him pause, and he amended it quietly. "Not for long. If that helps."

Ahead of them Gregor and Jack realized there was no one at their heels and stopped to listen. Jack scowled at Nick's statement. He did that at most things Nick did—talk, shift, breathe. Danny understood the reason for it—he had no fond memories of the prophet either, and Nick shared the sharp bones of his face with her, the relationship unmistakable—but that didn't make it easier.

"Freezing isn't a good way to go," he said. "We've seen that."

Nick shook his coat out around him, like a bird fluffed its feathers. He stuck his hands in the pockets and hunched his shoulders and collar up around his ears. "She didn't die of the cold," he said. "It was quick enough."

"He should know," Gregor said smugly. "He's a doctor. A real one."

Danny scowled. It was stupid to care. He'd never wanted to get into medicine, and the only reason Gregor even cared was the fact he could use it to get under Jack's skin. There wasn't much need of medical care when what didn't kill a wolf would eventually heal. Danny knew all that, but it didn't help. The jab still rankled.

He'd grown up a dog among wolves. They'd been bigger, stronger, and healed faster. All Danny had was that he was clever and that he fought dirty. The idea that he'd lost that advantage to someone who could love *Gregor*, bothered him.

But one thing he had learned from the wolves was how not to react when something drew blood.

"I hope he was a good one, then," Danny said. "I'd like to believe him."

"That's not how I knew," Nick said quietly, his eyes still focused on the face behind the frost-trail-obscured windshield. He blinked and looked away with a nervous twitch of his shoulders and pulled up a dry smile from somewhere. "But I am good at what I do."

"Did." Jack's curt correction dropped like a stone. "What you did, before you died."

Nick winced at the reminder. He rubbed his chest absently with a gloved hand, dislodging a fluff of snow that clung to his coat. "I'm not sure it counts," he said. "If you come back."

A growl trickled between Gregor's lips, the scrape of sound thinner than Danny remembered. He grabbed the back of Jack's neck and pulled him roughly close. "If you drop that in front of the Old Man," he warned as Jack shoved him away, "this truce will be over before the prophets are."

It was an empty threat these days, but it took Gregor longer to lose a habit than it had to lose a wolf.

Danny flinched as he caught the cruelty of that thought. It was hard to pity Gregor—and unwise, there was nothing more guaranteed to rile his temper—and easy to resent someone who couldn't be bothered to use Danny's *name*. Still, as often as Danny had resented what he was, he couldn't imagine being without his dog, alone in his skin. The discomfort of the idea made it hard to enjoy Gregor's fall from grace.

"You've taken a bird to bed," Jack pointed out with a snort. He scrubbed his hand over his nape as he stepped back. "I think Da'll notice that all on his own, even if I don't mention he was dead."

The potential for violence hung in the air for a moment, brittle as one of the icicles that dangled from the trees. Then Gregor snorted out a laugh.

"Look at that," he said. "After all these years, I've finally outdone you. Da's going to hate mine more than yours."

Reluctant humor warmed Jack's expression as he thought about that. After a second, he inclined his head in brisk acknowledgment, his dimple a faded mirror of the deep, crescent slash that scored Gregor's lean cheek.

"When you put it that way," Jack said. "You win."

Nick clicked his tongue. "I'm glad I'm good for something," he said dryly, a hint of something rough under his voice. If Gregor noticed it, he didn't think it mattered enough to apologize.

Danny used his nail to scrape a porthole in the smear of ice on the windshield. There was an empty white bottle of pills clutched in the woman's hand. He couldn't read the label, but it was unlikely to be vitamins. It looked like Nick had been right.

"We should get going again," Jack said as he looked up at the sky. "If we can, I want to get home before nightfall. The Wild's gotten strange as it's gotten stronger, and there were things in it that always liked the dark best."

They all, even Gregor, looked at Nick.

He scowled at them. "My world was perfectly normal until you came into it," he said.

Gregor laughed at him. "You cut up dead people to weigh their brains and read their past in their guts," he said. "You love a wolf. What's normal in that?"

"You love *that* wolf," Danny corrected, with a jab of his chin toward Gregor.

Muscle memory made him shift his weight, ready to run. Clever had been an advantage, but his smart mouth had only ever gotten him into trouble. Gregor took a step forward, but Jack put an arm in front of his chest before Gregor committed to the chase.

"Enough," Jack said. "If he hadn't said it, I would."

"You're my brother, like it or not. He's a dog," Gregor said. "He should remember his place."

"He does," Jack said. He dropped his arm. "That's always been Danny's problem. Let it go."

Gregor gave Danny a narrow, green-eyed stare warning, and Danny cowed as he hunched his shoulders and looked down. His chapped lips stung as he licked them in polite submission and gave Gregor enough of an excuse to back down.

"Fine. Let him run his mouth dry out here where there's no one else to hear," Gregor said. "He does it in front of the Pack, though, you won't be able to save him from a beating."

He turned and stalked away along the road. After a second, Nick coughed uncomfortably and followed him.

"He's right," Jack said. "You have to play the part."

Danny crossed his arms and tucked his hands into his armpits. "I know," he said as he walked away from the dead woman who he might have known if he'd bothered. "Don't worry. I'll be a good dog."

There had been a time when Jack would have accepted that at face value. Now he knew enough to look resigned as he waited for Danny to catch up with him. He caught Danny's arm and pulled him into a rough embrace, his lips rough with stubble as he grazed a kiss over Danny's mouth.

"It won't be that bad," he said. "You've just been gone too long, but once you get back, you'll get used to it again."

Danny supposed it would. He almost had before—whole weeks of time where being a dog in a wolf pack had seemed worth it if he was Jack's dog. Except he didn't plan to stay that long. It was a Wolf Winter and, like Nick's gran had told him as she collared him, the only place for a dog in it was skinned and butchered for meat.

There was no point telling Jack that, though, any more than there had been in his conviction that the dead dogs, whatever other use they had, had been left as a warning for him.

"Well, like you said," he noted dryly as he leaned into Jack's warmth, "at least they'll hate Nick more."

Jack chuckled his agreement as they walked. He didn't get it. The wolves might distrust Nick for his gran's sake or kill him because that's what they'd done with everything else in Britain that wasn't them. But he was too different to *hate*. People saved that for the things that were almost like them but not quite.

Like wolves hated dogs.

THEY DIDN'T quite make it before night. The faded winter sun didn't seem to give much heat during the day, but in its absence, the cold chewed down to the bone. Every time Danny stopped to catch his breath from the wind, he could feel his clothes stiffen and crack as they froze. Overhead the moon was a fat wheel with a single bite taken out of it, and he could feel the dog tug at the back of his throat as it wanted to howl.

Not yet.

He swallowed the sound as he stopped at the shore of the loch and stared over the dark, half-frozen water. Even without his glasses, he probably couldn't have picked out the landmarks he'd known. Under the snow, even the cottage he'd grown up in was lost among the crags and drifts. If he squinted, he could see the Old Man's run-down farmhouse, where it squatted halfway up the hill—gray walls and corrugated iron roof stark against all that white, the smell of generations of wolves worn thick and musty under the wood and mortar.

Old stones, mortared together in the old way. It was drafty as a barn, plagued with damp and vermin. Squirrels had given the stink of old predator a wide berth, but rats and mice, as it turned out, were no respecters of the Numitor's dignity. It had been Danny's job to set traps in the rafters and basements, his fingers blistered from the springs and bloody from the teeth of not-quite-dead rats when he cleared them.

Back then, Danny thought it stacked up poorly against the houses of his friends from school, with their hot-water boilers, radiators, and microwaves. Now….

Danny snorted to himself, breath white as hoarfrost as it smoked out of his body. If someone could offer him on-demand hot water and a pot of coffee, he'd still trade every hand-carved old block of granite from under the Old Man's nose for it.

The farmhouse would weather the Wolf Winter. The frost might crack the mortar or burst the old pipes—probably still lead, Danny had always darkly suspected—but the structure would be left intact. There was nothing there that the Wild objected to. In fact, rumor had it among the wolves that the Old Man's den stood unchanged in the Wild itself. If you could find it, of course.

Danny had never wanted to. He never planned to come back at all. The pipe dreams that other kids at university had—of going home in a BMW with a beautiful wife or handsome husband to rub their bullies' noses in it—had never worked for him. Wolves didn't value any of that.

Yet now he was here, and as he squinted across black water at the place he'd grown up, it didn't feel like home.

Danny was surprised to discover he didn't know how he felt about that.

"I should go," he said as he turned back to the others. "Alone."

"No," Jack and Gregor snapped at the same moment.

It made Danny blink uncomfortably. He'd never had trouble telling Jack from Gregor. Even though they had the same face, they wore it differently. It was moments like this, when who they were ran in lockstep, that caught him off-balance. Even if they'd reached that stop from different directions.

"What if Rose is there?" Jack asked. "Or the prophets are there to stop you from reaching the Old Man."

"So you can put Jack's side first?" Gregor said. "Get Da to back him?"

"Why?" Nick asked. He brushed snow off a rock and sat down with a sigh of relief. Once they left the road, he'd limped most of the last few miles. Birds and pathologists didn't do much hiking. He tucked his hands between his knees and looked curious. "I'd think this Numitor would want to see his sons first?"

Danny's cheeks hurt from the cold as he smiled grimly. "I forgot that you don't know him," he said. "Jack was told to leave, and now he's come back. Gregor was told to stay, and he left. No one told me to leave *or* asked me to stay. The Numitor probably won't be happy to see me, but he won't be angry either."

"That's what you think," Jack corrected as he stalked over to poke a finger against Danny's forehead. "You think he won't be angry. You think the prophets won't be ready for you. But thinking isn't knowing, Danny-dog."

Danny moved his head away with a flicker of annoyance. "What I know is that the Old Man doesn't like to be defied. He'll at least hear me out, long enough for me to convince him he needs to listen to what you and Gregor have to say."

"And if you're wrong?"

Sometimes Danny could still feel the choke of the prophets' collar on his throat, so tight that every time he swallowed it made him retch and strangle. The prophets had never cared one way or the other about him when he was a boy, but either that indifference had been an act or they'd coarsened themselves with their rites and rituals. They'd taken great delight in the petty torment of a dog.

It had cowed him. He didn't know why, maybe because, for the first time, he couldn't fight back or because he'd realized he was going to die before anyone came to get him. It turned out he'd been wrong about that, but.... If the prophets got him again, would they have to start from scratch or where the fault lines already were?

A wolf would have survived... better. Bounced back without scars. Danny hadn't, but he wasn't going to betray that to Jack. He wouldn't be the liability, especially not when others had suffered more than he had.

So he shrugged as he dropped his backpack to the ground.

"You get to play the hero again." He cast a glance toward the black, sullen waters of the loch, the ice crusted outward from the rocky shore. "This time, try and get me out *before* they dunk me in the water."

Jack growled under his breath. "If you get yourself in trouble again," he threatened as he scruffed the back of Danny's neck, "maybe this time I won't bother to get you out of it. Think about that before you dive headfirst into a fight."

Most of Danny knew that wasn't true. Even when they were kids, Jack was always there when Danny needed him. Even if he couldn't always interfere—some of the fights Danny had gotten into were ones he picked—Jack was always there to drag Danny back to his feet afterward.

But *most* wasn't *all*. There was always that cold sliver of doubt somewhere in his heart that believed his ma instead. She always told him to never depend on Jack, *"You need him, he wants you. One day you'll both realize it's not the same thing, but you'll be the one left bleeding."*

Danny never paid any attention, but that didn't mean he hadn't listened.

"Good thing I can swim, then," he said as he stripped down to his skin. Then he turned it for another. "Take the long way around. By the time you get there, they'll have either listened or not."

The dog sneezed and shook itself from ears to tail to shed rough gray hairs onto the snow. *Everything* that had worried at Danny sloughed away like dead skin, too full of *stuff* to fit into the dog's thoughts.

It knew where they were—for Danny, for later—but the dog was built for now. What mattered was the bite of cold in its nose, the itch on its back leg, and Jack's hand as he rubbed its ears. Tomorrow and yesterday, the prophets and their monsters, heartbreak and longing—it would worry about them when they got here.

The dog leaned against Jack's legs and grunted happily as Jack scratched under its jaw.

"Be careful," Jack said. "Don't get killed."

The dog thought about that for a second and then dropped it with the rest of the things that were for its Danny-self to handle.

It knew it was to go over the loch to find the Old Man. Once the dog had done that, it would do whatever came next. If it got stuck, then it would pull its skin back on and let Danny worry.

The dog pushed its cold nose into Jack's palm, snorted wetly between his fingers, and then scrambled down the side of the loch and onto the ice. The dog could feel the distant echo of Danny's exasperation as it slid over the frozen sheet and into the frigid water, but it ignored it as struck out for the far shore.

Halfway over, it realized there was already someone there before it. A figure crouched on the rocks, half hidden between them and with their scent deadened by the cold and the water, watched the dog get closer.

The dog barked, but the sound was lost in the wind that rippled the water. It hesitated for a second, tongue dangled out between its teeth to trail in the water as the wind pushed it toward the far shore.

Stubbornness was part of the core kernel of identity that passed between skins. The dog laid his ears flat to his head, sneezed out water, and forced cold-numb legs back into motion.

The stranger waited.

Chapter Four—Gregor

Jealous.

Gregor stood on the shore, his arms crossed, and watched the dog's long, narrow head as it cut through the loch.

Of a *dog*. He licked the back of his teeth and tasted bile. This was what the prophets had reduced him to, what they'd left him.

Fangless. Fixed. Fucking pathetic.

It was a familiar litany. Sometimes the words were different, but the sentiment was always the same. Gregor wasn't what he had been, and no matter how he postured and snarled the minute he stepped in front of the Pack, they'd all know it.

He'd been heir apparent—by default if not choice—and now he'd be nothing. No wonder he hated himself. Everyone else would.

Gregor curled his lip in a silent snarl at the taste of self-pity surrender. It wasn't his. He'd hated himself before—both the face he saw in the mirror and the one he saw on Jack—and he knew what *that* tasted like. It was resentment and scapegoated blame, all tied up with strings of raw, bloody anger that sharpened his fangs and clenched his fists.

He took his emotions—his grief, his disappointments, his frustration—out on other people, not on himself. The hunger to have Rose under his heel as he ripped her stolen skin from her sour flesh, revenge and the final fuck-you proof to Da that, even without his wolf, Gregor was better than Jack. That was his, not this self-pity that wanted him to go off somewhere and let the world rot for want of him.

That came from the raw hole the prophets left in him when they cut him open. They'd taken his wolf with their filthy knives and filthier teeth and left him an infection that festered under the thin scab that held him together. It bubbled out like emotional pus when he picked at it, like a child poked at the gap in their gum left by a baby tooth.

"What if Da doesn't listen?" Jack asked. He stalked a short, impatient circuit along the edge of the shore—three strides away and three back.

His boots packed the snow down to a hard crust of ice, streaked with mud churned up from the ground beneath. His scent was thin but sharp on the cold air, caught on the wind as it picked up, the burned-heather smell of anger with a sharp, saltwater-and-stone undernote of unhappiness. "He's always tolerated dogs born to the Pack, but that was when they were useful to him. It's Winter now, there's no more bills to pay, and Rangers have played their last match."

Gregor snorted. "What if he drowns before he gets there?" he taunted. "Or the monster gets him."

It wasn't a monster, of course, just old and too stupid to know it was dead, bones lost to the mud and silt at the bottom of the lake. As pups they'd all swum out to taunt it with pale, human feet or the bushy lure of a wet tail and yelped when it struck at them with a mouth full of cold-water fangs.

A chill. A scare if you'd gotten complacent. Nothing more.

At least not then. Gregor supposed it could be different now. The Wild had let other old bones back into the world, why not these?

Jack shuddered as though he'd forgotten and took a step onto the ice—it groaned under his weight, a drawn-out sigh that hung over the lake—and scanned the water for any sign. Nothing moved, but the water was dark, and it wouldn't have been much of a game if the pups had seen the monster as it came for them. Even the long-nosed prow of Danny's head, seal slick with water, was impossible to pick out as clouds covered the moon.

"Gods and monsters," Jack said softly, the attempt to convince himself the closest to a prayer any wolf could manage. "That's what the Wild has brought back, not some old fish."

He took another step, and the tone of the ice changed to a brittle note. Gregor reached out and grabbed his arm to drag him back to solid ground.

"If it *is* there, you're only going to make it worse," he said as Jack tried to jerk away from him. "It's more like to miss one body than two."

"At least I could fight it," Jack snapped.

Gregor laughed at him. The monster hadn't known to stop growing when it died. Its head was big enough to swallow a car whole, the spine that showed through its mud-and-kelp skin thick as Gregor's shoulders. Even Gregor wouldn't want to face that down, not in its own element, anyhow. Besides….

"The dog can take care of itself," he said. Not an admission he'd make if Danny were there to actually hear him. There were lines he didn't want to cross. "He did in Durham against Job, he survived Girvan, and he held his own against the Pack when he was a kid. I'd bet on him to reach the other shore before I would you."

Jack yanked his arm away. "He shouldn't have to."

"Then he should have better choice in men." Gregor smirked as Jack snarled at him. The hot pulse of the emotional poison faded into the background as he let himself enjoy the old simple pleasure of a dig at Jack. "Fine. Nick, is there anything in the loch?"

He glanced over at his mate as he asked the question and felt the odd tickle of pointless warmth in his chest. Nick's bony face, all nose and personality, also pleased Gregor, but he hardly looked attractive right then. His nose was pinched with cold and his lips were chapped raw, his skin blotched red from the wind. Still Gregor had to bite a smile off his lips, like he'd just seen Fenrir himself cross the snow, as he looked at him.

Idiot, he condemned himself.

Nick cupped his hands in front of his mouth to blow into them and then hopped up to walk to the edge of the loch. He toed his boots onto the ice as he peered down into the murky depths. After a second, he flinched backward and Gregor caught him, hand braced against one lean shoulder. He glanced down into the loch and caught a dark glimpse of bone and the weed-patched memory of skin pushed up against—through—the ice.

"Still there," Nick said after he swallowed. He gingerly shifted his foot back a step. "There's not much of it left, not even hunger. It doesn't want to live again. It just wants an empty lake. *Mine. mine.*"

His voice slipped away from him as he said that, the words wet and slippery in his throat. Gregor growled and tightened his grip of Nick's shoulder.

Nick was *his*. Without Gregor's wolf, Nick was *all* he had, and he already had to share him with a bird. A wet eel that couldn't even terrorize children didn't get to claim any more of him.

He dug his fingers down into Nick's shoulder and willed the sharp, doctor's wits back into vague black eyes. After a moment Nick blinked and rubbed his hand over his face.

"Can you make it leave Danny alone?" Jack asked, as though he had the right to ask Nick for anything after days spent filled with pointed mistrust.

Nick shook his head. "It's not slain, just dead," he said. "But the dead can't hurt the living, not yet."

Jack looked bleak. "Not comforting."

"It wasn't meant to be," Nick said as he turned up his collar and tucked his chin down into it. "Just true. The old loch monster isn't what you have to worry about."

"What is?" Jack asked.

Nick inhaled as though he needed to say the answer. If he did, it slipped away before he could spit it out. "I don't know," he admitted reluctantly. His scent, that distinct dusty sweetness, was cut through with the darker, fresh-carrion smell of his god. "Something older. Something worse. It's not here yet, but it's coming."

"But not tonight," Gregor said. He put his arm around Nick and tucked him into his side. "Let the dog prove its worth, Jack. Danny did well enough in Durham all those years, and you never gave him a second thought."

They both knew that was cruel, not true. It still worked.

Jack curled his lip in a snarl and, after one last look for a dog's head amid the ice and waves, he turned away from the loch.

"Fine," he grumbled. "We take the long way. Give Da time to bake a cake to welcome us home."

Gregor laughed, a low chuff with no humor in it. "Or gather the Pack to drive us back out."

"One or the other," Jack agreed with a shrug.

"YOU GREW up here?" Nick asked as they rounded the far end of the loch and started up the hill, away from the shore and into the Pack's territory.

Wolves hunted where they pleased, of course, but this was where they slept. Old crofters' cottages, some still thatched while others had been roofed with uneven shale slates, were scattered haphazardly across the property. Some were tucked into the shadow of Da's old stone box of a cottage, while others had been dragged stone by stone up past the boundary line of what man believed the Old Man owned and into the thin spaces where the Wild was easy to touch.

Usually there was a dirt track to follow, worn through the grass by heavy-footed hikers and runners who lapped the loch in their expensive trainers. Sometimes Gregor had kept pace with them in the trees, arrogant in how easily he could have caught them if he wanted.

Of course, he still could. His wolf was gone, but he was still more than most. It wouldn't be effortless.

"That's why it's called home," Gregor said. He hesitated for a second as he heard the words and fumbled for something to soften them. It wasn't easy. Harsh words came easier to him, and if it kept people at arm's length, that didn't concern him. It was only Nick he wanted to keep close, but his tongue couldn't seem to learn that lesson. "Or did you think I just walked out of the Wild a man?"

It was meant to be a joke, but it came out like a sneer. Gregor scowled to himself and swallowed the spiny ball of an apology. He *wanted* to be kinder to Nick, to say the right things and be gentle sometimes. If he couldn't, he'd rather no one knew he'd tried.

Nick laughed raggedly and stopped to push his hair out of his face. He pulled absently at the knots matted around his ears. "I just learned that my crazy grandmother wasn't crazy, just an evil wolf prophet who wanted to sacrifice me to a bird," he said. Despite everything the old bitch had done, there was still something like grief in Nick's voice. "So, I'm trying not to make any assumptions."

"We were both born and raised here," Jack said impatiently as he dropped back into pace with them. "We're wolves, not Sannock or something from a story. We can walk the Wild, but we don't belong there. This is our world as much as it is yours—as it is man's. It's just that they wouldn't share."

"Now neither will we," Gregor finished for Jack, the old lines of the catechism one of the few nearly as satisfying to say as to howl.

Nick looked around at the spare white lines of the frozen countryside and hunched his shoulders. "I was born and raised in Glasgow. The first time I left the city, I was eighteen and going to look at universities. The idea anyone grew up *here*?" He waved his hand at the wide, empty space between the loch and the horizon. "That's stranger than the Wild and the Sannock combined."

The only city Gregor had ever been in was Durham and then only when it was frozen to a near standstill under that first lash of winter. It hadn't troubled him—the streets and houses were a different sort of hunting ground to the moors and buried dens he was used it—but it was no place to live. The tarmac had been rough under his feet, and everything smelled-sounded-tasted of humans and human things, as though they thought they could keep the Wild at bay if they drowned it out. It was somewhere to pass through, not somewhere to stay.

Was that how Nick felt up here? The thought unsettled Gregor for a moment, but he shrugged it away. It was the end of the world, the winter of blood and fang, and where Nick wanted to live could wait until they knew they were *going* to live.

They'd have to decide one day, though. "Maybe the city is why your gran is crazy," he said.

Nick absently rubbed his chest through his coat. It was the scar on his stomach, sliced under his breastbone. Gregor had one that very nearly matched, although his was still raised and new even after the rest of his injuries had patched themselves together.

"Whatever she is, that's who she was before Glasgow," he said. "If anything, I suppose, it started here."

Gregor went to disagree but then held his tongue as he realized they both had a point. Maybe Rose had already been ruined when she started on the long trek to Glasgow, but the seed hadn't been planted here, on Da's land. He'd only allowed Job to stay in the shack behind the house, and the rest came and went as need. They certainly hadn't been made here… that was somewhere else.

"It'll end here too," Jack said bluntly.

Nick sighed but didn't argue. He looked mostly tired and cold as the wind sapped whatever protection the bird had given him.

There was a wall and a gate. A Beware of Dogs sign had lived there longer than Gregor had, the red letters updated every spring when hikers appeared. Some of the wolves had curled their lip at it in protest, but it was easier than the police turning up to look into reports of "large, unleashed dogs." Someone had scratched the cold, faded letters out with a rock so it read war of Dogs.

Nobody was there to either greet them or chase them back to the lowlands. But Danny had been here. His scent hung thick and salty on the air—blood and fear.

It was Gregor's turn to put his arm out in front of Jack.

"Find out what happened first," he said urgently. Blood and fear meant Danny was alive. The dead might want and fear—that was Nick's preserve—but all they smelled of was meat and rot. "Then you can kill whoever is involved."

Jack pressed against his arm for a second, all heavy muscle and a hot swell of smoky anger that had its own weight. Then he took a step back.

"Since when are you the voice of reason?" he asked grimly in a thin attempt to use humor to hold himself back. Words had always been more useful to him than they had been to Gregor.

Gregor snorted. "Trust me, I don't like it either," he said. "But the dog has always made you stupid."

Jack glanced at Nick, who'd climbed onto a rock to peer up the hill. The black tails of his coat flapped around his legs as he stretched onto tiptoe. "Pot and kettle, brother."

It wasn't the same. "I—"

"There's someone coming," Nick interrupted.

Gregor and Jack turned at the same time. The door of the house lay open, a flicker of firelight bright and unsteady behind, and a dark shape, hunched against the wind, picked its way down the path.

"That's not Da," Jack said.

Gregor snorted. He'd lost his wolf, not his eyes. Da was twice the size of whoever had just left the house, half-wolf even when he was human. But the Old Man had always done his own dirty work. Even if he'd washed his hands of his only living sons, he'd still come out to teach two… to teach a lesson to a wolf that trespassed.

"He's not alone either," Gregor said. He tracked shadows through the darkness, wolves in their winter coats with their ears flat to their heads as they skulked stiff-legged between the cottages. "I don't smell the prophets' monsters. You?"

At one time he wouldn't have had to ask. He'd spent more time as the wolf than Jack, kept the sharpness of his nose and his fangs. That had faded quicker than he'd imagined.

Jack shook his head once, the muscles in his jaw tight as he clenched his teeth. They both stepped away from the gate at the same time and ended up back to back in the middle of the path. Nick hesitated for a second as he glanced between them and the strange wolves, and then he stayed perched on the rock. He shifted his weight to get better purchase on its icy angles as the first wolf reached the gate and leaned against it. The hard-frozen wood creaked dangerously under his weight and the thick coat of frost melted under his fingers.

"Lach," Gregor said. Recognition relaxed his muscles and loosened the hard set of his jaw. They'd been… not friends exactly. Allies. Even if the Wolf Winter hadn't pressed the issue of succession, Numitors never died of old age. There'd been fault lines since the twins were inked with their first rank. Lachlan Givens had always been on Gregor's side of it, and even if that had changed, he wasn't wolf enough to be a problem. "We need to talk to the Old Man."

One of the wolves jumped over the wall in one fluid leap, all thick fur and muscle. Gregor felt that same tug of bitter envy he had when he saw Danny change his skin for fur. It was as sour as anything the prophets had left to fester in his wounds, but it didn't come from anywhere but him. The wolf—lean and gray with streaks of black in its ruff—circled around Nick with interest. She pinned her ears flat to her skull and wrinkled her lips back, all gum and teeth as a snarl gargled up from her broad chest.

"Ellie," Jack murmured her name in Gregor's ear. That was enough for Gregor to put a past to the wolf. They'd come up from Hull and fought for her place in the Pack. Most of the time Gregor didn't think much of the Southern wolves—even if they could fight, there was a softness to them—but she'd impressed him.

Then. He thought less of her now as she feinted for Nick's legs. Her teeth clacked shut an inch from his ankle, baffled in the flapping tails of his coat. Nick flinched in surprise and then kicked out sharply. The toe of his boot caught Ellie in the nose, and she stifled a yelp as she jumped back. Blood dripped from her nose onto the snow between her feet. She shook her head and pawed at her nose, eyes still focused on Nick.

"Yeah, well, you should have done as he said, then," Lach said. He met Gregor's eyes for a second in blunt challenge and then glanced away as he lost his nerve. To save face, he pretended to check the positions of the other wolves. "One of you was exiled, one of you ran away, and the Numitor said we didn't need either of you. This isn't your pack anymore."

"Pack or not, he's still our da," Jack said. "We want to see him. And my dog."

Lach skinned his lips back in an expression that had more of wolf's snarl to it than a smile. "Yeah, well, you ain't the wolf prince anymore, Jack. You better get used to wanting and not getting, especially where that dog is concerned."

A growl trickled out through Jack's teeth, a thin warning that the wind peeled off his lips. Maybe Lach even missed it. That would explain why he was stupid enough to stay where he was and keep that stupid sneer on his face.

"You sure that's a fight you want to pick, Lach?" Gregor asked. He stooped down and grabbed a handful of snow. It crunched in his hands as he wadded it into a hard-packed ball and the pricks of cold jabbed under his nails. He winged it at Ellie as she stalked a step closer to Nick, her tongue bloody as it poked out between her fangs. The ball caught her in the side, and she yelped a high-pitched yip of shock as the impact knocked her off her feet. She landed hard in the snow, breath knocked out of her. "And leave him be. If anyone's going to eat him, it'll be me."

Nick laughed. The cackle of real, gleeful humor cut through the cold and tension like wire, and everyone stopped to stare at him. He swallowed hard. The corners of his mouth twisted in an apologetic smile.

"Old joke."

One of the wolves still behind the wall panted out a laugh between white teeth as they got it. Lach's face darkened and red smears colored over his cheekbones as his control of the situation started to slip. He'd always been the sort of wolf that thought he was butt of every joke—one reason he'd never liked Danny—and that obviously hadn't changed.

"We don't like smart-mouthed strangers around here," he snapped at Nick and then glared around at the wolves as though to remind them of that fact. His point made, he turned his attention back to Jack and Gregor, his eyes hot with spite and old grudges. "And we don't like beggars at our gates either. You're not wanted here."

Our gates.

Two wolves climbed up onto the wall and crouched on the stones. Thick winter coats obscured the lines of their bodies, but there were fresh scars on their snouts and legs. Another wolf that had usually picked Gregor's side—Jamie, who was nearly as old as the Old Man but barely above a dog in the pecking order—only had half a ragged ear left on the side of his head. It might grow back, it might not, but for now it was a flap of scar tissue against his skull.

Gregor breathed in and felt the scar on his stomach tug at still-tender skin. It took… effort… to scar a wolf.

"What have you done to my pack?" Jack asked as he took in the same evidence.

The old rivalry hunched Gregor's shoulders, a sore point even more tender than the slow-to-heal injuries the Prophets had sliced into him. That he had no grounds to challenge Jack's claim now only stoked his resentment.

No wonder he hated Jack.

For the first time, Gregor wasn't sure if that was his thought or leakage from the infection. He swallowed the bile that stung the back of his throat. It hadn't even been the *right* question. Gregor's voice scraped like sandpaper as he asked, "Since when do you speak for the Numitor, Lach?"

Lach nervously licked his lips and looked away. He checked the position of the Pack around him, weighed his support, and then squared his shoulders.

"I don't," he said and lifted his chin defiantly. He dropped his voice to a rough imitation of the Old Man's bass rumble. "The Old Man's dead and gone, and this is *my* Pack, *my* territory. I'm the Numitor of the Scottish Pack now."

Gregor snorted.

"The fuck you are," he said. The competition to be the head wolf of the Pack had been his and Jack's birthright. It galled Gregor that he'd have to cede the position to Jack, but he'd die to defend his brother's right to it over someone like *Lach Givens*. "And if the Old Man was dead, the Wild would have rung with the news."

Doubt flashed through Lach's face and then he willed it desperately away. "He's gone!" Lach said harshly. "Now so are you."

He vaulted over the gate and lunged at them. The rest of the wolves followed, all red gums and white teeth as they snapped and snarled.

The smart thing would have been to let Jack take the brunt. He still had his wolf and he would be the Wolf King of Scotland one day, but no one had ever accused Gregor of being the smart brother. He flung himself into Lach's path and took him down in a tangle of limbs and snarls.

Chapter Five—Gregor

BLOOD DRIPPED into Gregor's eyes. It wasn't his. Lach straddled him, hands twisted in Gregor's shirt, and bled on him from a broken nose and gashed forehead. He held Gregor down with one arm, elbow straight and shoulder braced, and drove his fist down into Gregor's face.

His knuckles jarred against Gregor's cheekbone and sent a jolt of pain through his skull. Red and black smeared through his vision as Lach ground his fist against Gregor's eye.

"You left," Lach shouted. The wind had picked up as they fought. All around them Gregor could hear the snap of teeth and snarls of a fight. The storm had blown in from the north too quickly to be natural, the bruise-colored clouds tossed in on the breeze to clot thickly overhead even now. It was like the Wild wanted to come and see the fight for itself. Lach cocked his arm back for a second punch. "You should have stayed gone. The Pack's mine now. They gave it to me."

He threw the punch, but Gregor jerked his head to the side and Lach buried his fist in the snow, hammered his knuckles against the frozen ruts of the old hiking path. Even over the wind Gregor heard the stick-brittle snap of broken bones. It wouldn't last—bones were easy enough to stitch together—but it hurt enough to make Lach yelp and yank his hand back.

"Only for as long as you can keep it," Gregor snarled through stiff lips. The cold stung at his lips and made his eyes ache. He felt it more now than he had, but this was more than that. The chill was enough to make a wolf shiver and go to ground till it passed. "And you got your ass handed to you by a dog."

He punched Lach in the throat. Flesh and soft tissue gave way with the brittle sound of crumpled plastic, and Lach's mouth gaped open as he clawed at his throat. It was one of Danny's moves, vicious in the way you had to be when you knew you were going to lose. Lach's face went red as he tried to suck air in through his crushed throat, and Gregor flipped them both over.

Joints took the longest to heal. Sometimes, if the body was running hot to patch itself together in the middle of a fight, they'd get put back together *wrong*. They'd be stiff and locked, or bend the wrong way, or the muscle anchored too loose so the joint would slip in and out. Someone would have to hold you down afterward, break it with a hammer over and over till it worked again.

Gregor grabbed Lach's wrist, twisted it hard, and snapped the elbow the wrong way until it crackle-tore like a wing ripped off a chicken carcass.

"Fuck!" Lach groaned through a swollen throat as he writhed in the snow. He hammered a blind blow left-handed into Gregor's jaw. His teeth snapped shut on the inside of his cheek, and blood filled his mouth. Lach grabbed Gregor's throat and dragged him down until Gregor couldn't smell anything but the mutton-and-garlic stink of Lach's breath. He dug his fingers down into the soft flesh to cut off Gregor's breath. "We don't have any dogs in our Pack now. We've cleaned house for Fenrir."

Gregor spat blood into Lach's face and pulled himself free when the grip on his throat weakened in surprise. He rolled off Lach and scrambled to his feet.

When he fought Rose in the stagnant pond, the Wild dammed off for the Sannock Dead, he hadn't cared if he died or not. His wolf was gone, his lover dead—at least as far as he knew—and the Wolf Winter fairy tale of his childhood was tainted. Now Nick was alive, and Gregor tried to judge what he'd lost with his wolf as Lach lurched to his feet.

He wasn't as strong, and he didn't heal as quickly—the ache of the bruise around his eye would fade in hours rather than minutes—but he knew that already. With all his shortcomings he'd still beaten Rose. But since he made it back out of the wild, he wondered if he'd lost his edge—the brutally sullen anger that seethed under his skin, the killer instincts of the wolf that put his teeth in an elk's jugular, everything that had given him an advantage over Jack, with his charm and his wise tongue.

It felt like it was still there. The anger was spackled over the scab where his wolf had been tethered, a poultice of old resentments and disagreements to hold the infection in. And once Lach got up, Gregor would do his damnedest to kill him. That should answer all his questions.

Lach swiped blood out of his eyes and rolled onto his side, elbow dug into the snow as it took his weight. Before he could get up to start the fight again, Gregor caught a glimpse of movement out of the corner of his eye. He turned, clumsy in the knee-deep snow, as Jamie lunged at him with bared teeth.

He let the weight of the wolf take him down again. The snow should have broken his fall, but it didn't make much difference. Slaver dripped from Jamie's fangs, thick and sticky, and the stink of his breath made Gregor gag. Sharp teeth snapped in front of his nose as he buried his hands in the thick ruff of Jamie's fur to hold him back. He could feel the bulk of muscle in Jamie's neck, and the thick cords of it flexed against his fingers as Jamie fought him.

Gregor felt his arms start to give under the strain. He grimaced and, next time Jamie reared his head back, Gregor let go of his neck and shoved his forearm into the red, gaped maw as it plunged down. Pain ran black and irrelevant down his arm and into his spine, and a jolt of adrenaline spat out in response as Jamie tore his arm open.

It would heal. Eventually. Gregor gritted his teeth against the pain of being minced and reached out with his free hand. His fingers grazed over a stick, the wet tangle of a dead plant, and finally closed on one of the heavy chipped-granite rocks that the Pack's pups stacked up to rile the monster before they took their swim.

Not much changed in the Old Man's territory.

Gregor wrapped his fingers around the rock, hauled it out from under the snow, and swung it in a short, brutal arc. The edge bashed against Jamie's ruined ear, and a muffled yelp of surprised pain squeezed through Jamie's clamped-closed jaws. Gregor hit him again. His aim was better this time. He caught Jamie right on the temple, where the fur was too thin to cushion the blow. Bone cracked with a brittle, muffled snap.

Again.

On the fourth blow, Jamie's eyes dulled and his grip on Gregor's arm relaxed, torn flesh caught between his teeth as he staggered back. Gregor couldn't feel his fingers—his hand felt like it was overstuffed with wet sand—but his arm worked well enough to get him back to his feet. He wiped the slabber off his face and stepped forward to swing the rock again as Jamie lurched forward. The edge of the rock, ragged and thickened with ice, caught Jamie on the narrow point of his snout. Blood spurted from his black nose and his teeth snapped off like sticks.

That would take time to heal.

Jamie cringed and tried to stagger away, head down and haunches tucked under him. The unmistakable submission should have been enough. It would have been for the wolf.

Apparently without his wolf, he was worse.

He glanced around for Nick and caught the flap of a tooth-tattered coat as Nick dodged and feinted ahead of Ellie. Strips of torn coat hung from her teeth as she panted and spun to keep up with the dodges and kicks. Nick could have pulled on his feathers—human clothes were less of a hobble to a crow than a wolf—but the bird in him thought this was more fun. Stupid, but for now he was safe.

Gregor tightened his grip on the rock, his fingers grated raw on the rough surface, and started after the cringing wolf. Before he could deliver the final blow to Jamie's battered skull, Jack yelled his name. Two wolves had his brother down on his knees, teeth locked in his forearm and thigh. Lach, his eyebrow twisted where the forehead had stitched itself back together crookedly, fumbled his T-shirt up with a healed stiff arm and pulled a thin, ash-gall-stained knife out of his belt.

The rank blade was worn hard by years of use, the wooden handle dark from years of being gripped by bloody, sweaty fingers. Acid and ink had buffed the shine off the metal. By rights there should have been a legend around it—that the first Numitor had brought it from Rome, that it had been carved from a Pict's thigh bone before the truce—but it was too obviously just a knife. Practicality was worked into it, but so was the blood of generations of wolves.

Lach grabbed Jack by the hair and yanked his head to the side. He laid the blade against the thick pulse of the carotid artery and pressed. Tanned skin split easily and peeled back from the coarse stain on the knife, the thin strips of see-through skin dry and withered from contact with the oiled surface. Jack jerked away as far he could, weighed down with wolves and Lach's fist in his hair. It wasn't far enough.

"How long did you want to kill your brother, Gregor? How many years did it take?" Lachlan jeered as he dragged the knife back and forward in teasing strokes. "One fight and he's on his knees. You really think I'm not fit to be Numitor?"

Gregor spat in the snow. "I don't think you're fit to be a wolf," he said. Two big steel-gray wolves circled him on straight, stiff legs, heads down and eyes wary. Gregor shifted his weight and turned as he tried to keep them both in view. They were younger wolves, younger than him. Lachlan's chosen seemed to be either new or worn, handpicked from the bottom of the barrel either way. "No wolf would have the stink of a prophet's ass on their breath."

The jibe had been meant to cut, to confirm Gregor's suspicion that this—like everything else that had gone wrong since Job dripped his poison in the twin's ears and sent them south—was the prophets' doing. He hadn't expected it to slice down to the pus of an old wound. A sick knot of loathing and glee twisted Lach's face.

"When the gods come home," he said roughly, "the prophets will speak well of us."

He tightened his grip on the knife, ready to lay Jack's throat open down to the bone. Jack took a deep breath and threw himself backward. His arm ripped free of the wolf's fangs, flesh and muscle shredded, but he took the one locked on to his thigh with him as he pitched off the edge of the path. The two of them crashed down the slope, through rocks and shrub, toward the shore.

Lach stood for a second, mouth agape like an idiot, and then kicked the confused remaining wolf in the ribs.

"Go," he yelled. "Get him."

The wolf apologetically licked bloody jowls and clumsily went over the edge. Lach turned to face Gregor, a rictus smile twisted over his mouth.

"When the gods come home," he repeated the words like a mantra, "nobody will speak of you."

The two wolves went for Gregor at the same time—one low and one high, as though it were a hunt and he was prey. Maybe Gregor had fallen, but not that low. He reached for the Wild, the taste of stone on the back of his tongue, and a gust of wind and ice caught the wolf in the air and slammed it into the wall. Something broke, and the wolf huffed out a whimper.

The wolf on the ground was Gregor's toll. He dove to the side, landed hard on his shoulder, and kicked out with both feet. His heels hammered into the wolf's shoulder, knocked him off his feet, and Gregor jumped back to his feet before the wolf could recover. He spun toward Lach just in time for the knife to be buried in his shoulder instead of his back.

He'd been carved open on the end of that blade before. It had sliced open every line of ink on his skin and stained it with rowan gall to blister and scar. He'd expected to have the Numitor's rank scarred onto him with it one day. He thought he knew how rowan burned, but he was wrong.

The knife punched through skin and muscle to grate against his shoulder, and his blood caught fire from the old rowan oils worked onto the blade and carried it through his body. His mouth was dry and stung with blisters, his lungs squeezed tight in alarm behind his ribs, and his muscles spasmed in rock-hard, sting-hot spasms until his bones *creaked* with the pressure.

Nick screamed. Half human panic and half a crow's fury. The Wild—or the dour shadow of it—darkened around Lach as he wrenched the knife free and Gregor tasted Nick in the back of his throat. His knees wanted to give way under him, but he forced them to lock and hold him up. The shadow of a girl, draggle-haired and wet, leaned against Lach's back, and he shuddered. Her breath dripped like water, dank and misty, into his ear as she worked her fish-ragged lips.

Lach hesitated and something fogged over his eyes. His hand trembled as the dead thing cuddled closer, like a lover at a bonfire. Gregor's blood dripped from the point of the knife as Lach hesitated, but Gregor couldn't unlock his muscles enough to take advantage of the moment.

A hand—thin and ferociously freckled—grabbed Lach's wrist and hauled him out of the girl's embrace. For a second, Gregor saw her, gutted from clavicle to pubis and hollowed out by hungry things. Frayed bits of skin floated in the unseen currents as she screamed, face screwed in horrible, mute rage, and then drained away like suds down a plug hole.

Before Gregor could gather himself to react to the opportunity, rough hands grabbed him and forced him down to his knees.

"Enough," Kath Fennick snapped as she took the knife out of Lach's fingers. "Do you speak for the prophets now? We weren't told to kill them, and I won't be a murderer if I don't have to be."

No one in Lochwinnoch had ever looked at Danny and not realized he was Kath's son. They shared the same face—sharper on her, kinder on him—as though Lisa hadn't bothered to involve a man at all. People used to joke that was why Danny had come out tame, inescapably a dog no matter how Kath tried to make him fierce, but then Kath birthed her daughter. Still her face but so much a wolf that she howled before she spoke.

When Lach claimed to be Numitor, Gregor had assumed that Kath and the other wolves with more rank had scattered… or died. Instead, here she was, under Lach's thumb. Da wasn't dead—it was impossible, every wolf on the island would have felt that, even whatever hungry wolves still subsisted in Rome would have felt the balance of the world shift—but if Kath bent the neck to this, Da was *gone*.

The wolves scrambled up over the edge of the path, naked and barefoot in the snow with Jack dragging between them. Blood painted his face from forehead to jaw, and his arm had started to stitch the shredded meat back together with tender, pink stripes of new skin. Under the blood and clumps of muddy slush, his expression was drawn and bleak with anger as he was manhandled. As his muscles unlocked—agony soothed into agony he could work with—Gregor traded a grim look with his brother.

Lach wiped his forehead, greasy with cold sweat, and looked over his shoulder. When he saw nothing, he looked briefly relieved and then snorted as he turned back to Kath.

"It's the Wolf Winter. We're going to murder the world," he said. Contempt curled the corner of his mouth. "Or do you plan to stay in Scotland and mind the hearth, bitch?"

There was a flash of tension as everyone waited for Kath's reaction. Her spare, elegant face didn't show anything as she tucked the knife into her belt. The loose folds of her dress flapped around her in the wind as she moved.

"You don't murder a sheep or a cow," she said. "Man will be our prey once Fenrir comes, and I'll put my teeth in any throat he points me at. Wolves aren't meat for the slaughter, Lach. Even cowards and traitors."

Gregor growled at the insult, the sound thin as it squeezed through his still-tight throat. The "bitch" had been ignored, but the low snarl got him a scathing look from Kath before she dismissed him.

"If the prophets want them dead, let them do it themselves. They've enough blood on them that a few more pints won't make a difference," she said.

Lach scowled at her. "You're not my mam," he pointed out. "I don't need anyone to mind my conscience. I'm the Numitor now. I tell *you* what's right."

Kath made no attempt to hide the mockery in her thin smile. "Will you tell the prophets that?" she asked. "If they want them alive?"

The reminder of his leash made Lach blanch and backhand Kath across the face. The ridge of his knuckles split her lip against her teeth. Blood dripped down her chin, and she wiped it away on the back of her hand. She couldn't hide the contempt on her face, but Lach had used up his courage for the night.

"Fine, then," he spat as he turned his back. "Take them. Kennel them with the dogs. The prophets will be here tomorrow. I'll tell them of your loyalty."

Kath spat blood onto the snow. "Wolves don't need words, even prophets," she said. "They'll see my loyalty, not hear it."

She turned her back and stalked away. The wolves who had Gregor pulled him up onto his feet and marched him after Kath. After an uncertain look at the back of Kath's head, Lach's wolves dragged Jack along with them.

"Where's Danny?" Jack asked Kath in a harsh voice.

The question made Gregor flinch guiltily and look around for Nick. He hadn't forgotten about his mate, but it had been a long time since he'd cared about anyone outside his own skin. Back at the fence, Ellie showed a wet, torn coat to Lach, one hand shoved through a hole as though that would explain why a sort-of-human had gotten away from her. Lach raised his hand again but stayed it as she hunched her shoulders and curled her lip in a sneer. Another she-wolf—old enough to show silver in her muzzle and ears, so either Fern or Elsie, but without a wolf's nose Gregor couldn't tell which—growled and flattened her ears at him.

The Old Man could have beaten a wolf raw on the steps of his house and no one would have shown a tooth to him, not even the wolf on the ground. But then they all knew the Old Man never would. Da had always thought cruelty was inefficient.

It was good to know that Lach might call himself Numitor, but even the wolves that guarded his back didn't trust him entirely. Even better to know, as a crow cawed angrily from somewhere in the storm, that the bird had kept Nick safe.

He turned his attention back to the ground under him as he tripped over a rock buried in the snow. The wolf on his left yanked him back to his feet briskly and kept him in motion.

"The dog?" Kath asked in a harsh voice. She wiped her mouth again, even though it had already healed. "He's where he belongs."

"Kath," Jack said. The wolf's anger bubbled under his tongue, thick and harsh in his throat. "Kathleen. Where's your son?"

She turned around and walked backward for a moment. Her face was hard. "What's it to you, Jack? He's a dog. A pet. Nothing in the long run. Isn't that right?"

There was something expectant in her face, almost hopeful. Gregor hated the instinct that made him lean forward against his captors' hands. Two years ago, he'd have been happy to use his brother's weakness for the dog against him. But Gregor would never rule now, and Jack was a soft-hearted idiot.

"He's pack," he rasped out the harsh interruption. "Dog or not."

Kath gave him a cold look. She'd never thrown her weight behind either of them officially, but when the time came, she would have picked Jack despite the fact he'd ruined her son's chances of being a good dog… or a shit human.

"Not anymore," she said as she turned back around. Her hands were in fists at her sides and there was frost on the ends of her hair. "Dogs have a master, not a pack. They were a test we nearly failed, but the prophets have given us a second chance."

Jack snarled and tried to wrench free from the hands on him. The wolves wrestled him roughly to the ground and put their boots in while he was down. Jack made a thick, furious noise in his throat and curled into a ball to absorb the abuse against his hips and forearms. Gregor sagged in exhaustion, blood hot against cold skin as it soaked his shirt. One of the wolves snorted in disgust and the other shifted his grip to pull back up.

The second the grip on his arm slipped, Gregor kicked out sideways and took the wolf's knee out with a loud, grainy pop. Shock made the wolf's eyes bulge as he folded, and Gregor took advantage of the other wolf's surprise to pull free. He lunged forward, grabbed Kath by the throat, and dug his fingers down the tendons as he shoved her up against the wall of his da's house and pulled the knife out of her belt. He pressed the point of it against her stomach, through the pretty blue flowers of her dress.

Kath's eyes filmed over amber, but she held on to her skin as Gregor squeezed her throat.

"Call them off," he ordered.

Her bright yellow eyes flicked past him, and when she looked back, they'd faded to gray-flecked brown. She curled her lip in a sneer and leaned into the knife until it sliced her stomach open.

"Trust me," she whispered urgently against his jaw, the smell of fear acrid under the rich salt and metal of her blood. "Do what you're told."

Gregor could hear her heart as it stuttered against her breastbone. It could have been desperation or just pain from the sliver of poisoned knife he'd slid into her gut. Maybe, if he still had his wolf, he could have been sure. Instead he had to act on faith—something no wolf trafficked in.

She'd birthed her dog, raised him, taught him to fight. Of course, she wished he were a wolf—for her sake as well as his—but she loved him as much as Gregor had loved his wee broken daughter, and neither of them would give the prophets their due.

Gregor let her take the knife back. She scruffed him by the collar like he was her get and hauled him down the road. The others didn't bother to get Jack to his feet. They just dragged him along.

Prisons were for humans. The justice of wolves was usually clean and straightforward—exile or death at the Old Man's jaws. If the accused ran from it, that narrowed the options to death. Still, there were those who'd sinned enough that the Old Man didn't want the taste of them on his tongue or the responsibility of their future on him, even elsewhere.

Wolves sent for prophets—to be lamed, ruined, and bent over so they could lick the gods' feet—would run if they could. Anyone would. The loss of the wolf—that would have made Gregor walk into the snow to die if he didn't have rage and Nick to fill the hollow of it—was only the first step.

That was what the old icehouse behind the farm was for. Half-buried in the ground, the low hump of the roof thick rock padded with sound-muffling turf, the stone box was the perfect physical prison. And if the prophet-to-be was strong enough or desperate enough to reach the Wild....

Kath grabbed one of the hinged steel rings from the wall. It was cold enough to stick to her skin and freeze-dried scabs to the metal as she forced the collar open. She snapped it around his neck and padlocked it shut with competent hands.

"Where's your son, Kath?" Gregor asked quietly.

Kath glanced over her shoulder at the other wolves, her face sharp with reluctant suspicion.

"Safer than my daughter," she whispered through stiff lips. "Safer than you, if you aren't smart."

She pulled the gate open and shoved him down into the dark. He hunched his head from the memory of a low ceiling and staggered down the steps into the reeking dark. A second later, Jack, a matched collar bright against his bloody neck, rolled down after him.

"It won't be long," Kath told them. "The prophets will be back soon. You just have to wait."

The lock clanked shut, and Gregor was left in the dark with his twin and the source of the reek. Metal clanked in the corners of the room and eyes flashed dim blue in the scant light that filtered into the space as bodies moved away from the walls.

Gregor grabbed Jack's collar and hauled him to his feet.

They'd found dogs, just not the one they wanted.

Chapter Six—Nick

The dead girl bobbed in the storm, anchored to her corpse by an umbilical of old bones and slimy flesh. Fish had taken her eyes and her tongue—the bird envied them the tender tidbits—but it could still feel her accusation. Promises had been and were going unfulfilled.

With a flip of its wing, the tips of its feathers frost-painted, and a snap of its bone-white beak at her tether, the bird rejected the idea of a debt owed. It sheared a strip of rot-sweet tendon from its moorings and tossed it down, slick and slippery as a worm. The girl recoiled with a silent shriek of offense, her shed bones and old grudges caught up in her hands like a matron's skirts, and the bird jeered after her.

It had hooked her out of the broth of skin and marrow she'd brewed in and as good as spat the wolf up into her hungry mouth. That she'd given him a chill in his liver and a shadow in his brain was not the bird's fault.

In the back of his brain, Nick wondered if the wolf with the knife and the pale eyes had killed her. It was a mortal thing to think, a mortal thing to feel the sticky weight of pity and anger for the dead girl. The bird had no time for it as the storm buffeted it back and forth with no regard for its person or its calling.

A wolf killed her, it shrugged to Nick as it tried to orient itself in the storm. *That one or another. The living all look the same to the dead.*

The dead girl crawled back down her umbilical to the wolf she'd spat her death into her, fingers sunk in between the woven bones. The slick rope was plugged into his ear, gray tendrils of rot spread out from the root for those with eyes to see, and the wolf shuddered as the dead girl hung over his head.

Serve him right, the bird thought darkly. The aftertaste of Nick's desperate fear was still on the back of its tongue, tight in its chest. Another mortal thing, but it still *felt* like it belonged to the bird. The same as Gregor.

Their wolf.

Nick grumbled at that, but the bird ignored him as it labored cold-stiffened wings to climb higher. A frustrated croak of annoyance creaked out of it as it felt the weight of the Wild push down. It wasn't a thing of the Wild—it *looked* like a bird but had hatched from a… thought, a need for a thing with wings and hunger, not an egg—but it wasn't an enemy of it either.

Not as far as it knew.

It finally burst out of the sullen bubble of the Wild that hung over the old farmhouse, tatters of it caught in the bird's stiff feathers. The bite of winter was still harsh, bitter with generations of divine patience as it spread through the world, but the winds that battered the bird were impersonal.

After a moment the bird steadied itself, shook off the sour residue of the Wild, and drifted into a slow circle over the scattered collection of buildings. Through the veil of snow that blew sideways over the countryside, the bird's sharp black eyes picked out the shadowy outlines of wolves on the ground as they slammed the door to a hole in the ground.

Discomfort crawled under the bird's feathers and raised the ruff around its throat like a dog's hackles. Once things went under the earth, they weren't for it anymore. Corpses on battlefields or in ditches, strung from gallows or bloated in the street belonged to it. The slain, the murdered, the angry were its business. Maybe the occasional shallow grave could come under its remit, but tombs were its brothers' to stalk out.

Gregor, Nick thought from where the bird had put him. *He's safe.*

His relief was alien. The bird stitched it into his experience—wet beak, full craw—but it only mostly fit. Mortal things were a strange delight. It knew lust, the peacock preen of feathers and a well-chosen mating gift, but this?

Love. That was something it had only seen in the aftermath, when tears and blood had been shed.

Nick flinched at that thought. He believed it didn't have to end badly. People could just be happy.

People could, the bird agreed as it stooped on wide, black wings to perch in the bare, brittle branches of a wild hawthorn. The thorns poked at its toes as it shuffled into a comfortable perch and fluffed its feathers out against the cold. It tucked its beak in and preened at its breast feathers, flakes of snow cold on its tongue, around the knot of scar tissue that ran down its chest. *But* you *already ended badly.*

There was no answer to that. The bird chuckled to himself, smug that he'd won, and plucked a stray black feather from its breast to drop into the snow. It lay there for a second, like an arrow pointed to the wolves' den. Nick wondered, with a flicker of suspicion, why it had done that. The bird yawned, tucked its feather back under its skin, and croaked with laughter as Nick fell off the branch.

Fuck!

Thin branches whipped against Nick's thighs and back as he tumbled gracelessly out of the tree. With a jolt of pain and shock that ran from his tailbone to the back of his skull, he hit the ground backside-first and sucked in a shocked mouthful of air and iced needles. His chest cramped painfully, and his hips ached as he dragged himself to his feet.

The bird chuckled hoarsely at him as it nested down into his… soul, he supposed. Nick thought about that for a second, but it was too long, and he shied away from the idea as he felt his composure start to slip. He'd built his whole life, his surgical career, on the rock-solid foundation that his grandmother had been crazy, and he was nothing like that. The world made sense in a way that could be taken apart and pinned down, like an autopsy of reality.

Then he found out his grandmother was not only sane but right about the world, and that somehow made all her old cruelties worse. Superstition and fear were what stitched the world together against the monsters—the bird clicked its beak at him and he amended the thought—and gods outside, and the stitches had started to fray.

And he had *died.*

His life had fallen apart under him, the history he thought he knew snagged on gran's secrets and her murder of his mother, and he'd accepted that. In a way it was easier to stop his decades-long resistance to the fairy-tale reality his gran had constructed for him when he was a child. It was only when he poked at the edges—when he tried to find the logic—that he tasted panic in the back of his throat.

He would have to deal with it one day, let his new reality sink down into his bones, but not yet. Nick grimaced to himself as he chafed cold hands over his pale forearms—naked in the storm wasn't a good time to do anything.

We should go. He poked at the bird. It wasn't a *bird* exactly in his head, just a sense of something dark that was all hunger and wickedness. Despite that, it still managed to convey that it had tucked its head under its wing and wasn't paying him any attention.

The wind shoved at Nick to dislodge him from the sad shelter of the wind-blown hawthorn's bent trunk. It poked snow in his ears and pinched at his thighs and between his legs as he hunched over on himself. The old scar on his stomach—nearly the same age as him, where his gran had sliced him open—itched and flushed red against his pale skin.

Thirty minutes. That's how long it took hypothermia to set in. Less if you were stupid enough to go out naked in the snow. In the back of his head, the echo of his own calm, clinical voice diagnosed the cause of death in too many cold, stiff bodies back in Girvan. *"Reddening of the extremities due to frost erythema, damage to the extremities from frostbite, in the gastric lining, evidence of Wischnewski spots...."*

Nick exhaled, smoke on his lips, and pushed the nag of a voice to the back of his head. His body was used to being alarmed by the signs of extreme cold. It pulled the blood from his fingers and toes to make his heart race and make him shiver. But he'd already died, bled out on a beach in Gregor's arms, and the bird had brought him back. It wasn't going to lose him to a bad chill.

The bird chuckled darkly in his head. He ignored it too.

He gritted his teeth, pushed himself off the tree, and froze as the snow picked out the outline of one of the Sannock Dead. It looked tenuous as frost and shadows, but it was solid enough to leave footprints in the snow as it walked toward him.

Nick glanced down at the tracks and corrected himself.

Hoofprints.

It was what killed Nick the first time, the fossilized ghosts of rage and extinction that were all the wolves had left of the other Wild things that had lived in Britain. Maybe that was why they'd followed him up the coast—to see how he'd done it.

They'd fallen behind while he rode the train, the steel made their edges bloat and split. He still caught sight of them as they paced along through the trees and through the frozen, abandoned towns. Despite the horns and hooves, they somehow never looked out of place.

Nick swallowed as the Sannock joined him under the hawthorn. The pronged rack of its horns rattled the branches and dislodged thick, half-frozen chunks of snow, and it stamped neat, split hooves in the snow. There was no heat from its body, no wisps of breath on its lips. It did smell, though, with a faint bitterness that reminded him of mothballs and Sunday knit dresses.

It should have looked human. Other than the narrow hooves and horned brow, it was shaped like a man with bony callused hands and a wide, sensual face. Something about the eyes and the mouth—a little too wide set and green, too lush and red—made it off, unmistakably other. It compelled and repelled at the same time. Nick was reminded of a school visit to the zoo and the poison dart frogs in their damp glass aquariums. The bright colors warned of toxins, but he still wanted to pick them up and marvel at them.

"What do you want?" Nick asked, as his teeth chattered. It made his voice unsteady, the words stuttered as though he were nervous, not cold. Maybe he was both. "I can't help you. I don't want to help you."

The smile was close-lipped, as though there were something behind the scarlet pout that Nick wasn't meant to see, and the Sannock didn't look directly at Nick. It unbuttoned the stiff, high-collared coat it wore and shrugged it off. Without the folds of cloth to disguise them, the lines of the body were more obviously wrong—too deep in the chest, and the arms fit oddly into his shoulders, like someone had gotten halfway through making a deer into a human and given up. Yet it was dressed in what had been finery, with a faded red knot of silk at its throat and the glitter of cufflinks on its wrists.

"I don't—" Nick started to protest. The black bird, stirred from its fake sleep, croaked angrily at him. That, it insisted, would be stupid. It tried to push out of his skin, feathers sharp and itchy against his spine, but he held his ground.

The Sannock held the coat out and dangled it from one thin, hooked finger. It was a dead thing's coat, a ghost's memory of what it had worn, but as the wind whipped it, the faded lines of it thickened and grew heavy. It was dark and plain, with a high collar and frayed cuffs. The Sannock held it and waited. The fact it never looked directly at Nick made it appear casual, but the tension of the moment was strung tight as a tendon between them.

In the haze of snow around them, soft-edged silhouettes of almost-human and almost-beast shapes faded in and out of view as they drifted. The shadow of a dog, head huge and eyes like dimmed torches, came close enough to sniff the coat and then veered away. A slab of meat had been sliced from its flank, peeled away to show the white, bowed arch of its ribs.

Sometimes they remembered how they died, but not always.

"It's not a gift if it's not an exchange." The memory of his gran's harsh voice echoed from his childhood. *"It's just an obligation."*

The bird gurgled in disgust at being in agreement with Gran, but Nick knew he shouldn't take the coat. But he was cold, and they already expected something from him. If he took the first step of the exchange, maybe he'd work out what they wanted him to do.

He reached out gingerly, his fingers unsteady, and took the coat. His hand brushed the Sannock's as he did, and he felt it crunch and collapse under the touch. It was made of frost and will and dripped to the ground as meltwater as the Sannock withdrew.

The coat was heavy and unexpectedly warm to the touch, as though it had stored the long-dead Sannock's body heat for all these years. Nick hesitated for a second, the garment held at arm's length like roadkill he'd just picked up, but he could still feel the weight of the Sannock's attention on him.

He could do this. Nick pulled the coat on. His skin crawled at the rough, greasy touch of the wool, but the heat sank down into him.

"Don't suppose you have any shoes?" he joked nervously.

For a second, as the Sannock swung that heavy, horned head around to stare directly at him, Nick thought he'd misstepped. Then a smile cracked slowly across the Sannock's face, dry and stiff as its muscles and flesh tried to remember how it was done. The Sannock shook his head, the spread of horns tangled through the dry, rattled branches of the hawthorn, and stamped a hoof three times against the ground to make its point.

"I don't know what you want," Nick said.

The Sannock ducked his head and bent at the knees to untangle himself from the tree. Once he was loose, he turned his back on Nick and faded into the storm, the bloodless lines of him lost in the snow. After a thoughtful beat, the other Sannock faded away too, the taut expectation that strung the moment gone with them.

Last to leave was the dog and a golem of burned sticks and moss in the shape of a child. Two sets of empty eyes—one full of guttered candles and the other scraped down to green sap—studied him. The golem lifted a small hand—someone had gone to the trouble to craft it knucklebones, neat and stitched together with moss tendons—and pointed into the storm.

You will.

It wasn't a voice. There weren't even words, just an understanding that washed over Nick. He stumbled, shuddered, and looked away. When he looked back, they were gone.

In his soul the bird clicked in its throat and filled Nick with the affronted urge to preen. He caught himself as he pulled the coat straight over his shoulders and adjusted the worn cuffs. The buttons, he realized as he grazed his fingers over them, were dry bone. Glimpses of an old, old life flickered through his head, sucked up through the rough surface.

Dirt. A woman's ass. Dirt. A smile on rich red lips the bones would follow anywhere.

And he had, Nick supposed as he pulled his hand away from the button. Or at least he'd followed them to his end....

The bird didn't like it. It didn't like the gift or the smell of the Sannock that lingered in the air or that they wanted something from... one of them. The doctor or the bird. Neither option felt good.

"I thought the dead were what you were for," Nick said. Despite the greasy feel of the coat—and the idea he refused to dwell on that the layered, scratchy weave might not be from a sheep—he pulled it closed across his chest. He made a sour face at the thought he couldn't quite shift or the memory of some of the things he'd eaten since the bird brought him back. "I know corpses don't trouble you."

The bird was sullen, bleak, and blackly unresponsive, like a stone jammed uncomfortably into him. He started to walk, and his feet hurt. By this point they probably shouldn't if he was going to die of the cold.

What was it Gregor had told him?

"You feel the cold," he heard Gregor's harsh voice for a second, brusque, as though he resented being pushed to explain something so

simple. But he'd pulled Nick close to keep him warm, rubbed his back with strong, warm hands. *"You just don't have to mind it."*

It was easier said than done. The bird could do it, but Nick didn't have the knack. His feet stung with each step, the bones sore as they stiffened and ached. Despite how soft the snow looked, it was rough under his soles, gritty and full of sharp, frozen chunks.

Halfway down the hill, the sharp, feathery anger that shared his head faded away into the dregs of something uncomfortable. Or unhappy.

Some things, Nick's brain thought without any instruction from him as his hitchhiker gave in, aren't meant to be dead. They don't have the knack for it, the staying power to stick to it.

Nick glanced down at the stiff, strange coat that still felt warm against his back. The real version of it, the original, had probably been buried or burned with its owner hundreds of years before. The wolves who'd slaughtered the Sannock for their magic hadn't left much of them, just butchered meat and blood. If they could make this real….

He stumbled to a halt as his skin crawled. Only the thought of what might take offense in the storm stopped him ripping the coat off his back. He breathed through the revulsion and reminded himself of how cold he'd been without it. His balls still tried to squash themselves back up inside him.

Nick couldn't blame them. He pushed himself back into motion, but he had to take awkward, high-stepped strides to make progress, his body angled into the wind as it pushed him back and his thighs and ass tight and sore after a few yards.

Or a bit more than a few, he realized as he stumbled over the crest of a hill and into a low stone wall. Even if it wasn't as the crow flew, he should have been back to the wolves' town. The pitched roofs and matchstick chimneys he'd focused on resolved themselves into a rough-edged green hillock decorated with precariously stacked, narrow towers of slate and granite.

The bird shuddered, a feathery itch against his brain stem, and thought he was lucky that was all he saw. As they walked, it let Nick sneak a glimpse at what it saw—spires of old yellow bones stitched together with cords of dry sinew. A strung fence of unraveled tendons and nerves, brittle from the cold that silvered them, and inside it… something huge, damp, and moldered.

"What is it?" Nick asked as he drew closer. He was vaguely aware he shouldn't want to approach it, that the smart thing to do was turn and run, but he still climbed up the hill.

The bird didn't know what it was. It was also lying.

The stink of rotted flesh hung sour and sick in the air, and bile stung the back of Nick's throat as the bird made him hungry.

Carrion, Nick supposed for a second, another dead thing.

Except corpses, even the wet, restless bones that crawled through the corners of Nick's world, didn't steam like an overworked horse in the cold. And corpses smelled of rot or nothing in the cold, not that sugary, yeasty stink of infection and fever.

Nick reached out toward the brittle wires of flesh, but he hesitated, his fingers trembling, and the bird closed its eyes. He was left flat-footed in the snow, hand outstretched to pluck thin air. Whatever had been caged in the center of the stones was gone. In its place was a long, carved stone mounted on top of a low, rocky cairn half-covered with dirt and grass under the snow. Someone had left a bright red coat draped over the stone, the thick wool stiff with ice and welded to the granite. If Nick went inside, he supposed he'd find a sweater as well, or a shed pair of shoes left where they'd fallen in the snow. Then, somewhere in the dark, a cold, naked body curled up in the snow where they'd dropped once delirium couldn't take them any farther.

The cairn had probably seemed like shelter when the owner of the coat found it. Now it was serving double duty as a tomb.

"Enough," he said as he turned away from the stones. He squinted into the snow that blew in flurries and tangles around him. The cottages, roofs humped high with snow, had been difficult to pick out from the landscape, but he should have been able to see the big farmhouse, at least. Nothing. He'd gone the wrong way. "Whatever point you wanted to make, it's made. I need to get back to Gregor."

He reached for wings, and they were pulled away from him again. There was no reason why, but there didn't need to be. The wolves might change their skin at will, but Nick needed the bird's help. It didn't need his. Today it thought he needed to stay grounded, although it didn't share why.

Panic scratched at the back of Nick's throat. His head was full of the clammy memory of the first time he'd met Gregor, the bloody ruin that the prophets had left of him. Nick had felt Gregor's wet flesh and the pulse of blood between his fingers as he tried to keep the wolf alive. He'd known he was going to fail. That had been hard enough then, before Gregor had a name and before Nick had fallen in love with him.

In the back of his head the bird got distracted—briefly—as it dipped its beak in the memory. It knew, they knew, how Gregor tasted—his mouth, his skin, his cock—but it wanted this bit of the wolf too.

"Salt and copper," Nick told it shortly. "The same as a cow or a dog."

The bird didn't bother to argue. They both knew Nick was lying. Even before he'd had his feathered hitchhiker, warm blood had unsettled him with the sense of something potent and electric in it. That was why he'd been a pathologist, not a surgeon.

It had been easier to remember he wasn't crazy when he avoided the crazy things.

Nick raised his hands and exhaled onto them. His breath made the cold skin sting, the web between his fingers pinched with pain, and thunder grumbled overhead.

He hadn't been an outdoorsman either. The closest thing to the countryside he'd seen before he was twenty had been a scabby local park where the drug dealers—only a few years older than him, and then a few years younger—hogged the swings. If the bird wasn't going to help, Nick wouldn't find his way back to the wolves tonight. Not in the dark in a storm.

"He'll be fine," he told himself, the words stripped from his lips by the wind. "They don't lock someone up if they're going to kill them."

The bird didn't agree, but it wasn't going to take flight either. Not now. Not here.

Nick tried to put the memory of bloody, frozen strips of skin out of his head as he stepped past the narrow towers. His feet found gravel under the snow, the curve of an old path, and slicked his feet as he edged toward the cairn.

Something howled. Or… didn't, Nick realized as he spun to find the source of the noise. The back of his neck prickled in reaction to the almost-sound, and his heart pumped harder as adrenaline made him shudder. He licked dry lips and reached up mindlessly for his gran's pendant, the twist of iron that had hid the truth from him for so long. He'd left it back in Girvan, but sometimes he missed being able to lie to himself.

A dog with no… dog in it—just the skin draped over something that remembered the shape it was *meant* to have—leaped between the stone towers and raced toward him. Snow flew up from under its paws, but it left no tracks behind it.

It howled a throaty bell of alarm as it headed for him. Nick stumbled to the side, out of the way, but it never reached him.

Something else—some*one* else, because it looked like a man even if it ran on all fours—burst out of the cairn and caught up with the skin dog before it got more than a few yards. A big hand scruffed the black skin, flayed hide pulled up in clumsy, fatty folds, and ripped it off the dog underneath. With nothing to animate it, the skin went limp in the man's fist, blown backward in the wind while the dog faded away. Nick could still hear its aggrieved bark in his head, echoed as though it came from somewhere very far away.

The man sniffed the skin for a second and then tossed it away as he lost interest. He was massive, built like a bull with thick shoulders and layers of muscle under a dense fuzz of gray bristles. Salt-and-pepper hair hung around his face, tangled around chunks of ice and snow. Under the coat of fur, Nick could see thin red patches on the man's hands and on his cramped legs, where the skin had frozen, peeled, and healed over torn muscles.

Nick stumbled back a step. The crunch of his foot against the ice brought the man's head swinging around. Under the unruly bangs, his eyes were bright mindless yellow, and slaver dripped in wet, sticky strands from the corners of his mouth. The man peeled his lips back from broken shards of teeth, shreds of meat and hide caught between them, and growled.

That wasn't what made Nick take another step backward, a whimper caught in his closed throat. It was the face.

The Run-Away Man.

His gran had told him a lot of scary stories when he was a child, and the Run-Away Man was the star of a lot of them. The stories had all ended the same way, as his gran pinched his arm or thigh and demanded, *"And what do you do when you see the Run-Away Man?"*

Nick licked cracked lips as he took another step back. Panic tasted like a split lip, blood on the back of his tongue, and filled his hand with the blind, unthinking terror of his dreams. It even infected the bird, cold and insidious as it spilled over the graft that joined them. It filled his head with the batter of frantic wings and angry knock-sharp caws.

The man prowled forward, still on all fours as though he'd forgotten how to walk, and that low, dangerous growl dribbled out of his slack mouth along with his spit. There was something there that Nick needed to see, he could feel it, but there was no room for it in the panic-static that filled his brain.

There was only one thing to do when you saw the Run-Away Man, only one answer that Gran had wanted to hear.

Nick spun on his heel and fled, full of black, winged panic and his throat so tight he could hardly breathe. He tripped over a stone and went down, sliced his hands and knees up as he fell, and scrambled to his feet as a hand grabbed at the tails of his loaned coat. The Run-Away Man yanked him back for a moment, and then the fabric tore like tissue between coarse fingers. Nick staggered, caught himself, and fled between the towers and into the storm. He didn't question how he—barefoot and breathless and lost—stayed ahead of the man behind him or where his blind flight would take him.

He ran away.

Chapter Seven—Jack

THERE WAS coffee, two thermoses of it and an extra cup to share. Jack thought of Danny, his knee tucked between Jack's thighs and his nose cold where it pressed into the hollow of Jack's shoulder. Dogs weren't as immune to weather as wolves were. They felt it more. He supposed no one wanted the dogs—six of them, all chained to fresh, shiny loops sunk into the walls, some of whom Jack didn't know—to freeze to death down here before… whatever this was.

"Here," Millie Dance said, her voice scratched and raw as she thrust a cup out toward him. Her hand shook slightly as she held it, and the coffee spilled over the chipped rim to redden her chill-white knuckles. She ran the corner shop and post office in Lochwinnoch, with a brisk trade in Irn-Bru and gossip for the Old Man. It was a good life for a dog, and she had gotten used to playing human. Jack had never seen her without makeup and a sensible heel, never mind in a tattered dressing gown with blood matted in her hair. "Even a wolf would rather be—"

One of the other dogs—Hector Bates, a dour farmhand who'd been lying to local farmers about who ate their sheep for twenty years—backhanded the cup out of Millie's hand. It hit the dirt floor with a thud. Coffee spilled out to steam against the cold earth and rolled until Gregor put his foot out to stop it.

"Let 'em parch," he snapped, his shoulders hunched, and chapped lips lifted back from nicotine-yellow teeth as he glared at Jack. "We don't owe them anything. For centuries we've groveled for them, done their dirty deeds for them, and now they don't even have the fucking decency to put us down with dignity? You want to wag your tail for a pat on the head, Millie, that's on you. I'm done showing my throat."

Gregor laughed harshly and bent down to pick up the cup.

"Are we keeping you from your sheep?" Gregor mocked as he wiped the cup on his jeans. There was never a bad situation he couldn't make worse with his mouth, even when his fingers were wet with blood from the injury on his shoulder that wouldn't heal. "Scared they'll tup some strange ram while you're not there to watch?"

Hector lunged at Gregor and jerked to a stop at the end of his chain. The metal collar cut into the weathered slack of his throat and made him gag. Millie pulled him away by the back of his shirt.

"I'll do as I fucking please," she snarled at him as she shoved him against the curved wall. The old, shaped stones were limned with ice, thick glazed over the mortar and granite. She jammed her forearm up under Hector's chin, above the collar. "Give what I want, to whom I want. You're just another dog, Hector. Don't try and show your fangs to me."

Jack grabbed her shoulders, all wiry muscle under the greasy felt of her robe, and pulled her off the other dog. He didn't get any thanks from Hector for the save. He slouched sullenly against the wall.

"Enough," he said as he put his body between the two of them. He could feel Millie's growl through her collarbone—a dangerous, back-of-the-throat, almost whine that wasn't a warning anymore. "Fighting among ourselves isn't going to get us out of here."

It wasn't Millie who backed down. Hector was the one who turned away with a hunched shoulder and silence, and one of the strange dogs barked out a harsh, unhappy laugh.

"At least if we kill ourselves, they won't get the chance," the man—his voice burred with a lowland accent and the remnants of an expensive suit hanging in filthy rags from his body—interrupted. He tugged nervously at his collar, fingers curled around the rough round of metal, and his voice dropped as though the dread had real weight to catch in his throat. "You've not seen them—"

He broke off as a chunk of ice caught him on the temple. It split his eyebrow open and blood dripped down into his eye.

"Shut the fuck up!" Tom, a half-blind dog kept in the Pack on Da's charity, snarled where he huddled against the wall. He groped over the ground with clumsy, half-frozen hands for another projectile. "Monsters and murderers. You're full of shit. That's all it is. The prophets said they have a place for—"

"I know what I saw," the stranger shot back. "I know what I saw them *do*. Our *place* is on the end of their knives."

Tom grabbed a stone and cocked his arm back. Before he could throw it, Gregor stepped into the path of it and growled.

"You heard him."

The unexpected show of support from his brother caught Jack off-balance. He gave the back of Gregor's head a hard look and wondered if he could trust this. Probably not, he knew that, but for now it worked. Tom clumsily dropped the rock and lifted his chin in submissive acknowledgment of the reproof.

"Sorry," he muttered. "Ain't my place, but he isn't even pack. What's he know about our prophets?"

"Same thing you do, that we all do," Jack said. The question of where he stood with his brother could wait for later. The last thing Jack needed right then was to borrow more trouble. "That they're scum, the dregs and perverts that no pack wants, and no wolf with half a brain lends an ear to them?"

Tom gave him a resentful look through his matted hair, his one eye faded blue. "Well, I ain't a dog. The prophets told us the Winter was coming, and it did. They told us that the Old Man wouldn't come back from the loch, and he didn't. Now they told us that the gods got a special job just for dogs, that it's why we were born like this… instead of like you. Why shouldn't we believe 'em? They talk to the gods for us, don't they?"

A mutter of uncomfortable agreement ran around the room. Some of the dogs, like Tom, seemed entirely convinced, even seduced, by the new catechism. The rest, like Millie, who nodded uncertain agreement a second too late for conviction, wanted to believe, since they knew what the alternative was. Only the stranger, fingers pressed to his eyebrow to pinch the wound shut, openly rejected Tom's faith with a sneer as he spat onto the floor.

"We don't believe them because the gods fucked us before," Gregor snarled as he stepped forward to loom over Tom. "Or did you forget why we're on this side of the Wall?"

Instead of being intimidated, Tom lifted his chin and nervously licked his lips.

"You, not us," Tom said. His voice cracked as Gregor grabbed his shirt and hauled him roughly to his feet, but his words stayed steady. "Wolves, not dogs. The gods don't need you anymore. They need us. That's why they made us, to take your place now you've failed them."

There was something unsettlingly fervent in his face—almost religious, almost human. Sometimes, even with Danny in his bed, Jack forgot how *tame* some of the dogs were. Danny might claim it as a virtue, but there was too much wolf in him to thrive on a leash.

Jack caught Gregor's arm as it cocked back for a punch.

"For what?" he asked.

Tom opened his mouth, sure he knew the answer, and then nothing came out. He spluttered for a second and then rallied awkwardly. "To serve them," he said. His eyes flicked up to Jack's and then slid sidelong away. "To be loyal and stay by their side."

"Stay to heel, you mean," Gregor said with contempt. He shoved Tom back against the wall and turned to Jack. "They promised me your throat and the Pack."

Jack gave Gregor a thin smile. "To me too," he said. "And they gave Lach the Pack too, along with a promise they'd protect him."

"In Girvan they offered to save the children," Gregor said. There was a bite to his voice as he glanced around the shadowy cell. "But the children still died, and I'm not the Numitor."

Or a wolf, but Jack held his tongue on that. If the threat of his brother's fangs helped to keep people in line, Jack would use it for now.

"And my brother's still alive, and Lachlan might call himself Numitor, but the fuck he is," Jack said. The steadiness of his voice made Tom squirm as he looked away and wiped his nose on his sleeve. "The prophets make a lot of promises, try to be all things to all people, but they can't keep all of them. Once they don't need to keep you in line anymore—"

The stranger's cracked voice interrupted him. "Then they'll pull out your teeth, slice off your skin, and only when they're done do they cut your throat."

Uneasy silence fell over the cell as the stranger's voice cracked in a sob and he covered his face. The dogs shuffled their feet, and Jack turned away from the raw grief that squeezed through the man's fingers. He couldn't let himself see it, or feel pity for it, or it might seem real.

It wasn't—it *wouldn't* be—Jack's pain. He wouldn't be left cracked open for his pain to leak out like blood in the water. He'd find Danny, whole and irritating and *Jack's*, like he'd been since Jack first realized he wanted the lanky, older boy. Dog or not.

"Lies," Tom said, but his voice wasn't quite so sure. "And if it did happen, the prophets had their reasons."

Without looking around, Gregor reached back and grabbed Tom's jaw between thumb and forefinger. He squeezed down hard until the only sound Tom could get out was a whimper.

"Their reasons, not ours," Gregor said. "Since when do we trust the fucking prophets?"

Millie pulled a crumpled square of old cotton out of her sleeve and awkwardly offered it to the stranger as he groaned against his palms. He ignored it, and the tattered handkerchief dangled pathetically from Millie's finger. Maybe humans weren't the only ones who clung to the ideas of the pre-Winter world.

"What else can we do?" Millie asked. She balled up the handkerchief in her hand, her knuckles white against chapped skin as she squeezed. "Do you think no one said those things when the prophets came down from the hills and started to make demands? That none of the wolves told them to fuck off? The Old Man sent them away with a flea in their ear. Laughed them back into the storm. Maybe that's—"

She stopped, her mouth pursed around the words that wanted to get out.

"Killed him," Jack said for her.

An unhappy growl creaked out of Gregor's chest at the blunt statement, but he didn't argue. The idea that Da was dead and they hadn't *known*, not felt it echo through their blood like a drum, seemed impossible. Except no one had thought someone could find the Sannock Dead or that a prophet could stitch a dead wolf to their back and run in their skin.

It was the Wolf Winter, and a lot of things were possible. Jack didn't believe it, not yet, but Da could be dead. He didn't know how he felt about that. It was his *da*. He'd spent his whole life on the hunt for the Old Man's approval—and the flip-side disapproval of Gregor—but he also knew that one day he might have to kill his da. On some level he'd always accepted that.

Yet it still felt wrong to admit that his da's death would grieve him, but that Danny's would destroy him.

It was a weakness, and Da had always said the Numitor couldn't afford weakness.

"Maybe they just locked him somewhere," Hector said. It was obviously an attempt at kindness, not something he believed. "We don't know."

"Dead or trapped," Millie said. "Either way, the Old Man was gone, and that's when the prophets came back. They had dogs on leashes—"

"And empty leashes too," the stranger said without looking up from his knees. "Bloody ones. Plenty of those."

"They told them to round us up," Millie said. "That the gods wanted us. No one laughed this time."

"Kath did," Tom said. He seemed to have forgotten his conversion to the prophets' cause. Kath had always been kind enough to him. "She called them frauds and fuckers and tore the skin right back off that one man. Then that night, the Wild came down from the hills at *their* order."

"When?" Jack asked.

"A few weeks ago," Millie said. She paused and rubbed her hand over her face. Without the makeup she used down in the town, she looked younger. Not the effect humans went for, as Jack understood it. "A week? I didn't feel it. The Wild never spoke to me."

Hector shifted from his lean against the wall. "I did. I was up in the hills wi' the sheep. They'll be dead now, without me, poor bastards." He gave Gregor a dour look of accusation, and got an unapologetic, sharp grin back. "It didn't feel right. It hasn't felt right since."

Jack was about to dismiss that but hesitated. Dogs weren't attuned to the Wild like the wolves. Even Danny only really sensed it when the Wild reached out to him, and the Wild liked Danny better than most. Old stories let humans into the Wild if they were part of the warp and weft of fields or forests, absorbed them as though they were another part of the landscape. Hector had spent years in the hills with his flock and his frustration.

"Like what?" he asked. At his shoulder Gregor snorted in contempt.

Hector looked taken aback. He scratched his neck and took a second to think about the answer.

"Sorta sour," he said. "Like the old Graveland estate or the old Sannock haunts. Places where the grass has gone bad."

Jack thought of the beach in Girvan, the dead and the monsters laid out on the snowy shale. It hadn't felt like somewhere anyone would enjoy a picnic again. The stench had sunk down into the bedrock.

"That's bullshit," Gregor said. The hair on the back of Jack's neck prickled with familiar jealousy as Gregor reached for the Wild and it answered. He had to throttle back the urge to do the same, to prove he could. "I'd know if there was something wrong."

Hector tucked his chin in submission, but muttered, "You don't know everything."

"He doesn't," Jack agreed.

Gregor curled his lip in a sneer to express his opinion. "So the Wild went sour, and what happened then?" he asked. "Bad dreams? What did the prophets do?"

There was a pause as the dogs looked at each other. Reluctance pinched at the corners of their mouths and tightened their eyes. In the end it was the strange dog who answered, too caught up in his own losses to care about delivering bad news. Or maybe he enjoyed evening the scales a little.

"Whatever the prophets wanted," he said. "They walked in and out of your houses while you slept and took what they wanted. Flesh. Treasures. The bitch-goddess made the moon stand still in the sky to watch."

"Children," Millie interrupted sharply. This was pack news to share. "They took the children. Four of them, from their cots."

Tom shifted against the wall. "And Bron," he said, despite Millie's glare. "They took Bron. When the next prophet came into town to tell us what the gods wanted, he had Bron's finger with him. Kath didn't laugh at them after that."

No. If they had her wolf child, Jack didn't suppose she would have. He heard Gregor make a soft noise behind him—surprise and a scrape of concern. Bron had never forgiven Jack for her brother. She hadn't thought he should love Danny or that he should have let him leave. She'd run with Gregor and his friends once she was old enough to make her own decisions.

Bron was a grown woman, but if the others were young enough to be "taken from a cot," then Jack could guess who the parents were. Pack hierarchy was decided by strength, but the point of the pack was their children. Higher-ranked wolves were *expected* to have children.

It was the reason Jack had been exiled—because he wouldn't fuck a woman even to get her pregnant. Or, at least, that was why his da had picked Gregor to be the next Numitor. Jack had been exiled because no one believed he'd take the demotion well.

Back in Girvan, between the pain, he'd wondered if he should never have come down over the Wall. He could have picked a woman, closed his eyes, and thought of Danny. He hadn't seen why he should have to.

If it was the children that Jack thought it was—two named for him, one for Gregor, and the last after their dear, dead ma—the prophets had pulled the fangs of Da's loyalists. Kath was the only one who had what it took to lead, but the others would have backed her.

Would have.

So the kids had been taken to sideline them while Lach and his pack had been seduced by empty promises from the gods, filtered through a prophet's scarred lips.

"Fuck," Jack said.

Millie gave him a thin, tired smile. "If the wolves don't know how to fight," she said, "what's a dog to do but what they're told, and hope for the best?"

She gave him the courtesy of a pause to give him a chance to answer, but she didn't look surprised when he had nothing to say. Along with the other dogs, she turned away, either to curl up against the wall or pace the length of her chain.

"There's a plan," Tom said. He'd found his faith in the prophets again as they talked, plastered desperately over that hollow center of doubt. "There's always been a plan. Who were wolves to think they could deny it?"

While Gregor cursed Tom out, anger and frustration raw in his voice, Jack pulled impatiently at his new collar. He could taste the Wild in the back of his throat—*sour*, Hector had said, but it was grease and smoke on Jack's tongue—but he let it fade away again. The Wild could do a lot of things, but it could no more unlock a padlock than it could start a car.

The Old Man had said that if he came back, he'd end up here, caged for the prophets. Jack should have listened.

He found a spot on the wall and crouched down on the balls of his feet. The wolf itched under his skin, eager to shift, and he let it. If it came down to it, Jack thought bleakly as he rubbed his fingers over the cold metal, he'd rather strangle his wolf himself than go under a prophet's knife again.

He was afraid, and all the shame in the world couldn't shift it from his bones.

Chapter Eight—Jack

"HERE," GREGOR said as he slid down the wall to sit next to Jack. He handed Jack the battered, now-empty mug. It had taken him a while to work out his black, caustic mood on Tom and the walls. His voice was tattered, and his hands bruised, skin split and shredded over the bony jut of his knuckles. Careless. Even a dog would realize there was something wrong when the Numitor's son's knuckles scabbed over instead of healed. "Recognize it?"

Jack turned the mug in his hand. There was a fresh chip on the rim, and the cup was greasy with the residue of spilled coffee and dirty, sweaty hands. But even in the dim light of the cell, Jack could make out the bright, aggressive green of the glazed paint.

"It's Da's," Jack said. Coffee in the morning or whiskey in the evening, his da had drunk it out of this mug. A sour laugh squeezed out of his chest as he leaned his head back against the cold stones. "That's fucking pathetic."

Gregor snorted his agreement.

Da had smashed enough cups against the wall or floor from carelessness or temper. Or he used to catch rusty brown water from a drip in the pipes under the toilet or filled it with white spirit and vinegar to get rust off something. Once he'd used it to brew the mountain ash gall to ink a new wolf into the Pack, then sent Danny to buy a new one because his coffee gave him the shits after.

Only an idiot would think that the Old Man—dead or gone—would give a damn what anyone did with a cup he didn't have to drink out of. That was Lach, though.

"He broke your dog's ankle once," Gregor said. "Left him to crawl down from the hills on his own."

Jack paused for a second as a mixture of anger and jealousy twisted sickly in his stomach. He'd never fought Danny's battles for him. Da wouldn't have stood for that. Even dogs had to be able to stand up for themselves to stay in the Pack, but what Gregor had said sounded more like torture than a fight.

"He never told me that," Jack said once he'd swallowed the sour bubble of bile back down. "I would have—"

"Made it worse," Gregor said. "Lach threatened Bron if Danny told anyone, told him that 'things happened to reckless girls' who don't have people to look out for them. I guess he convinced Danny he should hold his tongue, because your dog didn't say anything to anyone."

Jack set the cup down and wiped his hands on his jeans. He gave his brother a cold look. "Then how do you know?"

Gregor shrugged unrepentantly. "Lach thought I'd be grateful he fucked with what was yours," he said. The corner of his mouth tilted with old contempt. "I wasn't. It just proved that he wasn't just a bully, he was a coward. He couldn't even beat up a dog without a girl to hide behind."

"And you didn't do anything?"

Gregor glanced at him in surprise, eyebrows raised. "He was your dog, not mine. Why should I care?"

Jack supposed he should have expected that, but sometimes.... Sometimes he thought this fragile alliance with his brother could work. It had always seemed like the world had only made enough room for one of them, that they had to shove and snarl to claim it for their own. With everything the Wolf Winter had carved out of them, Jack wondered if maybe there was *enough* left between them.

But then Gregor would open his mouth and remind Jack they still hated each other.

"I might have warned him off Bron, made sure he knew that wolves didn't have accidents, but I didn't need to," Gregor said. "Next time Lach got dragged over the loch to go to school, one of the town girls he'd been screwing threw coffee on him and accused him of putting something in her drink. When the teachers looked into it, they found a bag of drugs in his bag."

Jack frowned as a flicker of memory cut through his anger at Gregor. He'd been there when the local police arrived—sweaty-nervous as they ventured onto Da's land even if they didn't know why—and when his da dragged Lach out and beat him in front of the whole Pack, Danny had been there too, and Jack had thought it was a dog's weak stomach that made Danny look away from the beating despite the fact he hated Lach.

"You think he set that up?" Jack asked skeptically. "If Da found out that Danny had deliberately brought the cops up here, into pack business, he'd have exiled the whole family over the Wall. Hell, Da believed that the drugs weren't Lach's, and he still nearly sent him away just for being stupid enough to get into that situation. Why would Danny take that risk? It wasn't like he was scared of starting a fight."

Or losing one. Danny had never fought to win. He knew that most of the time he wouldn't. He aimed to hurt the other person enough to make them think the win wasn't worth it—dislocated knees, gouged eyes, and the humiliation that everyone knew a dog had made them yelp. But that had been a fight he hadn't wanted to lose.

Danny and Bron had never been close. Neither were Jack and Gregor, though, and they only made it back to Lochwinnoch because they weren't about to let someone else kill their brother. There were times Danny forgot he was a dog—sometimes even Jack did—but it was when he *didn't* that he was most dangerous.

Because a dog didn't have to play by the rules.

"A coward and a bully wouldn't risk exile to get payback," Jack said. "And Danny's always been stupid where his sister was concerned. So if he's not here, we know why. Why tell me this, Gregor?"

Gregor folded one arm over his chest to rub his shoulder. He didn't smell of fresh blood anymore, but under the hot, metallic tang of his temper, there was a murky hint of pain. It had started to heal, but it hadn't stopped hurting.

"Kath asked me to trust her," he said. "But I trust you. At least about this. Danny's your dog. You care, and you've always been stupid for him. So what are you going to do to get him back?"

He waited.

So did Jack, but nothing came to him. He pushed himself up the wall—the sudden focus of everyone's attention—and hoped that would change in a minute.

"Fuck the prophets," he said roughly. "And fuck any wolf that shows throat to them. The Wolf Winter belongs to us. We were promised it, and we do not forgive that promise. The gods should fear us. Not the other way around."

It was the strange dog who spoke up. "That sounds good, but what are we meant to do? Chained dogs and collared wolves, against the Wild and monsters and… gods?"

Jack still didn't know. His head was full of a sick storm of fear and anger. It would have to be enough.

"We do what we've always done, what we did to the Sannock." He felt a chill on the back of his neck as he said their name—murdered by wolves, butchered for their blood and meat. It was a deed to be ashamed of, not to hold up for people to rally behind, but Jack would use what they had. The Sannock, truly dead now the stagnant resection of the Wild they'd been trapped in had split open, were past being hurt by it. "We hunt them, we bring them to bay, and then we kill them."

It would have worked better on wolves. The words would have tickled their pride, and the excitement would have spread through the Pack like contagion. They'd have howled for him, a new catechism to add to the canon. Dogs were more cautious. They liked to sniff before they leaped. Maybe that was their nature.

It still lifted a few chins and lowered some shoulders as the dogs glanced from him to each other. Only Tom glared sullenly from the shadows and clung stubbornly to his faith in the prophets' half-promises. It was fragile, but it was faith.

Of course, it was Gregor who couldn't resist the urge to foul it. He had never been able to leave well enough alone, even when it was in his best interest. His voice cut roughly through the uncertain silence.

"Sounds great, but…," he said. Jack turned and scowled at Gregor, who lifted his chin and smirked at him. "Maybe we should get out of here first?"

Jack skinned his lips back from his teeth in a grin as an idea crystallized in his brain. The desire to spite his brother maybe wasn't the best source of inspiration, but he'd take what he could get.

"Why?" he asked. Gregor caught up a second later and grimaced, caught between understanding and their old, comfortable resentment. Jack turned to sweep his gaze across the dogs as they listened. "Let the prophets come. They're going to take us exactly where we want to go."

Despite their wariness, the ferocity of his words caught the dogs up. Teeth flashed in quick, determined smiles, and they nodded grimly as they traded looks in the dim light. Maybe, Jack thought with a flicker of grim humor, he wasn't the only one who found odd comfort in the old habits of hating Gregor.

The scuff of boots on dirt behind made him turn. Gregor met his eyes for a second and then looked away.

"You have the dogs," he said. "But to be Numitor, you'll need the wolves."

A ROUGH hand hooked through the ring that collared Jack and dragged him up out of the dark. He squinted at the sudden transition to the snow-bright morning glare and lifted his arm to shade his eyes. The world was white, the sky starched-looking with the next fall, and fresh, crisp sheets of white snow lay over everything. The prophet who had ahold of Jack had pockmarked cheeks and ginger hair that crept back from his furrowed brow. He slapped Jack's arm out of the way and looked surprised as he recognized his face.

"See?" Lachlan blurted as he stepped forward. "I told you it was them. The Numitor's bastards."

Gregor laughed at him as he was dragged up out of the hole. "Your parents get wed in a church, Lach?" he mocked. "Yer ma wear a veil over her fur?"

Color flushed up Lach's face, freckles sprayed in dark splatters over his forehead and across his cheeks. He stepped in and backhanded Gregor across the face, hard enough to jar Gregor loose from the prophet's grip and lay him out on the snow.

"Shut up," Lachlan spat down at him. He kicked Gregor in the ribs and then the stomach. "You aren't even a wolf anymore, and you were barely a man before, so who the fuck do you think you are to look down on me?"

Jack lunged at Lach, but the prophet who had him had a better grip. The metal dug in across Jack's throat and split open the slice on his throat as the prophet yanked him back and then kicked his feet out from under him and put him on his knees.

"He's the Old Man's son," Jack spat. He wrapped his fingers around the collar to pull it away from his throat. The nicest thing he'd ever said about Gregor, but whatever Jack felt about his brother, he was a golden son in comparison to Lach. "He's my brother. And he's more wolf than you. More man too."

Lach stamped down on Gregor's stomach. The impact made Gregor grunt, the breath shocked out of him, and curl up around the pain.

"He's nothing," Lach said. He bent down to grab Gregor's collar and pull him up off the ground. Spit strung his lips together like stitches as he snarled into Gregor's face. "The prophets will kill you, and I'll lead the Pack into the Winter. It's *my* name they'll remember."

Gregor snapped his head forward, and his forehead smacked against Lach's face hard enough to smash his nose in a welter of blood and pulped tissue. The pale, freckled skin puffed and purpled as it swelled, and Lach yelped in surprise as he staggered back. Blood snorted and spluttered between his fingers as he tried to fumble the mess back into place.

It would heal, but noses were like joints—it would heal but that didn't mean it would be pretty.

"They'll remember you were lacking," Gregor jeered. When he grinned, it showed bloodstained teeth. "Lacking Givens, the Prophets' Puppet."

Lach made a stuffy, inchoate noise of rage and let go of his half-molded nose to jerk his arm back and punch Gregor. His knuckles bounced off the side of Gregor's face as he turned his head to the side to save his nose.

"I should never have listened to that bitch. I should have killed you when I had the chance," Lach raged. "I could have made it last all night."

The cackle of low, dirty laughter that escaped Gregor despite his swollen eye didn't need any explanation. "That's not what I've heard."

Jack laughed. Someone else tittered with a stifled burst of repressed humor. Lach kicked Gregor again and turned to glare at the people who'd gathered to watch. Da's inner circle was there, grim but resolutely not involved, and Jack glanced around to confirm the kids were missing. He'd got one wrong. Jaclyn was there, with a dark scowl on her four-year-old face as her da tethered her in place with a tight grip on her arm. But her ma's stomach was flat, and the smell of sour milk hung around her. The baby had been born and taken while Jack was away.

She caught Jack's attention on her and glared at him. If she couldn't risk anger at the prophets, Jack supposed, he'd do to blame instead.

Kath was there too, her back stiff and her hair in damp, half-frozen elflocks around her face. She didn't look at Gregor, but her lip curled when Lach called her a bitch.

"Enough," the ginger prophet barked. He handed Jack over to one of his fellows and limped forward. If he had a new wolfskin to wear, he'd left it behind today. It didn't matter. Lach still grimaced and backed away from

Gregor like a pup who had to cede a kill to the alpha. "Call yourself the Numitor if you want, but the Pack is ours now. You don't decide who lives or dies. You're lucky we let you decide when you need to piss… and we can take that away from you too if we can't trust you to hold your own dick."

Lach flushed with a hot, humiliated misery that made his supporters lick their lips nervously and shuffle backward in anticipation of the payback being spilled down. The prophet ignored him as he bent down and pulled Gregor onto his feet. He even brushed clots of bloody snow off Gregor's shirt in an oddly polite gesture.

"Where is she?" Lach asked.

"Busy."

"When will she be back?"

"When she ain't busy."

Jack clenched his hand around the collar at his throat. Blood was slick against his fingers as it dripped down his wrist. "Where's the Old Man?" he asked. "What did you do with my da?"

The question pulled the air out of the day. Everyone caught their breath as they waited for the answer. Even gone—even assumed dead—the Old Man had to have a story, right? The prophet felt it too. He glanced around and then gave Jack a thin smile that acknowledged the move.

"Run off," he said. "Dead in a ditch. Lost in the Wild. Who knows? He was an old man, and now he's gone. Are you going to weep that you're an orphan?"

Jack's temper flared, and his anger pulled at the Wild for fuel the way he took a deep breath before exhaling. For the first time, he felt what Hector had meant about it being "sour." It was there, but when he reached for it, all he got was a slime of grease and reluctance. For the first time in his life, the Wild didn't want anything to do with him.

The prophet must have read that realization in Jack's face, because he smirked wide enough to show the withered gap in his gums where his eye teeth had been bedded. Jack let the Wild squirm away from his touch. He could destroy the prophets without it—or at least, he conceded to the skeptical undercurrent that welled up, hurt them—but let them think the Wild had rejected him thoroughly.

"When I kill you, any bastards you had before Da cut your balls off will dance in the streets," Jack said. The prophet behind him yanked on his collar, and he staggered before he caught himself. He braced his feet and looked around at the Pack. Da's best and Lach's dregs weren't going to shift yet, but there were wolves between those two poles. The prophets might have dismissed them, but even a middling wolf in the Scottish Pack was better than most. "Is this the fucking Winter we've been promised? On our knees to the prophets? Harnessed like sled dogs so they can keep pace with Fenrir?"

People listened. No one thought kindly of the boot on their neck, never mind a wolf. The ginger prophet scowled as he caught the taste of resentment on the air, and he gestured sharply to the man with Jack's collar. "Shut him up," Ginger ordered. "And hobble them both. Bring the dogs."

The other prophets dragged the dogs up from the cage, chains wrapped around rot-rashed hands. Protests and questions were silenced with backhands and kicks. Even Tom's attempts to testify to his faith were smacked out of him. He went on his knees with the rest.

The strange dog—Heath, Jack reminded himself, from Stirling—just kept his head down and did as he was told. He only glanced up once, to fire a bitter glance toward Lach.

"I'm coming as well," Lach blurted as he stepped forward. He hunched his shoulders like a whipped cur when the prophet growled at him, but he stood his ground. He scratched at the side of his face, where the skin was already raw and welted from being worried at. "I want to speak to her. I want to hear her tell what it will be like when they come back. For us. For me, for the Numitor. I need to hear her say it."

Ginger looked at him with contempt but gave in with a curl of his lip. "Fine," he said dismissively. "You can walk the dogs."

Behind him Ellie stepped forward. She looked like Kath, if she'd been left to fade in the sun. The same haircut, the same loose dress that most of the female wolves wore, and an attempt at the same confidence. It was all a little too blurred around the edges to convince.

"I'll go as well," she said. When both men glared at her, she ducked her chin quickly. Her hands were twisted in her dress, bony knuckles almost lost in the folds. "You're the Numitor, Lachlan, you need an honor guard. Even when you go to pay your respects to the gods. After last night… I need to prove myself again. Let me?"

It took a second as Lachlan was torn between paranoia and pride. It was Ginger who decided in the end.

"Let her tag along if that's what she wants," he said. "If she isn't happy to see you, maybe your guard will have the honor of being the next Numitor. And the rest of you… we only took some of the children last time. Don't think you could stop us, or hide, if we wanted to take the rest."

He turned and limped away, clumsy in the snow and his heavy, winter-weather garb.

"Like dogs," Jack said as the prophet behind him dragged at the collar. "When they whelp an unwanted litter, the owner just drowns them. Nothing they can do to stop it."

The prophet punched him in the kidneys until he gave in and let them drag him away. He locked eyes with Kath as he went, a quietly grim threat that was only for her. Jack didn't blame her for what she'd done to him or that she'd shown belly to the prophets. But if she'd traded her son for her daughter, that he wouldn't forgive.

At the edge of the lake, they punched holes through his wrists and ankles and strung them through with thick wire shackles so he couldn't run and if he changed, he'd cut his paws off. Da had preferred the collars, since people got to choose to change back or die. The hobbles maimed before they killed.

"Rose is looking forward to seeing you," Ginger said as he pulled Jack to his feet. His breath had the same sour stink as Lach's as he leaned in to mutter in Jack's ear. "You should have killed her while you had the chance. Whatever happens now, it's on you. We'd have never gone this far, never even dreamed we could."

Jack took a breath to ask, but before he could, Ginger pushed him into the Wild. It didn't want him. At least, it didn't want the metal locked around his throat and stitched through his joints. Jack retched with the rejection, hands and feet numb as he felt the metal vibrate like a plucked string. The slash on his throat flared with fresh pain, cold and electric as it spiked his nerves, and the collar choked him as it tried to anchor him to the world.

The Wild felt thin and slimy against his skin as it tried to kill him, like the membrane of an onion or the freshly peeled skin of a fish. It *clung* and *resisted.*

The prophets forced him, ripped at the Wild with the fetid *wrong* of their stolen wolves, until it let him through. He coughed and tasted the poison in the back of his throat as though it had been pressed out of his wound like juice. Behind him the dogs whined and begged, shocked by something they never imagined. Jack tried not to groan and locked his knees. Next to him Gregor gagged and then swore thickly through a mouthful of bile.

"It's sour," he said as he spat onto the snow. "I couldn't tell before."

Long strands of faded, frayed grass stuck up through the snow, which was churned up into hummocks and humps and frozen solid. The ice was pitted and gray, discolored and deformed.

Jack smelled something wrong first, and then he looked around....

It wasn't a whole place. Bits of it had been sliced up, grafted over the familiar highland Wild he'd grown up with. Gray sea waves, crested with a half-frozen scum of slush, spilled in over the dark, still waters of the loch. The high sea cliffs where the Sannock had been butchered faded in and out on the far side of the loch.

Old blood still stained the sand. It always would. It never had.

The whole landscape felt strained. It was pulled taut, drawn back like an elastic band used as a sling. Gregor had left Rose alive in the tied-off end of the Wild that Da had hidden the Sannock behind. Not for lack of trying, but prophets were harder to kill than they'd ever believed. They hoped she might end up trapped there, but expected she'd find her way out.

Instead she'd brought the Sannock's dead pocket of Wild north with her, dragged it at her heels like a cape. And the air was ripe with the smell of stagnant seawater and the sickly, poisoned stink of the prophets' monsters.

As though the recognition of them had called it, a monster appeared over the gray rocks of the Highlands, purple-gray skin pulled taut over great deformed sheets of muscle, and the blue lace band of a bra stretched over the barrel chest and strained ribs. Swollen yellow eyes popped from their sockets like a pug, oozed yellow gunge down its bony checks and into the loose jowls that flapped under its jaw. It snarled through a too-broad mouth—scar tissue stitched up both cheeks where flesh had torn to accommodate the new, undershot jaw—as it slid down onto the beach.

Legs that were too thin for its bulk sank into the loose shale and sand.

She came next, one hand on the knife-sharp shoulder blades of a lean monster with the hooked, whistling nose of a borzoi. She looked sickly smug at the sight of her prisoners.

Chapter Nine—Danny

"You said you'd warn them," Danny said. It wanted to be an accusation, but the tone caught in his throat and wouldn't come out. He was a grown man, an adult who'd had a job and paid his bills and answered to nobody. Never around her, though, and that left him the old habits of childhood to fall back on. "That they wouldn't walk into—"

Kath scowled at him from the door of the old shepherd's hut—four walls and a roof to keep out the storm if they were stuck up there overnight—and tossed the duffel bag she'd carried up the hill. He fumbled it out of the air before it hit him in the face, and he grumbled under his breath in irritation. It looked like he wasn't the only one to fall into old habits. Random objects thrown at his face had always been one of her tricks to make sure he was paying attention, hadn't dropped his guard.

Wolves can afford trust. You can't.

"Mind your tongue," Kath warned him bluntly as he dropped the duffel to dangle from his hand. "You're home now. No one here cares that you've got a bank account or that you're a teacher."

"Professor," he corrected her stiffly.

The ridiculousness of that occurred to him the minute the words left his tongue. Even if he could convince Kath the difference mattered, and he couldn't, that was all gone now. All those years he'd spent away—his almost perfect human act, the office that smelled of him and books, the comfortable life he'd made—felt like a pit stop. The first of the Wolf Winter's snow had only fallen a few months ago, but he'd already let go of the fantasy that he'd ever go back.

Even if there was anything to go back to—one day—Jack had ruined it. He'd been there, in Danny's bed and in his life, and now he wouldn't be. Danny didn't know how he'd live with that.

He dragged his hand down his face and sighed. "I don't suppose I'm either now."

Kath snorted at him. "It was what you did. That doesn't change who you are," she said as she stepped inside and dragged the door shut behind her. The wind rattled at it like it resented being closed out, and she had to latch it with the loop of rope nailed to the jam. "As for the Numitor's boys, I tried to warn them, but I was too late. Lachlan already knew they were coming somehow—"

"You knew I was here," Danny pointed out as he sat down on the edge of the narrow metal cot, the smell of mildew worked down into the stuffing of the bedroll he'd found propped up in the corner. "Why wouldn't Lach?"

Kath huffed and shook her head. "Dog or not," she said, "I carried you, I *birthed* you. You think you could come back to Lochwinnoch and I wouldn't catch your scent in the Wild? Besides, once the snows came, I knew to look out for you. Whatever you pretended to be down over the Wall, we're your blood. Your family. Where else would you go?"

Guilt cut through Danny's anger and made him look down. He focused on his fingers as he wrenched the buckles of the duffel loose. It had been his once, the stitches still strained where he'd stuffed it with books and errands, but the canvas had gotten discolored and stiff with disuse since he left.

There was an old glasses case on top, patched together with duct tape where he'd broken it. The glasses inside had heavy, battered rims, and the prescription was a few years out of date, but they'd do. Danny unfolded the legs and put them on. The world came back into focus and didn't make him feel any better about himself.

If Jack hadn't come to find him and brought the prophets on his tail, Danny would never have come back here. The idea that he might need to check on Bron and Mam had never occurred to him. He'd have stayed with Jenny and the others, kept his mouth shut and his head down. Maybe he'd have gotten back together with Jenny, because he was still a dog and he wanted a pack.

What good would he have done back here? They were wolves, and this was their winter. All he could do was remind people their bloodline had thrown a dog.

Kath had always thought she knew him better than she did, though.

"However he knew, he knew. You should have—I should have done something," he said.

"What? Die?" Kath asked. She leaned over and rapped her knuckles on the top of his head. "I told you when you were a little boy that if you read too much you'd get stupid. Squeeze too many other people's words in there and where is there for your wits to live?"

Danny leaned his head to the side out from under her hand. "I could have warned them. When you told me what happened, I could have gone back and stopped them before they reached the wolves."

She grabbed his ear and pulled his head back so he had to look at her. "I make pretty kids, Danny, but not that pretty. If you told them their da was dead and Lach had taken their crown, they'd have gotten back quicker, been taken earlier. Nothing would have changed, except the prophets would have you as well. What good would that do anyone? What good would it do your sister?"

Danny grabbed her wrist. He didn't know which of them was more surprised.

"Don't."

"Or?"

Another of her old lessons. Danny hadn't forgotten any of them, though.

"I make pinching my ear more trouble than it's worth," he said. "Let go, Mam."

She did and then startled him by pressing her cold palm against his hot ear. Like a balm, or an apology. Except Kath never apologized to anyone.

"I swear," she said earnestly, "when I asked you to do this, I didn't think Jack and Gregor would be in danger. There should have been time to warn them, to plan what to do next. They're the Old Man's only sons. The last thing I expected was for Lachlan to try and murder them on their own doorstep. That's not how we do things. Whoever this woman he talks about is—this prophet—she's fucked the good sense out of him."

Danny rubbed his neck. Sometimes he could still feel the constriction of the leather when he swallowed.

"Nick—the dark man with Gregor—said she was his grandmother," he said. "Rose Blake."

Kath abruptly pulled her hand away. "No," she said. "He's wrong."

"More than you know," Danny agreed with a grimace. It bothered him a little that he still had a wolf's insular rejection to anything different to them, but he couldn't help it. It bothered him more that Gregor was more adaptable than he was, but he couldn't help *that* either. He leaned his elbows on his bag and looked up at Kath. This close he could make out her face, but it blurred as she stepped away from him. "But he probably knows her name. Do you know her?"

"No. I *knew* her," Kath said. She raked her fingers through her hair to slick the half-frozen curls back from her face. "She was no prophet, though. Just a mad bitch of a wolf that the Old Man had to put down."

"Why?"

"Because she deserved it," Kath said flatly. "It doesn't matter why. Whoever raised this Nick, it wasn't her. I threw the dirt on her face myself."

There was an uneasy undertone to her voice. Danny hesitated, but the other prophets in Girvan had known the name too. They'd never questioned it….

"What if it is?" Danny said carefully. "If I knew what she did—"

"If it was her—if it *is* her—then Bron's already dead," Kath said quietly. There was no doubt in her voice. "So why would I send her my son to gut too? You want to try and save Jack, don't convince me it's her. I won't let you go. Let the Old Man worry about his blood, and I'll worry about mine."

"You can't stop me." Kath turned toward him, and Danny smiled crookedly at her. "Dog or not, I'm your kid. When did anyone ever stop *you* doing what *you* wanted?"

He waited and Kath finally walked back to him. She sighed heavily and stroked his hair back from his face.

"I brought the books, the maps you asked for," she said. "Do you really think you can do it? Find the prophet's temple on this side of the Wild? Find where they took the children and the dogs?"

Danny glanced down at the bag still in his lap. He could feel the weight of the books against his thigh. He wanted to say no, to shed that responsibility, but now it wasn't just his sister he needed to find.

"I can," he said. "Mam, if it is Rose Blake, do you know why she was exiled?"

Kath's fingers tightened around the back of his head, and then she leaned down to press a cold-lipped kiss to his forehead. She didn't pull away immediately but rested her head against his. Uncertain of how to respond, Danny froze awkwardly. His mother loved him as best she could. He'd always known that, like he'd always known it wasn't enough. Kath wasn't a woman to be casually demonstrative. A sentimental moment was hand on a shoulder or nod of approval as she hauled you up out of the mud. The last time she'd kissed him had been his first day of school. Under the expectant eyes of other parents, she realized more than a sandwich and a brusque "Do well" was expected.

From what Danny remembered, he'd felt a lot like this about it—frozen uncomfortably to the spot. He hadn't understood school at that point, and the kiss had seemed like a formal goodbye. Someone had been there to take him home at the end of the day, but it had felt like something released. This had the same finality, and for a moment, Danny felt the old, frantic desire to cling to his mother.

"She wasn't exiled, she was executed," she said as she drew back. "But did you ever wonder why the Old Man was kind to dogs?"

Danny shrugged. "We're useful," he said. The rationale was one he'd heard often enough to have off by heart growing up. There was always a wolf ready to grumble because the Old Man kept his dogs, insisted they be treated as pack even if they were at the bottom of the pecking order. "It makes dealing with humans easier, and there's nowhere to live anymore where you don't have to deal with humans."

"You are, and that's why he let Millie and the like hang around. He was never kind, though, until he had a dog," Kath said. "A daughter, before the twins, but with their ma."

That was new information. Danny blinked as he tried to absorb it and then grimaced as his mind made grim sense of it. He'd always known that his mam loved him, because she kept him when she had old, dark options she could have picked instead.

"He got rid of her," Danny said. "Sacked her."

That was the traditional way—a sack, a stone, and the loch. It surprised Danny how much that thought troubled him. He'd never put that much value on the Old Man's fondness for him—Danny had been smart and useful—but the thought that the Numitor would have preferred to drown him threaded a chill through his memories.

"No," Kath said. She twisted her mouth as though the memory was sour. "He would have. He was expected to. Fiona, his mate, she wouldn't have it. Dog or not, it was her wain, and she wouldn't give it over to the prophets. Fiona would have taken the girl and gone south first, rather than give another litter to the man who killed his own get."

No one ever talked about the twins' mother, the Old Man's mate. Death had rubbed the human edges off her and left this idea of a perfect wolf. Danny had known his mam knew her, but until he heard this story, he hadn't realized Kath *liked* the other wolf. It occurred to Danny that he might have too. She sounded a lot like Jack.

"What happened?"

"The Old Man let Fiona stay, and let her keep the baby," Kath said. "He wasn't gracious about it at first, but dogs love like it's easy, and that's hard to resist. By the time she died, he cared enough to grieve. I think that's the only reason Fiona was able to stay."

Danny absorbed that. It was a story that he'd never heard even whispered in all his years in the Pack. Not a secret, exactly, just unspoken because it was too tender a scar to poke. He supposed it explained a lot about the Old Man, but so far it didn't answer his question.

"Did Nick's grandmother kill the wee girl?" Danny asked.

"See?" Kath said. "You don't need books to be smart, Danny."

"Why?"

"She was rabid," Kath said. Her lips curled back in an expression that hovered between a sneer and a scowl. "No one saw it, though, not until that night. Rose was the highest-ranking wolf in the Pack, the Old Man's right hand, and if she was a traditionalist, it wasn't any more than some of the other old wolves. Then one night she got up, stole a baby, and we found her at dawn by the loch with a wet, still sack. People said she was moonstruck, that she'd gotten too close to the moon goddess's heels during the hunt and been maddened."

"And you?"

"I think she was jealous," Kath said. "All those years she'd spent at the Numitor's side, his loyal wolf, and what did she have for it? Bad enough Fiona had the Numitor's heart and his cock, but now she had his ear and his child too. I think that was the final straw, that all the wolves Rose whelped had been sent away for being too weak, but Fiona got to keep her dog. She dressed it up with rants about purity and fate and the gods, but in the end, it was her spite. It doesn't matter, though, because the Old Man killed her, and we buried her out in the moors."

Danny rubbed his neck, the phantom bite of leather still there, and remembered the contemptuous bite in Rose's voice as she booted him in the ribs. *"You'll wish your ma had been brave enough to put you in a sack."*

Dead and buried should have been good enough, but Danny had seen enough over the last few weeks that he didn't think it was that simple. The prophets had kept secrets.

"What does that have to do with Bron?" he asked. "Why would Rose hold it against her?"

Kath looked away. "Because, until that morning when we found her at the loch, I'd agreed with her," she said. "I thought Fiona should have gotten rid of the baby. I thought the Old Man should have gotten rid of Fiona. I didn't know what Rose had planned, but I'd heard every word that came out of her mouth and nodded my approval. So when I turned on her, dragged her back to the Old Man with the others, she cursed us for it. If she had a chance to pay me back by killing my daughter, she would."

Not her son, though, Danny thought, not the dog. That was why Rose hadn't killed him in Girvan—she thought it was more of an insult to Kath to leave him alive.

"Check her bones," Danny said. "Make sure they're there. It's the Wolf Winter, Mam, a lot of things are coming back."

MAYBE SHE would. Danny hoped she did, but it was up to her.

This was up to him. He jogged into the storm, head down and shoulders up. The snow had finally let up but was replaced by an icy rain. It was full of splinters of ice sharp enough to draw blood when the wind found the right angle, and it froze in his hair and the scruff of stubble on his jaw. Danny clambered over a low stone fence and stopped in the shelter of a twisted ash tree, lightning-struck and charred, to pull the map out of his pocket. The rain quickly soaked the map, and he cursed as the paper tore under his fingers.

A wolf wouldn't need a map. They knew every rock and piss-scented tree of the territory the Pack claimed. Sometimes that wasn't an advantage.

Wolves ran with the Wild at their heels, their paws sometimes on this world and sometimes on rocks that had been gone for centuries. That was the problem—sometimes the geography and the distances didn't match.

Danny had spent his childhood on the long way around the moors and the old stone roads. He knew the lay of the land, the shortcuts and landmarks, in a way that only the footsore and irritated did.

And he liked to know things. The prophets left no trail to follow to their temple, no path worn through the heather, no scent trail on the rocks. The only way to get there was through the Wild, but no one had been able to find it there either.

That was because it didn't exist there. Danny coughed cold water out of his mouth and ran his finger over the map to the blob of gray at the fold. There were some things in the real world that left a stain on the Wild, altered and odd as it would be to the people who knew the original. It was hard to tell what, though, the same way people could read a book but only remember a single extract twenty years on.

Some places, though, were just empty boxes with no soul. Like Glenlough—a folly built out here on an industrialist's whim in the 1900s that was neither inhabited nor left for the weather to wear into dereliction. It was neither home nor ruin, like a shell on the beach a crab could move into to disguise itself.

Danny reoriented himself and struck out over the field to the east. The dog stirred in the back of his head, restless at being penned up in his skin. But Danny needed a human brain for this and human shoulders to carry the duffel.

At least he would if he was right. Danny wiped his hand down his face to scrape off the film of water and ice. He hoped he was right. Back in Lochwinnoch, with Kath's expectations dropped back onto his shoulders, he'd felt a lot more confident.

He found the crick at the boundary of the Glenlough land when he stepped on it. The thin skin of ice cracked under his weight and the frigid water seeped in through the eyelets of his boots and soaked his socks.

"Shit," he muttered between cold lips. "I'm going to lose a toe."

Back in Durham he'd watched the end of the world a dozen times on TV and speculated with his ex and friends what they'd miss most.

The internet.

Music.

Thai food.

Socks hadn't even made the list. Dry socks, *spare* socks, were something they'd taken for granted. Even Danny, who'd always privately assumed he was better prepared. After all, he hadn't had Thai food until he was nineteen.

Wet wool rubbed against his heels and squelched with each step as he climbed up and struck out across the field. There were no roads to Glenlough, not anymore. The land had been sold off over the years, repurposed for crops or left for the moors to reclaim. On Danny's old ordnance survey map it was a ghost-gray ribbon that wriggled across the hills. He found it under his boots, chunks of macadam and rock under the frozen heather, and the thought that it was close made him walk faster.

A sudden gust of wind hit Danny from the side and made him stagger. It parted the rain for a second and he saw the outline of the old building appear like a ghost ahead of him. It was closer than he'd thought.

It had been a grand house once. Gargoyles peered out from under the few intact sections of roof, ice frozen over spouted mouths like muzzles, and the remnants of stained glass glittered in the window frames. Someone had taken pride in it. Now wet blisters on the Virgin-Mary-blue front door bulged out of the grain of the wood and ice-crusted scaffolding had been erected to hold up the bowed old walls. No Trespassing signs rattled like tuneless wind chimes on the chain-link fence that marked out the boundaries of the property.

Danny stared at the building until he realized he was in plain sight of anyone inside. With a muttered curse he hunched over and loped into the shelter of the wind-twisted old ash. The trunk was lightning-scarred and blistered where the frozen sap had exploded out of the living wood. It creaked softly in the wind as Danny crouched down in the roots, the sound of something not quite dead yet.

He leaned his head back to rest against the tree and waited. The rain soaked his face and ran back into his hair and down under his collar. Danny strained to hear something, *smell* something, over the storm. If there was anything that he could have sensed—even with his nose and ears muted in this skin—it was lost under the storm. The clatter of the signs against the fence and the aggressive drumbeat of the rain against the old stone building drowned out everything. Any scent in the air was washed away before he could catch it.

Or had never been there.

Danny squeezed his eyes shut. He'd left Jack to be taken by the prophets and hiked miles across the frozen hills on a hunch he'd had as a nosy teenager. He had to be right.

He shrugged the duffel bag, now soaked and worse for wear, off his shoulders and fumbled it open. His stomach turned as he pulled out the frosted Tupperware box that his mam had brought up from the village. Something inside rattled like dice as he popped the lid.

It was an index finger, still gray and half-frozen despite being pressed against Danny's sweaty back for the hike. The nail was broken down to the quick and the knuckle scuffed and torn from a fight. It jiggled like something still half-alive in the Tupperware as Danny's hands shook.

Bile retched miserably up the back of Danny's throat, and he closed his eyes to force it back down. He was a dog, the best thing you could be if you weren't a wolf, and he could deal with this.

His brain disagreed. Maybe if he'd stayed here, it'd be different, but he was a professor at Durham University. The worst thing he'd seen for the last decade had been the rampant privilege of rich twenty-year-olds, and he liked it that way.

It wasn't wrong.

"Yeah, well," Danny muttered through chattering teeth as he opened his eyes. While they'd been closed, the rain had turned to snow. "Tough shit. Deal."

Bron was his little sister. She hated him for that—no wolf wanted people to know that about their bloodline—and he'd resented her for… being everything he wasn't. That wasn't the point. She was irritating, prickly, and didn't know nearly as much as she thought. She was also the tiny, bloody blob of a person his mam had let him hold after she was born, even when the midwives *thought* the dog would be jealous of the new baby.

Maybe Danny didn't want to share a room with Bron again, but he couldn't imagine a world that she wasn't in, somewhere, being better than him. And if she was here, then Jack would be too soon enough. The Wild tolerated a lot, but it didn't like prisons. Nothing that wanted free stayed caged in the Wild for long.

He wedged the Tupperware solidly between the roots of the tree and stood up to strip off. Goose pimples prickled his arms as the cold hit him, and his balls tried to squeeze back up inside him. The film of sweat and rain on his back and stomach froze thin and brittle against his skin.

He stuffed his jeans and T-shirt into the duffel. They'd still get soaked, but if he needed them later, there was a chance they'd be there. His coat he rolled up and put under the bag.

Then he crouched down, breathed out, and let his skin shift.

The dog sneezed, shook its head hard enough to make its ears flap, and hopped clumsily out of the boots Danny had left on. The cold made its feet ache, and a skitter of something nearby, under the snow, caught its ear and made its stomach grumble.

Other things to do, the core of Danny that survived the change prodded. The dog could eat after that.

It put its head down to the Tupperware box and nosed at the dead thing in the corner. The smell of half-frozen meat usually would have made it drool. It had pawed over the cold box in the old den often enough, choked down plastic and hard chunks of mince despite the not particularly convincing knowledge it would be sick when it changed back. But this smelled like pack.

The dog whined softly and nosed the finger again. Dead flesh, not quite turned, and the milky, almost-me smell of the wolf it had denned with. Complexities of emotion weren't the dog's strength—the conflict of resentment and affection that made Danny's feelings murky—it just knew they were family.

And that she was hurt. Fear hadn't stuck to the finger, the acrid gray flash of it picked apart by cold and time, but the black stickiness of pain was embedded in the splintered bone. The dog gave a soft, dangerous growl and pawed at the box until the finger fell out.

Bron smelled peppery, mixed with milk and sweetness. Caught under the broken nail there were shreds of dead flesh that smelled tainted, that made the dog want to bite. It remembered that smell from back in Durham, the stink of it on the monsters that came into *its* territory.

The dog pulled the smells apart and filed them in its brain so it would know them again. Then it assiduously scraped snow and dirt over the finger until it was hidden. Once it was satisfied, it lifted its head and cast about for a scent.

Snow. The brittle, translucent scent of the lightning-struck mountain ash, cooked sap, and singed wood. On the roots of the tree, under them, the ghost of rodent musk hung yellow and papery until the dog growled a warning at it. The urge to unearth the finger, to move it somewhere the rodent wouldn't find it, plucked at its brain.

No.

It shook itself bristly, nose to tail, to shed the compulsion and a layer of snow. The scentscape here was bleak, just ice and see-through ghosts and not as familiar as home. Even the finger was preserved, the scents it picked up dry and powdery.

Houses always smelled. Scents lingered in corners and worked into carpets—old food and sweat, anger and happiness, sex and death. Humans did all that inside.

The dog growled at the rodent that might be under the tree—just so it knew—and headed off toward the house. It was too lanky and dark to go unnoticed, but it skulked through the trees and slunk up on its belly to the house. The long roll of chain-link was stapled to wooden posts hammered into the ground around the house, but it had bagged in the storms. It wasn't hard for the dog to flatten itself and squirm under, even if it lost some hair in the process.

Some skin too. It smelled its own blood, a bloom of salt in the cold air, before it felt the itch of pain across its shoulders. Nothing else. The dog prowled, stiff-legged and careful, across the snow. With each step its paws left deep, perfectly round prints in the virgin snow, but there was no help for that.

Besides, the snow that eddied around it would fill those in soon enough. The dog shook its head to get the tickle of ice out of its ears and then cocked its head. It heard the same creaky sound of something under the snow, but it couldn't smell mole or rat. The sound didn't move either.

The dog paced back and forth in front of the house as it tried to pin down where the noise came from. It got closer and closer to the steps and then pounced, paws first, on the sound. Instead of warm body, its feet found metal, and the sound stopped.

It dug down into the snow, kicked white, frozen chunks back between its hind legs until it had uncovered a heavy, metal grate sunk into the concrete under the stairs. The sharp smell of pepper and milk leaked up on the damp hair. The dog flagged its shaggy, whip of a tail in excitement and barked, one sharp yelp, into the grille.

There was a pause.

"Danny?" the voice was smaller than Danny remembered, pinched in by fear and walls. It wobbled for a moment and then hardened. "You stupid dog. What are you doing here? Get out. Go away. I don't need your help!"

The dog wagged its tail and stuck its nose against the cold metal. That was her. Definitely Bron.

CHAPTER TEN—GREGOR

FADED RED hair hung in frizzy hanks around the old bitch's head as she limped down the beach, hunched and ruined-looking in a stained Aran sweater and long skirt…. The monster kept pace with her while the other watched them and growled through its deformed mouth.

Last time Gregor had seen Rose, she'd fled the cave of the Sannock Dead—their slaughterhouse and resting place—with a single hide. It didn't look like it had made it out intact. The freckled skin had been sliced into scraps and used to patch Rose back together where the hot oil Gregor had doused her with had sloughed the skin off muscle and bone. It was stretched over her face like a mask, the thin skin under her eye puckered with small, black stitches, and she'd used long strips of it to pull her singed scalp back together. Patches of her own hair, gray and brittle, stuck wirily through the matted hanks of corpse hair.

It was a horror—Gregor could see that—but the *idea* she was beautiful caught in his brain like a fishhook. That was somehow a fact, even as the stitches gaped to show the waxy burns and hints of bone below. The dissonance of it made Gregor's brain ache and his cock twitch with an interest that turned his stomach. He breathed in the *wrong* stench of the monsters instead, the reek of sick-poison flesh almost welcome, and let the revolted anger push everything else out.

Had this been it? The unearthed dead and the murdered children had just been to make her beautiful again. That wasn't much to show for all her trouble.

Her trouble, Gregor recalled bleakly, and the life of her grandson. Nick had come back, but that didn't undo what Rose had done. It didn't erase Gregor's memory of Nick's twisted corpse on the beach or the wash of raw, sour anger that clawed up his throat.

The thin, furious snarl trickled down his nose. One of the prophets yanked on his collar hard enough to bend him backward. The hobbles laced through his ankles tore the skin as he staggered. He choked as the metal dug into his throat and cut off his air along with the growl.

"Leave him be," Rose ordered. Her voice was harsh, the accent burned off her words but still clotted. "They came a long way to die for me. The least I can do is let them do it on their feet."

The prophet relaxed his grip with a disgusted grunt, and Gregor straightened up. He hunched his shoulder in a clumsy attempt to rub the bruised, torn skin of his neck. Blood dripped down his ankles to stain his bare feet and soak into the almost-there beach.

"Bitch," he said.

She shifted her chin at the sound of his voice, tilted her head toward him, and he realized she was still blind. One eye socket was empty, the edges melted like wax, and the other had been stitched closed with a stolen lid. Something moved under it. Gregor wasn't confident it was an eye or even what was left of one.

"Where's my grandson?" she asked.

"Gone," Gregor said harshly.

She had the gall to flinch as though she had the right or the ability to give a fuck. Her head snapped around and she raised her hand at Lachlan, finger reconstructed from stolen skin and splints.

"What did you do to him, boy?" she demanded harshly. "Where is Nicholas and my little god?"

Lachlan stumbled forward, propelled by a shove, and dragged Ellie with him. His hand was locked on her arm as they stumbled through the misplaced seawood and stopped just in front of the old woman. His face was greasy with sweat, and an uneasy stink of fear and lust seeped out of him.

"The dark-haired man? I didn't know he was anything of yours. If I'd known, if we'd known, we'd have welcomed him better," Lachlan blurted out. He yanked Ellie forward, grabbed the back of her neck, and shoved her toward Rose. Ellie struggled in his grip but couldn't break away. "I barely saw him. It was Ellie who chased him off."

Ellie stammered out a shocked denial. She buttoned her lips together midword as Rose turned her ruined face toward her. There was an accuracy to the movement that gave the creepy impression she could still somehow see through that ruined eye.

"What did you do to him, girl?" she asked as she leaned down into Ellie's face. Her lips, smooth and pink, sagged and slipped as she talked, her own wrinkled seam of a mouth visible underneath. Ellie squirmed uncomfortably, her face puckered with revulsion and attraction, and tried to turn away. Rose pinched Ellie's chin between her fingers and held her in place as she sniffed. "Did you bite my boy? Did you fuck him? I can smell him on you."

Ellie whimpered. Behind Gregor, among the row of dogs, a chain rattled, and a man made a low, strangled sound of protest. He looked around, past the prophet behind him, to see the strange dog cuffed to his feet.

He registered that and glanced at Jack to make sure he'd seen it too. He had, and his jaw was set unhappily. Before Gregor could pick the expression apart, the prophet behind him cracked him around the ear.

"You look at her," the prophet ordered over the ringing in Gregor's ears. "She wants you to see her."

Gregor exhaled and reluctantly turned his attention back to the patchwork woman of scars and stolen skin. He could see her, but his brain didn't question the belief in her beauty. Some Sannock skin, he supposed. The myths of them claimed they were beautiful, yet when he saw the remnants of them in the Wild, they'd been mismatched, none of them just one thing entirely.

In Rose's grip, Ellie gulped audibly and choked out through her pinched jaw, "I fought… no, I chased him. He got away from me."

Rose snorted. "How did he do that? He's all leg now. And I taught him what happened to boys who can't run fast. But you're a wolf. How did one lanky boy get away from you?"

Ellie hesitated. She tried to turn toward Lachlan again, but Rose didn't let her. "He… he turned into a bird."

"Crazy bitch," Lachlan blurted. "She just doesn't want to admit a human got away from her."

Rose finally let go of Ellie, who staggered back and wiped her face on her sleeve. Then Rose reached out for him. She patted the air blindly, and Lachlan moved under her hand, a shudder of something going through him as she gripped him.

"No, he does that," she said pleasantly. Then her fingers tightened, dug down through the wool sweater to dig into flesh and muscle. Lachlan staggered under the pain but managed to throttle the whimper that tried to escape his throat. She dropped to a guttural growl. "And do I look like I'd have a human grandson?"

Lachlan choked out a strained "No" and "Sorry." Rose finally let him go with a shove. He staggered out of the way, blood dark as it stained the cable knit of his sweater, and nearly into the heavyset, flush-skinned monster. Its growl was a thick gargle of a sound in its throat, and Lachlan jumped away from it.

"Nicholas will find me," Rose murmured to herself. Her eyes flicked over Gregor, and she tightened her lips behind the stolen ones. Her voice was bitter as she grudgingly admitted, "Or he'll find you."

Gregor spat at her. It hit the freckled mask and dripped down onto her shoulder. She backhanded him, her knuckles like a bag of dice, and only the prophets behind him kept him on his feet. Gregor's ears rang with a brittle buzz as they dragged him back upright. He could taste blood in his mouth, and his cheekbone throbbed with the hot pressure of a fractured bone.

"Do not let it slip your mind," she told him coldly. "You are not what you were. Nor am I."

Gregor shook his head—the wash of red-tinged nausea drowned out the drone in his ears—and spat the mouthful of blood onto her. It speckled her face, a bright addition to the faded freckles, and the beautiful/hideous mask slid for a second.

The prophets cursed and kicked him in the backs of his knees until they gave way. He went down hard on the stones, and the prophet grabbed a handful of hair and yanked his head back. Rose found his face with fumbling, uncertain fingers and dug her thumbnails into the soft skin under his eyes.

"Leave him alone!" Jack yelled at her. There was a sound of scuffle, a dull crack of bone on flesh and muscle that ended with a grunt and a stifled whine of pain. Gregor didn't need to look over. He could smell his idiot brother's blood on the air. "What the fuck do you want with us anyhow?"

There was a pause, and then Rose pulled her nails out of Gregor's flesh. He felt blood run down his face like tears.

"I want what every new bride wants. To get to know her new family," Rose singsonged mockingly as she stepped backward. Gregor licked his own blood off his lips and watched as she pulled the sweater tight across the front of her body with both hands. The cable knit stretched over her stomach where it swelled, drum taut and round, over skinny hips. She looked like a snake that had swallowed a pig. "And to get your blessing for your new brother. The Numitor's true son."

The prophets threw back their heads and howled, triumphant and deranged. A few of the dogs were carried away enough to join in, their undying loyalty to Jack forgotten in the moment. Lachlan's wolves looked at him for a guideline on how to respond, but he looked as poleaxed as any of them.

"The fuck it is," Jack spat out as he recoiled back a bloody, confused step.

Gregor threw back his head and roared with laughter. He laughed until the prophet at his back choked him on it, but even with a knee in his back and metal cut into his throat, he sniggered.

"My brother?" he rasped as he hooked his fingers into the collar. "More likely a rat crawled up in there and died."

The wolf rippled under Rose's face. It bristled, moldy gray fur patched with stolen bits and grafted skin, and bared yellow, chipped fangs. The stolen skin sprouted fur too, dandelion white and matted, but whatever it was made the pelts around it wither and go dry.

Rose sucked in her breath and the stolen wolves, stuffed the change back into her bones. The stolen face had frayed at the edges, torn where the stitches held it behind her ear, and she had to hold it in place with one hand.

"You don't need to give your blessing," she said from behind lips that had slid out of place. "I can take it just as well, but ask your brother if you want to spend any longer than necessary under my care. Take them to the *valetudinarium*."

The hospital. But wolves didn't need hospitals. Anything that they couldn't heal from, they either died of or lived with. Gregor had never heard another wolf talk of a hospital, but as he was dragged to his feet and beaten around the head until he shuffled forward, he doubted anyone was in the mood to answer his questions. As he edged past the monster, he supposed that he'd find out soon enough.

THE THING snarled at him, and thick strings of pus and blood hung from ruined gums as he passed. Its stink scraped on his nerves, dug down into his guts where the same infection festered, but he ignored it in favor of one last hard look at Rose.

Once upon a time, Nick had loved that raddled old witch, whatever was left of her between the grafted wolf and the Sannock skin, and now Nick had to live with the knowledge that he'd only ever been meat for her ambitions.

One day Gregor would kill her for that.

Two months ago, the Wild here had been as familiar to Gregor as his own face in the mirror, and he'd known it as well as his own body. Now he wasn't comfortable in either. The Sannock's old prison spread like a sour infection and made the native Wild swell and crease in reaction. It hung *odd* across the landscape.

Gregor counted his footsteps. Three hundred of them, his stride constrained by the wire that sliced him with each step. Yet he could feel the hot looseness of distance in his thighs and between his shoulders, and his sense of where he stood—on the Pack's land, *his* territory—moved like sand under his feet.

"What did she mean?" Ellie asked, her voice so low it was almost inaudible as she fell in next to Lachlan. He growled dismissal at her and walked faster through the snow. "She can't be pregnant—"

Lachlan turned on her with a snarl, closed his good hand around her throat, and pulled her up onto her toes. "Whatever Rose says she is, that's what she is. Understood?"

The Old Man had never had to get physical to make an out-of-line wolf back down. Lachlan couldn't get the job done even with Ellie's throat as good as in his teeth. She slapped his hand away roughly and took a cautious step back but held her ground.

"She says she's pregnant with the true Numitor's brat," Ellie said sharply. Her fair curls blew into her face and she swiped them away again. "If you aren't Numitor, Lach, then what right do you have to put hands on me?"

He glared at her. "The right she gave me," he said. "That… what she said… was just to hurt these two."

Ellie glanced at Gregor and past him to Jack and then spat in the snow. "If she just wanted to hurt them, then she could have broken their legs," she said. "Not written a play. I came up here, gave up everything, to follow the Numitor. Old Man or the Young Wolf, I don't care. If you aren't even the Numitor, why should we be at your heels?"

"She told you to," Lachlan said flatly. He tilted his head toward the front of the group where Rose walked with her fist twisted in the monster's slack ruff of raw skin. "You want to cross her?"

"She told the others to follow you," Ellie pointed out defiantly. "Took their brats as surety they'd obey. I'd already thrown my lot in with you, and she told me nothing. But if something happened to you, I think she'd tell me to take over."

"You think too much," Lachlan said. "The Old Man's dead, and his heir, if that's what that is, isn't even born yet. Maybe he never will be. Right now I'm Numitor, and if you question it again, I'll slice your throat."

He tossed her into the snow and stalked away.

"Wise wolves don't make threats," Gregor said. "They just do."

Ellie gave him a bleak look as she scrambled to her feet. The smell of adrenaline and fear rose off her like a cloud of steam—thin and sharp as snapped fingers—and she bared her blunt human teeth at him. "And you're wise?" she asked. "To come back here where you aren't wanted? None of us asked for your help, neither of you, and we don't need to hear you mouth off either. The Wolf Winter isn't what we thought. So what? I'll survive."

She glanced down the row of prisoners, the tip of her head almost unconscious, and then immediately away. Her mouth twisted with bitterness.

Gregor would have asked, but Jack jabbed him with his elbow to shut him up. Habit made him want to ask *anyhow*, but he choked it off behind his teeth.

"You trust her?" Jack asked quietly. He pointed his chin toward Rose and her monsters. "What's left of her."

Ellie let a flicker of confused horror show for a second. Then she slammed a game face over it. She rubbed her throat and glared at Jack. "I trust power," she said. "Of everyone here? She has it, and we don't. *You* don't. Not anymore."

She wrenched the buttons of her dress loose with one hand. Gregor got a flash of lean sides and flat stomach, the inner curve of high breasts, and then the wolf sucked it down. It wasn't like the change the monster went through, a torture of broken bones and fever-malleable flesh. The wolf knew the template it wanted to use—the prick of its ears and the length its legs were supposed to be—and it stuck to that.

Ellie's wolf dropped to all fours and shook itself out of the dress. It gave Gregor a curious look out of amber eyes and then trotted away. He watched her go with sour envy in his gut. Maybe the prophet's poison and maybe just him. Sometimes it was easier to be a wolf, to shed the *noise* of humanity. Gregor missed it.

A misstep in the snow bumped Jack's shoulder against him. Gregor reminded himself of their new alliance and didn't shove him away. "What the prophets don't know," Jack murmured, "won't help them."

The prophet chained to Jack yanked him away with a growl before Gregor could respond. Jack's ankles ripped open again and spilled fresh blood, musky and potent in the snow as he stumbled. Something would eat well tonight, Gregor thought as he glanced back and tracked their trail along the blood-splattered snow.

What was in the Wild was real, but it was a memory of a thing. Catch and eat a squirrel and it would satisfy in the teeth and on the tongue, but it wouldn't linger or satisfy, not like meat in the world, where an hour later you could lick your chops and taste the meaty gravy of the prey. In the Wild anything from the world was a seductive treat, a lure as good as the smell of grease and fried starch from a Lochwinnoch chip shop on a Friday night.

The prophets had grown in confidence if they weren't worried about what they'd bring to their door. Or.... Gregor waited for the rest of the thought to form, but it didn't. It felt like he'd missed something, but he couldn't pin down what.

At least it gave him something to think about as he walked, one step after the other, the weight of a collar around his neck and the itch of pain in his feet. Then, between one step and the next, he caught the tail end of a familiar scent—salt and candy floss, Nick and blood. Even the cold-thinned hint of it caught in Gregor's throat like a hook and jerked his gaze away from his grim study of the pimple on the back of Lachlan's neck. He looked around quickly, his eyes drawn first to the white, snow-heavy clouds in search of a cruciform black silhouette and then back down to earth.

A cliff of ancient, black trees loomed along the ridge of a nearby hill, dense as a thicket of brambles, and a herd of elk skirked along the outskirts of it. Snow lay thick over their humped backs, and as the lead male swung his head around to study the wolves as they passed, Gregor saw that he was long dead. Icicles dripped like knives from his antlers, and the skin had sloughed off his head to leave weather-scrubbed planes of bone.

Then he moved again, and instead of an elk, there was a man—most of a man, although he was still skull bones and icy horns wrapped in old rags. The Sannock locked its empty eye sockets on Gregor—a flicker jolt of stolen life battered against Gregor's mind as if it *needed* in—and then pointed down the slope with an oddly mortal ugly hand.

Blood splashed on the snow three steps left to stain the ice.

Then Gregor's foot came down, and the Wild spat him out. It clawed at him as he went, tried to hold on to his bones as it ejected the metal, and he had to struggle to keep himself together. He landed somewhere else. The scent of Nick was ripped out of his nose, and the flat, acid fear in the back of his throat turned hollow in confusion.

The prophet behind him laughed and jabbed a finger into the back of Gregor's skull. "Finally smart enough to be afraid," he mocked as he caught the edges of the scent. The moment with the Sannock at the tree line had been quicker than it felt. No one else had noticed. "Too fucking late."

Gregor spat the bad taste out of his mouth and looked up. The ruins of an old manor house, stitched together by scaffolding and ice, sulked in front of him. There was a sense of something unfulfilled about it, like it was the architectural equivalent of a miscarriage.

Something had also slaughtered a sheep in front of it. Half of the gray, matted corpse of a black-legged Highland sheep was impaled on the fence, its head dangling back to stare with bulging black eyes at the new arrivals. The other half had been ripped free and been dragged over the ground in front of the house. Entrails lay in long, purple streamers, blood had soaked into the snow and frozen in fat, red targets, and the bones had been torn apart and dragged away to gnaw on.

The stink of dead sheep and offal hung in the air. Gregor resisted the urge to turn and look at Hector, as though the dog might recognize one of his flock like this.

"What the fuck?" the ginger prophet blurted as he took the scene in. "How the hell did that sheep get up there? Look at the mess."

He sounded exasperated, like a Lochwinnoch housewife who'd just had mud tracked on her clean floors. It was Jack who laughed first, a snort of amusement, and then it spread even to the dogs, who tittered and then cringed as the prophets beat them with the ends of their chains.

Ginger flushed angrily all the way to his scalp, bright through his faded hair, and yanked on Jack's collar to shut him up.

"Maybe we should get you to clean it up," he spat. "The Numitor's sons can finally do something useful."

Rose turned her head as if she could still, somehow, see the mess. The monster under her hand turned its head at the same time, as much as it could around the exaggerated bulge of muscle under its jaw.

"There are things in the Wild that have fasted for a long time, Ewan," she said, an edge of mockery to her voice. "Now they are free, we should begrudge them mutton? Soon enough we'll be gods, and this old place will have outlived its usefulness to us anyhow. Let the sheep rot."

She absently touched the ruin of her face as she spoke and picked with her nails at the stiff, dry edges of the stitches.

"It'll stink," Ginger Ewan protested.

Rose turned her shoulder toward him. Her matted, stolen hair blew back from her face, revealing the nub of her ear. The edge of mockery had sharpened in her face as she waved her hand in an expansive, encompassing gesture.

"It's winter, Ewan," she said with withering contempt. "It will freeze."

She took a step toward the house, stumbled, and had to catch herself with an arm across the monster's back. One hand lifted to check her face again, and the skin pleated between her fingers as she pressed it back down against the raw edges of her face.

"You need to go," Ewan said. He didn't hide the satisfaction in his voice.

She pushed herself back up straight on the monster's back. Pus dripped down her wrist in a thick gray trickle.

"Get on with our preparations. I don't want to have to wait until the New Year to get this done," she ordered sharply. The pus dripped onto the snow, and the monster lapped it up. Rose kicked it away with a hiss of disapproval. It withdrew, and she shot her hand out to grab Ewan's wrist and dig her fingers in. "And find Nick. Do one thing right and I'll be pleased. Get both right and I'll be amazed."

She threw his arm back at him like it offended her and stepped—no, Gregor corrected himself—was taken back by the Wild. Lachlan made an inchoate sound of protest before he managed to choke it off.

"Burns heal badly," Gregor said. "But they heal. The old bitch looks as raw as when I tossed the oil on her."

With the side of his boot, Ewan scuffed snow over the pus stain. "And she has neither forgiven nor forgotten that," he said.

"Didn't want her to," Gregor said bluntly.

Ewan snorted, half amused. "Aye, well," he said. "Piss off the Wild and you won't heal at all. What she's done—"

"You talk too much!" one of the other prophets interjected. "If the wolves know all our secrets, what use are we to them?"

"If her plan works, what use are they to us?" Ewan countered. He didn't sound excited at the idea, just grim. When the other prophet spluttered out a half-formed protest, Ewan impatiently waved it away with a freckled hand. "Besides, they'll be dead soon enough. Who will they tell? Take the dogs inside, put them with the rest."

Tom protested as they dragged him inside, promised that he was a loyal dog and they could trust him. He was still marched through the sheep guts and into the old ruin with the rest.

"And us?" Jack asked.

"She has set aside special accommodations for you," Ewan said. He sounded almost regretful, as though he'd realized what he'd thrown his support behind too late. "So you can properly appreciate what's to come. Now everything is in place, it will be over soon enough."

He stepped back and gestured for a prophet to take them away. Gregor resisted the yank at his collar and dug his heels until Ewan actually looked at him, bloodshot blue eyes reluctant.

"If you hurt Nick, I'll kill you," Gregor said. "Alive or dead, I'll find a way."

"Gregor," Jack warned softly.

Ewan straightened his shoulders and glared indignantly at Gregor. "He's my grandson," he spat out. That was new information. Nick had only ever spoken of his gran, but Gregor supposed there had to have been a grandfather or two. Maybe even a father somewhere. The flicker of jealousy in his gut resented that. He wanted Nick to be his alone, but it made sense. "My flesh, my blood. All I have left. You think I'd hurt him?"

"She did," Gregor said. He wanted his wolf, wanted the bite it would mark on the edge of his word. But it was still gone, and he had to make do with his own anger. "And Nick's *mine*, prophet."

Ewan looked taken aback. Maybe Rose hadn't told him everything about why Nick had been willing to come north. But it only made him hesitate for a second, and then he gestured sharply for the prophets to get on with it.

This time Gregor went when they dragged him away.

Chapter Eleven—Gregor

Old moisture stains blotted the eggshell-blue walls and warped the once-glossy wooden floorboards underfoot. The dark oak was scored from neglect and pitted with round, golf ball dents from the hail, rough-edged chunks of which still lay along the skirting.

Gregor glanced through a door as they passed it, into a room with bowed, empty shelves and a smashed desk. He craned his neck to look up the stairs, and he could see right up through the roof, to the span of pale sky that floated overhead. The Winter had reined its storm in, but it would be back soon enough.

A prophet punched him in the back of the head. The impact made Gregor stumble forward, and he felt the wire rip something important in his ankle. A jolt of pain slashed up the back of his leg, and his toes went numb and unresponsive. They folded under him as he forced himself forward, bloody and ripped with splinters.

Jack staggered over and braced his shoulder against Gregor's to keep him on his feet. The fact he needed the help, and from Jack, tasted like rotted meat on the back of Gregor's tongue. He swallowed it anyhow.

"There's nothing to see up here," the prophet said. He sounded almost proud of the run-down den the prophets had moved into like hermit crabs on the beach. "Our lives aren't spent where wolves can see them. Ailsa, get the door."

The prophet who ducked past Gregor was small and dark haired, with a sallow, mean face dominated by nothing in particular. She'd already shed her coat to reveal the patchy silver-and-black hide of a wolf that Gregor did recognize. Jess had been old, maybe even older than Da, and only part of the Pack by courtesy these days, since she preferred to keep to herself in the hills.

But she'd been alive and well when Gregor had left for the Wall, and from the gore-tatted hole ripped between the shoulders of her hide, she hadn't died well.

It looked like the prophets weren't willing to wait for a corpse to skin anymore.

"I hope Jess took her gelt from your guts on the way out," Jack said before Gregor had the chance. Irritation scratched at him, one more thing his brother took, but he ignored it. "She deserved better."

Ailsa spat on the ground and crouched down to unlock the thick, iron padlock that hooked through a hasp sunk into the floor. Once it was undone, she unlatched the two steel bars and hauled up the trap door with a stink of old dirt and fresh musk muggy as it escaped.

"I deserved better," she spat. "I deserved my wolf. The boy was only human anyhow, what business was it of the Old Man's—"

"Shut up, Ailsa," a prophet ordered. "It's bad enough to have to know you, without being reminded what you are."

She rolled her lips back to snarl at them. Not satisfied with the wolf's fangs when she changed her skin, Ailsa had pulled two eye teeth from something and jammed them in her gums. They were gray and chipped, dead-looking and full of infection.

"What we all are," she spat back at him. "Whatever we did, they made us all prophets the same. Now we'll make ourselves gods."

She pulled her hand off the ring and left shreds of skin frozen to the metal. Her frost-burned hand didn't bleed, not yet, as she scrambled out of sight down the sharp curve of gray stone steps.

"Some of us," said a prophet behind Gregor, his voice indistinct but thick with disgust. "Not all."

He was told to shut up, and then it was Gregor and Jack's turn to go down into the ground.

"What's going to happen to the others?" Jack asked as he struggled down the narrow steps on hobbled feet. It hadn't occurred to Gregor to care. He supposed that whatever Jack's plan was, it wouldn't work if the dogs died first.

"The dogs?" Ailsa asked with a snort. "You would be the one to care about them."

She lifted her foot and kicked him down the stairs. An odd, breathy laugh escaped her as he tumbled down into the dark. Gregor lunged for her with a snarl, but the collar pulled him up short as the prophet yanked the chain tight with a laugh. Gregor gagged and stumbled back a step.

"The dogs are kenneled out back where they belong," Ailsa said. She stepped forward, ignoring the other prophet's hiss of warning, and stroked his face with a soft, fever-hot hand. The stink of her—rot and misery stitched to whatever sickness had sent her for a prophet—sweated out of her skin, and Gregor gagged. She smiled at him with those stolen fangs. "But you keep the breeding stock away from the curs. Someone should have told your brother that years ago—"

She was mean, but she wasn't smart. Gregor grinned at her and then snapped his head around to sink his teeth into her hand. Hot blood filled his mouth, the familiar taste cut through with the bitter sweetness of rot as he bore down. Ailsa squealed and tried to wrench her hand away, but her flesh tore between Gregor's teeth.

Human teeth weren't as efficient as a wolf's, but they could do the job if you put your mind to it. Greg ground his jaw, tearing her skin, and jerked his head viciously from side to side. Bone cracked and tendons stretched, caught between his teeth like gristle. Ailsa punched at his head with her free hand and finally got away from him as the prophets dragged him back. She clutched her bleeding hand to her chest and glared at him.

"When it's time," she said, "I want to be the one who kills him."

He grinned at her, hard and bloody-toothed, and spat her little finger out onto the stones. She whined in her throat and checked her mutilated hand as though she hadn't realized she was short one.

"You get what you're given," the other prophet said. He dragged Gregor over to the trap door and roughly shoved him through. "Like the rest of us."

Gregor pitched down the stairs headfirst. Instinct made him try to break his fall, but with his hands and feet tethered, that just made it worse. He gritted his teeth, raised his arms to cover his head as best he could, and tried to go limp. Shoulder and hip bashed against the hard, stone edge of the step until he landed in a heap at the bottom, half on top of his brother.

He rolled over onto his back, legs still propped up the stairs, and stared up at the dim square of the trap door.

"Don't bother," a familiar woman's voice said. "Even if you crawl up there, the door won't budge. I've tried. And they have those things stand guard."

"Their monsters," Gregor said. "I've killed them before."

Jack grunted as he shoved Gregor off him. "Not easily."

"We just need practice."

Gregor got his elbow under him and scrambled awkwardly to his feet. The taste of Ailsa's blood lingered like sour grease in his mouth, and he glanced around the cellar. It had been a larder once, probably, shelves and cupboards on the walls and hooks strung from the ceiling. The prophets had lined the room with cots, thin bedrolls stained with blood and fluids and the metal frames scratched and warped. It was, he supposed, no easy task to become a prophet. In the corner of the room, huddled on the cleanest sheets, two toddlers and a still-blue-eyed pup stared back at him. Candlelight flashed green in all their eyes.

"I thought they took five?" he said as he looked back at Bron. "Four children and you."

She scowled and looked off-puttingly like her brother for a second. "Greer got away from them in the Wild," she said. Her mouth twisted around the words. Gregor's namesake had been nearly five, one of the oldest of the children taken. He'd been a stocky little brat of a kid, always in trouble. "He ran. I hoped he'd gotten back, but…."

But he hadn't, Gregor finished the sentence for her. Sometimes children didn't. The Wild kept lost children, hid them. Even the humans told stories about that, although they blamed it on the Sannock.

"He's not dead," he said. "That's some comfort."

Bron grimaced. "Is it?" she asked skeptically as she reached down to rub her stomach.

Gregor followed the gesture, and his brain went blank as she spread her bandaged hand on the taut, high bulge of her stomach.

"You're pregnant," he said.

"I know," Bron snapped at him. "I worked that out for myself."

Jack snorted out a halfhearted laugh. He wiped his bloody face—from a gash on his forehead where he'd caught the stairs wrong—on his sleeve.

"Whose is it?" he asked, and a sudden thought turned the corner of his mouth down. "Not Lachlan's?"

It was an understandable assumption. Lachlan had sniffed after Bron since she was barely old enough for it not to be creepy, as much to do with her brother as her.

"No," Gregor said. He warily extended his cuffed hands, not entirely sure what he should do with them. "Mine. Right?"

It had seemed like a good idea at the time, or good enough. Their blood had been up from the moon hunt, and Bron had grinned at him and dragged him into her bed. An itch to scratch and, she admitted, a way to get Lachlan to back off. Lach might have been willing to play rank games with other wolves over Bron, but he wouldn't risk Gregor's temper.

Most people didn't want to.

It hadn't meant anything, but it had been the full moon, when the wolves and the Wild were strongest. Two-thirds of the Pack had been born nine months after the moon waxed, he should have wondered. He had other things on his mind, though.

Bron twisted her mouth into a thin smile. "Well, they didn't drag me down here and chain me up for the pleasure of my company, did they? It's yours. Congratulations. It'll be dead like the other one soon enough."

She looked sorry for that almost immediately as she bit her lower lip, but she didn't try to take it back. That was Bron for you, sharp as a nail and as unwilling to bend. And hurtful or not, Gregor thought bleakly as he dropped his hands, it wasn't as though she lied. Even as a wolf, he hadn't been able to save his daughter, and what could he do for this baby now? He couldn't defend himself, couldn't *find* Nick let alone protect him, and now he might have to let another baby die.

The thought curdled in his chest, cold and rancid. Gregor could feel the slow burn of the prophet's infection as it leaked from under the picked-at scab on his soul. It was just harder to ignore when he knew the sour self-loathing was right.

"It's better," Bron said. "Better than what that raddled auld prophet has planned for him."

"What?" Jack asked.

She shrugged. "I don't know," she said, her hand still pressed protectively to the bump. "I don't expect it's a nice party, though. No wonder my brother likes you, you're both idiots."

Jack glanced up and then stepped toward Bron. He tilted his head toward her as he mouthed the words almost silently. "Is he here?"

"Do you see him?" Bron sniffed as she glared at Jack. She met his eyes for a second and then flushed uncomfortably as she looked away.

She tapped wait on Jack's shoulder and turned to look at the children still cuddled together in the corner. "Shut up! Stop whining, you little mutts. Everyone's already dead for all we know."

The older girl, Shauna, wiped her nose on her sleeve, coughed, and then wailed like a banshee. Her voice, piercing as only a child's could be, dug down into Gregor and found the one tender spot that flinched to comfort her. The boy didn't quite have the lung capacity, but the undulating shriek he pumped out was still impressive. Even the pup threw its head back and tried its best to howl gummily toward the ceiling.

"Did you send Danny here?" Bron asked under the cover of the cacophony. She shoved at Jack with one bandaged hand, and he stepped back. Once. "He's a dog, you dick. You can't just use him to get what you want. What if one of those things had got him?"

"Where is he?" Jack asked.

She scowled and shoved him again. Jack grabbed her arm and moved her back a step.

"Where is Danny?" he growled.

Gregor moved forward with a soft snarl of warning in his throat, but he didn't intervene. Bron wasn't helping, and it wouldn't hurt her for Jack to put her back on her heels, but Jack wouldn't hurt her. The children faltered, but Bron hastily gestured for them to keep it up.

"He's outside," she said, her eyes focused acceptably on Jack's chin. "He said he had a plan, but we had to wait for you. All these years, and you can still get him to heel."

Jack's fingers tightened on her arm, blood around his wrists as the wires dug in, and Gregor thought he'd misjudged his brother. He tensed, but Jack let go before he had to do anything.

"What's his plan?" he asked, voice clipped.

Bron huffed in annoyance. "Like he'd tell me the details," she said. "Clever dog's plans are too complicated for his dumb little sister to follow. He just told me what to do when you got here."

"And?" Jack prodded.

Shauna's voice finally gave out, and she sniffled herself into silence. She wiped her eyes on her grubby sleeve, lower lip wobbly as though her performance had reminded her she had plenty of reason to cry. Bron patted her hands together in a silent clap and then gave her a thumbs-up.

It earned her a watery smile from the little girl, who slouched back and stuck her thumb in her mouth.

Gregor wasn't a tender man. He didn't think often of his dead child if he could help it. It hurt when he did, so what point was there to it? But the sight of the grubby, frightened little wolves made Gregor think of her. What point was there to a pack that couldn't keep their own pups safe, alive, and fed?

He let himself be angry. It was easier—a simple emotion that didn't leave room in him for anything else.

"Whatever it is," he said harshly, "get on with it."

Bron glanced nervously at the ceiling, waited for a second, and then crouched down to pull a pair of wire cutters out of her boot. She fumbled them in her bandaged hand as Jack thrust his out expectantly. Blood dripped from his torn wrists as Bron pinched the wire in the cutting hinge of the tool. She caught her tongue between her teeth as she snipped through the strands, first on his wrists and then his feet. The collar took longest, the hasp of the padlock too thick for the cutters, but she was able to wear through the steel enough for Jack to twist the lock till it snapped.

As he freed himself, Bron turned to Gregor. Dark curls hung over her face as she did, and this close, Gregor could smell the faint milk-and-honey smell of pregnancy on her skin.

"I'll kill him myself," he said quietly, "before I let her take him."

Her prickly mask slipped, and she gave Gregor a grateful look. Then she tucked her chin and went back to work on his cuffs. "Danny will try and stop you," she said quietly. "He's soft, stupid dog. Don't let him."

"I'm not the brother that loves him," Gregor reminded her.

She snorted. "Wolves don't love dogs," she said. "They use them. Danny was fine where he was. He liked humans. He liked coffee. Now he's here."

Gregor shrugged. He hardly cared about his brother's soft spot for the dog, but he supposed that someone could say the same about him and Nick. That idea put his hackles up. "Everyone's here now, Bron," he said. "The end of the world isn't just in the north."

She cut sharply through the last wire and left him to do the rest himself. He sucked in air through his teeth and pulled the wire from between the bones of his wrist. It didn't hurt like the knife in his shoulder had, but the hot sting of it as it sliced through raw flesh caught the same nerves that nails on blackboards put on edge. Done, he crouched down to do his feet. They were bruised and puffy-looking, the skin so swollen that it folded around the wire in fat pleats.

He had to dig down into the raw meat, almost down to the bone, to get to the strands.

"What now?" he asked as he discarded the bloody slinky and dragged the cuffs of his jeans down to cover the raw-meat mess of his ankles. He tossed the cutters to Jack in a mute request for help with the collar. Their truce still held, apparently, since Jack cut him loose without comment. Gregor scratched the back of his neck once he was loose and looked expectantly at Bron. "You whistle?"

Bron shook her head and produced a battered lighter from her pocket. She tightened her fingers around it like a talisman. Her wolf glittered ferociously in her eyes, wild and dangerous from being caged.

"We burn their fucking hospital down."

OR AT least smoke them out. Gregor balanced on his brother's shoulders as he stuffed wads of petrol-greasy cotton into the cracked plaster tubes that went up inside the walls. The fumes rose like rainbows, sweet enough to make his mouth water as he packed the fabric tightly.

"Danny said there's speaking tubes that go all through the building," Bron said under the cover of the kids' renewed wails. She unraveled the bandage from her hand—the missing finger healed into a smooth stump—and clambered up the stairs to wedge it around the edges of the trapdoor. On the top of it, something shifted and gargled out a suspicious growl. She snatched her fingers back an inch and then shook the chill off and finished the job. "It should get everywhere. He'll see it."

"How'd he know?" Gregor asked.

"The house isn't exactly well-secured," Bron pointed out as she flicked the lighter. "He was able to look around. That's why he slaughtered the sheep. You saw the one outside, and he dragged another one all through the house."

She ran the flickering flame of the lighter along the dry linen. It smoldered sullenly, unwilling to step on winter's toes, but eventually it caught. Bron tossed the lighter to Jack, who snatched it out of the air. The gas-soaked rags flickered, spat, and caught much more willingly. It singed Gregor's fingers as he fed it more fuel, one of Surtr's littlest demons hungry for flesh. It writhed through the flames and then, with a leered wink, crawled into the pipes.

Gregor wiped the Wild out of his eyes and stepped back. He licked his blistered fingers and wrinkled his nose as the smoke backed, thick and black, into the basement.

"I hope your brother thought of this," he said with a cough.

"At least he thought of something," Bron said. She stripped her dress off and stood, pale and freckled in the fire light, as she ripped it to shreds to feed the flames. Her voice pitched up as she screamed, "Help! Help! There's a fire! Help us."

Gregor's fingers were still scratched with white scars from his last encounter with a fire. As it caught and spat, cracks spread up the way as it rose through the pipes like a chimney, he couldn't move. In the shadows of his mind, the flayed, scorched hides of the Sannock billowed and tore and the smoke caught in his throat as he got ready to die.

Then Jack shoved a handful of rags into his hand, and he forced himself back to work. Jack stripped down, naked as Bron, and fed the fires, since clothes would only slow him down. Damp, bloody denim made the smoke thick and ripe with the charred smell of skin.

It didn't take long for the smoke to reach the upper levels. Over the children's wails and the crackle of flames, Gregor caught the sound of curses and scuffling as the prophets upstairs tried to work out what was going on.

"Where's your brother, Bron?" Gregor asked. The kids had backed away against the wall, hands over their faces. "Or are we just the turkey in the oven, stoking the flames?"

She ignored him.

"Trust him," Jack said. "I do."

"You trust me," Gregor pointed out sourly. "So, your judgment is poor."

Jack made a face, half amused and half acknowledgment, and shrugged. "What other choice do you have?"

"Move that thing," someone snapped overhead, harsh and thickly Lowland. "Don't just stand there like idiots. What do you think she'll do if she comes back and finds we let her wolves burn?"

The monster tried to hold its ground. Gregor could hear its claws scrape against the wood and the snap of its teeth, but in the end, it gave in to the prophets. As it was dragged outside, someone rattled the padlock against its hasp.

"I was going to get them out," Ailsa said, her voice nasal and self-serving. "Just before you said that, I decided to—"

She hauled the door up.

Bron and Jack were already in their fur. They shot for the slice of light the minute they saw it. Bron had always been fast on her feet, and she wasn't pregnant enough for it to slow her down as a wolf. She went up the stairs like a missile and slammed into Ailsa's chest. She bowled the mean-faced prophet backward onto the floor and sank her teeth into her upraised arm. Dead skin and hot flesh ripped and tore under her teeth.

Only a second behind her, Jack went for Ailsa's legs and ripped chunks of them as she tried to get back onto her feet.

That left Gregor to grab the children, like the toothless old wolf only good to scavenge bones and watch the pups play. He grabbed the pup by the scruff with one hand, slung John up onto his shoulder, and dragged Shauna along by the arm as they scrambled up the stairs.

Ailsa had finally remembered the stolen wolf she'd stitched to her back. Her body twisted as the fur sank down into it and the poor, dead wolf crawled out. One eye was split open, eyelid peeled back and the gray-pink of old liver, and Gregor got a glimpse of Ailsa's desperate, bloodshot eyeball underneath. She grabbed at Shauna with a hand that was short a finger.

She tore Shauna's pajamas with her claws as Gregor pulled the little girl out of her reach. She shrieked and clung to him with bony little hands. Gregor stamped down on Ailsa's hand, heel ground down into the heart of it, and jumped over to get to the far side of the hall.

He staggered and caught himself, the wood hot under his feet as Bron sunk her teeth into Ailsa's throat and ripped it out. She let the meat drop from her mouth and let Ailsa splutter, jaws big and broken, her blood out. A wild blow of Ailsa's arm threw Bron off, and she thumped against a wall hard enough to make Gregor wince. She writhed away from Jack and staggered away on bloody, half-ruined legs, Ailsa's voice a raw gargle as she tried to raise the alarm.

Gregor started to lose his grip on Shauna as she squirmed and grabbed at him. Out of the corner of his eye, he saw a prophet in a dirty brown hide grab for her. Gregor snarled, dropped Shauna, and pushed her behind him with his knee as he shoved the prophet into the wall. The reek of dead, badly preserved skin slid into his nose and down his throat. He dug his fingers into the other man's throat until he gagged, and Gregor could feel the brittle strands of cartilage creak under his fingers. On his shoulder, John hiccupped with quiet panic and tightened his arms around Gregor's throat in unconscious mimicry.

"Don't!" Jack grabbed his shoulder and yanked him back. "It's Danny."

Surprise loosened Gregor's fingers, and the prophet slumped back against the wall. Now that he looked, he could see Danny's face under the skin of the wolf, the narrow muzzle draped over the frame of an old pair of heavy glasses.

"Finally got to play wolf, huh?" he said roughly.

Jack shoved past him and dragged Danny, stinking hide and all, into a hard, desperate kiss. He slid his hands up under the wet hide to tangle through Danny's soft curls.

"You smell like shit," Jack said as he leaned back. He grazed his thumb along Danny's cheekbone. "Are you okay?"

"Kath was meant to warn you," Danny said. He pulled the skin off with a shudder and dropped it through the trapdoor into the smoke. "You weren't meant to get hurt."

Jack cupped his hand around the back of Danny's neck with rough affection and pressed their foreheads. "We wanted to find Rose and her prophets," he shrugged. "We did that."

"Gross," Bron said. "If you're done slobbering on my brother, can we go?"

Danny looked at her and then away. He had played human too long if he was embarrassed by nakedness. A split second later, Danny jerked his head back and looked down.

"Are you pregnant?" he blurted.

Bron rolled her eyes at him. "No, I've just not farted for a while," she said. "Is that what you learn at your fancy human schools, how to state the obvious?"

"I just…. Mam never said," Danny spluttered.

"Why would she?" Bron asked. "You've not met it. Why would you care more about it than your own sister? Gods, you're dumb."

"Yeah, well, I bet that baby can't wait to be born so it doesn't have to listen to you all day," Danny shot back. "I just rescued you!"

"Rescued by a dog," Bron said. "I'll tell everyone that."

Jack tightened his hand protectively on Danny's shoulder. "Danny, come on," he said. "She's what she is."

"Don't tell him what to do," Bron snapped. "He's not your pet."

She shoved him out of the way, getting a growl from Jack, and threw her arms around Danny. For a minute she must have forgotten that he was the dog, because she squeezed him so tightly he grunted.

"I bet you were scared," she said. "But I told you it'd work."

Danny rested his face against her dark curls. "Yeah. You did." He looked up at Jack. "Now we need to get out of here before the prophets realize we're alone. Mam's looking for a fire, but—"

Jack gave Gregor a baffled look for a moment—at least their sibling hatred was straightforward—and then shook his head. "But we're not," he said. "Danny, get Bron and the kids out of here. Gregor and I will cut the dogs loose. They might be prophets and monsters, but they're still just blood and bone. We can end this."

No. They couldn't. The dogs would die, and Gregor supposed he might too in his current state, but they could hurt the prophets enough that they'd be easy prey for the wolves.

"Let's go," he said as he peeled John from around his neck and passed him and the pup to Danny. Shauna scowled at the dog but allowed Gregor to pass her off to Bron.

No one questioned them as they joined the prophets, ragged furs stitched tightly around their naked bodies, as they fled from the thick, oily smoke that filled the house and into the heart of a storm.

One prophet stumbled over Shauna, gave her a startled look, and opened his mouth to raise the alarm. Gregor grabbed him by his stolen skin, dead fur rough and scratchy against his fingers, and yanked him.

Wolves killed with their fangs and their endurance, long bloody hunts over hills and woods until they'd worn their prey down for the end. But Gregor had grown up a farm boy too. He'd wrung the necks of chickens, snapped a car-struck fox's neck to put it out of its misery. He broke the prophet's neck with a sharp twist before the man could shout anything. The prophet wasn't dead, but he didn't need to be. Gregor dropped him to the ground and left it to the snow to cover him.

Bron flashed him a quick, sharp smile, scooped up Shauna, and ran after her brother.

The dog was probably more use to her and the baby than he was.

It was harder to dismiss the thought than it had been—even anger wasn't enough to burn it out—but Gregor pushed it to the back of his mind and followed Jack's footprints around the side of the house. He'd already broken open the kennel cage and was dragging them out.

He stopped, caught on… something.

Rose stepped up behind him and laid a rebuilt hand on his shoulder. The nails still hadn't grown back on her fingers, and she pressed down with the tender nubs.

"I ruined you," she said. "Hate me for it if you want, but you hate him more, don't you? I can help."

Gregor steeled himself against the terrible lure of her beauty, tried to believe in the ruin he could see out of the corner of his eye. "I already told you," he said. "I don't want any wolf from you."

"Liar," she purred. The alien bulge of her swollen stomach pressed against him, hot and too soft. He wanted her, a hook in his balls, and he wanted to scrape off the skin she'd touched. "You are a wolf born, Gregor, your da's true heir. All you are is *want*. You *want* your wolf, my grandson, your pack… and I can give them to you. Just give me him."

"How?" he hadn't meant to ask.

He could hear the slime of satisfaction in her voice. "You'll know."

Something cold pressed against Gregor's palm and she was gone. He glanced down and then shoved the dented metal flask into his pocket. The dogs were out of the kennel and fell in behind Jack—a pack of sorts. Gregor swallowed the gross taste in his mouth, the temptation, and pushed his heavy legs into a lope.

"You don't need me for this," he spat the truth out like a weapon. "I'm going to find Nick. Whatever Rose's plan is, Nick's part of it. We can't let her get him again."

Jack looked torn. It was probably a lie. They both knew that without his wolf, Gregor wasn't much use. Or maybe Jack hoped Gregor would get killed and let Jack off that hook.

"If we wipe them out here, her plans are done anyhow," Jack protested. "Without the prophets…."

"They're just tools," Gregor said. "Just like Lachlan, just like the monsters she made back in Girvan. As long as she's not here, this isn't over."

Jack pressed his mouth together in a grim line, but he couldn't argue.

"Go," he said as he clapped Gregor on the shoulder. "I'll take care of Bron till you get back."

Gregor curled his lip. "I don't need your permission, Jack," he said. "You aren't anything yet. A pack of dogs won't make you Numitor."

He reached for the Wild, and it answered. Even through the silt of the Sannock Dead's rot that streaked through it, it pulled him sideways out of the world.

CHAPTER TWELVE—NICK

"YOU'RE LUCKY you still have your toes."

The clipped voice didn't give Nick any clue as how he should take that. Was he lucky that they'd been able to save his toes, or that the owner of the voice hadn't cut them off? He lay on what felt like an actual bed and stared at the inside of his eyelids as he debated whether to open them and find out.

"Mister, if you don't want to go back out in the snow," the voice said harshly, "you better sit up and tell me what you're doing up here."

Doctor. The prickly correction stung the tip of Nick's tongue. He swallowed it before it got away from him. Until he knew where he was, and why, let them make the assumptions.

Nick gave in and opened his eyes. It turned out to be a grim-faced man in a suit—in a *tie*—flanked by two soldiers, assault rifles cradled across their bodies as they stared at him. Nick was sprawled over the thin mattress of a narrow cot, padded cuffs around his wrists attached to the raised sides. An IV was plugged into his arm, the familiar itch of surgical tape against his skin, and the walls were the yellowed white of a dozen wards he'd been in over the years.

For a second Nick wondered if he'd had the psychotic break he'd spent his life afraid of, if the last weeks had been the hyperrealized work of a brain destined by nature and nurture to slip out of true eventually. It should have been a relief—that none of the monsters were real and his evil gran hadn't sacrificed him to… something—but all he felt was a terrible hollow loss in his chest.

"Gregor…," he muttered… or tried. His tongue was so dry it was nearly leather and stuck to the roof of his mouth. His eyes burned too with a hot, sun-scorched itch that his cuffs stopped him rubbing at.

"Is that your name?" the suited man asked. He gestured for one of the soldiers to lower his gun and get some water. Nick reached for the glass as it was held out but was brought up short by the rattle of his cuffs.

The soldier had to hold it to his lips for him so he could suck the tepid water down. "Gregory?"

Nick waited for the bird to cackle. It was mute. His head felt empty.

"No, I was.... Nick, my name's Nick." He lifted his arm as far as the shackles would allow. "Why am I in these? What did I do?"

"James Malloy," the suit introduced himself instead of answering. "Do you remember how you got here?"

Nick thought about it and then shook his head. He remembered the Run-Away Man, childhood monster given flesh and bones, and that he'd done what Gran had always told him. Run.

Smart as budgie.

A slideshow of memories flickered through his head, out-of-sequence and oddly framed. Snow and fear, pain in his feet, the panic in his head that the bird picked up from him like an attack. A road. That image flicked sharp and clear into Nick's mind—the snowed-crusted lorry wedged under a bridge and the trail of cars abandoned behind it. Belongings—important enough to pack in the car but not carry on your back—piled up at the side of the road.

Then he was here. Nick squinted and tried to peek through the bird's eyes to see the Wild, but there was nothing there. His head was quiet, and the world was as solid as he'd spent years and pills determined to believe it was.

"I don't remember," he said carefully. "I was on the road, looking for a sign to follow into town—"

"I thought everyone up here had evacuated?" Malloy said pointedly.

"Not everyone," Nick said. "Some people, the crofts have been in their family for generations or everything they own is in their sheep herd. And some people don't like to be told what to do."

"And you are?"

"A doctor. I didn't want to leave my patients, and then I couldn't leave," Nick said, because it seemed to make sense. He rattled his cuffs again. "What did I do?"

Malloy considered that answer for a moment, his eyes narrowed, and then nodded toward the guards. They backed off to the door, and Malloy pulled a chair over to the edge of the bed to sit down. He crossed long legs.

"We found you in the snow outsides, naked and raving," he said. "You mustn't have been out there that long, though, because you seem… intact."

The glance at Nick's groin under the threadbare white sheet was obvious enough to make Nick's ears hot. He shifted uncomfortably.

"I don't remember anything," he said. "Where am I?"

The odd, lewd distraction in Malloy's face snapped off as he pulled his "give nothing away" mask back on.

"Somewhere you shouldn't be," he said as he stood up. "But another doctor might be useful. We'll discuss it. Get some rest, Nicholas. You'll need it."

There it was again, the flash of furtive lust that made Nick squirm uncomfortably. He wasn't a prude—a loner but not a prude. People had found Nick attractive before, but they hadn't looked at him like that. Malloy eyed Nick like he didn't care if the interest was mutual, like maybe it would be better if it wasn't.

"Could you?" He held his arm up.

A small smile folded Malloy's mouth, and he licked the corner of his lips. "No," he said. "Not yet."

Nick accepted that with a nod and lay back against the thin pillows. He let his eyes flutter closed and evened his breath out into the slow patterns of steady sleep despite the itch that intensified. Malloy didn't move for a second, and then his hand touched Nick's thigh, warm through the sheet. It took an effort of will not to twitch as his skin crawled and his balls tightened, but Nick managed it.

The hand slid higher, and then one of the guards shifted with a creak of leather and stiff canvas and cleared their throat. Malloy snatched his hand away.

"He seems harmless," Malloy said, a thread of tension in his voice. "And he could be useful."

One of the two soldiers spat. "We should have killed the bastard," he said flatly. "He's not supposed to be here, and we're meant to let him eat our food? Breathe our air? Ewan should have left him in the snow. It would have been kinder. At least Big-Nose wouldn't have seen it coming."

"He can earn his keep," Malloy said, his voice starchy.

Someone laughed crudely.

"Enough," Malloy snapped. "We have other things to do. Tell Ewan that he found Nicholas here, so he can keep an eye on him."

There was a grunt in answer. Nick listened as the door opened, feet scuffed over the floor, and it closed again. He waited for a moment and listened to the room. After a few years of working in a morgue, you learned what a room where no one else was breathing sounded like.

Once Nick was satisfied he was alone, he lifted his head and opened his eyes.

The room was silent. There was nothing pressed to the sliver of reflection in the metal-covered cupboards, no dry, dead eye that watched him through the crack under the door. When he rattled at the inside of his brain, nothing shed feathers or croaked laughter at him.

None of it had been real—to the monsters, not the Wild, and not even Gregor and his awkwardly sweet mouth. Or that's what they wanted him to think.

Nick snorted to himself as he braced his feet against the mattress and pushed himself as far up the bed as he could with the cuffs limiting his movement. He sounded paranoid, Nick knew that, but his world had never been this normal….

Maybe he'd believe the Wild and the horror he'd not quite survived back in Girvan was the result of a break with reality, that the stress of that endless rote delivery of cold sad corpses had made his brain fold back into his memories of Gran's old stories to make sense of it.

Nick could even doubt Gregor, although that one hurt like a knife in his gut. The idea that someone could love him when even his gran had struggled with it had always been hard to buy.

The monsters and the dead things had always been there, though. Dry, dead eyes that watched him through the crack in a cupboard door or things that scraped bone-fingers against the mirror in a dark room. Nick had learned to turn a blind eye to them, afraid that no matter how many times he told himself he wasn't crazy, the evidence was right there. But when he looked, they were always there.

Even, Nick glanced from the cannula plugged into his arm to the IV stand, medication hadn't ever shifted them before. The straps on the cuffs were too short to let him reach the needle, but he squirmed over onto one hip and caught the thin plastic tube between his teeth. A yank of his head ripped it out of his arm with a quick, dry flash of pain that should have been worse.

He left the IV to drip onto the floor and his arm to drip bright red blood on the sheets as he reached down over the side of the bed. The metal rim of the bed was cold under his fingers as he followed it along until he found where the strap was fastened.

Medical restraints weren't prison shackles.

Nick caught his tongue between his lips as he twisted his hand around so he could pull at the buckle. The tendons in his wrist pulled tight as he fumbled at the rough leather, his little finger curled in a cramp, but he stuck to it. He finally worked his thumb into the loop and pulled it out. A tug unraveled the stiff leather from around the bed frame. It dangled limply from the cuff still around Nick's wrist, and he twisted over onto his side to do the other hand.

They weren't actually that hard to get out of if you weren't panicked.

Once his hands weren't leashed to the bed, Nick pulled the heavy, padded cuffs off and rubbed his eyes. Then he threw the sheet back. He was naked, all pale skin and the old scar on his stomach, but all his bits were still there. Someone had bandaged his feet in fat, overstuffed socks of gauze and surgical tape, but when he wiggled his toes, it didn't hurt.

If he'd somehow made it from Girvan to here without the bird inside him, he wouldn't have toes or fingers.

He scrambled out of the cot, goose bumps pimpled over his skin at the chill, and hunted through the cupboards and drawers—pills and rolls of bandages, a scalpel left in a tray, shreds of gray flesh still stuck to it. He grimaced at it but set it aside for later. He didn't know where he was exactly, or why anyone else was there, but he knew doctors. Every last one of them would have a spare set of scrubs stashed somewhere to change into after you were bled on, barfed on, or both.

Bottom drawer beside the single cot. The gray tracksuit bottoms were a bit short on him, the cuffs just above his bony ankles, but they'd do. He zipped the hoodie on over his bare chest and left the bandages on as he shoved his feet into the grubby white sneakers. It meant they almost fit.

Now what?

It wasn't a hard question. Or it shouldn't have been. It doubled Nick over, his hands braced against the edge of the counter, as he tried to convince his lungs to let in the air he'd sucked up. His brain felt pinched, and behind the scar on his chest, he could feel his heart batter against his breastbone.

The old go-to mantra bounced around his head—*Gran was crazy, I'm not*—but it didn't help the way it used to. He reached up and dragged his fingers over his collarbone, but there was nothing there. The old nail pendant had been left behind in Girvan, and it had never been meant to help him. Not really.

Nick squeezed his hands into fists until he felt his nails slice into his palm. The pain cut through the fuzz of panic like a razor and let in clarity.

He couldn't do this.

The first time he'd stood over a corpse in medical school, with a scalpel in his hand and his voice still Glasgie-thick, he'd realized the same thing. Then he sliced that cold body from sternum to pubis, because that's what he had to do to get what he wanted.

This was the same. Whether he could or not, he had to.

"Goddammit, Gregor," Nick muttered as he pushed himself upright. "You've got to learn to time your rescues better."

Because he knew Gregor would find him. All he had to do was not die or get turned into a monster by his gran until then. Nick shoved the sleeves of the stolen hoodie up his arms and turned to grab the scalpel. He caught a glimpse of his reflection in the mirror hung on the back of the door as he did so. It didn't look… right.

Nick wiped the scalpel on his jeans and walked over to the door. He had to crouch down slightly to see. The mirror had been hung at the right height for the doctor whose too-short trousers Nick wore. When he saw his face, he flinched in surprise. Hectic red stained his cheekbones, stark against his pale skin, and his eyes were pink and sticky. He leaned in closer to the glass and pulled his eyelid down with one finger. Strings of the discharge stretched between the white of his eye and the lashes. The skin exposed was tender red and splattered with hard, white blisters. It stung as the air touched it.

That Malloy had looked at that and still wanted to feel Nick up was testament on its own that there was something *wrong* going on here.

It looked like an allergic reaction or—Nick drew back from the mirror as it occurred to him—like a reaction to a caustic agent.

Nick let go of his eye and scrambled around the bed. There was a puddle of saline on the floor, pinkish with diluted blood. Most of the liquid had drained out of the bag and it dangled flaccid from the hook. Nick reeled up the tube and licked the needle. It tasted like blood—salt and metals, nothing that made his stomach twist or the bird in his head ruffle—and something sharp and ethanol sweet. Nick spat it out on the ground, twice, to clear it off his tongue and wrenched the tainted bag off the hook. He threw the bag against the wall, where it hit with a wet slap and flopped down onto the floor.

Gran had said it made wolves see *farther*, not that it blinded them. But his gran said more than her prayers, and whatever Nick might have been born, he wasn't a wolf now.

He roughly rubbed his knuckles over his eyes until they smeared oily color across the backs of his lids. It wasn't likely to help, but Nick couldn't stop himself. He couldn't help but imagine what he'd see if he weren't half blinded.

It would wear off, Nick reminded himself. He'd seen that in the people his gran had poisoned before.

Eventually. Mostly.

Nick shuddered that thought away before it could root. Most of his life, he'd wanted to *stop* seeing things that weren't there, but now the thought of being blind to them made him flinch. Without the carrion bird, what would he be to Gregor? Not that he'd had much time to spend with the wolves so far, but they didn't seem like they needed a pathologist or even a surgeon, if he could remember what it was like to work on living people.

Worry about that later, he told himself. Blind was better than dead. Maybe.

He padded over to the door and pressed his ear against it. All he could hear was the panicked rush of blood in his ears.

Shit.

He rolled the dice and opened the door. There was no one outside. Nick let his breath out between his teeth and stepped out the door. He hesitated in the starkly lit hall as he weighed up his choices. Left or right? The flip of a coin in his head made him turn right. The soles of his sneakers squeaked on the floor as he padded down the hall. Just before he reached the end, a familiar voice stopped him dead in his tracks, feet nailed to the floor.

Between one breath and the next, he was a little boy again, damp with night terrors and holding his breath in case his gran knew what he was doing.

"What about Nicholas?" Gran asked. Her voice was still rough, scorched from fire and smoke. Behind her he could hear the sound of laughter and things being broken over the dull thump of bass-heavy music. "Is it still in him?"

"… yes. The carrion god is still inside him," a man said. He had the same accent as Gran, same as Gregor and Jack. Highland born and bred, without any attempt to soften it for the English. "I've just blinded him to it for now—"

The crack of a hand against skin made Nick jump. He could almost feel the sting of the slap against his cheek, and he had to bite the inside of his cheek to keep from yelping.

"If you have damaged him or it, I will crack your ribs open and use your beating heart as a snack to lure the bird back to us," Gran said flatly. "He's a god, Ewan. The first god to walk our world in millennia. The others need to see that before they'll trust us."

"And once they know they can't?" Ewan asked. "What will it do to him then? What will we do with him? He's your blood, your grandson."

Gran huffed an impatient breath through her teeth. "Don't borrow trouble, Ewan. Once the gods come to our table, everything is possible. Look at me."

There was a pause, and Ewan's voice was thick with longing as he said, "You're as beautiful as the first day I saw you, like fire in a meadow. But it's not real, Rose."

"Does it matter?"

"… no."

The sound of wet kissing jarred Nick out of his paralysis, and he gagged as he recoiled from the sounds. There were some things that you didn't want to imagine your gran doing, especially when she was an evil old monster.

Something bigger than a glass smashed down where the party was going on, and a roar of approval and anger rose up.

It reminded Nick of the rest of the medics back in Girvan after they'd swigged the prophets' tainted brew.

He licked his lips and tasted the sharp poison on his tongue again. What was his gran doing here? What did she want with soldiers and civil servants like Malloy? And what did the Run-Away Man have to do with it?

The answers lay—probably—somewhere ahead of him, but escape didn't. Nick closed his eyes, turned, and jogged back down the corridor. This wasn't Girvan. He didn't owe these people anything.

He'd set Jepson's ghost free back in Girvan, cut her loose of her bones and her duty to go to whatever reward the ex-army surgeon had earned. Even if he hadn't, he couldn't have seen her right then. That didn't matter. The memory of her still haunted the windows he passed, her face pinched with disapproval.

Yeah, well, she was dead, so she didn't get a vote.

Someone had stenciled directions on the wall at the end of the hall where it branched. Nick stopped to read them.

Mess and Med-bay were behind him.

Barracks straight ahead.

Labs to the right.

Nothing indicated what was to the left, so Nick went that way. Two more turns and the floor started to incline upward. It got colder too, and Nick shivered as the chill worked under his hoodie to bare flesh. If whatever they'd done to him had killed the bird, would he still be able to survive out there?

It didn't matter. Gregor would find him. He just had to make it easier to be found.

Two sets of heavy doors got him to the end of the corridor, where heavy, snow-damp coats and insulated boots had been left to drip in front of a heavy steel door painted with a sharp white three.

Something about that seemed important. Nick stared at the door as he tried to work out *what*, but it wouldn't stick. He grabbed one of the thick, pixelated-gray camo jackets and dragged it on, then swapped too-big sneakers for too-big boots. Once he zipped the coat up, he could smell the man who'd worn it before him—rank sweat and a meaty, sour undertone that reminded him of typhoid.

He had a feeling none of the others would smell better.

The door was sealed with a heavy-duty door bar. It was meant to keep people out, though, not in. He supposed most people wouldn't want to go back into the storm. He yanked it up with both hands and shouldered the door open against the drift of snow that had formed outside.

An alarm went off as the door opened, flickering red against the walls for a second before a siren kicked in. No going back now. He pulled the hood up with one hand and squeezed out through the crack of the door.

The wind caught him and shoved him forward as he stumbled outside, as though it thought he needed to get away too. The snow was so thick it was like fog. Nick stretched his hands out in front of him and lost sight of them. When he drew them back, they were blanched white and frost rimmed his cuticles.

He clumsily shoved his already numb fingers into his pockets and pushed himself into a shuffling jog through the snow. The direction didn't matter. He didn't know where he was or where he should be going, so "away" was the best he could plan.

Voices yelled through the snow behind him, almost lost under the mournful drone of the wind.

"… how'd he get…."

"… go and freeze…."

The stutter of gunfire made him flinch and fold his arms over his head. Bullets zipped past him and slammed into the thick-packed snow on the ground. One hit a tree and took a frozen chunk of bark with it.

"Shit," he muttered between his elbows.

Weeks of being a sort of god thing and he'd almost forgotten what it was like to be afraid. That had reminded him.

"Stop! Damn you, hold fire!" a thickly Scottish voice roared, sharply audible. "Don't shoot him. We need to get him back."

"… not your call… make," Malloy said, voice muffled by the snow. "… in charge here, Ewan."

There was a pause, and then, even with half his brain still tranquilized, Nick felt the world shift around him. It felt like the tide.

"Not anymore," Ewan said, his voice still eerily clear. "Find him. Bring him back. In one piece."

There was a pause and then easy mutters of agreement. Nick dropped his hands from over his head, exhaled raggedly through his teeth, and veered to the left away from the noise behind him. He scrambled over a low wall and, almost on his hands and knees, up an unexpectedly steep field.

The air was like splinters when he breathed, and it made his lungs cramp painfully. But at least the wind, unruly as it shoved him back and forth, filled the tracks he left behind with soft snow.

A shadow in the corner of his eye caught his attention, and he stopped in place, shivering, to track it through the snow. He managed for a few steps, and then the snow thickened, and he lost sight of whatever it was.

The Sannock?

Nick creaked out a stiff laugh at the madness that he hoped to see one of them. He still turned and headed toward the last place he'd seen it. The muscles in his legs ached as he kicked his way through the snow and then nearly tripped over what he had to assume was the shadow he'd chased.

A weathered stone bench was perched on top of a hill in the middle of nowhere. He leaned on it to catch his breath, and something snarled—a high, thin noise from somewhere in the storm. Nick turned, hands raised, and a heavy, cold body crashed into him. The impact knocked him off his feet, the air shocked out of his lungs, and he pitched backward down the hill. A rock caught him on the hip and dug into the small of his back, and rough ice scraped across his back where the coat rode up.

They tumbled to a stop at the bottom of the hill, the other man on top of him with his arm cocked back for a punch. Nick swung first in a wild arc that cracked his knuckles against the sharp line of a heavy jaw, and he twisted his hip to try and throw the other man off. It didn't work. He was slammed back into the ground hard, and the man leaned down to scowl at him.

"How come every time I lose track of you?" Gregor asked in a rough voice. He curled his lip as he sniffed the air. "You turn up smelling like shit?"

Nick didn't have the air in his lungs to laugh. He grabbed the back of Gregor's neck instead, fingers twisted into the snow-matted knots, and dragged him down into a cold, eager kiss. The heat of Gregor's breath warmed his mouth and slid through him.

Even half-frozen and battered, Nick felt the hungry tug of desire under his skin as Gregor shifted his weight on top of him. It wasn't the time, but his body didn't care, and neither did Nick really. There was something reassuring about *this*, the private bubble of hunger and unexpected love that pulled them together.

It wasn't about the carrion bird or the wolves, his gran or Gregor's brother. This was theirs.

"My gran's here," Nick confessed as Gregor broke the kiss and pulled back. "Back there, with some old wolf."

"I know," Gregor said bluntly, still no fan of wasting words. He glanced down between their bodies. "You're bleeding, Nick."

Nick started to disagree, but then he looked down and saw a splash of blood spread from under his arm across the white crust of snow. The minute he saw it, he felt the hot, dull ache of pain between his ribs and his head swam with woozy discomfort.

"Oh," he said. "Can you die twice?"

Chapter Thirteen—Jack

THE OLD house shouldn't have burned so easily. It was halfway to a ruin, but it had stood for decades and was riddled with frozen damp. That made no difference. The flames caught and spread inside the walls with giddy spite for what made sense. The bricks cracked, the mortar crumbled as it was kiln-dried, and unruly licks of flame poked through the shattered roof like hair from under a hat.

It wouldn't be Surtr's turn at the world for seasons yet, but fire was never patient, and he wanted the world for kindling. He took what he could.

Winter wouldn't have it. Already the wind had picked up to dash thick flurries of snow into the flames where they turned to steam and made the fire crackle out thin curse words in the giant's sizzle-and-pop language.

A prophet threw himself from a window on the top floor. Ungainly in his stolen skin, he landed badly, with a crack of bone, and lay broken on the snow until he could pull himself together. Others milled out front, half-blind in the smoke and snow as they tried to pull themselves together.

The dogs harried them with sharp teeth and quick strikes, louder than any wolf as they barked and yowled to each other. It made Jack want to put his ears back, annoyed at the noise as he used his fangs and the bulk of his dire-wolf muscle to keep the two monsters Rose had left behind at bay.

Bulldog shoulder-charged him with a pig grunt of a growl and slammed him into a tree. A rib popped, loud and hollow in Jack's ears, and snow dropped off the tree's branches onto him. It was heavy, almost solid, and studded with chunks of ice that battered his skull and back. His ears rang with an oddly pitched tone that made him feel unbalanced as he shook the snow off and staggered back to his feet.

Millie shot in from the snow, low to the ground and with black lips wrinkled back from her teeth. She still had something of the terrier about her, with tricolored fur and wiry muscles, but mapped onto the body of a much larger dog. She grabbed at Bulldog's tail, a naked knob of bone and twisted nerves, and clamped down. Bulldog screamed in affronted pain, an unexpectedly shrill noise for its size, and spun around in a clumsy circle to try to grab Millie. She slipped in the snow, tumbled paws over tail, and scrambled back to her feet in time to snap at Bulldog's nose.

It stung Jack's pride to leave a dog to fight his battles for him, but as a wolf, he was too practical to dwell on that. He ducked his head to paw blood out of his eye, the skin over his forehead laid open from a sharp bit of ice, and let Millie keep the Bulldog busy while he shot after the long-nosed, mad-eyed monster who pranced through the snow on fingers and toes pulled out long and braided together. Its jaw unhinged all the way back to its ears, revealing serrated rows of thick, see-through teeth that it snapped at Bron as it tried to get around her to the pups.

"Fucking *abortion*," she spat as she turned to keep between them. "Get away from them."

Blood dripped from gouges in her arms and legs. The monster feinted to the right to try to shoot around her, but she grabbed it by the ear and pulled it like taffy up onto the top of its skull to haul it back. The ear ripped off and took a long patch of skull with it, revealing porous bone and oddly knit muscle, and Bron yelled her disgust and punched it in the eye.

It made a glottal, angry noise as it fell back and shook its head. Jack assumed it had been told that it could hurt, but not kill, the prisoners. Otherwise Bron would have been dead. She had a mean streak in a fight, like the rest of her family, but the monsters didn't care for damage. The skin had already started to pinch together over the raw wound in its scalp.

Jack hit it before it could gather itself. He sank his fangs into its back leg, braced his feet, and dragged it backward. Overclocked strands of lean muscle pulsed like a heartbeat in his mouth as the thin bones cracked and flaked. Sour blood flooded his mouth and made his tongue squirm back in revulsion. The trickle that ran down his throat made his stomach cramp and try to retch it back up.

The longer the monsters lived, the worse they smelled, corruption like a layer of fat under their skin. Most of the ones that followed Rose didn't even have enough of an identity left to pity.

Jack snapped his head from side to side. The monster's leg snapped, and it staggered clumsily in the deep snow as it tried to get its balance. He dragged it back, one step after the other, while it clawed at the ground to try and drag itself back toward Bron and the kids. Five feet from them and it suddenly shifted its focus to him as it bent impossibly at the narrow waist to snap at him. The bony, nail-toothed snout struck out at him like a snake and laid his shoulder open in a raw mess.

Pain sliced hot down Jack's leg, but he hung on. A muffled growl filtered through his mouthful of meat and bone, and he wrenched again. Flesh and tendons slid against bone, thick and slippery in Jack's mouth. The monster made a strangled, nasal squeal of frustration and struck out again.

This time Jack let go and dodged back on three legs, his foreleg hitched up as he waited for the shoulder to knit.

"Danny said the Pack would come!" Bron yelled, frustration and disbelief in her voice. "Where are they?"

She reached up and grabbed one of the denuded branches from the tree that Jack had hit. It snapped off in her hands, frozen and heavy, and she swung it like a bat at the monster.

Jack snarled in frustrated reproof at her as the monster lost interest in him and turned back to her. He wanted to distract it from her. Bron showed him her teeth in unrepentant response and swung again. The monster grabbed the branch out of the air, sank its teeth into it, and shook it violently. Bron managed to hang on but ended up on her knees with a gash in her shoulder where the branch had caught her. One of the pups—Shauna—had changed her skin, and the lanky yearling wolf yapped shrill and angry as it bounced forward.

She, at least, had enough respect to back off when Jack growled at her, but her ears stayed pinned and her needle-sharp puppy teeth bared.

"Bron!" Danny yelled, his voice cracked as he pitched it to carry over the storm and the fight. He was in front of the house, lanky frame barely visible through the angry flurries of indignant snow. "Get over here."

"What?" Bron yelled back as she let the monster have the branch and staggered back "Why?"

It was Shauna who listened. The young wolf shot between Bron's legs, fluffy tail clamped between her legs, and made a beeline for Danny. Even from this distance, Jack could see Danny's horror in the way his body flinched. The monster hesitated, pointy head swung between Bron and the pup. Then, like the sight hound it was built to resemble, it went after the prey in motion.

Jack snapped his teeth at Bron, growled a wordless command for her to stay, and went after the monster. He stripped chunks of flesh from its haunches, the splintered bone of its leg visible through its stitched-together skin, but he couldn't catch it.

It strained its neck out and snapped a divot from Shauna's back leg that made her yelp a high-pitched puppy whine that caught in the back of Jack's brain.

Danny darted forward. He grabbed Shauna by the scruff just as she reached the steps into the house. Her heavy, dark-furred body dangled from his fist, and he tossed her aside like a football. The monster twitched its head to follow the arc of its prey's body—and maybe there was still enough of a being there left to be surprised—and crashed into Danny. They tumbled over each other and kicked up snow in grubby arcs as they wrestled in front of the house.

"Get it into the fire!" Danny grunted as he landed on his back, hands locked around the monster's throat as it snapped at him. "It won't heal as fast."

That could work, Jack supposed. He slammed into the monster with his full weight and sent both of them crashing through the blistered front door and into the flames. Fire singed his fur and blistered the pads of his feet. The smoke was sharp in his throat and eyes, but maybe Surtr remembered who'd set him loose. It was the monster who caught. The blond strings of what was left of its hair flared, and the naked, drum-tight skin blistered and scorched as the fire hit it.

Again, something of the person the monster had been scraped out of its throat as it screamed in panic. It writhed away from Jack, still lamed on that ruined leg, and fled blindly into the house. The charred floor gave way under it as it ran, and it fell with a whinny of miserable confusion, into the hot, red flames that filled the basement.

The house shuddered and groaned around Jack, the floor under his scalded paws rolling like a ship's deck. It could have been cracked stones and weather, or it could have been the low, grating laugh of Surtr. This might not be his time yet, but he'd gotten at least one god-thing to burn.

Jack clamped his tail and backed out of the flames. The bitter cold outside was almost a comfort as it hit him and stole the heat from his burns.

"Are you okay?" Danny asked as he dropped to his knees next to Jack. There was blood on his arms, freckled skin raked down to raw meat as he slapped out the charred spots on Jack's fur. "Jack?"

Jack pawed at his stinging muzzle and then leaned his weight against Danny's shoulder. He smelled like blood, smoke, and fear… but still home. Shauna crawled over and put her chin on Danny's foot, her sides fluttering as she breathed raggedly.

"Mam's on her way," Danny said, staunchly hopeful. "The dogs are holding their own."

They weren't, but Jack appreciated Danny's view of the world. It took a dog or a human to lie that stubbornly to themselves. Jack pawed his nose again—the blisters itched—gave Danny's face a quick lick, and threw himself back into the fight.

If Shauna had been a bit faster, Danny's plan would have worked. The monster's own bulk would have carried it straight into the fire without help from Jack. He headed for the heavyset, bulldog-shaped thing as it pinned Millie to the ground. The dog made a weirdly alien sound as the heavy, twisted head dropped. Jack went between a prophet's legs, threw the snarling woman in the air for the dogs to pile on as he landed, and darted in to grab a mouthful of the slack folds of flesh that hung from the monster's throat. It split under his teeth but stretched rather than tore as he snarled and shook it like a rat.

"… gro… oof," the thing grunted as it threw its head back. It almost sounded like words. Jack hoped it wasn't. He loathed the monsters, instinctive as the hackles that pricked at the smell of him, but whatever they'd been before didn't deserve to know what had happened.

He let the folds of musty flesh drop, blood and fluid wet on the skin as it dripped out slowly, and went for the stomach instead. There was more mass to this monster than the other one, muscle layered over muscle in knots that threatened to split its skin, so it wasn't as limber. It shook its head and lumbered around to snarl at Jack. Blood and flesh were clotted between its broken fangs.

Millie was still alive. Jack could hear the rattle of her breath, and that was all Jack could buy her. He lunged in and snapped at the monster's face. The flattened features, eyes puffed out over slab cheeks and nose flattened over its broad mouth, held more of the human than the other monsters. Jack set his teeth in that snot-wet snout and tore it open. The monster screamed, reared up onto its bowed back legs, and slapped Jack off like a bug. The splintered bone claws that poked out of its paws raked his ribs open to the bone.

With a grunt, Jack landed in the snow. He made himself stagger up onto his paws, each breath a stab of pain down his bloody side, and growled a challenge at the thing. It squealed and rubbed its ruined face into the snow. As it looked up, a bloody frost crusted around the hole he'd left on its face. The blood-rimmed bulge of its eyes glittered with spite as it lumbered toward him.

"Wolves!" someone yelled, panic in their voices. "The wolves are here."

Shauna's da, a sable-brown wolf big even in the dire-sized pack, went through the chain-link fence instead of over it. It came down on top of some of the prophets who were still human-shaped, and the rest of the Pack trampled them underfoot as they stormed the prophets' den.

It didn't take long. Kath, sleek-furred and silver-gray, went for the hamstrings. The prophets who dropped behind her, enraged or screaming, she left for others to clean up. It had been a hard winter, the Old Man was still lost, and not all the Pack had fallen in behind Kath. Some of Lachlan's wolves weren't there, and the ones that had traded camps had torn ears and chunks of fur missing. If the prophets had rallied, ghoulish and alien as they pulled patched and rotten wolves over their bones, they could have made a fight of it.

Maybe not a long one.

They didn't. Prophets were cowards and killers, oathbreakers and perverts. A few of them had hammered their flaws into horrors, but without a Rose or Job to rally behind or kidnapped children to hide behind, the prophets weren't suited for conflict. Even magic and stolen skins couldn't change that.

They broke and fled on lame feet, the ripe stink of carrion trailing behind them whether they fled into the storm or into the Wild.

Jack snapped and snarled at the bulldog to keep it hemmed back from the fight. His ribs were broken, sharp against his lungs as he twisted and jumped, and the vision in one eye was smeared gray and red from a claw that had scraped down his face. The bulldog had signs of wear too.

Thick strips of flesh hung from its shoulders and gut, left to bleed as the monster's body repaired more important injuries to throat and bone. He'd ripped off a strip of muscle from its cheek on the last pass, thick as gristle between Jack's fangs, and the grotesque jaw hung stroke-slack on one side. Tendon and skin writhed like worms as the prophet's curse worked blindly to reshape the monster into something that killed easier.

Gray and black fur blurred through the compromised vision in the corner of Jack's bad eye. He thought it was backup and wasn't sure if he was grateful or resentful that they thought he needed it. Then the wolf barreled into him, breath sour as rancid cheese, and they tumbled over each other as sharp fangs tore at Jack's ears and thick ruff.

His first suspicion—always read—was that it was Gregor, but even if Jack's brother had his wolf, Gregor wouldn't try to kill him now. It would be a fair enough fight when that happened.

Lachlan.

The mouthful of fur that Jack ripped from Lachlan's throat was dry and matted. It stuck to his tongue and the roof of his mouth, annoying and scratchy. Lachlan landed on top of Jack and used his weight to pin him down.

Snow hung between them like smoke as Lachlan peeled his lips back in a snarl, teeth dull against the bright red of his mouth. His breath was hot enough to steam and more even.

There was something wrong with him. Jack wasn't sure what exactly, half-blind and his brain fogged with blood lust, but he didn't question it either.

A massive paw swung out of the snow and slapped Lachlan off Jack's chest. The huge wolf yelped like a puppy in surprise as he was flung into the air. Then the monster screamed, and the sound gargled out of its loose throat as it lumbered after Lach. Bad wolf or good wolf, it didn't matter. The prophets might have twisted their monsters into caricatures of the wolves, but they couldn't tell them apart.

Jack huffed out a wolf laugh, and his bloody tongue dangled out of his jaws as he rolled onto his feet. He shook himself and quickly ducked his head to scrape his paw over his eyes and peel away scabbed blood and dead flesh so he could see—more or less—again. There was still a taint of pink to the world, and the cold burned his face, but his peripheral vision was back.

His legs trembled with exhaustion under him. Whatever reserves he'd scraped together since Rose peeled his skin off were gone. He shook his head and found more from somewhere as he went after the monster.

It was easy to track them. Blood and a trail of churned, stained snow. Until it wasn't.

The trail stopped cold, between one step and the next, and the scent filtered away on the wind, just like the site of Job's bloody slaughter back in Durham, where he'd stepped away from guilt and into the Wild.

Footsteps crunched behind him, and Danny nearly ran into him as he dashed through the snow. He stumbled to a halt and crouched down next to Jack. His breath steamed on his lips as he gave Jack a concerned look and then turned his attention to the straight line division between there and gone.

"Was that Lachlan?" he asked as he put his arm over Jack's shoulders. His fingers twisted in the thick hair of Jack's ruff. The gesture pulled at the fresh wounds hidden under the mats, but Jack ignored that. It was worth the discomfort to be able to lean into the embrace and sigh out his weariness.

He folded his wolfskin away and knelt in the snow, naked and stippled with ruined ink and fresh bruises. Blood scabbed his skin over almost healed injuries. Danny hissed in concern as he gingerly prodded at the edges of the deep punctures bruised into Jack's shoulders.

Without the wolf, the simple pleasure of the embrace fanned out into something more complicated. Familiar and sweet, a dull hint of desire twitched under the dull weariness of the fight It was layered over with need and fear and, unfair though it was, anger.

"Saved by a dog," he heard Bron's voice hiss inside his head. *"I'll tell everyone that."*

Let her.

"It was him," he said. His lip curled in contempt. "The new Numitor that was."

Danny rubbed his hand over his face, and his nose wrinkled as he squinted. "He couldn't do that," he said. "Lach could hardly touch the Wild."

Jack snorted and pushed himself to his feet. "And prophets used to be toothless, and monsters were for stories," he said. "It's the Wolf Winter, Danny, things change."

He offered Danny his hand and hauled him up out of the snow.

"No," Danny said. "You don't get it. Lach couldn't touch the Wild at all without another wolf's tail to chase. Why do you think he hated me so much? He was practically a dog. He only made it as a wolf by the skin of his teeth. The Wild's not gotten strong enough to change that. Has it?"

Probably not. Not here, where the skin of the Wild was shot through with the dead flesh of the Sannocks' prison.

"Maybe," he said. There was something there—woven in with the certainty that there was something *wrong* with Lachlan—but Jack couldn't pin it down. Either he didn't want to look at it, or he didn't want to admit he needed Danny to tie the threads. He shrugged it off and wiped his nose on the back of his hand. Back at the prophet's den, he heard a thin, territorial howl challenge the drone of the wind. "The rest? Your sister?"

"Wiping up the prophets who couldn't run," Danny said. He pulled a befuddled face. "Still pregnant."

Jack could have told Danny then, but he didn't. Something like jealousy caught painfully at his ribs. It would have been so easy for Gregor. His brother could have had what he wanted *and* what he loved. Instead Jack would have to give up one or the other and then live with it.

It wasn't fair, but that wasn't new. He also didn't have to deal with it just yet.

"We should get back," he said. A crooked smile twisted his mouth. "Before they think it's over."

He started to limp back on scorched feet, blood still hot on his thigh where Lach had raked him during their brief scuffle. Danny edged over and unselfconsciously tucked himself under Jack's arm and cupped his hand around Jack's hip, fingers callused and familiar.

It was easy. He was Jack's.

"I wouldn't have gone if I'd known you'd get hurt," Danny said. "Mam said it was bad, but you and Gregor are the Old Man's sons, and—"

He was cold, shivering as he thought too much about the wind that nipped at his skin. Jack wasn't sure if the body pressed against him was there to hold him or steal his heat. He didn't mind either way.

"Sometimes you have to do things you don't want to," Jack said.

They limped back into the aftermath of the fight. The fire had finally given in to the inevitable and guttered—just embers and black smoke as the storm dumped snow down on it. The bodies of the prophets who hadn't escaped lay where they'd fallen. Snow already covered their bodies in a white blanket, stained with faded pink as it soaked up the spilled blood.

Ellie was on her knees in the middle of the wolves, the back of her neck scruffed unkindly in Kath's thin, bony hand. One of the dogs—the stranger—was yelling a protest, but the dogs' help in the fight had already been forgotten. The wolves snarled and cuffed him, eager to get him to shut up or go away. On the outskirts, the rest of Lachlan's wolves watched sullenly.

Shit.

He pulled himself away from Danny and squared his shoulders as he stalked across the bloodstained snow and dirt.

"Let her go," he said.

Kath tightened her grip instead. "She's the prophets' lapdog."

Ellie writhed in the painful grip on her neck. "Fuck you," she spat. "Lach was Numitor."

"I'd sooner have a goat," Bron said with a contemptuous curl of her lip. "What sort of wolf would follow the likes of Lach?"

"Everyone did," Jack said, his voice harsh. "Kath. Connor. Tom the dog. Maybe for different reasons, but the prophets had you all on a string. If you want her to pay for that, you'll be accountable too. Let her go."

Kath studied him with hooded, dark eyes. Then she glanced past him to where he'd let Danny fall back.

"You the Numitor now?" she asked dryly. "Here to give us all orders?"

Kath had always believed that it was best to rip the plaster straight off. The pain would have to be faced eventually, so why not make it clean? It was a wolf way to be, but Jack had spent too much time with prophets and humans over the last few months.

"I'm the Numitor's son," he said. "And if he contradicts me, then do what you want. Until then, let her go."

She did. Ellie rubbed the back of her neck and gave him a grateful, thoughtful nod.

Jack felt the Pack settle in around him, the structure of it clear as glass as he was folded back into the hierarchy. Just like that.

"What now, then?" Hector asked from the back. He didn't mean immediately, but Jack decided to take it that way.

"We go back to the Old Man's," he said. "And work out what to do next. This isn't over, and I am done with being prey."

Someone howled, sharp muzzle thrown up to the sky in defiance, and a low mutter of agreement rolled through the Pack. It felt good for a moment, heady as a draft of the prophets' poison drink.

Then he looked over at Danny—always the last person he looked for at the end of a fight—and Danny dropped his gaze in polite submission. Jack's stomach sank with it, because he supposed he'd made that decision.

Jack was the Old Man's son, and the only thing he'd ever wanted was to take Da's place one day. He'd been willing to kill his brother for it, because he knew he'd be the chosen one. Everyone had.

It didn't matter that he'd changed his mind. Who else was going to step up and lead the Pack through the Winter?

Jack let himself look at Danny for a second longer and then turned his attention back to his wolves.

"We have until the next full moon," he said. Then he nodded to Bron. She instinctively curled her arms around her stomach and scowled at him. "And we have what the prophets want."

Or at least what one mad old wolf wanted. They just didn't know why.

CHAPTER FOURTEEN—JACK

THE SHOCK of snow-melt water against his skin made Jack's balls tighten between his legs and his toes curl. Wolves might not let the cold bother them, but that didn't make it pleasant. It was still better than the stink of smoke and the hackle-prickling offense that the prophets' monsters reeked of. Even secondhand, mixed with Jack's own blood, it made anger scrape at the back of his throat and tighten his fists.

He grabbed the half-melted bar of soap from the sink and scrubbed until his skin was raw and all he could smell was the sharp, antiseptic smell of tar. Blood and suds dripped down his legs and made pink puddles on the old gray slate tiles. Jack leaned over the basin and splashed a handful of water into his face. He raked his fingers through his hair and down to cup the nape of his neck.

It was a shame he couldn't wash the inside of his brain clean.

"That's a smell that takes me back," Danny said from behind him.

Jack snorted, unsurprised. Even at his worst, his nose stuffed with rot and the wrong smell of the monsters and the last dregs of energy carved out of his bones to keep on his feet, he would know when Danny was there. He knew how Danny walked, the sound of his breath, and the rhythm of his heartbeat.

"Why's that?" he asked as he straightened up. There was a mirror on the wall. It was old and specked with wear, but good enough to shave in. Jack ignored his own reflection and looked at Danny's in the glass instead. The dark-haired man was propped against the frame of the door, and Jack felt a twinge of surprise as he took in the shaggy hair and the old sweater, ragged at the collar and cuffs, that Danny had unearthed from some cupboard. At some point Jack had forgotten that Danny could look like he belonged here. Danny didn't meet Jack's gaze through the glass, but his eyes had drifted lower than courtesy demanded, down the lean lines of his back to the curve of his ass. Jack couldn't complain about that. "They're too soft for carbolic down over the Wall?"

He reached for the towel and scrubbed himself more or less dry on the bleach-rough cotton.

"Not as much blood to scrub off," Danny said.

Jack snorted.

"So I was right. Too soft." He turned around the lobbed the towel at Danny. "Catch, Danny-dog."

It was an old trick. Danny caught the towel, looked annoyed with himself, and tossed it down on the tiles to sop up the water. It annoyed him enough that he finally looked up to meet Jack's eyes. Jack waited for it. He knew Danny hadn't missed what happened out on the moors, in front of the ruins of the prophets' house. That was the disadvantage of taking someone smart to bed.

Then Danny let his breath out on a ragged laugh, stepped over the discarded towel, and pulled Jack into a kiss. With one hand he cupped the back of Jack's neck, fingers tangled in the damp, dirty-blond hair, and his mouth was mint-fresh and determined.

For a moment Jack was too caught off guard to respond. He'd expected anger, even if it was Danny's quiet, precise version of it, not a tongue in his mouth and a rough thumb grazed along his jaw. He stumbled back a step, the curved porcelain edge of the sink cold as it dug into his hips, and Danny nudged his thigh between Jack's legs. The scrape of denim against his cock made Jack hiss against Danny's mouth with a jolt of unexpected sensation that knotted in his gut.

It wasn't how it was done.

Danny was a dog, bottom of the pack hierarchy from now until eternity. He had the right to say no to Jack, not that he ever had, but he was meant to wait to be asked. That was how it worked.

Not like this, with Danny's hunger chewed over Jack's mouth and Jack left flat-footed and breathless.

Jack's pride spluttered up from under the crap of the last few months, the cocky young wolf who thought he could just turn up and take what he wanted. Except this *was* what he wanted, and the raw honesty of Danny's *want* somehow made him into the supplicant even as he shoved Jack back into the wall.

That didn't mean Jack was going to go along with it, just that he didn't exactly object to being wanted that much.

Jack grabbed a handful of Danny's hair, grown out curly and shaggy enough to tangle around Jack's fingers, and pulled his head back. He admired the taut line of Danny's throat and the hunting-fit sharpness of his jaw. Danny had always been lean, as lanky in human form as he was in his dog skin, but he'd gotten soft down in Durham. A layer of good living had softened his jaw and sheathed his muscles. It was gone now. He was no wolf, but he didn't have to be dangerous.

The pulse point in Danny's throat fluttered erratically under the skin, uncertain and aroused. Jack scraped his teeth over it, bit down on the bubble of it hard enough to make Danny squirm at the warning.

"I just need some time," he said. It was a lie—they could both smell that on him—but maybe if he wanted it enough, it could become true. "Da would have listened, but the wolves need to be led. And after what happened with Lach, with the prophets, I need to be what they expect for them to follow."

"I get it," Danny said. "A Numitor wouldn't be mated to a dog, especially one with a dick."

That made the pulse between Jack's teeth flutter in nervous anticipation before Jack had the chance to growl. Danny wasn't wrong, but the truth wasn't what Jack wanted right then.

"Danny—"

"I *get* it," Danny insisted. He stroked his hand over Jack's shoulder and down his side, over the taut slats of rib bone and muscle. "It's all about the next generation. How could they trust a wolf to lead them that doesn't have an investment in that future? Without your own pups, why would you care about theirs? You think nobody ever explained to me why I couldn't have you?"

Jack chewed a short-lived bruise into Danny's throat, a livid splash of red and blue that would fade soon enough. He leaned back and narrowed his eyes in a glare.

"Who?"

Danny looked amused. "Who didn't?" he asked, his fingers curved around Jack's hip. "Maybe some of them didn't put it in so many words, but they made sure I got it. You were the prince of the Pack, the Numitor-in-Waiting. And I was a dog who nobody thought you needed."

Nobody had tried to tell Jack that. Neither of the Numitor's sons had ever taken kindly to being told what to do. It hadn't stopped his own version of the lesson from sinking in, though. No one had a problem with Jack's dalliance with a dog—he could do as he liked—but they'd all thought it was just a fling. Even Jack had stalled at imagining a future further away than the idea he wanted Danny around past "tomorrow."

Jack tightened his fingers on the nape of Danny's neck, enough to make Danny hiss through his teeth. "They were wrong."

A shadow of regret passed over Danny's face for what he was about to say. He tilted the corner of his mouth wryly, and Jack could think of better things to do with that mouth than argue. He shoved Danny down onto his knees in front of him and pulled his head back to exaggerate the submissive stretch of his throat. Tendons pulled tight for a second as Danny resisted on instinct, but then he relaxed back into it. Brown eyes watched Jack curiously through his glasses, at least until Jack reached down and plucked them off his face.

"Don't—" Danny protested as he reached up to take the glasses back.

"Show me what your humans taught you," Jack said as he put the glasses behind him on the sink. He remembered the heat of Danny's mouth on him in Durham, his knee-jerk scrape of arousal and irritation at the reminder that Danny liked playing human, that he might be Jack's, but he hadn't wanted Jack to come and get him. That still chewed between Jack's ribs sometimes, like a squirrel at the root of the world, but he wanted *all* of Danny, even the bits Danny had never meant for him. "Make me want you."

Danny glanced at Jack's cock, already flush and half-hard between his thighs at the thought and swiped his tongue over his lower lip. The gesture made Jack's cock twitch in interested response. It might be a human thing, but Jack liked being *in* Danny, so why not in his mouth too?

"I need to try now?" he asked.

There was a crack of something other than Danny's clever mouth in the question, a hint of uncertainty, as though he thought it wasn't just a fact, like the fucked moon getting fat. Jack supposed it hadn't been—since he'd let the old bitch in his head—but that was something in him. Nothing to do with Danny.

"I meant use your mouth on my cock," Jack said. He leaned back against the sink and spread his legs slightly, his cock thick and *obviously* not in need of anything more than Danny there to get its interest. "Not talk until I give up and fuck you to shut you up."

Maybe it wasn't what Danny needed. Another dog—a human—might have been kinder, gentler about it. Vulnerable. That wasn't in Jack. It wasn't something he could stomach. The blunt honesty of his lust seemed like it was enough for Danny. The hint of uncertainty, the hesitancy, bled away.

"When did that ever work?" Danny asked.

Jack snorted. He didn't mind when Danny ran his mouth, to be honest, but that was a challenge, and he had definitely reduced Danny to nothing but ragged breathing and whimpers before.

"Remind me to show you later," he said.

Danny gave him a quick kiss and ran his hands up Jack's braced legs. With his thumbs he traced the tight run of muscle through the pale, sensitive skin of the inner thigh. He hesitated at the spot where the black lines of ink tore away and left his skin new and naked. Something in Jack tightened, a knot of tension behind his breastbone, but it felt… the same. He didn't know what he thought it would feel like—tainted somehow by Rose and her sharp little knife—but all it felt was good.

Danny lifted his cock and leaned in to press a wet, tongued kiss to the base of it. He worked his way up the length of it, hard, flushed flesh slick and wet under the attention of lips and tongue, to the come-slick head already only barely covered by Jack's foreskin. The tip of Danny's tongue swiped around it and then flicked across the eye to taste the bead of come.

"Shit," Jack groaned as Danny took him in his mouth. Pleasure jolted down his cock and clenched in the back of his thighs and his gut.

The wet warmth of Danny's mouth was more tease than the instant satisfaction of Jack's cock in Danny's ass. It made his nerve ends fire off slivers of electric sensation that twitched under his skin and pulled anticipation tight as a wire through his stomach.

Like a lot of human things, it was unnecessary. Jack could have bent Danny over the bath and fucked him. That wasn't a thing that needed improvement or adornment. The only reason he didn't was the sticky, undemanding intimacy of it.

Danny was on his knees, mouth wrapped around Jack's cock, and Jack got to watch. He raked his fingers through Danny's curls to pull them back from his face and watched the way Danny's mouth stretched around the width of his cock, his lips already flushed from kissing and now slick with spit and come. It was the vulnerability of it that dragged on the hot thread of pleasure that ran into Jack's stomach.

Danny took nearly all of Jack into his mouth, the back of his throat tight and wet as he swallowed him. He pushed his tongue up against the underside of Jack's slick, hard cock, and Jack braced his arms against the sink as he came. His hand tightened around the back of Danny's head, fingers tangled in his air, as he jerked his hips roughly forward. Then he spilled his come over Danny's tongue and watched Danny's throat work as he swallowed it.

Heat flushed up Jack's spine to the base of his skull. Maybe, he thought hazily as Danny leaned back and let Jack's cock slide out of his mouth, the humans had a few good ideas in them. Beyond Celtic football club.

"So, I'm done," Jack said, his voice thick with satisfaction, as Danny sat back on his heels. He cupped Danny's chin between his fingers and tilted his head back. "Who's going to take care of you?"

It was just a tease. He wasn't about to suck Danny's cock—his pride bristled at the idea even as his tender balls tightened with interest—but he could still get him off… or get it up again. His cock was spent and wet against his thigh, but he could feel a twinge of interest.

"I can always take care of myself," Danny said as he scrambled to his feet. His jeans were wet over the knees and the faded denim pulled tight over the hard rise of his erection. "You don't have to worry about me."

It didn't take years spent in dusty rooms reading dusty books to pick up that Danny didn't mean he could just use his own hand. Jack snorted as he grabbed a handful of Danny's sweater, laced his fingers through the rough knit, and shoved Danny back against the door frame. He leaned in and breathed in Danny and sex, the musky smell of it a shot of hunger that flowed straight down to his cock.

"I guess I'm going to have to fuck you after all," Jack rasped into Danny's ear. "Otherwise you just keep talking, huh?"

Danny tilted his head to the side until their mouths almost touched. For a moment, as brown eyes met his, Jack thought Danny was actually going to force the conversation. Instead, the corner of Danny's mouth tilted in a half smile and he drawled, "Well, we've got time to kill, and that didn't take that long, so—"

Jack kissed him hard enough to press Danny's head back against the wood and mash his teeth against Danny's lips. He chewed whatever smart-arse comment had been on the seam of Danny's lips and swallowed it.

Maybe, one day, the memory of that smart mouth would be all Jack had. But for now he had Danny. Or he'd have him in a minute.

"Next time," he said as he broke the kiss, "maybe I'll suck your cock."

He didn't particularly mean it… maybe, not until the suggestion made Danny flush a bright, flustered pink from his collar to his temples. That clever tongue was left to splutter, something about "he could" and "didn't have to."

Clever as Danny was—and Da had always described Danny as "sharp-witted enough to cut himself"—all it had ever taken was a look or a well-placed hand from Jack to leave him blush-red and bumbling.

It would be a lie if Jack pretended he didn't appreciate that. Enough to play human games in bed.

He pressed a dry, closed-mouth kiss to Danny's cheek. It would have been almost chaste, but Danny had Jack's cock on his breath and they both knew Jack was going to fuck him next.

"When was the last time I fucked you in my da's house?" he asked.

He knew Danny well enough to know that would throw him off for a second as he tried to remember. While he counted back, Jack scruffed him and dragged him out of the bathroom and down the hall to his bedroom. Danny tripped over his own feet and growled in protest for the sake of it but went along anyhow.

Given time, his da would have cleared it out. Or Gregor would have marked all the corners to make a point. The end of the world hadn't given either of them a chance to get around to that. Instead his bedroom was much as he'd left it, sheets tangled on the bed and clothes hung limply over the open drawers on the scarred old chest in the corner. Clean—Da had chucked their clothes out the windows and hosed the rooms down a couple of times when they were pubescent—but with the distinct, comforting scent of mine worked into the fabrics and walls.

"Asshole," Danny accused with a snort as Jack shoved him toward the bed. "I wasn't going to argue."

He unbuttoned his jeans, and they slid down over lean hips to flash a slice of pale skin across his stomach. The jeans caught there, held up by the jut of Danny's hard cock as Danny grabbed the bottom of his sweater. He dragged it half up, tangled around his arms, and Jack smirked as he shoved him back onto the bed.

Danny sprawled back over the mattress, elbows braced behind him. Half dressed, his cock trapped under his jeans and stomach taut as he squirmed out of his sweater, he looked ridiculous and fuckable at the same time. Jack eyed the thick bulge of Danny's cock and considered his offer to suck it. The images that flickered through his head—the noises that Danny would make, his hands on Danny to pin him down as he squirmed—appealed enough to get him hard again.

The ache of his cock—and the pressure of the full moon deadline neither of them wanted to acknowledge—dissuaded him. If he only had time for one thing, he wanted to be buried in Danny.

Jack flipped Danny over on the bed, grabbed the waistband of his jeans, and yanked them down enough to expose the pale, firm curve of Danny's ass. Sprawled out on the bed, Danny swore indignantly as he tried to get out of his sweater. Muscles tightened in long strips along his back and made his asscheeks clench.

"Tell me what you want me to do to you," Jack said. He reached down and wrapped his fingers around his cock. It was already hard, still sticky from his spilled come, and the rough jerk he gave it made him clench from his balls to his ass. He rubbed his thumb over the wet head and then worked his hand down to roughly squeeze the base. The pressure built in his balls. "Tell me you want me to fuck you."

First time he wanted to be *sure*. It was easy with wolves, but humans did things differently. Just because they smelled or moved like they wanted to fuck didn't mean they did. After Danny had spent so many years away, Jack didn't want to misread anything.

Now he just liked to hear Danny say it, his voice raw with hunger and impatience as he begged for Jack's cock.

"You know I do," Danny rasped out as he finally pulled his top over his head and tossed it off the bed. He pushed his shaggy curls back from his face and looked over his shoulder with irritation as he propped himself up on his hands. Something he saw—and Jack didn't want to know what it was—made his face soften. "I want you to fuck me, Jack. Please?"

The plea sent a shudder of reaction down Jack's back that ended somewhere tight and tender in his balls. He gave his cock a last jerk, the ache of it almost uncomfortable, and then reached out to grab Danny's cheeks and pull them apart. The pucker of his asshole tightened as the cold air reached it, and then it relaxed as Jack pressed the slick crown of his cock against it. It stretched open under the pressure, tight around the thickness of Jack's shaft as he buried himself inside Danny in one hard thrust.

Danny groaned and dropped his head between his shoulders as Jack filled him. His hands twisted into the sheets and his ass squeezed around Jack, warm and firm as it squeezed around his cock. The muscles in his back tightened, taut as cords under his skin. Despite the need that ached in Jack's hips and thighs to just pound into Danny, to fuck him breathless and compliant into the bed, he held back for a moment.

Just until Danny's shoulders loosened and he rocked back against Jack in silent encouragement. Then he hooked his hands around Danny's hips, anchored in the jut of his hipbones, and thrust into him with rough, eager strokes. His hips slapped hard against Danny's ass and jarred him forward each time his cock slid deeply inside him.

Danny fell back onto his elbows as he braced himself against the mattress. He groaned desperately and pushed his ass back to meet each thrust. Sweat slicked their bodies and seeped out of Jack's freshly soaped skin as they ground against each other.

Heat pulled at Jack's balls—a dull, almost too tender ache as they got ready to spill their load again with each hard stroke. It itched under his skin with a prickle of sensation along his nerves that settled tight and vibrating in his gut. He leaned forward and grabbed Danny's shoulder to pull him back up onto his knees. The wiry length of Danny's body pressed back against Jack's chest as Jack's cock was buried deep inside him.

"You'll never want anyone else the way you do me," Jack promised against Danny's throat, words punctuated with the scrape of teeth. "I'm the only one who knows you like this."

He reached over Danny's hip and grabbed his cock. Thin skin pulled taut around the solid shaft creased under Jack's fingers as he dragged his hand down in a quick, rough stroke. There was probably a smart retort somewhere in Danny's head, but all he could muster was a ragged groan as he bit down on his lower lip.

Jack rocked his hips in two slow, deep strokes, his thighs taut as he stretched up onto his tiptoes to get his cock in deeper. He felt Danny suck in his breath and the taut tug of his stomach and spread of his shoulders in reaction.

"Please," Danny groaned as he reached back and tangled his fingers through Jack's hair. He turned his head, and Jack felt the graze of warm, damp lips across his temple. "I need you."

That was enough to wrench Jack right up to the edge until he could feel himself balanced on the brink of orgasm. He spilled them both back down onto the bed, legs tangled around each other, and pressed his mouth against the crease of Danny's shoulder as he hammered his cock into him. Danny squirmed, caught between pushing back into each thrust and the urge to grind his cock into Jack's tight fist.

He came first with a spill of thin, sticky come that smeared Jack's fingers and dripped onto the bed. It was Jack's name on his mouth, as close to a prayer as any wolf with pride would spit out, as his cock twitched and his balls tightened. His breath hissed raggedly between his teeth, and he grunted into the mattress, as Jack worked his cock the last few strokes to orgasm into Danny's ass and it fluttered around him in reaction.

As he came, pleasure wrung roughly from his gut as his balls cramped, he bit down on Danny's shoulder, his mark chewed into the swell of muscle in the smell of his spit and the shape of his bite. Sweat salt and blood stung on his tongue, the sharp intake of Danny's gasp a pinch of pleasure on its own.

This was his—Jack sprawled boneless and comfortable over Danny's back. He licked the blood off Danny's skin and growled annoyance when Danny finally jabbed him in the ribs to make him move. They lay on the bed, legs lazily tangled, and waited for whoever would be the first to come hammer on the Old Man's front door for solutions.

"Nothing has changed," Danny said. He pressed a kiss to Jack's throat. The cut Lach's knife had opened had healed, but the ache was still there under the bones. Danny's kiss didn't ease that, but Jack appreciated it anyhow. "Nothing has to change."

"No," Jack said quietly, because everyone got to lie their own way.

When Jack asked Danny when they'd last been together under his da's roof, he already knew the answer. It had been his birthday, a month before Danny left. Even as Danny had straddled Jack, sweet and long, easy muscle spread out for him, he'd had the offer from university folded away in one of his books. He'd known he was going to leave the Pack and not see Jack again, because he couldn't stay and still be *Danny*.

And nothing had changed, had it?

The sound of a fist on the door downstairs saved him from having to admit he had no answer.

Chapter Fifteen—Danny

"I DON'T know," Ellie said. "That wasn't something that Lach told me. Told any of us, as far as I know."

She sat on the low, scarred stool in the middle of the Old Man's living room. Her head was tilted back submissively to show her throat to Jack, her eyes tipped down and to the side, so she wasn't even looking at him. The handful of the Pack Jack had handpicked to have their say—the accusers, the survivors, the wronged—stood around her in a rough, judgmental circle.

Danny sat to the side, not quite part of it, but no one was ready to face down Jack and get him thrown out.

"You were willing to sell the Pack out to the prophets," Jack said skeptically. He crossed his arms and leaned back against the Old Man's desk. "And you didn't even know why?"

Her eyes flickered to him and away. "He was the Numitor," Ellie said. Behind her Kath growled, an angry scratch of noise in the back of her throat. It made Ellie cringe, for which Danny had some sympathy, but she didn't back down. "I did what I was told. Besides, you were exiles, and the rest were only dogs. Not my pack."

Kath clipped her around the ear with the back of her hand. "You don't get to make that call," Kath said through gritted teeth. "And Lach had no claim to be Numitor."

"So *you* get to make that call?" Ellie asked sarcastically. She ducked her head to avoid another slap and beat her fists against her knees. "You didn't tell him that to his face, though, did you? No, you were a good wolf and fell in line. Same as me."

Kath grabbed a handful of blond hair and yanked Ellie's head back to roughly expose the tight line of her throat again.

"And you know why."

Bron, in a borrowed coat that hung down to her thighs, curled her lip in a toothy, humorless smile. “And I wasn’t a dog or an exile,” she said. “Neither were the children.”

A mutter of agreement ran around the room. Danny bit at the inside of his lips to hold back a cynical comment about how disposable he was. He didn’t doubt his mam would have tried to save him, or that she’d mourn if he was gone, but would she have bent the neck for *his* sake or put the Pack at risk?

Danny doubted it.

The future of the Pack lay in their children, and even if Danny had a bit more interest in women than Jack did, a dog couldn’t sire a wolf. It didn’t help. Danny raked his fingers through his hair, which was overgrown and tangled in knots from Jack’s hands, and tried to swallow the sharp edges of that.

He could have sworn it never used to bother him this much. Too many years away had weakened his tolerance. Or maybe it hadn’t. He’d left, after all. If it hadn’t bothered him back then, he could have stayed.

Danny glanced sideways at Jack from behind the glasses he’d retrieved from the bathroom sink—sharp green eyes and the compact, lean lines of a body that had been wrapped around Danny an hour before. If he *could* have stayed, back then, he would have, wouldn’t he?

“And I’m ashamed I didn’t help you,” Ellie said. “But that was the prophets’ doing, not Lachlan’s. There wasn’t anything we could do about them other than do as we were told so they didn’t end up an object lesson.”

“Yeah, well, one of those dogs managed to get us out,” Bron said caustically. “So maybe they’re more useful to the Pack than you.”

This time Ellie bit her tongue. Jack glanced away from her and at Danny, as though the backhanded compliment had reminded him he was there. Bron followed the direction of his gaze and glared at them both.

“For what *that’s* worth,” she said caustically, and then irritably blew a stray curl out of her face. “And what does that mad old bitch want with *my* pup? It’s not even out of my belly. It might not even live that long.”

It might not. If it did, *she* might not live long enough to see. Wolves lived a long time, but they lived hard and the Wild took its tithe. Danny didn’t particularly want to think about it. He couldn’t stand his little sister—the sharp-nosed apple of their mam's eye, a sneer given legs and a mouth—but he loved her. Nothing should happen to her.

"She claims she's pregnant," Jack said. He curled his lip at the thought.

The glimpse of his teeth made Danny's shoulder remember to ache under his itchy sweater. He ignored it as he leaned forward, interest hooked. When the prophets brought Jack and Gregor to the hospital, he'd stayed as far back as he could. In the cold the sheep hadn't stunk nearly enough for him to feel confident it would cover his scent.

Not from her. Danny still woke up to dreams that *this*—his thumbs and his legs, the words in his throat and his freedom—was a dream. He was just a dog, his brain slower every day, on the end of her leash.

"Is she?" he asked.

Wolves, after all, lived long.

Jack made a disgusted sound in his throat. "Even if her womb hadn't dried up years back," he said, "what man in his right mind would touch that? She looked like something that rolled off a barbeque."

On her stool Ellie shuddered. "I thought she was beautiful," she murmured.

Jack looked at her as though she were mad. By the door, James, whose son had been taken but not found, spat on the floor. "Her child. Your child," he said bitterly. "Why should I care when none of you brought my son home?"

"That's no one's fault," Kath said. "The Wild—"

"Fuck the Wild," James spat. His mate gripped his arm with one hand and tried to soothe him with what little emotion she could spare from her own grief. It was brittle and distracted. James yanked his arm free and swung his red-rimmed, furious gaze around the group. "And fuck all of you. All of you got your children back—alive, whole, *here*—and Kath's dog even found its way home—"

Someone growled. Danny thought it was Jack and then realized the scratchy sound came out of his own throat. James glared at him and seemed to swell with anger as he hunched his shoulders and tensed his muscles.

It would have been intimidating, but.... Danny had fought monsters, he'd fought Job in the plague-skin of a dead wolf, and he'd spent too much time stuck in his own hide for his temper's sake. What was one grief-struck wolf compared to that?

Danny wasn't stupid. He knew, if it came to a fight, James would wipe the walls with him. It just didn't scare him anymore.

"I have a name," he said bluntly as he straightened up off the stool. "So you can call me Danny or he, or you can shut your—"

It was Kath who stepped between them, her back to James as she faced Danny down.

"That's enough," she snapped as she took a step closer and gave him a shove. "Maybe I didn't teach you prudence, Danny, but I know I taught you manners. Apologize."

Danny snorted.

"Your dog needs to spend a night in a muzzle," James rasped out. "Lach might have been a poor excuse for a Numitor, but that he got right. Dogs have their place, but it's not here."

"Da would disagree," Jack interrupted. He sounded angry, probably with them both.

"Your da's dead," James spat. He laughed when Jack snarled at him. "You expect me to care about your feelings? I served the Old Man well. I was loyal, but he was *old*. He had decades under his belt. My son didn't even get five. Until he's back, Jack, fuck your mourning." He turned to pin Bron with a hard look. "And fuck you too. You think I care more about what's growing in your belly than my own lad? Why? It probably won't even live. Gregor's other child didn't."

"The fuck?" Danny blurted, his voice sharp and oddly clear as shock brought the professor out of him.

At the same time, as though to underline Danny's shock, Bron backhanded James across the face. Her knuckles split his cheekbone and knocked him back a step. He shook his head, blood splattered on the floor, and he instinctively pulled his fist back.

"No!" his mate cried out, her emotions snapped back into focus. "That won't help him!"

She grabbed James's arm and the scruff of his neck to wrestle him back. At the same time, Kath shed her dress and pulled her other skin on as she crossed the room, from woman to massive, thick-furred wolf, and put herself between James and her daughter.

James threw his mate off and swung a kick at Kath. She absorbed it against one heavy shoulder and sank her teeth into his leg. Blood stained his jeans as she bit down into the meat of his calf. James snarled and staggered on one foot as he tried to shake her off, but it didn't work. She braced her legs against the floor and threw her head from side to side to tear the wound open.

Shocked by the outbreak of violence, Ellie jerked to the side and fell off the stool. She squirmed on the flagstones, onto her back and away from the fight. Jack grabbed her by the shoulder and hauled her out of reach before he waded in. She showed her throat to him in submissive gratitude, and James finally ripped his leg out of Kath's jaws.

His leg was tatters of muscle and meat, his jeans shredded. Blood puddled under his feet as he grabbed Kath by the throat and waist, ignoring the snap of her teeth that tore his arm open, and threw her at the wall. Then he reached for Bron.

Danny cursed under his breath and scrambled to his feet. He dove across the room to the Old Man's desk and grabbed the shotgun leaning up against the wall next to it. It was old and rarely used—just to scare birds away when they got on the Old Man's nerves, but enough for him to make a show of himself by chasing them in his fur—but it was clean and well-oiled.

The Old Man always believed it was a virtue to maintain your weapons, even if you didn't really need them.

Danny pointed it at the puddle of blood around James's feet and pulled the trigger. The recoil smacked the butt back against his hip, and smoke belched from the muzzle. Buckshot pocked the old granite slabs of the floor and punched a few holes into James's foot as well. Danny had never had to aim before. The Old Man didn't want to eat the gulls or the crows, so all he'd sent Danny—or whatever dog was playing assistant that week—out to do was make a loud noise at the sky.

The unexpected noise made everyone flinch, their ears even more sensitive than the birds, and James swung his head around to glare at Danny. His lips peeled back from teeth that looked too cluttered for his mouth, his fangs pushed against his gums as his wolf tried to get out.

"You think that will stop me?" he asked thickly as he stepped toward Danny. Bron took a step after him, but Kath—human again—dragged her back. "Go on, then, boy. Shoot me and I'll take that thing off you and—"

"How long will your eyes take to grow back?" Danny asked as he lifted the shotgun to his shoulder. Faced with the steady, black barrel of the weapon, James, despite his faith he'd survive the shot, hesitated. "How fast will your spine stitch itself back together to get your legs working?"

Bron shoved Kath away. "Not fast enough," she answered for James. "I'll have his throat before he stops pissing himself. I don't care if they're dead *or* a dog, you keep your mouth off my brother and my baby."

Doubt flickered over James's face, and he uncomfortably shifted his weight on his mauled feet.

"You wouldn't dare," James said. "You know I'll get back up and beat you worse."

Danny bared his teeth in a dog's grim smile. "When did that *ever* stop me?" he asked.

"And you won't get back up," big, genial Craig—who was barely above Danny in the Pack because he didn't like to fight—said in a soft, dangerous voice that sounded odd from him. "Those dogs you don't think should be in our pack? They saved my daughter. I like them better than I ever liked you, James."

James turned awkwardly to glare at him. "And my boy?!" he demanded. His voice cracked. "Why didn't they save Greer when they were about it, then?"

"He never got there," Ellie said. She leaned against Jack's leg, her head on his thigh, and visibly defied the need to cringe when James turned his glower onto her. "The prophets lost him, and the Wild took him. He wasn't there to bring home."

James's face flushed red and twisted. It could have been rage or grief. Jack stepped in before the emotion could decide what it was and gripped the back of James's neck.

"We'll find Greer," Jack promised as he held James in place. He dug his fingers into the tense cords of James's neck. "We'll bring him home. But first we have to end the prophets and put the Wild to rights. Otherwise he could be lost in the miles between one step and the next."

James shuddered and relaxed, his shoulders slumped and his chin dropped. Tears spilled down his cheeks as he decided on grief. He leaned against Jack, relieved to let go of the responsibility. That was part of the comfort of the pack—that you could let someone else make the decisions if it got too much for you.

Danny had never accepted that, but he could acknowledge the attraction.

Jack let James grieve for a second, then kicked his bloody feet out from under him to put him on his knees. He dug his fingers into the scruff of James's neck and bent down to growl in his ear.

"Next time you disrespect me or my brother," he rasped, "I'll put you on your back. If you ever touch Danny? I'll put you in your grave."

He waited for James to lick his lips and bend his neck to the side in submission, weather-tanned skin pulled taut from collarbone to jaw, then he dragged him back to his feet.

"Go home and clean up," he said gruffly as he turned James toward the door and gave him a shove. "The sooner we put the prophets down, the sooner we get your son back. All of you. Go. Get some rest."

James looked away from Kath and Bron in apology as he limped toward the door. His mate went with him, and with that, the meeting dissolved without fuss. Danny let out a slow breath and felt his muscles quiver with aftershocks of adrenaline.

"As for you," Jack said. He walked over and put his hand on the barrel of the shotgun to pull it down. Danny resisted for a second, but only because he'd forgotten he still had it raised. Jack took the shotgun off him and then wrapped his free hand around Danny's neck. His thumb pushed Danny's chin up until his throat was exposed and Danny swallowed nervously. "Don't shoot my guests with my gun."

Danny nervously licked his lips and glanced down. "It's actually your da's," he said.

"Da's not here," Jack said. He leaned in to sniff the soft skin under the line of Danny's jaw, skin that still smelled of Jack. "And I don't need a guard dog."

"Fuck you," Danny said roughly.

On the floor, where he'd forgotten her, Ellie choked in surprise. Jack leaned back from Danny and glanced at her.

"Spend too much time with humans and you pick up their bad habits," he said as he let go of Danny's throat. He dropped his hand, possessive and familiar, to Danny's shoulder instead. "Although Danny's always had enough of his own."

Ellie's attention shifted from Jack to Danny and then down to Danny's collar where it pulled down enough to expose his bite-bruised throat. Her mouth twitched awkwardly in an attempt at a smile. "It's hard to love a dog," she said. "So close to us, but—never enough for us."

She trailed off with a shrug as she glanced down at her scuffed knees. Her scent had the dull, dust-and-ash smokiness of regret and loss. Maybe she expected someone to be sorry for her. It wasn't going to be Danny. He didn't need any reminders of what he was and wasn't.

"Maybe you just didn't try hard enough," Danny said as he ducked out from under Jack's hand. He ignored Jack's "stay" gesture, because he might be a dog, but he wasn't trained. "I should go and check on Bron."

"*Gregor*?"

Bron wrinkled her nose at Danny as she chewed on a hunk of dry venison, her cheeks puffed and her hands greasy with it. They were in the kitchen of the house they'd grown up, in clothes pulled from wardrobes in their old rooms. It was probably less strange for Bron, who'd never left. The fire was stoked, and the embers burned a dull, stubborn red. An old copper kettle sat on the tiles in front of it, burnished with the flames, and the air around the uneven stone chimney rippled as the heat sank into it.

"*Jack*?" Bron parroted back, with a pointed nod at his shoulder. Danny flushed from the pit of his stomach and pulled his collar up uncomfortably. It wasn't the sex. In the Pack, everyone knew when someone had sex. The tangled smells stuck to your skin like honey. A bite was possession, a claim that Jack knew couldn't count for anything.

"That's different," he said as Bron finally ripped a chunk of venison free to chew.

She boggled at him, mouth too full to speak, then spat the half-chewed cud of meat back into her hand to demand "How?"

"That's disgusting!" Danny said.

"I'm pregnant," Bron snapped back at him. "You can't call me that."

"I saw you eat your own boogers once. I can call you what I like." True but, Danny supposed, off-topic. He stepped back and took a deep breath as he tried to find the years he'd been away and grown up. "I'm just saying that… Jack is *Jack*."

"Oh, well, I see why the world couldn't get on without your wits at their university," Bron said. She tossed the wet bite of venison into the fire and chewed on the edge of the rest with sharp, white teeth. "Jack is Jack, and Gregor is Gregor. Congratulations, you explained twins."

"Gregor's a nutcase," Danny snapped. "He saved my life, and I've travelled with him, and I *still* think he's an unpredictable lunatic. Why would you want to tie yourself to him?"

Bron shrugged. "It wasn't a *plan*. I just screwed him and then realized I was pregnant with this one." She poked the high, distended curve of her belly. "Why not? Get it over with early, prove to them all that I'm not going to throw a dog."

It could have been cruel, but Bron was too blunt for that. It was the difference between a cut and a body blow. Danny grimaced anyhow.

"At least you'll get to sit out the end of the world," he said.

Bron rolled her eyes. "Don't be an idiot," she said. "I was never going to raise it, you numpty. Gregor would have while I went to Glasgow or somewhere, took a pack and proved I wasn't *just* my mother's daughter. I'd have come back, but I'm not sitting out the Winter to babysit some wean."

"*Your* wean," Danny said. "It's not babysitting when it's *your* baby."

Bron gave him a sharp sideways smile. "Modern women don't stay home, Danny. They join Fenris's Pack and winnow the world. Didn't your fancy education teach you that?"

He glared at her. She looked smug as she ripped a bite from her venison. Her jaw moved as she chewed noisily just to annoy him.

"Leave her alone," Kath said as she came downstairs. Her hair was wet, slick to her head like a seal, and a mosaic of green and blue bruises ran from her cheekbone down under her dress. They looked a week old already. "Your sister knows her own mind. If the baby makes it, they'll thrive with the Pack. Most do."

Not all, Danny thought, *but fine*.

Danny swallowed the old, prickly urge to defend the "normalcy" of the nonwolf world. It was Bron's decision. Maybe she'd change her mind when she held the child. Or she wouldn't. Danny imagined the look on Nick's face when he realized he was going to have to raise his mate's pup. It tried to be funny, but he was too tired to appreciate it.

"Did you check her bones?" he asked. "Rose?"

"Who?" Bron asked.

"No one," Kath said. She ran her hand over her head and flicked water away from the nape of her neck. "Go and have a bath, Bron. You stink."

Bron glanced between them and then curled her lip. She tossed her jerky onto the table and stalked to the stairs, past Kath.

"Fine," she spat down at them. "You talk about your smart things. I'll go upstairs and think about proper wolf things, like deer and biting."

Kath sighed and waited until she heard the door slam upstairs. "She's always been so jealous of you," she said. "It's childish."

Of him? Danny gave Kath a dubious look. His sister wasn't jealous. She was too cocky about her wolfskin to spare time on anything else. It probably wasn't the time to disillusion his mam that she'd royally spoiled her youngest.

"Did you—"

"Yes," Kath said sharply before he could finish the question. "She's gone. Just old stones and rags where she was. It doesn't mean she's alive. The Wild could have claimed her."

"It didn't," Danny said. "Do you have any idea what she wants with Bron?"

"Because I crossed her?" Kath asked as she hooked a stool out from under the table with one foot and sat down. "I could have worked that out myself."

"It might not be about you," Danny said. He leaned against the table and fastidiously poked Bron's gnawed strip of meat to the side of the platter. A smaller bit did for him, old habits about taking the last pickings from the bone. It was only when he took a bite that he realized how hungry he was. Through the mouthful, he said, "Did she have a daughter?"

"Yes," Kath said slowly. "Alice. We were… friends?"

"You aren't sure?"

Kath shrugged and held her hands out toward the fire. The light of it shone through her fingers and picked out the shadows of thin bones.

"I admired Rose," Kath said. Her mouth twisted as though the admission left a bad taste in her mouth. "Back then, I admired her. Alice never did."

"Do you know what happened to her?"

Kath shook her head. "She left the Pack and moved to the Lowlands. I thought she was weak. After I found out what Rose was, I thought she was smarter than I'd known. But we're wolves. We don't send letters. I've no idea what happened to her after she left here. You think she was this Nick's mother?"

"Would she have let Rose take him?"

"I don't think Rose would have given her the chance to say no," Kath said wearily. She glanced upstairs, to where her daughter and the potential of her first grandchild splashed in the bath. "Could he just have been some child she found?"

That was a question. Danny wiped his mouth on the back of his hand and shrugged.

"Nick wasn't a wolf or a dog, but Gregor said he never smelled *human* either," he said. "And…."

The taste of venison turned sour in the back of his throat as he thought back to the days he'd spent collared. They weren't his memories, although they lived in his head like they were, and the dog stirred as he poked at them. It still felt smug over its rescue of Bron and happy—in the simple, uncomplicated by human doubts and complexes way—to see Kath. The thought of Rose, her height exaggerated and her scent cut through with *mean*, wasn't quite as scary in the familiar warmth of the kitchen.

"… she loved him. She killed him, or tried to kill him, and didn't hesitate, but for what it was worth, she loved him."

"Babies are meant to be loved," Kath said. "They're good at it. You can love a baby you don't share blood with."

"Could she?"

Kath acknowledged that with a grimace, the corners of her mouth turned down. "Why does it matter?"

Sometimes all it took was someone to ask the question to shame your brain into the answer. Danny hesitated. He could feel the answer. It was on the tip of his brain, but it didn't conveniently spill over.

"I don't know," he said. "But she took, or tried to take, three children. Three pups. It's her signature."

"She's a wolf," Kath said as she got up from the stool. She leaned over the fire, wrapped her skirt around her hand, and lifted the hot kettle. "Not a human-sickness killer."

Steam rose from the spout as Kath filled a cup and then tossed a tea bag in. She gave Danny an inquisitive look and lifted the kettle slightly in question. Danny shook his head.

"She's a prophet stitched into a dead wolf," he said. "She broke into the Sannocks' cairn—"

Kath nearly dropped the kettle. She caught it with her bare hand and hissed as her skin blistered. The smell of burned skin was a sharp note against the smoke of the peat in the fire. She shoved the kettle back onto the hearth and shook her hand as though she could shed the pain through her fingertips.

"She what?" she asked. "Did they escape? Wolves or Sannock?"

"No," Danny said… maybe lied. He'd seen Nick's bird-bead black eyes flick toward shadows and linger in the gaps between trees. And even if that was the normal dead the carrion god saw, if Rose had found her way out of the old prison, then surely the Sannock had followed. "We closed it again. We hope. But she kills, and there's something sick in her, something that's made the Wild lay… strange."

Blisters spotted the palms of Kath's hands and in long welts on her fingers, full of serum so they stood out tight. Danny scratched his palm as he glanced at them.

"Like blisters," he said. Then he rubbed his eyes. "But whatever she is, three times she's tried to steal someone else's pups. That has to mean something."

Kath pierced the blister on her palm with the edge of her nail and blotted it against her thigh before she picked up her cup. She curled both hands around the heavy china and studied him through the steam.

"Maybe just that she's wicked," Kath said gravely. "And something my dog son should leave to wolves."

She loved him. It had never been enough, but she did. Danny hugged her awkwardly, mindful of her bruises, and was surprised when her wiry arms squeezed him tight. She got tired of it first, though, and shoved him away with a snort at his softness.

"You're the one who taught me that if someone hurt me, I hurt them back more," he said over his shoulder as he grabbed his coat and headed for the door. "Besides, this is my world too."

Kath waited until he'd opened the door and banished the illusion of warmth. The cold sucked the breath out of him and made his eardrums ache, a sharp shock to the system as snow blew in between his legs.

"It's the Wolf Winter," Kath said. "And sleeping under a wolf doesn't make you one."

CHAPTER SIXTEEN—GREGOR

"THERE WAS a time when I would have asked for this on prescription," Nick said dryly as he tilted his head back for Gregor. His mouth twisted into a wry grin that didn't hide the nerves underneath. "Even with the itch."

Nick was perched on the side of an overturned kayak, the man-made fiberglass hull crazed and cracked from the cold, in the boathouse on the edge of the water. The wind outside whistled through the tarred cracks in the hut, thin streams of snowflakes scattered over the floor, and irregularly timed waves came up the gravel shore to batter at the door. His eyes were blistered and scabbed along the lashes, red where it should have been white, and lightly clouded like mist on a window.

Gregor took Nick's chin in his hand and tilted his head to the side. He felt Nick's affronted grumble against his palm at being manhandled. The inside of Nick's ears was irritated as well, wet and red, as though the skin had been scalded. Gregor leaned in for a sniff and caught the bitter scent of the prophets' drink under the sweaty musk of whoever had owned the coat.

"Gross," Nick protested as he shoved Gregor away from his ear. He stuck his finger in to scratch at the inflamed skin. "Did you see anything? Is there anything in there?"

"Not now," Gregor said. He grabbed Nick's wrist and pulled his hand down. "Don't scratch it."

Nick sighed. "Easier advice to give than take," he said as he wiped his hands on his jeans and then hugged himself. He tucked his fingers under his armpits and hunched his shoulders up toward his chin. Despite his pink rabbit eyes and restless knees, he still looked like a bird, just an ill one. "Do you… how long do you think it will last?"

"Does it matter?" Gregor asked.

Nick huffed out a laugh and then sniffed. "I'm not exactly much use like this," he pointed out. "Human again."

"You were never human," Gregor corrected him.

Not that it mattered. Human, bird, or whatever slice of wolf his gran had made of Nick, Gregor loved him. He liked Nick's restless hands and dry humor, his beaky, stern face, and the ridiculous way it creased around his sudden, delighted smiles. He liked Nick, the ability to turn into a giant bird or work out how someone died from their liver wasn't anything to do with that.

"Human-ish," Nick said. "Human-adjacent. I'm useless."

Words worked better for Jack. He knew how to put things to make people follow him, cheer for him, fight for him. To make them love him. That had never come easily to Gregor. Most of the time, he didn't care—except for the expected irritation that his brother existed to be good at anything—but Nick made him wish for a clever tongue.

"Fuck that," Gregor said.

He cupped Nick's face in his hands and leaned in to kiss him. The faint sourness that stuck to his skin—humans, sickness, and fear—faded as the familiar popcorn scent that was Nick thickened and sweetened. Cold lips warmed under the kiss. Nick reached up to grab Gregor's shirt and pull him down. His long, lean body sprawled out under Gregor's, all bones and wiry muscle like a stoat, and he moaned around Gregor's tongue.

Gregor thought about it. It would make him feel better, remind him that Nick was his and there and the old bitch hadn't managed to take him away again. He twisted his fingers in Nick's hair and dragged his head back to kiss him deeper.

His cock thickened to a tender ache under his jeans, and then a muffled, distant retort cut through the drone of the wind. Nick went still under him, and Gregor lifted his head to listen. His breath silvered cold around his lips as he breathed heavily.

Sometimes Gregor thought he was used to the loss of his wolf, that he'd accepted the castration. Then he'd try to do something as simple as *listen* and it split the crusted scar back open.

"They're still looking for you," he said as he pushed his weight up off Nick. "The Old Bitch wants you back."

"She won't find us here," Nick protested as he tried to pull Gregor back down. "Let them look."

Gregor snorted. "Don't be stupid," he said. "The snow covered our tracks, but this is the only shelter for miles. If they're willing to keep looking, they'll find us."

"Me," Nick said. "They're not looking for you, Gregor."

There was a *smell* to martyrdom, a light, sickly smell of righteous determination and fear. Gregor had smelled it before—off his brother and his dog for each other, from the woman in Girvan that the monsters had taken. He'd always felt an itch of resentment for it—no one had ever wanted to die for him—but now it turned his stomach in a sour roil.

Gregor pulled Nick to his feet. He leaned in close enough to feel the scrape of Nick's stumble against his jaw and growled, "No."

"They'll stop looking," Nick pointed out, uncowed by the thrum of danger against his skull. "Once they take me back, I can find out what Gran wants with them."

Gregor hissed out a sigh. He didn't want Nick to be afraid of him, but wary might be useful sometimes.

"If what she's doing matters so much," he said. "Why did you try so hard to get away?"

Nick turned his head and kissed him quickly, tenderly. "You weren't here," he said. "Now you are."

"No," Gregor repeated through the metallic taste that clung to his tongue. The last time Rose got hold of Nick, she killed him. Gregor didn't care what happened to the humans in their burrow, but he wouldn't risk that death would give Nick back again. He rested his forehead against Nick's and breathed him in. "Stay here. Heal. I'll deal with them."

Nick grabbed his arm and lifted it. The cuff slid back to reveal the still-raw welts that wrapped around his wrists, crisscrossed over the bone where they'd twisted the wire.

"You're hurt," Nick said, "and the soldiers out there are ready for trouble. If I hand myself over, it would buy us time. And if they were going to kill me, they'd have done it already."

Gregor took his hand back and flexed his fingers. It still hurt, but the sharp sting of raw meat had faded to tenderness and itchiness.

"No."

Nick narrowed his eyes. "You can't just keep saying no."

"I disagree." Gregor caught the nape of Nick's neck and pulled him in to plant a kiss on his forehead. "Stay here. I won't let Rose take you again. So, turn yourself in? You'll get us both killed."

That warning finally sank in. Nick made a reluctant sound of agreement and stepped back, out of the way. He hunched down into his quilted jacket, nose tucked into the collar despite the reek, as Gregor manhandled the door open. The water from the lake had frozen on the door, a thick rime that worked its way into the seams and cracks. Gregor put his shoulder to it and shoved. It creaked—a low, ground-out sound that hooked some atavistic "get off the ice" reaction in the pit of Gregor's stomach—and held. He stepped away and put his back into the next shove.

The impact made his bruised collarbones ache, but it broke the frozen seal and the door cracked open. Chunks of broken ice dropped onto the ground outside.

"At least take my boots," Nick said.

"You need them more."

"I can sit on the boat."

Gregor kicked a last chunk of ice out the door. "They'd just get in my way.

"Like me," Nick said. The frustration and self-hatred in his voice was familiar. And the fear. "If I weren't *blind*, I could help. I could—"

"Maybe," Gregor said. "And if I still had my wolf, I'd have killed Rose in the Sannocks' graveyard, and she'd have never touched you again. What you've lost is like the cold, Nick, you've got to learn not to mind it."

A hoarse chuckle—and maybe Nick couldn't hear the bird anymore, but Gregor could in the rough edges of the laugh—made Gregor look over his shoulder. He raised his eyebrows. Nick shrugged at the mute question.

"I can't imagine you any *more* dangerous," Nick admitted. "Even if you were a wolf."

Gregor couldn't help but preen at the compliment, even though he knew Nick wouldn't say the same if he'd ever *met* him as a wolf.

"You'd have been terrified," he said with a smirk.

Nick canted his head to the side so he could rub his jaw. "Maybe," he admitted. "Gran's stories never painted wolves in a good light—gluttons and killers, the Run-Away Man, all her monsters."

"I guess we weren't monster enough for her," Gregor said as he put his shoulder to the door again. "So she had to make better ones. Stay here. I'm getting sick of having to track you down."

He kicked the ice out of the way and squeezed through the gap. Frozen water curled up over the edge of the small loch, braced on icy fingers that dug into the gray slurry of churned-up snow. The water was gray, a scum of fresh-fallen snow on the surface that curdled as the wind stirred it up like stew.

"Jack has his wolf," Nick said. "*Had* his wolf when Gran took him. It didn't do him much good."

Gregor breathed in. It was so cold that the air didn't feel like something that should be in his lungs, and it eddied from his lips like smoke as he exhaled. Rose had skinned Jack to make monsters, stitched wolf skin and rank ink to curse-putrid flesh. Neither of them—the wolf or his shadow—had been good enough to end Rose.

"I was always better at being a wolf. Jack's the better man," he said. "Ironic. Close the door."

WARM SPIT hit Gregor's cheek and dripped down onto his shoulder. It was chased with guttural, ranted curse words as he pinned the woman up against a tree. Her lashes were scarred with the same blisters that puckered Nick's eyelids, and the ripe smell of her hatred pulsed in the air like a heartbeat.

"They'll flay you, and I'll wear your skin for my winter coat," she ranted, strings of bloody saliva strung between her lips. "I'll see out the winter in your guts to keep me warm. They'll make me a god! They've told me your secrets, whispered them in my ear at night! One day—"

Useless. Like the others.

Gregor dragged her off the tree and broke her neck. She fell silent midword, her inflamed eyes wide open and blind as snow filmed them. He set her down at the base of the tree, her hands in her lap and her tangled red hair pulled out by the wind, and left her there.

The cold had sharpened as though a frost giant had belched the storm out from the Wild. Gregor could feel the pressure of it in his bones as he looped away from the dead woman. His joints felt swollen and rigid, as if they'd seize up if he stopped moving. Like the people they'd seen on their way north, naked and stiff in the cairns they'd scooped out of snowdrifts.

He didn't think the cold would kill him, even now. But the idea of being stored like a trout in the icebox until Surtr brought a brief spring and fire to thaw him out didn't appeal either.

A radio crackled somewhere in the white. Gregor paused, weight balanced on the ball of his feet, and cocked his head to the side as he listened.

The radio blurted out static again, a few words buried in the noise, and then a muffled man's voice growled an impatient response.

"Not yet," he snapped. "And after he dragged my ass into the cold, if I see the bastard, I'll shoot him rather than bring him back."

The other end of the radio snapped something but was clicked off midword. Something dark, a shadow against the white, arched through the snow and cracked against a tree or a rock—something hard enough to make it crack and splinter.

A second later the muffled voice in the storm growled a frustrated "Fuck it."

Gregor loped toward the voice. Wolf paws, with broad pads and thick fur, were made to hunt in the snow. Human feet weren't, but barefoot was better than booted. Gregor could feel the ground underfoot, adapt to the bite of a sharp rock against his sole or the hip-jarred drop of a snow-concealed hole.

The man was a squat block of gray and white against a world of white and gray. His heavy, winter-hued camo gear padded him from the shoulders down and smudged the edges of him into the landscape. It worked well enough, but camouflage only worked until it didn't. Enough winter-coated rabbits had learned that lesson at Gregor's fangs over the years.

Something made the hair on the back of the man's neck stand on end. He started to turn in reaction, heavy rifle half-raised in his hands just as Gregor tucked his shoulder down and tackled him. A startled grunt escaped the man, and as they crashed down into the snow, his finger tightened on the trigger. The gun fired blindly into the storm and hit something that howled. It sounded human… until it didn't.

Gregor's ears rang from the retort of the gun, a pulse of blood against the bones of his skull, and he had to struggle to ignore the pain.

He threw a quick punch at the man's black-masked face, but the man jerked his head to the side. Gregor's knuckles caught the smoked-lens goggles and knocked them up onto guy's scarred forehead. Brown eyes, whites blotched with blown red blood vessels, squinted up at Gregor.

"Get the fuck off me," the man spat through his frost-crusted mask. "You crazy son of a bitch."

He jabbed the gun up in a quick, harsh blow that caught the side of Gregor's head. Blood dripped into Gregor's eyes and he snarled in frustration at himself. Weeks of fights against the prophets' monsters, just violence and flesh that almost healed around Gregor's fangs, had made him careless. Even a human could be dangerous.

Not as dangerous as Gregor—still, even now—but still.

The man drove his knee up into Gregor's groin. The impact was blunted by the thick padding of the snowsuit, but it still hurt, and then the man tried to throw him off. Gregor spat a curse between his teeth and yanked the gun out of the man's hands. He tossed it away and grabbed the hood pulled tight around the man's head. Then he punched the screwed-up, half-masked face with a balled fist until his knuckles came away bloody and the man went limp under him.

He was still alive. Gregor could hear his heartbeat hammer against the inside of his chest and smell the sharp, acrid chemicals pumped out with fear and pain. When Gregor slapped his battered face, he groaned and tried to turn away. Conscious too.

Gregor rolled off the man and scrambled to his feet. He wiped his bloody face on the back of his wrist and bent down to grab the guy by the collar.

"You and me need to talk," he said.

THE MAN—THE tag sewn onto the front of his jacket said BOYD—leaned back against the tree, shivering as the wind battered him with icy snow. The dense grove of trees was some protection, but not much. They creaked in the wind with a deep groan like frozen dark water. Blood hung in the air, metallic and salty-appetizing, and Gregor could feel the Wild's expectation close in around him. The Wild was built of things that had happened before, and a bloody warrior in an isolated clearing was made for sacrifice.

He ignored it. This once he found himself disinclined to serve the Wild any more than he already had. It was a glutton, but it should have had its fill today.

If Gregor killed the man, it would be for Nick, nothing else.

The Wild still waited. Blood was blood, and Gregor knew it wouldn't care why he shed it. But he did.

"Not going to tie me up?" Boyd asked thickly.

"Why bother?" Gregor asked. He picked up a handful of snow to scrub his face clean. Cold and impossibly clean, it stung in the gouge over his eyebrow. He rubbed the pink melt over his fingers, worked it into the creases between his knuckles to scrape out the blood. "I don't need to keep you long."

Boyd laughed, a choke with no humor in it, and reached up to peel the bloody, half-frozen mask away from his face. His skin was pale, blotched with chilblain-raw blisters, and bruises stood out like paint against his skin. He'd been handsome in a blunt way before his nose was broken, canted to the left as his eyes puffed up around it.

"You're not a professional," Boyd assessed. He was breathless, his words choppy as he spat them out on smoky lungfuls of cold air and shivered as the cold soaked through his suit. "Otherwise you'd know to try and… put me at ease. Make me think… I can trust you."

Gregor brushed his hands together and thought about that. "I don't care if you trust me," he said after a second. "If you answer me, that'll be useful. If not…."

He tilted his head to the side to listen to the storm. The sound of occasional gunfire could be heard over the wind as anger and blindness made the other soldiers twitchy.

"You aren't out here alone," Gregor finished as he turned back to Boyd.

Boyd licked chapped lips. "That's not—" He stopped, and some shred of wit clawed through the murk the prophets' brew had filled his head with. "Who do you work for? What do you want?"

"Stupid questions," Gregor said. "Look around you. Does this look like the world you made? A world where your alliances mattered?"

"It's just a storm."

Gregor shrugged. It wasn't his job to teach some stranger the catechism of the wolves. Ignorance might be a kinder state to die in.

"There's an old woman at your burrow," he said. That was where the Wild had spat him out, above the ground the soldiers had filled with tunnels and concrete. It offended him somewhat that they'd come into his country to build their bolt-hole and no wolf had noticed. This was outside of the scent-marked borders of the Pack's land—distances in the Wild were still off, folded in on themselves around the dead tissue of the Sannocks' grave—but they should have noticed. Maybe the prophets hadn't wanted them to. "You want to fuck her."

Boyd flushed, two swipes of red hectic on his cheeks—guilt and disgust stitched together with confusion.

"I don't know what you're talking about," he forced out through his teeth as they chattered. "I'm not going to tell you anything. Go to hell."

"Her brother's claim predates any she might make," Gregor said. "The old woman. Or you're useless to me. Like the others."

Boyd pulled a face, his expression exaggerated as stiff muscles moved clumsily, and he ducked his chin down into the padded collar of his jacket.

"She's not there," he said. His eyes flickered nervously toward the blind white gaps between the trees instead of to Gregor and his sharp grin. "Not officially. But nobody says anything, they just act like she's always been there. Or that she's still *not* there, like half the time they can't see her. Only the doctor talks to her."

Gregor crouched down next to Boyd. He ignored the flicker of calculation in Boyd's brown eyes and tapped a finger against his scarred forehead. It was a still-tender scar, the skin still thin and damp where it stretched over the bone, but it should have been raw meat and pus still.

"A bird did that," he said. "A raven the size of an eagle."

Boyd coughed out a nervous laugh and reached up to touch the same spot Gregor had. He touched his hairline with gloved fingers and grimaced as the seams scraped the half-healed spot. "Size of a fucking Labrador. I swear—" He stopped abruptly, and his eyes shifted back to Gregor, a quick check that went from his shoulders to the wolf-coarse tangle of his hair. "You. Was that you there, with the bird and the dark-haired man?"

"I'm with the bird, my brother was with the dog."

"I didn't see a dog."

"You just said you did."

Boyd rubbed his eyes with the heels of his hands and let it drop. "The woman. Who is she? Why is she there?"

He leaned forward, his body tense as he focused on the answers. Apparently, he'd misjudged his role. Gregor braced his hand against the man's chest and shoved him back against the tree with a thump.

"I ask. You answer," he said.

Boyd exhaled, the moisture from his breath frozen into the stubble of his beard. "I don't have any answers," he said. "You're right. None of this—fuck it's cold—none of this is how it should be. Okay? The fucking weather. The fact we got here… and nobody is here. Nobody that's meant to be. And everyone's… they're not right. And it's so damn cold. It's so cold, and I've been cold places. Not like this. Even when I dream, it's cold."

"I don't care."

Boyd fumbled his jacket open, the raw rip of Velcro surprisingly loud over the wind, and reached in to pull out a flask wrapped in the same camouflage print as his uniform. Glove-clumsy fingers popped the cap off, and he lifted it to his lips.

"I'm not right," he said. "Should have told you to fuck off. Should have let you kill me. But—"

Gregor slapped the flask out of his hand. The bottle flew through the air and bounced off a tree. Green-tinted amber liquid ran down the bark of the tree and puddled on the snow. Boyd howled in furious loss and elbowed Gregor out of the way as he lunged after the flask. He scrambled over the ground on his hands and knees in a desperate bid to save something.

The liquor had soaked into the snow. Boyd scraped up chunks of frost with both hands and shoved them into his mouth to chew at the ice. He sucked at his gloved fingers where the cloth had stained.

Gregor grabbed the back of Boyd's collar and dragged him away from the mess. It went against his nature to save someone from their own weakness, but Boyd was only useful because he hadn't drunk as much of the liquor as the others. Or it hadn't had enough time to work on him yet, at least. Nick thought that, with time, the prophets' converts would recover, whatever the liquor burned out would regrow, but he wanted to believe that. Gregor wasn't so sure.

The soul didn't heal, or at least not well. The scabbed-over hollow that Rose had left in Gregor when she cut the wolf out of him was evidence of that.

For now, Boyd was reasonable enough to talk, and Gregor wanted to keep him that way. He shoved him back against the tree, and it shed snow and chunks of ice around them.

"That stuff isn't good for you," he said. Curiosity prickled, and he paused long enough to ask, "Haven't you noticed?"

Boyd sucked the frost off his lips. "It's medicine," he said, a slice of something blank in his eyes. "Doctor Ewan gave it to us. He said it's like quinine… or something… it works on the blood. It helps with the cold."

"The doctor," Gregor interrupted. Ewan was the ginger prophet's name, the one that had no stolen skin and carried on Rose's work out in the world. Nick's grandfather. "This Ewan, he's the one who talks to the old woman?"

"She's so beautiful," Boyd said, horror in his voice. "All raw meat and blisters, but I want her. I don't even know why she's there. It was meant to be—I don't know—politicians. Scientists. People who get to put the world back together. And us. To keep them safe."

"Guard dogs," Gregor said with contempt. Even before Rose put her rotten teeth to them, they were trained to come to heel. And kill. "What is she to the doctor?"

Boyd impatiently tossed his head back. It cracked against the tree hard enough to make Gregor twitch at the noise.

"What is it to you?" Boyd snapped. He leaned forward, his chest braced against Gregor's arm, and got into his face. His breath stank, the oily, sharp reek of the drink caught on his tongue, and he stared into Gregor's eyes. Too close, too direct. It made the back of Gregor's itch with the urge to rise to match the aggression. "I don't know you. You could be part of this."

"Obviously," Gregor said. "What does this doctor want with Nick?"

"Who?"

Gregor growled at him. The sound made Boyd recoil uncomfortably, his nerves on edge at a sound that didn't belong in a human throat.

"The bastard that dragged you out in the snow," Gregor said. It was easy to let the anger into his voice as he remembered Nick's body in his arms, cold again and sour with the smell of fear. "The one you were going to shoot."

"What?" Boyd asked with a sneer. "You want to fuck him too?"

Gregor punched him with a short, sharp strike to the nose that bounced Boyd's head back against the tree again. Blood splattered down Boyd's chin, bright against his pallor, and he grabbed Gregor's wrist with one hand. A hard yank pulled Gregor forward as Boyd rammed his elbow into his chest, hard enough to jar his heart through his breastbone, and then swung it up at his jaw. Gregor grunted, realized he didn't have time to dodge, and took the forearm to the base of his jaw.

He gagged as his throat spasmed shut and something popped distinctly under his ear. Pain stabbed from the nape of his neck down to the small of his back, and he felt a shadow of chill numbness weaken his muscles. Boyd grunted in satisfaction. If he'd run then, he might have gotten farther. Not far, but farther. Instead he pushed his luck as he twisted at the hips to try and hammer his knee into Gregor's side.

Gregor blocked with his forearms, tucked his shoulder, and rammed it into Boyd's stomach. The breath escaped Boyd on a grunt, and he pawed angrily at Gregor's shoulders. With a quick heave, Gregor lifted the other man off his feet and then tossed him into a packed drift of snow. Boyd landed awkwardly and writhed as he tried to suck in half a lungful of frozen air.

"… fuck…." He tried to roll over onto his stomach to scramble to his feet.

"Stay down," Gregor told him. He craned his neck from one side to the other to make the bruised joints pop. Then he stalked over. Boyd tried to ignore his advice, but Gregor put his boot between his shoulders and bore down until Boyd's braced arms gave way. He went facedown into the snow, body tight and resentful. "You broke your radio. If you had someone else's, could you use it to call this doctor?"

Boyd spat and slapped his hand against the ground. It was surrender or frustration. Human body language was hard for him sometimes—the broad strokes were the same, the monkey was still there under the wolf, but the subtleties had never interested Gregor. Scent usually filled in the gaps when he needed it to, but after they drank what the prophets gave them, it pumped anger out with their sweat.

"Yeah," Boyd forced out through his teeth. "I could do that."

Could, not would. Gregor understood the difference, but it would do for now. He yanked Boyd up from the snow and tried to remember where the nearest body he'd dropped was. This had taken long enough. If he left Nick on his own any longer, the crow would get himself in trouble.

He had a talent for that.

"Why do you even want to speak to them?" Boyd asked raggedly as Gregor dragged him into the storm. "What good will it do you?"

Gregor thought of Rose's promise, and then he buried it.

"That's my business."

Chapter Seventeen—Gregor

"Her name was Harris," Boyd said. He stood to the side, hunched down against the wind that battered him as Gregor ripped the woman's jacket open to frisk her. "Katie Harris. She had a daughter down in London."

Her radio was buckled to the inside lining of her jacket, a strip of tape on the back with Blake written on it in black letters. Gregor wordlessly showed the label to Boyd, who grimaced and looked away.

"She still *had* a name," he said. "Even if I hadn't had a chance to learn it. She could have a kid. A family."

Gregor glanced down at the dead woman. Her red hair was frozen stiff, fanned in a short halo around her face, and frost glazed her brown eyes to a shabby gray. Whatever she'd been was gone.

"Do you think I thought she didn't?" He got up and held the radio out toward Boyd. "Call in, say you need to speak to this doctor."

If anyone knew what Rose wanted—today *and* tomorrow—it was him. And Gregor had something he wanted.

Boyd took the radio. He pulled his mask down, coughed dryly as the wind caught him, and thumbed the button.

"Command, this is Alpha 4," he said. "Come in. Over."

He let go and waited. Silence except for the drone of the wind and the distant grumble of thunder. Gregor's skin itched under his clothes as he remembered the lightning that came to the snap of Jack's fingers back in Durham. Maybe, he thought dourly, the Wild had already had its favorite, then, long before he lost his wolf.

"How long will it take them?" he asked.

Boyd shook his head. "I don't know," he said. "Soon. If they answer. It's been…."

He trailed off as he glanced toward Blake. His eyes lingered on the flask tucked inside her jacket, and nervously he licked his lips at the temptation.

"Chaotic," he said.

Gregor used the toe of his boot to close the flap of the jacket over her chest and disguise the bottle. "Try again."

"Command, this is Alpha 4," Boyd repeated. He stopped to cough. "Come in. Over."

Nothing for a long moment, and then the radio crackled. The voice that came through was distorted and unidentifiable.

"What the … going on out there?" it demanded, broken by silence and static. "Half the Alpha squad … back empty-handed. The … radio silent. Do … the target in custody?"

Boyd looked at Gregor. Anger warred with self-preservation as he visibly weighed his options, his thumb stalled over the Call button. Gregor's smile was sharp.

"Alpha four?" the static prodded.

Gregor leaned forward. "Say they drank all their medicine," he instructed. "Lost their wits. Ask for the doctor."

"That won't work."

"Then tell them what will."

Boyd grimaced, hesitated for a moment, and then squashed the button roughly under his thumb.

"Target acquired," he rasped out. He took a quick look at the dead soldier and then turned away from her. "But Blake lost her fucking head and shot him."

Silence except for the crackle of the radio.

"Is he dead?" It was almost a whisper, the voice of someone who knew they were in trouble. There was something almost childish about it.

"She's dead," Boyd said. "Him, not yet. He's bad. I don't think he's going to make it back to base. Get Doc Ewan. If I can stabilize him, I'll hole up somewhere until you get someone out here to pick us up."

"I don't—"

"Command, get me a goddamn medic," Boyd barked harshly. "I need to speak to him now! Or else, when this guy dies, it's on you."

That did it.

"Wait. Over," the static muttered.

The line cut out. For a second it felt almost quiet, and the wind whined around them, a muffled roar that rolled down from the hills. Gregor reached for the Wild and folded it between his mental fingers, but instead of the familiar scent of heather and old stone, it stank of seaweed and cold salt. He cast it away with a scowl and wiped his hand on his leg, as though that was where the smell lingered.

"How badly is he hurt?" the radio spat out suddenly. It was hard to recognize the attenuated voice, but it was more thickly Scottish than the rest. "Do you know where you are? I can get there on one of the snowmobiles."

Gregor plucked the radio out of Boyd's grip. He held it for a second in front of his face, the plastic thick with the smell of a dozen sweaty hands, as he considered his options. It was just a hunt, he reminded himself as the choices available weighed on him, and if things didn't work out, he could change his plans.

"The junkyard by the loch," he said. "Come alone, no need to worry Rose over this if you want to see your grandson."

The snort of laughter bounced down the connection. "When will I see him, then?" he asked. "When we both get to heaven after you kill us? I have put my faith in the judgment of wolves before. It never ends well."

Gregor lifted the corner of his mouth in a quick snarl at the suggestion that he'd hurt Nick. He knew the prophets were evil, but that they were this stupid and still a danger offended him.

"Do you want an oath, prophet?" he asked. "After you swore you'd never hurt Nick, but you put out his eyes?"

"That was for his own good."

It was the sort of lie that was only meant for the one who told it. The words slipped off Ewan's tongue too quickly, practiced and ready. But Gregor's laugh punctured the thin veil of the excuse.

"Liar."

He lifted his thumb from the button and picked absently at the crust of ice matted into his stubble. Any information Gregor gave Ewan would probably make its way to Rose's stitched-back-on ear, no matter what he promised. Or she could already be there behind him, Ewan's strings wrapped around her fingers.

It didn't matter. Gregor already assumed he couldn't trust Ewan. If prophets had any honor, they wouldn't have been sent to be maimed. Still, something of the man he'd been had survived. Enough that he wanted to believe he could care about his bloodline.

"Do you want to know what Rose did to Nick?" Gregor asked. There was no answer. He'd take that as a yes, or close enough. "I told you what to do. If you can still think for yourself, I'll see you there."

Gregor tossed the radio back down onto the dead woman's body. It crackled, voices lost as he turned to look at Boyd. The soldier stared back at him with a grim expression on his bruised face. He pulled his lips back in a humorless smile, blood on his teeth as his lips split.

"Don't tell me," he said. "I've outlived my usefulness?"

It was past the point he could put up a fight. Whatever benefit the drink offered required a steady top-up of it in the bloodstream. Boyd still hunched his shoulders and lowered his chin aggressively. It would almost be admirable, in a wolf. In a human, it was deluded.

Still—Gregor dodged the punch, and Boyd tripped forward over the corpse and went face-first into the snow—not quite yet.

"HE'S GOT frostbite and the early signs of hypothermia," Nick said. He winced as he turned Boyd's hands over, his nails a pale blue that shaded into black toward the beds, and tied blunt fingers together with vinyl strips torn from the kayak's covers. Boyd sweated silently through the treatment, sweat beaded on his forehead from the pain. "There's a chance he'll lose some of his extremities, even with proper treatment. Which I can't provide in a boatshed, Gregor. He needs to go back to the base. The infirmary there was full stocked, and I might not have agreed to being drugged blind, but whoever did it could at least put a line in."

Boyd laughed. "British military equipment," he said bitterly. "Our boots melt in the desert, and we get frostbite in the winter. Who are you, anyhow? Why is it so important we get you back?"

"That doesn't matter," Gregor said. "Just accept you won't."

"Is it because of Doctor Ewan?" Boyd pressed on despite the warning. "Is he really your grandfather?"

Nick fumbled the knot, the pinch of wrinkled fabric yanked tightly enough to make Boyd hiss in pain.

"Is my what?" Nick asked. His attention was on Boyd, and then, as the question sank in, he turned to look at Gregor. He narrowed his dark eyes. "What's he talking about?"

Gregor shrugged. "You heard him."

Nick stared at him for a second, face blank and composed. Then he nodded slightly to himself, gave Boyd his hands back, and pushed to his feet. He walked over to Gregor and punched his upper arm.

"Go to hell," he said, his voice tight. "You don't do that. Not to me."

Gregor caught his wrist and tightened his grip to keep hold of Nick as he tried to pull away. The fact his hand still fit easily around the narrow joint made him loosen his fingers slightly. Even if they were more evenly matched these days, the reminder he could have ever hurt Nick always reined in his temper. Not that he had to show that.

"I could say the same," he reminded Nick in a low, dangerous voice. "Do that again, and you'll find out why not."

Nick didn't even flinch at the barely veiled threat. He leaned in until they were almost nose to nose, his breath warm against Gregor's face.

"You think I should be scared of you?" he asked. "That's what you want?"

The temptation of Nick's mouth caught at Gregor. He resentfully ignored it.

"I want respect," he said. "I'd accept fear."

Nick leaned in and kissed him, his free hand cupped around the back of Gregor's neck. It was a quick hard press of lips, breath mingled between their mouths, and obviously meant to make a point. Gregor didn't care. He pulled Nick closer, twisted his hand in the padded folds of the oversized jacket, and bit at the soft curve of the lips pressed to his.

His human, his carrion god. The prophets might have fucked to make Nick and the gods might have brought him back to life, but they could all fuck off if they wanted to take him back. He was Gregor's now, the only thing other than his wolf that Gregor had ever loved without hating at the same time.

The one thing he'd ever beaten Jack at, because Gregor wouldn't have to choose between the Pack and his mate. That choice had been made for him already.

Nick sighed into Gregor's mouth and pulled away. He tightened his hand around the nape of Gregor's neck and rubbed his thumb along the tight ridge of tendon in his own version of possession. His eyes were soft and vague for a moment, and then he blinked them back into focus and cleared his throat.

"Then don't be a dick," he said as he pulled away from Gregor. "Don't leave me in the dark. I've had enough of that."

Nick pulled his jacket tight around him and stalked over to the door. He wrestled it open and squeezed out through the gap. The wind pulled the door out of his hand and it slammed behind him hard enough to dislodge chunks of half-frozen ice from the corners of the hut.

Lust and anger were both volatile scents. They hung in the air behind Nick as he slammed the door behind him, hot and red, but the gray thread of old, worn fear pulled through it. He'd grown up with no idea of what the world really was, afraid of the inside of his own head as people told him that what he saw made him mad. The things people hadn't told him had gotten him killed.

Gregor resented the idea that Nick would lump him in with the prophets and the ignorant. It sat in his throat, thick and rancid like a lump of sour meat he couldn't quite swallow.

"He's a bit high-strung," Boyd said, his voice pitched to needle. He shifted position on the floor, with his weight braced on the heels of his hands to keep his roughly splinted fingers from being jarred. Gregor hadn't bothered to leash him. Where would he go? "You'd think he'd be grateful you came to get him. I'd have left him to rot, ungrateful bastard."

He waited for a response. Gregor crouched down and grinned at him, all teeth. "Is that how a professional does it?" he asked. "You're trying to, what, divide and conquer? Because my lot invented that."

Boyd shifted back. The complexity of his smell had been stripped, and only the coarse notes were left to dominate. It made it difficult to track his emotions, like someone who shouted every word.

"Your lot? Who is that? You're not military, but you know how to fight. What, some Glasgie brawler that hooked up as a merc with some PMC? Get to kill people without having to do the time? I've seen it before. No judgment here. But what's the likes of you doing up here, and who's he that he matters so much? You didn't chase him up here into the blizzard for his sweet ass. Neither did we, I'm guessing."

He said guess, but there was confidence in his voice.

"You'd be surprised," Gregor said. He shifted his weight onto the balls of his feet and stood up. "About a lot of things. If you had the time. If you drink that, you'll still die."

Boyd held his face still, but his hand twitched toward the pocket of his jacket. He'd stolen the flask from the corpse when he tripped over it. The sleight of hand had been smooth. Gregor might have missed it entirely if Boyd had been able to resist a nip on the long walk back.

"I don't…." He started the objection and then gave up in the face of Gregor's disinterest. "Maybe, but at least I won't feel it."

It wasn't Gregor's business. He didn't care how—or where or when—humans died. They did it so easily, after all, how was he meant to keep track? Yet he hesitated before he followed Nick outside.

"Die as yourself," he said. "It might come quicker, but it'll be cleaner."

Boyd snorted out a harsh laugh. "I'm a soldier," he said. "If I wanted to die clean, I would have stopped living a long time ago."

It was as much effort as Gregor was willing to make. He left Boyd with his poison and headed out into the storm.

The loch was entirely frozen now, rippled with sharp, chipped ridges where the cold had caught the waves midlap. The haze of cold rose from the black glass surface, the bite of it sharper by the hour. Tomorrow the moon bitch would open her lazy eye to track how far things had progressed toward the end, and it felt like something had been brewed to give her a show.

Nick was perched on a rock at the edge of the water, his arms braced on the shelf of his knees. It looked a lot less elegant in the padded, stolen snow gear than it did in his trademark long coat—still birdlike in the hunch of his sharp shoulders and the tilt of his head, but more like a fluffed-out sparrow than a raven.

"What does it matter?" Gregor asked. Despite his best intentions to be kind and loving, the words turned harsh as he spat them out. "What do you care if Ewan is your grandfather? Rose is your grandmother, and you have enough sense not to care about her."

Nick didn't turn around. The wind stripped his voice from his lips when he said something, and Gregor had to stalk closer to make him out.

"… should have let him drink it."

"What?

Nick impatiently rubbed his hand over his eyes with a quick, frustrated flick of his fingers and looked over his shoulder.

"You've more faith in that than me," he said. "She's my gran, and she killed me, but…. The first thing I learned in this world was that I had to love her."

"Doesn't mean you do," Gregor said. "I was told to love my brother, and we can barely stand each other."

"You saved his life," Nick pointed out wryly. "You can't hate him that much."

"I hate him enough to want to kill him myself," Gregor said bluntly. It sounded like he was trying to convince himself as much as Nick. That troubled him. Who was he, if he didn't hate Jack? How could he justify what he did—what he might do—if thwarting his brother wasn't an excuse in itself? But he couldn't deny Nick's point, so he shrugged awkwardly as he crouched down next to Nick and leaned against his leg. "Maybe one day I could tolerate the idea he's still alive, somewhere else, but he's not *mine*. You're my family. I don't need anyone else."

Nick reached up and tangled his fingers in Gregor's cold-stiff hair. His fingers were icy.

"I picked you over her," he reminded him. "I chose *you*, even if you don't talk to me."

"Not really had the time," Gregor said. He paused and then pointed out, "It might not even be true. Prophets lie. Rose lies."

"Does she?"

Gregor stiffened at the question. Had Rose gotten to Nick while he'd been lost? Had she something to offer him that was as seductive as what she'd offered Gregor?

"You know she does."

Nick shuddered at something and then nodded with a brisk dip of his sharp chin. "Not about him, though. The Run-Away Man. I saw him, out on the moors."

"He's a fairy tale," Gregor said. "A bedtime story from a lunatic."

"I *saw* him," Nick insisted. "In the Wild. In this world. He was there. They led me to him."

Shadows on the snow with nothing to cast them, the glint of wet human eyes in the darkness between the trees, and the faded scent of something alien enough that it could have been the remnants of grief or rage on the air and he couldn't tell which. Gregor didn't need to ask who they were, and he didn't want to know if Nick would lie about them.

"The Wild is full of things," he said. "Some old troll that the Winter woke up. Or a berserker who never remembered he wasn't a bear."

Nick shook his head. "I knew his face," he said. "Gran had a picture of him that she hung in the hall. It was the same man. I knew him. I think he knew me."

Gregor hesitated, uncertain of what to say. He doubted that some man whose photo was nailed up in her hall had ever known Nick existed, never mind someone found his way into the Wild and up to the Highlands. But Nick believed it. He could feel the tension of it strung through his body.

"Was he ginger?" he asked.

That surprised a laugh out of Nick. "No," he said. "He had dark hair and—"

"Then it wasn't Ewan," Nick said. "He's a little ginger prophet. And Rose, even if she told the truth about the Run-Away Man, doesn't mean she told the truth about anything else. Or she ever planned to. You don't need them."

Nick unfolded from his perch on the rock and stood up. He moved stiffly, his joints chilled, and offered Gregor a hand to get to his feet. Gregor didn't need the help, but he accepted the offer just to feel Nick's long, restless fingers tangle through his.

"I know," Nick said as he hauled Gregor up. He clung onto Gregor's fingers once he was done. "I just… don't want to *know* that everyone who made me is a monster. That I was going to be a monster, even before—"

Gregor kissed him to shut him up. "You were always going to be mine," he said. "Monster, god, or human. I don't care."

"I do," Nick said as he rested his forehead against Gregor's. "I get it. We need to know what Gran has planned, but don't blindside me, Gregor. Not again."

With Nick so close, Gregor could smell the sickness on him. It wasn't as *wrong* as the monsters, but something bitter still clung close to Nick's skin. Whatever the prophets—whatever Nick's grandfather—had done to him, it hadn't worn off yet. Thinned out, but not faded away. A whole layer of reality just wiped out.

Gregor stepped back and tucked his knuckle under Nick's chin to tilt his head up. "I decided to keep you when you were human," he said. "I want you, Nick, not the bird."

"If it can still hear you, you'll hurt its feelings," Nick said. "It likes you."

"I like it," Gregor said. He did. The bird's personality was distinct from Nick's when he pulled on his feathers—a creature who cackled humor over the dead. Carrion gods, he supposed, had a particular view of the world. "But I need you."

Nick grinned with a flash of that unexpected, ridiculous sweetness that he pretended wasn't there. Then his face fell into serious lines and he reached up to cover Gregor's hand with his, fingers slotted between Gregor's knuckles.

"I love you," he said.

Of course, he did. Gregor knew that already. Why else would Nick have come back from the dead for Gregor or followed him north to the harsh welcome of the wolves? The need to say it anyhow was a human thing, as though a feeling could be domesticated like a dog.

Gregor still wanted him to say it again. Maybe the prophets had sliced more out of him than he thought and left room for sentiment to creep in.

"Why wouldn't you?" he asked.

Nick gave him an exasperated glare but leaned in for a kiss. His mouth was desperate, his lips cold and tongue warm as he pressed against Gregor's body. He cupped Gregor's face with his long-fingered hands, buried his thumbs in the stubble that crawled along the clean edges of his jaw, and muttered something that Gregor didn't catch between their mouths.

It didn't matter what the words were, Gregor could taste the tenderness of them on his tongue. He swallowed it greedily and pulled Nick closer, his hands twisted roughly in the thick jacket that rustled in his grip. The lean body under the thermal material relaxed against Gregor with easy, seductive compliance. Nick wasn't *easy*—he argued with Gregor more than anyone but Jack had ever dared before—but he always melted when Gregor touched him.

The ache of lust in Gregor's balls was heavy and hot, almost painful as it reminded him how cold his thighs and ass were. Temptation knotted in the small of his back, equal parts desire and the need to mark Nick with his scent.

Mine.

"We'll freeze," Nick muttered into Gregor's mouth. Despite the objection, he didn't pull away. "*I'll* freeze."

"I'll warm you up," Gregor teased. He pulled away from Nick's mouth and licked his way down to the taut skin under his jaw. The flutter of Nick's pulse against his lips made Gregor's mouth water. He bit down on the bubble of it, just hard enough to make Nick gasp, and then licked the spot better. Temptation had settled into intent as he nuzzled his way down Nick's throat to his collarbone. "You still aren't human, no matter what they did."

A whimper caught in Nick's throat. He slid his hand back and twisted it into Gregor's hair, and the tug of his fingers in the dense curls was echoed in the clench of Gregor's balls.

"I'd still rather not freeze my cock to a tree," Nick protested halfheartedly. "And that soldier could get away—"

"Let him," Gregor said. It had been a whim that made him drag Boyd back with him. He might be useful, but if he got away, then Gregor would just change plans. He scraped a kiss along the hard wing of Nick's collarbone and offered slyly, "You can go on top."

The whimper escaped Nick, thickened to a moan as it spilled over his lips, and Gregor could almost ignore the sound of an approaching ATV under the storm. Almost.

He peeled his lips back in a frustrated snarl as he lifted his head and stepped back. Nick stumbled as the wind took advantage of him being off-balance to shove at him. Gregor caught him by the shoulder and then jerked his head back toward the abandoned house they'd passed earlier.

"They're here," he said.

Nick hunched his shoulders and swore, the guttural Glaswegian accent dragged from his childhood in frustration, when nothing happened. He roughly scrubbed his hand over his eyes, as though he could scrape the poison out.

"Alone?"

Gregor strained his ears. He isolated the rumble of the ATV and the howl of the wind to filter out and tried to pick out any other noise. If the wolves were out, he wouldn't know they were here until one had their teeth at his throat. They could hunt silently in the snow. Humans lumbered and talked, the crackle of radio and confidence of something that hadn't realized it was prey.

"No, soldiers." He licked the back of his teeth and caught the greasy aftertaste of the monster's off-putting reek on the air. "Maybe one of their monsters."

Nick shuddered and didn't stop as he remembered he was meant to be cold… or that he was afraid.

"I guess Grandad is on the same child-rearing book as Gran," he said bitterly. "Good to know."

Gregor grabbed the back of Nick's neck and pulled him into a quick, rough hug. He pressed his face to the tangle of dark, fine hair and breathed in the odd, candy sweetness that was unique to Nick.

"Fuck him," he said. "I was going to kill him anyhow. Now I don't need to make up an excuse."

Nick laughed unsteadily. He pulled his jacket over again and ducked out from under Gregor's hand to head back to the hut. "Since when do you *need* an excuse?" he asked skeptically.

"I don't," Gregor said. "But I'll pretend it matters if it makes you feel better."

Nick snorted and hunched down into his coat. He leaned forward against the wind as it tried to push them back to the lake.

"Should have let him drink," Nick said. "It would be easier."

Gregor hesitated, eyes narrowed against the snow. It was Nick's voice, the sanded-off vowels and quiver from the cold, but Nick was in front of him. The voice came from the lake.

He didn't turn around. Whatever was there—dead thing or Sannock ghost—wanted to play games, and this wasn't the time. If they wanted to haunt him, they could wait their turn.

Maybe when they saw what he'd do to Ewan, the prophet who'd been dumb enough to think Gregor would trust him, they'd give up Nick's voice before Gregor had to reach down their throat and rip it out for them.

He grinned at the thought and broke into a jog to catch up with Nick.

Chapter Eighteen—Nick

Pain pecked at the inside of Nick's skull. His head throbbed as though it were about to crack open like a melon and misgivings would spill out like guts.

Something is wrong.

Nick rubbed his finger up the bridge of his nose and pressed against the span of skin between his eyebrows. The pressure didn't help, but the small new pain distracted him from the dull thump in his brain as he hunched down behind a heaped mound of frozen snow. Gregor was only a few feet away, folded in behind a scrawny tangle of threadbare bushes, but it felt farther. Every time Nick looked over, it took him a second to pick Gregor out from the frost and branches. They were stationed across from the lonely little house tucked onto a pocket of land just off the road. It had been all straight lines and modernity a few months ago, from the look of it, but now the white plaster had broken off the walls from the cold, and hailstones had smashed out the windows.

Boyd stood at the door, wrists laced to the handle with his back to the drive. From behind, with the hood of his filth-blackened jacket pulled up over his head, he could pass for Gregor. At least he could if you didn't know Gregor. Nick was confident he would have been able to tell from the breadth of shoulders and the way Boyd stood.

Hopefully his grandfather had spent less time watching Gregor move.

The drift they were behind was gray and clumped under the fresh coat of new-fallen snow, a relic of the locals' last attempt to clear the roads and pretend this was just a hard early frost.

"Good for potatoes," people had told each other in the shops, "There won't be a shortage of brussels sprouts this year."

That little bit of self-delusion hadn't lasted long. Anything that had grown through this had been left to rot in the fields.

On cue, Nick's stomach remembered it was empty and growled. Gregor frowned over at him, and Nick shrugged an apology. The last time he'd eaten had been a bag of jerky as they headed around the lake.

Crunchy. Meat. Slippery. Sweet.

Nick gagged at the unexpectedly vivid memory of something the bird had eaten, peeled off the frozen corpse of a sheep. He'd thought he'd gotten used to the bird's appetite, but apparently that was one of the bits they shared. Now that it was quiet, his stomach had turned fastidious.

A flash of black humor reminded him that he'd see the sheepsicle again if he puked. That helped to choke back the bile.

Nick ran his hand through his hair, ice-matted knots cold against his knuckles, and wondered if that dark thought was him or if *maybe* his gran's bitter liquor had worn off.

Or started to, he reminded himself, which wasn't going to be any help over the next few hours. He shifted his weight and kicked away the snow that had built around his feet. The rumble of the ATVs' engines rattled under the howl of the wind with a deeper note, but it carried oddly through the snow-dense air, and Nick couldn't tell where the noise came from.

"Where are they?" he muttered to himself.

He wasn't sure if Gregor heard him—for all his complaints about the loss of his wolf, Gregor's ears were still sharp enough—or if the gesture to catch Nick's attention was just well-timed. When he looked over, Gregor pointed down the road and then pressed his finger to his lips in silent direction.

Nick nodded and strained his ears. At first the noise was lost in the wind, but then he caught the low growl of an engine in the stillness.

A moment later two ATVs bounced through the trees and up the hill, snow spraying out behind them with waves. Two men sat on each ATV, heavy black guns slung over their backs and gloved hands wrapped around the handlebars of the machines as they jarred to a halt in front of the wall.

Boyd made a muffled howl of protest and yanked at the door until the reinforced wood rattled in the frame. He threw his head from side to side to try and dislodge the hood.

"Hands up," one of the men shouted as he scrambled off his bike. He moved stiffly after an hour in the saddle in the cold, but his hands were steady as he raised the gun. "Get away from that door."

Two of the other men followed his example, guns cradled ready in their arms as they fanned out around the house. Nick didn't have a wolf's sense of smell, except for the ripe, red threads of carrion, but he could read tension in tight shoulders and jerky movements. Gloved fingers twitched on triggers as Boyd kicked at the door with black-booted feet and swore through his gag.

"We should just fucking shoot him," the man on the left yelled over the wind as he hiked the gun up to his shoulder. "Shut the fuck up!"

The last man stayed in the saddle of the ATV. He pulled his gloves off, hands very pale at the end of his thick-cuffed sleeves, and tucked them into his pocket as he turned to search the white-blanketed landscape. The crest of phantom feathers that weren't there on the back of Nick's neck bristled as he felt the man's attention linger on him. Even hidden behind smoked glass goggles, the weight of his attention felt… heavy, thick with something that sucked at the pain in Nick's head like it could taste it. That was his grand—Nick's brain stalled over that idea, the word weighted down with a leaden ball of panic. He let it go. The prophet, he corrected himself as the man turned his attention back to the soldiers. That was the prophet.

"I told you to—"

The flat retort of gunshot cut the ranting short. Blood sprayed through the air as the prophet shot him in the back of the head. It splashed a gory red against the faded white walls of the cottage. Boyd stayed upright for a moment and then pitched over, face-first into the snow. Blood seeped out from his head, watered down from scarlet to a faded pink as it filtered through the crystals.

One of the men flinched in surprise and his finger tightened on the gun. It spat a short judder of bullets that studded the door and caught Boyd in the shoulder. The impact smacked Boyd into the door with a grunt. He slid down the door onto his knees and Nick started to his feet. It was instinct, years of training taken over from the lessons learned in the last few weeks. Gregor growled loudly enough for Nick to hear and impatiently gestured "stay."

"Wait," Gregor mouthed as the prophet put a bullet through the shooter's throat.

Nick flinched at the noise, his heartbeat loud in his ears. After everything that had happened—the monsters, the dead, the strange things—it was the sound of a gunshot that still hit every socially installed, pop-culture-panic trigger he had. His breath caught in his chest, hot and anxious, and he covered his hand with his mouth to hide the steam as he panted.

The last soldier realized where the shots came from and spun around. He didn't bother to ask why, just pulled the trigger and pumped two bullets into the prophet's gut. One spat out his back, just above his ribs, but the other caught something inside. The prophet groaned, pressed one hand to his gut, and hunched over.

"What the hell?!" the soldier got around to. His voice was ragged, and he swung the gun in quick, unsteady arcs to threaten shadows in the snow. He shot one in a quick spray of bullets, and it burst apart to reveal nothing but ice and emptiness. Nick flinched again as his ears reacted to the noise with a hot whine of feedback. "What the *fuck*!"

The prophet slouched to the side, nearly off the ATV. There was no blood on his jacket, absorbed by the thick stuffing, but *that* Nick could smell on the wind. With his head slumped down toward his chest, he muttered something.

"What?" the soldier shuffled forward warily. He poked the prophet with his gun, which made the slumped man moan and drop his gun from weak fingers.

Nick cursed through his fingers but obeyed Gregor's glare to stay where he was.

The soldier kicked the gun out of the way and reached out to grab the prophet's shoulder to push him upright. His fingers dug into the mottled gray fabric, and the prophet came up with a thin, over-sharpened knife in his hand.

From where Nick crouched, he couldn't see him cut the soldier's throat, just the flash of the knife at as it started the stroke under one ear and then ended it at the other, but he could imagine the damage. A short, oblique cut that sliced neatly through the carotid artery, split the windpipe and larynx open, and maybe nicked the jugular on the way out.

Neat. Professional. Unusual in presentation, since a forward slice to the throat was usually in a fight and the victim would have more hesitation marks and defensive injuries. Most killers couldn't open a throat as deftly as the prophet had.

Gran had always been good at getting the meat off the bone too, Nick remembered queasily.

The prophet pulled the soldier close for a second and then pushed him roughly away. The man staggered back a couple of steps and turned, one hand clutched to his throat as though that would be enough to pinch it closed. He stumbled toward the other quad bike and almost reached it, but his legs gave way in time to leave him draped over the black plastic seat. Blood dripped down the side and puddled on the dredged-up snow beneath the tires.

"You could have helped," the prophet said, voice pitched to carry. He wiped the knife on his sleeve and made it disappear again. "I don't relish murdering my own."

Gregor finally stood up. He shook his head to shed the snow and brushed it off his sleeves. The branches of the stunted trees cracked and rattled as he stepped through them. Nick hesitated but then scrambled to his feet to follow. He crunched uncertainly through the snow.

"So, you'd rather watch someone else do it for you, Ewan?" Gregor asked as he stepped over the dead man. His lip curled up in a sneer. "No wonder you were sent for a prophet."

Ewan—*Grandfather*. Nick tried the word out for size in his head and flinched away from it. Ewan pushed his hood back. His face underneath was spare and bony, freckles stark against pale skin. A thick woolen hat covered his head, and his eyebrows were thin and gingery over deep-set eyes.

"You make it sound like I had no choice. I choose to be a prophet rather than an animal, a man and not the Old Man's beast." His attention shifted to Nick and his face… tried to soften, but it couldn't quite find the lines. "Nicholas. Are you okay?"

It was Nick's cue to answer, but he didn't. His tongue just refused to move. He felt like he had the first time he drove up to a foster home in a social worker's Ford Fiesta, the crisp-bag-and-old-receipt detritus of a nonstop day under his feet, and hadn't wanted to move. As though life might miss him if he just stayed still enough.

No encounter with Nick's family had ever left him better off than before.

Gregor stepped closer to him—not quite in front of him, but near enough that Nick could feel the comforting threat that coiled under Gregor's skin. Despite the situation, he felt warmth slip down his spine as he remembered that lean, dangerous body bent over his.

It was hardly the time, but he stole courage from the heat as he lifted his chin and swallowed.

"Who?" he asked. "Me or the bird?"

The prophet stared intently at him. His eyes, intent behind a sandy fringe of lashes, flickered over Nick's face—lingered on his eyes, flicked away from the beak of a nose—as though he thought he might recognize him.

"I couldn't see it when you were asleep," Ewan said. "I can now. You look like your mother."

The unexpectedness of that made Nick flinch. It made sense, he supposed. To have grandparents, they had to have had something to do with his parents. At least one of them.

"Don't. I—" He stopped and took a deep breath. The lungful of cold air steadied him, even as the ice-cream headache jabbed deeper between his eyes. "We're not here for a family reunion. That's the last thing I need."

"Whatever they've told you," Ewan said, his voice low and earnest. Something in the rhythms of it tried to lull Nick into trust while, at the same time, it made the hair on the back of his neck stand up in unease. "You can't trust it. You can't trust any of them."

"I trust Gregor," Nick said.

Ewan's lip curled, and he lifted his hand from his side to show the blood that coated his palm and fingers.

"Never trust a wolf."

The sight of blood made Nick grimace and look away. It wasn't as bad as if he had to touch it, but fresh blood always made him dizzy. His training tugged at his fingers—muscle memory of sliced-open flesh and neatly lined stitches—but he curled them into his palms.

"You'll heal," he said.

"Of this, yes," Ewan said. "But some hurts wolves do never knit back together."

"Enough," Gregor said. This time he stepped in front of Nick, as if muscle and shoulders could stop words. "I didn't shoot you. The humans did, after you dosed them with your sacrificial wine. What do you want with them, Prophet? What does Rose have planned?"

Ewan pushed himself up off the quad. Blood stained the metal, frost roses of pink around the edges as it froze.

"What we should have all planned for," he said grimly as he stepped forward. Blood ran down his leg and stained the snow behind him. The wind staggered him as he walked, his legs unsteady under him. He might heal, but it wouldn't be quick. "What we were made to do—save the world from the teeth of wolves."

Nick laughed, the ghost of the god harsh around the edges of the sound. The reaction made Ewan rock back on his heels in surprise. He had the gall to look affronted, and then his face settled into grim lines.

"Save the world," he repeated, "and finally get justice against the people who killed my daughter. Your mother. This is the winter of the wolves, and they will not see spring again. You have my word on it."

Out in the storm, something tried to howl. It sounded wet, like it tore at the throat as it got out. Gregor turned his head toward it, and something answered, the garbled shriek more distant but close enough to make Nick's shoulders twitch with the instinct to fly.

This time he felt something under his brain *push* at a shape that wasn't him. Feathers and scaled toes, the weight of a carved, bone beak where his nose was. The shadow of the crow fluttered over his vision and then was gone again.

"That's why you killed the humans," Gregor said. "No witnesses."

Ewan glanced at the dead men and looked regretful. Maybe even guilty. "They aren't far gone enough yet. We thought military men would be *more* susceptible to Loki's brew, but it takes longer. The venom eats away their inhibitions, but duty is harder to erode. Maybe we should have let the politicians in, after all, but too late to change plans now."

"Why?" Nick demanded. He shoved Gregor out of the way and stepped forward. Decades of frustration cracked his voice as he confronted his grandfather. "What is Gran doing to do?"

"I told you," Ewan said. He reached up and grabbed the back of Nick's neck, his fingers slippery and warm. There was something desperately hungry in his eyes. "Save the world. Save you."

"Fuck off," Nick spat out the coarse Glasgow retort of his childhood as he pushed Ewan away. "Whatever Gran's done, it was never for me. *To* me, sure. Next time you want to lie to me, run it past her first. She'll tell you what ones she's worn out."

Ewan frowned. "What do you mean? She loves you."

"Yeah," Nick admitted. It would have been easier if she hadn't. "That's never stopped her."

Gregor took his arm and pulled him away.

"We need to go," he said. "Can you drive the bike?"

Nick hesitated, all that pent-up anger and pain caught in his throat like a knot. He couldn't get past it.

"He hasn't told us anything," he protested. "Nothing true, anyhow."

Gregor gave him a shove toward one of the quad bikes. "Not yet," he said as he grabbed the shoulder of Ewan's coat. "Don't worry. This isn't over. The prophet's coming with us."

He dragged Ewan with him back to the bloodstained quad and shoved him into the saddle. Of course, Nick remembered as he grabbed the dead soldier by the shoulders, Gregor couldn't drive. The dead weight was a familiar strain against Nick's shoulders as he lifted the corpse off the saddle and dragged him out of the way. The dead didn't usually bother him—he'd have picked the wrong job if they did—but the slack red slit in the man's throat made Nick's skin crawl.

He thought that maybe it was some sense of guilt, that his family had done this. Then he realized that, while he couldn't see them, he could feel the thread snakes of the potion slither dry and cold between his knuckles and the prickle-bite as they tried to hang on to him.

The cold, he thought as he pulled away with a shudder. It wasn't the weather for snakes. He wiped his hands on his coat and scrambled onto the saddle. The wind had already cooled the blood. It was sticky and wet under his backside.

"Where are we going?" Nick asked as he shook his hands again and fumbled with the ignition.

"Just follow us," Gregor said. He took the slim knife from Ewan's sleeve and pressed it under his ear. "Head home, Prophet. The Numitor wants to speak to you."

Ewan laughed. The sound scraped the blade against the side of his throat, and a drop of blood dripped down into his collar.

"The Numitor is gone," he said with grim, unapologetic satisfaction as he started the bike. "He's the god's dog now. Maybe it will teach him humility."

Nick hesitated, his hands clumsy as he struggled with the handle of the bike. He'd never really driven one before this winter, and only had a single, short lesson when they landed on the coast. It hadn't been enough to make the controls second nature. Something Ewan had just said was important, but he couldn't put his finger on what. Maybe that part of his brain was blacked out along with the bird.

"Death comes to us all," Gregor said. "The Old Man knew that as well as anyone."

"He wishes," Ewan said.

That was it. Before Nick could chase the thread back down into his head, Ewan gunned the engine and headed down the slope toward the lake. Nick started after them and then hesitated when he heard Boyd groan. He cast a glance over to the door and realized Boyd wasn't dead. Not quite yet. The soldier lifted his head woozily off the door and tried to pull his hands free.

"What about him?" Nick stood up on the bike to yell after Gregor and Ewan, his hands cupped around his mouth. "He's alive. We can't just leave him."

Ahead of him Gregor looked around and yelled something back. The wind snatched the words from his lips and spun them away before Nick could catch them. It didn't matter. He knew what Gregor would have said.

Leave him.

Nick exhaled, a ribbon of white steam caught around his lips, and he gave Boyd a guilty look. The prophets' monsters had no reason to be interested in Boyd, and the prophets wanted him for… for whatever they had planned.

He couldn't help Boyd. Doctor or not, he had no supplies, and the monsters were on his heels. The vibration of the engine between his knees underlined the urgency. Nick still didn't move.

Leave him.

That was good advice, but Nick couldn't do it. He cursed under his breath and reached to turn the quad off.

Something made of shadows and splinters of ice came together out of the storm and flung itself into Nick's face. The cold sank into his bones, locked his jaw, and glazed his eyes with frost. He tried to suck in a breath to scream, but his throat was choked up with wet slush. Hard, thorn-sharp fingers dug into his ears, and a wet-mulch tongue licked at his eyes and poked up his nose.

It smelled of graveyard dirt and death. Some dark part of Nick, lodged in the crack of his breastbone, breathed it in with delight. The dankness of it refreshed him somehow.

LEAVE HIM.

This time the thought shook the foundations of Nick's brain. He cowered from the rage in it, huddled back into the corner of his own skull like a child in front of his gran's unpredictable temper. When he pulled himself back together again, his fingers were tight around the throttle and the cottage had been left behind in the storm.

Nick shuddered. He could still taste stale breath on his tongue, and the corners of his brain still felt stiff and unresponsive. His fingers were locked around the handles of the bike, although he couldn't tell if it was the compulsion or the cold that stiffened his knuckles.

Ahead, Gregor twisted around to check on him. Even through the snow, Nick could feel the concern as Gregor's eyes fell on him. He shuddered, took a breath, and forced one hand free to lift his chilled fingers in acknowledgment.

Whatever had happened, it was done now. Nick couldn't go back. Alive or dead, Boyd would have to fend for himself.

Gregor accepted Nick's reassurance. He gestured with one hand, forward and then a sharp curve to the left. Nick didn't know what he meant but nodded anyhow. He would follow Gregor's lead.

Irritation pecked at the inside of his head, and he heard the dry rustle of mantled feathers. It felt distant, muted, but a thread of tension in Nick's stomach finally loosened at the promise something was still there.

He didn't know if this was the life he would have chosen, but it was what he had. It was what he *needed*—to survive this, to keep Gregor. Love was one thing, but nobody would trade a partner for a burden.

Nick blinked as the world ahead blurred. He thought it was the Wild until he felt the pinch as the tear froze on his cheek. He sniffed and wiped his sleeve over his face. His tears stained the fabric with salt and blood, but now wasn't the time to worry about that.

Ahead of him Gregor took a sharp left up an unevenly steep hill and into a copse of trees. Nick spluttered out a curse under his breath and followed suit. The quad slid under him, tipped, and then steadied. The engine complained and spluttered as it bounced over rocks and potholes hidden under the snow.

He caught up with Gregor and Ewan just past the tree line. They'd stopped next to an old yew tree, the bike tilted up almost sideways on the scored roots. Nick made a messy, precarious stop a few feet away but didn't turn the ignition off. The thought of the silence that would fall once he killed the low growl of metal and petrol was daunting.

Gregor dragged Ewan out of the saddle and over to Nick. He ignored Nick's instinctive protest and kicked Ewan's feet from under him to put him on his knees in the snow.

"Keep him here," Gregor said. He flipped the knife in his hand and held it out, blade first, to Nick. "I need to see how close they are."

Nick reluctantly took the knife. He supposed that technically he could use one, but it sat in his hand differently than a scalpel or a bread knife.

"If anything happens, kill him and run," Gregor said. He cupped his hand around the back of Nick's neck and pulled him into a quick, rough kiss. "I'll find you."

Nick smiled against Gregor's lips. "I know."

Gregor rested his forehead against Nick's and then pulled away and jogged back out of the trees. Ewan watched him go.

"Was that a promise or a threat?" Ewan asked. He spat in the snow, phlegm streaked with red, to make his opinion clear.

"He finds me, or I find him," Nick said. He finally turned off the bike. The sudden silence was as oppressive as he'd imagined. "That's how it works."

"Not this time," Ewan said. "You can't outrun them. Once Rose sets them on your trail, they won't eat or drink or stop until she's satisfied. They are tenacious things, her new breed."

"And that's what you call salvation?" Nick absently worked his shoulder, the memory of his gran's wolf-mawed bite still locked into the tendons and marrow long after the bird had healed him. "I'd rather freeze."

Ewan gave him a hard look. "Easy to say, boy," he said. "You don't know what you'd pick until the choice is put to you. Death is a cold place, and you're there a long time."

"I know," Nick said. His voice was empty, the trauma stripped out of it. "Better than you. Better than those soldiers you're marinating for her, softening up the meat. Even if she gives them a choice, they don't *know* what it's going to do to them."

"You misjudge her gift," Ewan argued. "The ugliness of it now will pass, like a fever, and they'll—"

"They'll still be monsters," Nick said. "And that's what she wants. Trust me, I don't misjudge my gran."

"Rose is a visionary," Ewan said. "She's made hard choices, but only the ones she had to make."

"Like killing me?" Nick asked. "Or killing my mother, your daughter—"

"Don't believe the wolves," Ewan insisted. "She'd never do that. Whatever the Numitor's boy told you your whole life, Rose was looking for you. She'd never hurt you."

Nick snorted and yanked down the zipper of his coat. The cold nipped at him, but he ignored it as he dragged the sweat-stained T-shirt up. His shoulder had healed when he died and came back, but the older scars lingered—the one across his stomach, stretched tight and rucked where it had stretched with his growth. Ewan glanced at it and then flinched away, but he couldn't stop his gaze being drawn back to the betraying scar.

"She hurt me plenty," Nick said. "Gran tortured me as kid, terrorized me, and then, when she found me again… she killed me."

Ewan shook his head. "You're wrong. You… she didn't have time to explain. You never knew her."

"Or maybe you didn't, or didn't want to," Nick said. He swung his leg off the saddle, his hips sore from the long, cold ride. Even if he didn't remember half of it. He let his shirt drop and zipped up his jacket again. Whatever warmth had been in it was gone, and he shivered. "Rose Blake raised me until social services had to step in and stop her. I know how she likes her whiskey, and she never slept more than three hours a night. I know she whipped me for pissing the bed even though she terrified me with the monsters that were under it. I love her, even though I know there's nothing there to hang it on, and I know when she's lying, Ewan. And when she's not."

"What—"

"You said the wolves killed your daughter?" Nick said. "I guess that's true, because Rose told me that she cut me out of her daughter's stomach herself."

Ewan's bony face twisted away from the truth as though Nick had punched him with it. The muscles in his jaw bulged as he shook his head.

"You're wrong," he said. "I know Rose. She has done terrible things—for lust, for pride, and even to save us all—but she'd never hurt Ashley. She loved her. Maybe she couldn't show it, too much the wolf, but everything she did was for Ashley."

Had that been her name? Nick had never known. Or if Gran had told him at some point, he'd lost it under the gorier stories.

"So?" Nick asked. "She loves me too. Otherwise when she killed me, it would have been a murder, not a sacrifice. Why did she do it, Ewan? You owe me that much. What was more important than her daughter? Her grandson."

Ewan pulled off his hat. He dug his fingers into the wool and twisted at it unhappily. Underneath it, his hair was sparse and red. Some small, hived-off part of Nick that he tried not to think about much wondered if his mother had looked like that.

"I turned my back on everything, let them cut my wolf out of me, because she told me that the Old Man had murdered our daughter to punish her. An eye for an eye. A child for a child. That he'd taken the pup she was going to have—taken you—and sent you down over the Wall to raise."

Nick shrugged. "She lied. Rose does that."

A distant yelp made them both flinch. Ewan let the hat drop to the ground. He wiped his hand down his face and smeared wet from the corner of his eyes.

"I loved her," he said. "She never loved me, but I knew that. It didn't matter. I knew what she'd done, what she would have done, but I told myself there were limits. That there were lines she wouldn't cross."

Nick edged away from the bike, caught between keeping an eye on Ewan and one on the trees.

"That's your problem," he said bluntly. "What is she going to do? Why did she come back here, back to where she knew they'd try and stop her?"

Ewan stared at him. Conflicted emotions warred visibly on his face.

"I don't know you," he said. "Why should I trust you? Over the woman I've followed for decades?"

Nick shrugged. He didn't have an answer, and it didn't matter. "We'll find out eventually," he said. "One way or another."

The monsters spilled into the clearing, half made and still raw from the fever that birthed them. Broken bones stuck out of wasted skin as the—curse, infection, whatever it was—pulled muscles loose to reknit their bodies to order. Plates of Kevlar were stitched roughly into their puffy pale flesh with seams of gray-green scabs and the rags of their old uniforms still strained across their swollen, hunched shoulders and thick thighs.

Gregor was in the middle of them, flesh torn to shreds and his teeth bared in a blood-streaked snark as though he'd forgotten he couldn't turn. He shoved his forearm into a monster's mouth, muscles shredded down to bone, and dug the fingers of his free hand into its eyes. They split and seeped pink fluid down its face. It shrieked and lurched backward as it clawed at its face. Wet, white skin slipped off its bones in ragged sheets as it pulled at it.

"Run," Gregor yelled as he wrenched himself free and tackled the other monster. It went down in a tangle of limbs it wasn't entirely used to yet. "Get out of here. I'll catch up."

Liar.

Nick tightened his grip on the knife and lurched forward, but a hand on his shoulder pulled him back. Ewan bore down hard enough that Nick felt his collarbone creak.

Ewan's fingers tightened and he took a breath as though he had something else to say. It never came out. Instead he threw Nick aside into the snow and stalked forward to wade into the brawl. Like a man with a misbehaving terrier, he grabbed the monster by the ear and dragged it off Gregor.

"Enough," he ordered. His voice was harsh and thick with authority. "If we wanted him dead, we'd have told you. Back, you fucker."

He bullied the two monsters and got them to crouch beneath one of the trees, slabber hanging in strings from badly hinged jaws. They growled and shifted uneasily on blistered, flayed paws, the compulsion to obey their master's voice conflicting with the bloodlust in their swollen eyes as they stared at the bloody mess they'd left of Gregor.

"You should have let them finish," Gregor said. He propped himself up on his other elbow, his breath ragged and his arm slack and bloody. "I won't give you the same quarter."

Nick dragged himself out of the snow. His hips and ribs ached as he staggered to his feet. It wouldn't kill him, so he ignored it as he limped over to Gregor. He dropped back to his knees in the snow and tried to patch the gory wounds with wads of cloth and pressure. The blood oozed between his fingers, wet and potent with life, and Nick tried to focus through the woozy nausea.

He'd eaten an eyeball—or the bird had. He wasn't going to puke at the sight of some blood. It was a lie, and it didn't even help. Gregor sucked his breath in between his teeth at the pain and gave Nick a hard, green look.

"I told you to run," he said.

"And I didn't," Nick said. The cold slowed the blood but not enough. He knew Gregor would heal if he got the chance, but some lizard-instinct in Nick's brain didn't believe that. Every wet red flower of blood that bloomed on the rucked-up snow made the tension in his chest ratchet tighter. "What are you going to do about it?"

Gregor rasped out a laugh. "One day you'll do as you're told."

"Not today."

Ewan turned to look at them. The two monsters crouched at heel on either side of him, and he put his hands on the bony jut of their deformed shoulders. He looked small and oddly normal between them—a neat, slightly weathered man with a tired face. But Nick's shoulder still ached from the iron grip of those fingers.

"I would have been a bad grandfather," Ewan said. "I was a bad father, and I learned nothing from it. That's why my daughter's dead, no matter what the Old Man did or didn't do. All these years, all this god fuckery, because I didn't want to admit that."

Gregor used Nick's shoulder to push himself up onto his feet. He folded his arm over his stomach to hold the wound shut with his forearm.

"They're not alone," he said. "Prophets. They'll catch up soon."

Ewan smiled thinly. "I know. I brought them," he said. "It was a trap."

"Yeah," Gregor said. "We got that. And now?"

There was silence for a moment as Ewan glanced at Nick. His eyes were dark with unsaid things, and then he let his smile stretch ruefully over his face. "I don't know," he said. "Call it my bid to be the favorite grandparent."

Blood had cooled stickily on Nick's hands. He wiped them on his trousers as he struggled to his feet. His heart thumped in his ears, too fast and too hot.

"What's she going to do?" he asked.

One of the monsters raised its head. It flared its nostrils, split like petals, and slurred something out of its broken jaw.

"… now y'r plas," it rasped, raw lips peeled back and wet with blood.

Nick felt the itch of the bird's feathers behind his eyes as it stirred and pecked irritably at him. In the shadows, between the trees, he caught a foggy glimpse of a dead woman. Dark stains clotted on the front of her oversized Aran jumper and gloved her hands. Nick couldn't make out her face, and he didn't want to.

The monsters saw her too, or at least knew she was there, since their eyes didn't track her. They growled at the air where she'd been, thick runs of goose pimples on their spines as they tried to raise their hackles while she walked around them and stood behind Ewan. Her mouth moved close to his ear.

Nick couldn't make out the words. He tried, but the bird croaked and flapped to drown it out. It—they—might be a god, but not everything was meant for them.

Ewan tilted his head as though he could hear her too. Then he sighed and shook his head to dislodge whatever it was.

"Rose made you a god, but only a small one. She made herself… something. That won't be enough when the real gods come back. They'll still expect us to bend the neck. That's why she's here. That's what the humans are for… will be. Gods, ones who will bend the neck to her and do as they are told. So when Odin sets his one eye on us and Selene finally comes down to earth, we'll meet them as equals." He tightened his grip on the monsters and glanced over his shoulder. Nick thought, at first, that he'd heard something the dead woman said. Instead he hissed under his breath. "The others are coming. You have to go. Go as far as you can. It's too late to stop Rose, but maybe if you run far enough, she won't come after you. My daughter thought she could do that, but I guess she didn't go far enough."

Fragments of voices carried on the wind—curses and Ewan's name.

Gregor grimaced and grabbed Nick's arm to pull him away, although Nick didn't know where they meant to go. He dug his heels in and looked at Ewan.

"What's the dead thing on the mound?" he asked. The rot-musk of it was strong enough in his memory that he could taste it. The oil of it coated his tongue. "And why did Rose leave the Run-Away Man to guard it?"

Ewan looked confused for a moment, but he didn't have time to puzzle out whatever part he'd missed. The monsters were restless at the approach of the other prophets, and they pulled against the restraint of his hand on their shoulders. He dug his fingers in and wrenched them back, sweat on his face despite the cold.

"God or not, she needs to have the wolves at her heel," he said through gritted teeth. "And when the Old Man wouldn't bend his neck or give her his cock, that only left her one path."

Ewan spoke like he'd shared something profound. It meant nothing to Nick.

"I don't understand." he said. "What path? What's she going to do?"

Maybe Ewan would have answered, but he didn't get a chance. The prophet limped into the clearing on malformed legs. She was half-wolf, but the rotted hide was torn to rags and it couldn't cover her. The long, fanged muzzle of a wolf was unfinished, her ribbon of a tongue shredded as she tried to fit it between broken teeth crammed in a human jaw. Her eyes—one clouded amber and the other human as it peered through a split in the hide—flicked from Ewan to the bloody Gregor, and she leered.

"Kill the whoreson," she said. "I'll pluck the bird."

Ewan smiled. "You make it easy, Ailsa." He dragged the monsters around by the scruffs of their neck, skin loose and too elastic in his fists, and set them on her with a snarled command. She went down with a shocked screech as the mass of twisted bone and claw hit her. Ewan shot a quick look at Nick and Gregor and snapped. "It won't work for long. Run."

Guilt pinned Nick in place. It felt like he should care, but he couldn't. Gregor growled and dragged him away. The last thing Nick saw as the Wild closed around him was the monsters lurch away from Ailsa and turn on Ewan.

He held his ground.

Nick didn't need to see the end of the fight to know it wouldn't make much difference.

Chapter Nineteen—Jack

THE HARE, scrawny in its patchy winter coat, threw itself across the snowy field in a desperate dash for safety. It jinked and turned in a frantic attempt to stay ahead of Jack's teeth. A snap of his jaws caught him a tuft of tail fluff and the sweet bloom of blood on his tongue. It wasn't enough to bring the rabbit down, and as Jack collected himself from the lunge, it gained an inch on him. It might have been enough.

On a summer's day, with the Old Man's sheep penned up in the field and someone willing waiting for him, Jack might have called it a day. The hunt then had been as much about the chase as the catch, a sop for the wolf who sometimes chafed at even the barely there domestication of the Scottish Pack.

Jack would have spat out the shit-matted fur, rolled off his frustration in the heather, and mocked Gregor for running his paws bloody for a stringy mouthful of squirrel. It would have been the hare's lucky day.

In the summer, but this was winter—The Winter—and Jack needed the kill. His world narrowed down to the slip of snow under his paws and the yellow flash of the hare's hind feet ahead of him. Cold air scraped at the back of his throat, caught like glass in the lungs that labored in his chest as he ran. Snow sprayed up from under his feet as he pushed himself faster, each millimeter of space the hare claimed with an impossibly tight turn won back on the straight stretch. Ellie fell back, the reserves of speed in her muscles exhausted.

Jack flicked his ears. Even over the rasp of his own breath in his throat, he could hear the hare—the stutter-fast beat of its heart as he ran it down, the panic-fast huff of each breath that powered the desperate stretch of its body.

It went left, but it should have gone right. Jack had solid ground underfoot and lunged as the hare's body twisted. He bowled it over into the snow and tried to pin it down with his paws as it squirmed. It rammed a foot into his eye, hard enough to make him yelp, but then his teeth closed around its neck. Jack bit down, bone crunched, and the hare went limp.

He lifted his head, the long hare body dangling limp in his jaws, and looked around. There was nothing there, but his wolf still wanted to retreat to shelter before he ate. Jack tossed the hare up into the air and then snapped his jaws back around its midsection as it fell, so he could carry it easier.

As he loped toward the shelter of a nearby cairn, he felt his hackles go up between his shoulders. It felt like eyes on him, but there was nothing to watch him. The world might not be empty, but this particular stretch of moors was. The half-fed hare in his jaws was the only living thing he'd seen since he left Danny sleeping to check out the boundaries of his—*his*, now—territory.

Alone like an idiot, a mental voice that made the effort to sound a lot like Danny noted inside his head.

Jack snorted at the thought, for all his wolf agreed. The wolf wanted the comfort of the pack, the reassurance of a dozen kin at its heels.

And a dozen hungry bellies who could have seen him bested by a hare.

The stomach always won for a wolf. They were a hungry breed.

Despite the distraction, he still felt watched. He hunkered down under the stones and tore into the softness of the hare's stomach. It was still warm, full of sweet meat and the bitterness of guts. He wolfed it down, cracked the bones between his teeth, and scraped the fat from under the fur.

A single hare shouldn't have been enough to fill a wolf's belly, but Jack's hunger was more than just physical. Whatever prayers the hare had for the God of Chased Things added spice to the meat and thickened the marrow. The prophets left their kills uneaten for the gods, but the wolves took it all for themselves.

Let the moon bitch climb down from her chariot if she was hungry, tear her white robes on the briars and stain her pocked skin with blood. Jack hadn't sired her that he should chew her meat for her.

When Jack finished his meal, there was nothing but a stain in the snow and plucked hanks of fur left. He licked up the bloody frost as though it were a Popsicle and crunched it between his teeth. The shock of cold stabbed into his skull, just behind his eyes, and he shook his head until his ears flapped to dislodge it.

The wind sidled around the stones and pulled at his fur with cold fingers. There was a storm on the horizon, the sky bruised purple with the weight of it. Tonight was the moon hunt. The Wild would wax as the bitch-goddess opened her blind eye, and the prophets would try to put their twisted plans into action.

Whatever they were.

Apparently, it was too much to hope for the Winter to sit it out.

Jack finished, licked his chops of any dregs of blood, and stood up. Chunks of ice were matted into his fur, and the cold had bitten down enough that even a wolf could feel it in their bones. He shook himself and stretched to enjoy the feeling of a full stomach against his ribs.

Speculation and prediction were human things. There wasn't room for them in Jack's fur-skin. The wolf knew that the Scottish Pack would survive whatever the prophets threw at him. What else could the prophets do but lose? They were made for it.

Then….

Then.

The wolf hackled at the thought of losing Danny again, but the Old Man's son knew his duty. Jack couldn't remember the last time the two had been at odds inside him.

He shook himself again as though he could shed his thoughts as easily as the snow and raised his nose to the sky as he howled. In the odd stillness that hung before a storm, his voice trailed upward, thin and sharp, and hung in the air.

Someone answered from down the hill. It had the raw-edged scrape of a dog's voice—not Danny—but somewhere between the cell and the fight, his brain had fit them in as pack. The sound rippled back across the landscape—call and response—until something to the north, near the storm, squalled a coarse gargle of sound into the mix. It was an old, ruined voice, cut through with other voices. It was dissonant, with a pus-thick edge of sickness that made it glottal. Other ruined voices picked it up—the shades of dead friends stitched to coarse throats—in mockery and challenge.

Prophets didn't raise their voices to the pack. They held their tongues except to howl the catechism. Or they had.

Unnerved, the Pack fell silent. Jack waited until Rose's distant voice raggedly trailed off.

He snorted to himself, twitched his ears, and headed back along the rucked-up trail he'd left on his hare hunt. The Pack already knew the prophets were out there. Now they knew where and how many were left.

The sense of being watched dug into his shoulders again. He froze, his hackles raised, and growled low and scratchy in his throat. All he could smell was frost and empty air, a hint of icy heather and oak. When he twitched his ears, he could hear the creak of the snow as it settled and the distant crackle of frozen trees.

On the wind the echoes of the wolves' voices drew back together and stitched into a stale exhalation from the wild.

Little wolf, little wolf...

It was barely there, a breathy whisper that faded when he tried to actually listen to it. Cold, bone-hard fingers pinched the end of his tail and yanked. Jack pinned his ear and spun around. He snapped his teeth at the empty air and felt cold bite up into his nose as *something* laughed.

...run away home....

The cold fingers shoved and jabbed at him. Jack stumbled and spun, teeth bared, as he was buffeted and pinched. They stretched out his lips, wet and tight, and flicked the end of his nose.

Through the thin huffs of laughter, his assailants found their words again. The voice was clearer now, but not louder. It was a dozen voices layered, not quite perfectly, on top of each other as they singsonged,

Your father is gone...on...on...

The fingers pinched his ear and bore down, suddenly hot as the skin split under the force.

...and your brother soon too!

A yank made Jack stagger as a quick rip of pain jabbed down into the corner of his eye, and then the itch at the base of his neck was gone.

He was alone. Blood dripped down onto the snow in fat red drops from his split ear and crystalized on the snow. Habit made him reach for the Wild and then recoil from the cramped muscle tightness of it. It felt like a sprain did under your skin, the rubber-band tension and soft, inflamed tenderness of infection.

If he needed to, he could still drag it to heel, rip it open and see what spilled out, but not easily and with no guarantee that the infected grafts wouldn't slow him down. So he'd wait until he needed it. The Wild always took a kinder view of need than it did of pride. Even with the Wolves.

Jack snarled at the emptiness, hair still bristled down his spine like a hog, and wrinkled his lips back until he could feel the cold on his gums. Sannock Dead or just dead, he didn't care for his new visitors.

Harbingers never helped anyone.

He pushed himself into a ground-eating lope. The familiar singsong rhythm of the song carried the stand-in words around his head on a loop. Worry ate at his bones like acid and released a cold broth of anger into his blood.

They might never know what happened to the Old Man, but the prophets had been behind it, behind everything. It had been Job's poison in Da's ear that saw Jack stripped of position and exiled. They'd taken his da, his tattoos, and—accidentally or not—given him Danny only so they could take him away too.

It was enough. Jack would be damned if they got the satisfaction of killing Gregor too.

He barreled back into the wolves' settlement on ice-raw paws, his breath hot as it smoked over his tongue and between his lips. Sweat matted his fur down from his shoulders to his tail. He stripped it off like a sodden coat. The slap of cold air against his spine and between his legs felt good against his overheated skin, even as his balls tightened and goose pimples pricked his arms and legs.

Nothing.

Jack had expected bloodshed and confusion, to find whatever was left of his brother dead or dying in the heart of their territory. Instead it was quiet, almost peaceful under the thick quilt of snow.

Except Jack *knew* he was too late. He could feel the awful weight of it in his gut, an anticipation of something terrible held back by a single thin thread of ignorance. Jack stood there for a second with the bleak knowledge that he was going to find out what it was.

"Get the fuck off me!" It was Danny's voice, but raw and broken. "This was *your* fault."

Jack moved before his brain caught up with his feet. He sprinted through the snow toward Danny's voice, between the houses and across the neglected scrub at the back of the Old Man's house.

The old barn was there to pen sheep in the winter, when the hunting was thin and the pups needed mutton to wolf down with scraps of deer. Da had always said it was always easier than trying to fill hungry bellies from their neighbors' farm stock and pets. But this was the Wolf Winter, when the wolves expected to get fat on easy prey, so no one had bothered. The old building, weathered wood patched with tarred planks where it had rotted into holes, should have been empty.

Yet what looked like half the Pack were huddled around it. The rest were trying—and failing—to drag Danny away. He was naked and battered, blood half-dried on his skin and gloved on his hands, but that didn't stop him. He spat every swear word he'd ever learned at Gregor—battered and with a bloodstained, makeshift bandage around his leg—as he struggled against the wolves who had their hands on him.

In that second, Jack didn't *care* what had happened. The harbinger's warning took on a different tone in his head—if Gregor had hurt Danny, then Jack could learn to do without his brother—and he snarled through human teeth as he threw himself at Gregor. He rammed his shoulder into his brother's stomach and took both of them down into the snow.

Numitor or not, he couldn't fight the whole Pack. Wolf or man, both of them agreed on that simple fact. It didn't matter. If they'd hurt Danny, he'd fucking try.

He threw a punch at Gregor's face and barked his knuckles against skull as Gregor twisted out of the way. They scuffled in the snow, all fists and knees and the strange release of years of animosity. It always felt good to split Gregor's lip, in Jack's experience, but for the first time, he could appreciate how simple it was too.

No complicated prophet schemes. No reluctant alliance or grudged respect.

Just the old, easy hatred of each other and the satisfaction of being in the right.

Gregor spat blood into Jack's eyes and followed it up with a headbutt. Stars flashed black across Jack's field of vision, and Gregor managed to get him on his back and by the throat. Hard thumbs dug into Jack's windpipe, and he choked as he tried to suck in air. He groped around for something and wrapped his fingers around a rock, but before he could swing it, Gregor was dragged off him.

He managed to get a kick in to Jack as they dragged him away. Jack wheezed out a thin "fuck" as he felt his ribs bow under the impact, but they didn't break. He sucked in cold air through his raw throat and scrambled to his feet to go after Gregor. Or whoever had broken up the fight. In the red of his temper, he wasn't sure what he intended.

Millie stepped in front of him, her good hand up to hold him back, and the other—the one she might still lose after she saved Jack's ass in the fight with the prophets' monsters—held gingerly across her body. She smelled like blood and pain, sharp and sour on her skin.

"Stop it," she said, her voice thin. Then she glanced over her shoulder. "Both of you."

There was a sudden scuffle around the wolves that held Danny and a startled yelp. It wasn't Danny.

Millie took a deep breath and let it out raggedly. "All of you," she shouted. "Just stop it. This isn't going to help."

Behind her, Gregor sucked blood from his split lip. He looked as frustrated as Jack did to have their fight interrupted.

"He started it."

Jack stepped forward until Millie's hand was braced against his chest. He ignored her as he glared at Gregor, into the grim mask of his own face.

"You touch Danny again, and I'll throw you off the fucking cliff," he snarled.

"Try."

Ellie stepped up next to Millie. She met Jack's eyes as though she thought she had the right.

"Nobody has laid a hand on your dog," she said. "We're trying to stop him hurting *himself*."

The same old instinct that had made Jack punch Gregor made him look to his brother for confirmation. Gregor was a lot of things, but he'd never been much of a liar. After a sullen moment, Gregor shrugged away from the wolves holding him and nodded.

"Your dog has more bark than brains," he said. There was respect in his tone despite the words Gregor had never much respected prudence. "He wants to run off after the prophets on his own and get himself killed."

To the side, apart from both factions of the Pack, James curled his lip at them all.

"I told them to let him go," he said, his voice still rough with misery. "If your dog can take a bite out of that old bitch, more power to his jaw. And if she kills him… who gives a fuck? No one does about my boy, and he was a wolf, not just a dog."

Gregor turned to glare at James. "It won't bring your son any closer to home either," he said. "The Wild has him, not Hel."

"And you're not even a wolf anymore," James sneered. There was a glitter in his eye that spoke of wanting to hurt anything—Gregor, Danny, or himself. "Not a prophet either. So why don't you mind your betters or, better still, you can—"

Gregor punched him in the throat, and something popped under his knuckles. James's eyes bulged as he choked on the words he'd been about to say, and he clawed at the collar of his jumper with blunt fingers as he gaped like a fish for air.

It would heal and it probably wouldn't take that long, but it was an unpleasant few seconds to spend choked while it did.

"Anybody else have anything to say about what I'm not?" Gregor asked as he glared around him. Lost wolf or not, nobody quite had the courage to hold his gaze as he caught theirs. Eyes dropped in silent acknowledgment that, for now, they'd submit to him. "Whatever the prophets cut out of me, I'm still the Old Man's pup. That makes me more wolf than you."

"You're still an asshole," Jack said, to make the point that he wouldn't.

Gregor just showed him bloody teeth. It wasn't an insult that bothered him. At his feet James sucked in thin ribbons of breath through his broken throat. He glanced up, bloodshot eyes bleak with a rage that needed *something* to chew on.

"Tell them to let me go," Danny said. His voice was steadier, the curses bitten back between his teeth, but still raw. He was on his knees, his arms twisted up behind his back and a wolf's arm around his throat. His face was flushed and puffy, with a stain that spread from his jaw halfway to his eye where someone had hit him "Jack. They're hurting me. Get them off me."

Jack swallowed the order instead of spitting it out. It didn't want to go. His throat felt raw with the need to get the wolves off Danny, but the calm was a lie. In all the fights that Danny had lost over the years, he'd never admitted that it had hurt him, not even when he had two dislocated shoulders and was sobbing with the pain of it. He'd never asked for help either, not from anyone.

Not for himself.

"Danny. Danny-dog." Jack pushed through the wolves and crouched down in front of Danny. He started to reach for Danny's face, but the self-conscious awareness of the wolves watching made him settle for shoulders instead. It was the wrong choice—he could feel it in his gut, in the tension under his fingers—but it was too late to change his mind. "What happened? Who hit you?"

"I did," Gregor said. He didn't sound sorry or amused, just grim. "It was the only way to stop him till someone else got here to hold him down."

Danny snarled like his dog, lips wrinkled back from his teeth. He twisted angrily against the wolves holding him, until his joints twisted weirdly under Jack's hands. Tears dripped down his face, cutting through the grime and blood, as he spat at Gregor "You should have let me go. Coward."

A growl rumbled out of Gregor. "I'll give you one pass, dog," he said.

"Fuck off," Danny said.

Jack shook him hard enough to make Danny's teeth audibly click together and pull his focus back to Jack.

"What. Happened?" Jack repeated. He tightened his grip until he could feel bone under the layers of cloth and muscle. It was the Numitor who asked. "Danny, tell me."

For a second the mask of anger slipped and Jack saw something terrible and raw underneath.

"They killed my mam," Danny said. He sounded like a kid again, all shocked at the unfairness of the world. "They cut my wee sister to bits. I wasn't there, and they came in the night and... *slaughtered*... my family."

"Kath?" Jack asked Ellie. It was stupid. He knew that even before Danny creaked out a bitter laugh at the question. What did he think Ellie was going to say, that Danny had panicked and mistaken a nap for death? It seemed impossible. Jack had expected blood when he raced back to the village, but not this distinct, unheralded murder. So he still waited for Ellie's nod before he let himself believe it. "Gods. Let him go. Let him up, for fucks sake, I've got him."

The wolves at Danny's shoulders hesitated but did as they were told. Danny slumped, the fight gone from him now that he'd put his grief into words. His hands lay limply on his knees, fingers curled, and he stared at the lines of his family's blood worked into the creases.

"Danny. Come on, get up," Jack said. He pulled Danny to his feet and gripped his shoulders tightly. "Not yet. Not alone. You're pack. We hunt together."

The corner of Danny's mouth twitched slightly, and then he pressed his lips together in a thin line. He wiped tears and snot off his face onto his sleeve and nodded. It was resentful—a short dip of his chin—but Jack supposed it was what he'd get.

He wanted to say more, to make Danny promise not to get himself killed, because.… Gods, Jack could barely accept the idea of Danny gone from his side. The thought of Danny gone, *dead*, and not somewhere that Jack could imagine going to someday? That dropped dread through Jack like a stone, from the pit of his throat all the way down to his wolf.

"Danny.…" The words stuck in Jack's throat, and he couldn't get them out. It felt too naked, too *raw*, like he was laid out on Rose's table again. The Pack didn't need to know their Numitor was so weak. Jack cupped his hand around the back of Danny's neck with the old familiar affection. "The prophets won't take anything else from us."

"Won't they?" Danny pulled away from Jack and walked away. He was barefoot, but he didn't seem to care as he headed toward the barn.

Gregor stopped him on the way past, a hand on his chest and a brief, unfriendly look traded between them. Then Danny nodded and went over to fold himself down on the wall outside the barn. He pulled his knees up and hunched over to rest his head on them.

"Go get him some shoes," Jack told James. The big wolf sneered at him, defiance in every line. Jack grabbed him by the collar and hauled him to his feet. He leaned in until he could smell James's breath on his lips, sour with what was going on inside him. "Do as you're told. Or, if you're no use to the Pack, I'll flay you for the prophets myself."

The words were enough to make James flinch. He staggered away and glared when Jack let go of him, a flush on his throat and under his stubble. Then his resistance spluttered out. He muttered his surrender under his breath and stalked away, making a point to shoulder past the assembled wolves.

That left Jack with no more excuses.

He turned to Gregor. "What happened?"

Gregor shook his head. He had to swallow before he said anything. "I don't know," he said. His mouth twisted in a humorless smile. "It was already… done… when we got back. Kath was dead, Bron… they cut her open to kill the baby. Then they left them both to die. Your dog wasn't in a state to tell us anything."

It sounded brutal, almost careless. Jack knew better. Gregor had always swallowed pain whole instead of in bites, as though letting it hurt all at once was easier.

The neat little terrier woman from the town was gone. She looked like a scrapper now, in borrowed jeans and a too-big sweater. But her hair was still neat, and her lips were primly pressed together.

"It was our fault. The dogs," she said. One of the wolves snarled, a low, ripped-from-his-throat sound, and she flinched. Jack didn't bother to look, he held up his hand to shut the wolf up.

"Go on."

Millie swallowed hard. "Tom, our Tom," her voice cracked as she said his name with the hardness that only came from betrayed love. The cowed dog from the pen, with the milk-glazed eye—as though the gods had thought being a dog wouldn't be hard enough for him. Jack felt the old, lazy stir of pity, but it flickered out as it faced what Tom was involved with. "He went to talk to Kath. She was always… kind to him, you know. After Danny left, he'd do odd jobs for her that she couldn't be bothered with. Or she'd send him down to town for errands, to me. Kath could never abide Lochwinnoch."

"Does that matter now?"

Millie had to think about it. Then she shook her head. "No, I suppose not," she said. "She let him in. I saw him going in, but I didn't think anything of it. He loved Kath. He followed Bron around like a lost puppy. If anything, I thought he'd finally spit the prophets' poison out of his gut, once he had the chance. He wasn't a *bad* lad, you know. He was angry, resentful of the gods, but we *are*, us dogs. We know what else we could have been."

It wasn't an excuse. She sounded baffled.

"What. Happened?"

This time Millie pressed her lips together so hard they turned white.

"He poisoned them," Ellie said instead. "From the smell. Something mixed in their tea. It smelled like the potions the prophets gave their favorite wolves."

"That wouldn't kill them," Jack said. It would make them sick. It might have twisted Bron's baby out of her—pregnancies could be fragile even if the wolf wasn't. They would have been sick and weak, but not dead.

"No," Ellie admitted. "He used a knife for that."

He finally turned to look at her. It stung. She'd made herself over in Kath's image, just younger and weaker. She was like a shadow… or a ghost.

"Who else?"

Her mouth opened, but the name didn't come out at first. When it did, her voice was weak and thin.

"I don't know," she said. "There was too much blood. It drowned out any other scents."

"Did it? She turned her coat once," someone muttered under their breath but loud enough to hear. Ellie flushed, but she kept her eyes on Jack. "Maybe she helped."

"I didn't," Ellie swore. "But there was a wolf. Or a prophet. They left by the Wild. I wouldn't do this, Numitor, and I'll kill whoever did."

"If you're lying, I'll kill you myself and make sure your wolf never finds the Wild," Jack told her. He glanced over at Danny, who had twisted his fingers into his hair while the wolves didn't look at him. "And if you didn't, then you don't have first claim to the killer's throat."

Gregor put a hand on Jack's shoulder. "If you want an answer, ask Bron," he said.

"What?" Jack said as he jerked around in surprise. "I thought she was… that she died."

"No," Gregor said. His voice was thick and rough in his throat, the way it had always gone when he needed the wolf to hide from something. But he was alone in this, the only one of the Pack who was really alone. "Not yet."

Without really thinking about it, Jack reached up and gripped Gregor's hand in sympathy. The fingers were cold and stiff under Jack's, and it took a second before he pulled away.

"I don't need your pity. Save it for your dog," he said flatly as he jerked his head toward the barn. "Or for Bron."

Chapter Twenty—Jack

Bron lay on the roughly swept boards, sliced open from one hip bone to the other, like a bizarre zipper. There was an apron of blood that dripped down to her thighs, the rags of her nightgown shredded and plastered to the floor. She was unconscious, her face slack and tear-stained.

The silence was the shock. Bron was so rarely quiet, even as a wolf on the hunt.

Jack grabbed a pair of jeans from the basket by the door and pulled them on. The cuffs folded under his heels and the waistband sagged around his hips.

Nothing should have been funny right then, but part of Jack's brain insisted that he register how ludicrous it was.

The Numitor in a pair of pants—and a title—that were too big for him.

And then there was Nick—harbinger, carrion god, collector of the dead—fish-belly gray and sweaty as he worked on her. His hands shook every time he lifted them out of her guts to wipe his face on his sleeve. As though Jack hadn't seen him in bird form peck a frozen eyeball from a corpse's skull like it was a melon ball at a party.

It wasn't humor, just a bleak recognition of how ridiculous they all were.

"He doesn't like blood," Gregor said quietly, the same faded, terrible shred of acknowledgment in his voice. "Not when it's come out of the living."

Faint as it was, the macabre flicker of amusement faded as Jack walked gingerly over, as though a creaked board might be what made her slip away. He took in more injuries as he looked her over, cuts to her arms and feet, bruises on her shoulders. The smell of blood was bright and metallic—the tang of the rabbit's blood caught in the back of Jack's throat and made his stomach turn—with a sour undertone of infection.

Bron's chest fluttered in fast, shallow breaths and her sallow face was wet with tears. She looked like Danny, so much it grabbed Jack's guts and twisted. If she hadn't healed yet….

"Just let her go," Jack said. His throat was so dry the words hurt. "We're wolves. We live or we die, but we don't linger. We don't suffer. This isn't right. She's—"

"Shut up," Nick said through his teeth without looking up. "That's the choice everyone gets. You're not some special case. Life or death. And I know what kills people a lot better than you do. It was my—it is *our*—job. She can survive this."

It was Gregor who put his hand on Nick's shoulder, although he stopped short of trying to pull him away from what he was doing.

"In your hospitals, maybe," Gregor said. "Here? On the floor of a sheep byre, with a storm on the way?"

Nick grunted. "Good. She's going to have a fever soon. If the temperature drops, that will keep it down. You. Hector? Get her to drink more of the tartar."

Hector hesitated as his eyes skipped from the gory scene on the floor to Jack and Gregor. His worn hands worked nervously around the large brown bottle he held.

"I don't know if—"

Nick lifted his head sharply and fixed Hector with a bleak glare. "Good thing I do, then," he said. "Pour it down her throat."

He didn't bother to wait and see if Hector did as he was told. Nick's attention dropped back to Bron's ruined stomach as he grabbed a bleach-white sheet to sop up the blood. He visibly gagged as it squelched under his fingers, his lips a thin, white line. Then he dove back in with bare fingers and a needle that Jack had seen Hector use to sew up a ewe's fox-shredded stomach.

The first jab of the needle made Bron flinch and choke out a moan. She dug her fingers into the barn floor until she gouged up splinters with her fingernails.

Jack lunged down and grabbed Nick's wrist. It was slick with hot blood, sticky under Jack's fingers.

"Stop it," he ordered thickly. "This is torture."

"It's medicine," Nick corrected him sharply. "Done right, sometimes there isn't much difference."

"If she's going to die," Jack said. He tightened his grip on Nick's wrist until he could feel the tight play of tendons under his fingertips. "Let her die. Cleanly. I can smell the prophets' taint on her. It's a bad way to go."

A hand grabbed his ankle. It was weak, but Jack was surprised enough that Bron could grab at all that he nearly jumped out of his skin. He recovered after a breath and crouched down next to her. However else he'd fucked up as Numitor, at least he could do this. A Scottish wolf should die with her Numitor by her side.

"I'm here," he said. "You don't have to fight anymore."

"Fuck. That," Bron gritted out between chapped lips and clenched teeth. "I am. Not. Gonna die by dog."

Gregor snorted a startled laugh, but the brief moment of humor faded quickly. He came over and squatted down beside Jack.

"Bron, I don't think pride has healing properties," he said. "You aren't healing, and Nick's not really much of a doctor."

Nick grumbled under his breath. "I don't *like* working on the living," he said. "It doesn't mean I wasn't good at it."

Bron swallowed and tried for a smile. It didn't quite make it. Her lips twisted down in a grimace as Nick grabbed the torn sides of her gut and pulled them together.

"You. You puked. When you saw me," she gasped out, her eyes closed and hand on Jack's leg.

"It was puke or faint. I'm not much good unconscious."

"I don't want to die," Bron said as she opened her eyes. "There's people I need to kill. Can't depend on my dog brother to do… can I? Give me the fucking drink."

This time when Hector looked for approval, Jack gave it to him with a nod. Gregor put his arm under Bron's shoulders to prop her up, and Hector poured the thick, acrid liquid down her throat. She swallowed, throat working with each gulp until the taste got too much for her and she had to turn her head away.

"What's that for, anyhow?" Jack asked.

Nick lifted his head briefly. His eyes were black and bright in the sweaty mask of his face as he glanced at the bottle. "To make sheep puke," he said bluntly. "We didn't have any activated charcoal and no time to make it. If blood loss and infection don't kill her, that won't."

Jack recoiled. "Why the fuck would you give her that? She's—"

"To get out any of the prophets' potion left in her stomach," Gregor interrupted. "You think it'll be the same as you? That she'll heal once the poison's out of her system, the same way you got the bird back in your head?"

Bron retched and then tried to curl up around the pain. "How's there even any left in there?" she groaned. "They sliced me open like a fish and emptied me—oh gods—out."

She rolled her head to the side as much as she could and retched again. Thin streams of black bile dripped from her lips. Hector wiped it for her on the sleeve of his sweater and then offered her the bottle again.

"They didn't," Nick said. He sounded detached, almost polite in a weird way, as though he didn't have a naked woman on the floor with his hands covered in her blood. "It was quite a neat job. They knew what they were doing."

Bron lurched up to try and grab him, her fingers clawed as she reached for his throat. That wouldn't make his stitches any neater, so Jack grabbed her shoulders to push her back down.

"Their *job* was to kill my baby," she spat out and then twisted to glare at Gregor. "*Our* baby, Gregor. So it's no fucking comfort they did it well."

Out of the corner of his eye, Jack saw Nick's hands, all gore and neat movements of the needle, pause midstitch. He hadn't known that. Of course not, why would Gregor do something that might not backfire on them all.

Then Nick started to stitch again. His hands were steadier than they had been as he dragged the thread through her skin. Anger worked well when you needed to focus. Jack had always found that too.

"It wasn't," Nick said. His jaw tightened, the muscles drawn taut under pale skin, and he reluctantly corrected himself. "They might have, essentially, but it wasn't what they were there to do. Look at where they cut. It was a Cesarean. The job was to take the baby out of her, and it looks like they did it neatly enough."

There was a crack as Hector dropped the big glass bottle. It was heavy enough that it didn't break, but the liquid spilled over the floor and stank. Hector cursed and stooped down to pick it up.

"Tom helped me with the sheep during lambing," he said as he righted the container. "Sometimes we had to cut them open to get the lamb out. He… he always had a steady hand with it."

Bron shoved Jack out of the way and dragged herself halfway up into a sitting position. She curled her hand over her stomach to hold her guts in and glared at Nick.

"You're telling me… that they cut my baby out of me. Like I was some… half-dead sheep? And I didn't notice?"

Nick grabbed more towels and pressed them over Bron's hands to soak up the fresh blood that oozed out of her.

"You weren't at your best," he said dryly.

Bron laughed. Her rusty throat worked as she swallowed her first reaction and then tried again.

"It would have still died," she said as stoically as any wolf could fake. "It was too soon for it to be born."

Nick hesitated as he glanced uncomfortably at Gregor. "It's not dead," he said. His attention dropped back to Bron's stomach as he peeled the clothes away from her stomach to peer at the injury. "I—we—can tell that much. Not yet, at least."

"How can you be sure?" Bron asked. Her eyes were fever bright, and she was shaking as she twisted her hand in Nick's coat. Her fingers left stains on the fabric, but they'd blend with the rest of the blood and filth. "Do you *know*? Are you *certain*?"

Blood squelched between Nick's fingers. He looked sick again, his skin greasy with sweat.

"I know." He made a faintly revolted face. "Dead things—*murdered* things—are what we do. If they killed the baby, we'd know."

Bron let go of him and sagged back down. It was almost a fall, but Gregor caught her before she hit the ground.

"Keep me alive," she ordered roughly. "I don't care how much it hurts."

"That's what I've been trying to do," Nick muttered as he plucked thread out of torn stitches to start again. It made Bron suck in a hard breath through her teeth and hold it. The tense muscles in her arms and legs trembled under the skin. "Hold as still as you can."

Jack waited for a second and then put his hand on Bron's arm to catch her attention.

"It *was* Tom, then?" he asked.

She exhaled hard through her teeth—almost a scream—and nodded jerkily. Tears swam briefly in her eyes, but she furiously blinked them away.

"Tom, first. He was sorry, he *said* he was sorry, over how he'd behaved. Mam…." Her voice broke and she breathed raggedly through the grief and the pain. "She felt bad for him. He's a *dog*, you know? Not like Danny. So she let him in and he must have put something in the tea. It made me and Mam weak and stupid. Human. I could have still *hit* him, I could have *fought*, but I didn't. Mam did. She fought, but… then Tom let Lachlan in. Stinking bastard. She couldn't fight them both, and they… they…."

She stopped again. At some point she'd grabbed Gregor's hand and her fingers were twisted around it. His tanned skin was bled white under her grip. Tears squeezed out from under her lashes and down into her ears and already-matted curls.

"Did they say anything else?" Jack asked. "Anything that might help us find them?"

The baby was gone, sliced out and stolen, but Bron panted like a woman in labor as Nick finished his work on her stomach and swabbed the raw, puckered stitches with smears of powdery, old iodine. Her face was gray, the years of tan floating on top like a film, and her eyes glazed over before she closed them.

Jack hated himself. Maybe that was part of being Numitor. He slapped her face twice with a sharp, stinging impact that made Nick curse. Bron's eyes fluttered back open again. She glared at him.

"Bastard," she said weakly.

"Bron, we can't wait for you to heal," Jack said. If she did heal. Whatever Nick claimed about his familiarity with death, Jack had killed a lot of things in his life. Bron smelled like she was dying. "What did they say?"

She squinted and licked split lips with a dry tongue. "Tom couldn't do it, not at first. He kept cryin', saying he'd not meant to hurt us. Don't know what the fuck he thought he was going to do." She trailed off for as her mouth trembled, and then she took a deep breath through her nose.

"He couldn't put the knife in me. So Lachlan did it. He cut me open and told me, told me not to worry because… because Rose had done this before. I figured he just meant the bitch had killed a lot of babies."

Gregor clenched his jaw so hard that Jack could hear his teeth grind. He tightened his grip on Bron's hands.

"Not this one," he said. "I promise, Bron. Whatever happens, the prophets won't have your baby."

She curled her lip. "I'm not letting your mate juggle my guts so I can cheer you on," she rasped. "When I heal, I'll get the baby back myself. Then I'll cut Lach open and stick a badger into his guts. See how he takes it."

Jack leaned over and put his hand over Bron's eyes. He'd seen their da do that to wolves that had lost the run of themselves to grief or who couldn't pull themselves together to face punishment. It wasn't something Da had ever taught them. He probably thought they had more time. Jack reached for the Wild and… asked. The Wild knew Bron better than he did, so it would know what she needed better than him.

He tasted fresh blood on the back of his tongue and the sharp bite of that first gulp of cold water after a run. When he took a breath, he could smell Danny, all sweet sweat and musk, and a flush of self-consciousness made him pull away.

That was his, not even the Wild's for sharing.

"Oh," Bron said in a small voice. Her body relaxed, muscles loose and shoulders lowered, but she fought it. She forced her eyes open wide and grabbed Jack's hand. "Where's Danny? Is he okay?"

The Wild probably didn't have the ability to be smug, but Jack imagined it would try in response to his hubris. It hadn't conjured Danny for him, from him. That had been for Bron, because Danny had been her brother long before Jack ever noticed that the lanky, stubborn dog was beautiful.

Not everything was about him, he supposed. Danny had probably told him that sometime. It sounded like him.

"He's not hurt," he said as he focused on his injured wolf. "Nobody touched Danny."

Bron looked at him like he was stupid. "I know that. I was *there*," she said. This time when she blinked, it lasted longer. She had to fight to open her eyes again and only made it to half mast, her eyes hazy with sleep. "He's stupid, and he never remembers he's a dog. Never. You made him come back. Y'gotta take care of him. Make sure he doesn't get hurt."

The protest that he hadn't *made* Danny come back caught on the back of Jack's tongue. He hadn't—he didn't think he had—but if Danny hadn't come around? It wasn't as though Jack would have given up and left him back in Durham.

"I'll take care of him," he said.

"Promise?" Bron insisted.

"I love him," Jack said. He felt the weight lift off his shoulders as he made the admission out loud. It settled again as he realized it was only to people who already knew or, in Hector's case, would never repeat it. "I won't let anyone hurt Danny, not even himself."

"You always loved him," Bron said. "Never changed anything, did it? Never did, never will. Promise."

The air tasted like blood and birth, even if it hadn't been willing, and it scratched on the back of Jack's throat as he swallowed.

"I swear," he said. "On my da. On Danny."

She sighed and closed her eyes. That was apparently enough. The ragged hitch of her breathing evened out, and the hard lines around her mouth softened.

"I always thought she hated him," Jack said.

Gregor shrugged as he retrieved his hand from Bron's lax fingers. "Not everyone is lucky enough to have an uncomplicated relationship like us."

"Still?" Jack asked.

It took a second before Gregor answered, and then it was just a grunt as he stood up. From Gregor, that was a concession of… something. Jack was too tired to care what.

He wiped blood on borrowed jeans. "I should have killed Lachlan the first time he hurt Danny," he said bitterly. "Been done with it then."

"Da would have been thrilled," Gregor said dryly. "Me too."

Jack shrugged and tried not to think what would have been different if he'd just… left with Danny back then. Not that Danny had asked him, but… even the Wild didn't really let you travel back in time.

"I guess we just have to do it now," he said. "Call it practice for Rose."

Nick taped the makeshift dressing over Bron's stomach with a last strip of duct tape. He smoothed it down over her hip and then scrambled unsteadily to his feet. He lost his balance and Gregor grabbed him before Nick staggered into the wall.

"Later," Gregor promised roughly as he steadied Nick. "And I know."

After a brief exchange of looks, Nick accepted the promise with a brief dip of his chin. Then he turned his head to look at Jack.

"If you're looking for prophets," he said, "we know where to find them. Some of them, at least. They're up in the hills, near the Run-Away Man. Gran likes to keep all her monsters close."

DEATH WASN'T complicated when you were a wolf.

A hole to bury the body and a howl to see the spirit through to the Wild. That was all the dead needed or the living wanted. The Pack had thought the Old Man sentimental when he put a marker on the twins' ma's grave.

Danny wasn't a wolf.

He'd lived in the human world, loved humans, and even nearly convinced himself he was one of them. Maybe he'd learned to grieve like them too.

Someone had washed the blood off Kath's face and wrapped her loosely in a white sheet that was now smeared with streaks of crimson. It ended at her collarbones and left the raw gash in her throat exposed, enough flesh scooped out to reveal tendons and bone.

Danny took a corner of the sheet and pulled it up to her chin. His hand, the knuckles split and bleeding, was steady, but he flinched away from touching cold skin.

"What do you want to do?" Jack asked. "About the body."

"Burn her," Danny said flatly, the words clipped off between his teeth. It sounded too hard for Danny, but Jack bit his tongue on the disagreement. Then Danny relented enough to look at him. "If we lose—"

"We won't."

"We might," Danny contradicted him. "And if we do, I won't have some prophet walking around in my mam's skin. Burn her. It's just meat now. She's gone."

Jack crossed his arms. He'd changed into jeans—his own—and dragged on a T-shirt. For once he felt like he might need a jacket. The cold in Kath's cottage was understandable—the fire in the hearth had gone out—but it felt deeper than that.

There were still bloodstains on the floor, and the odd hormone-and-saline pickle of amniotic fluid hung in the air.

"You don't want to say anything?" he asked. "I'll listen."

Danny shook his head. "Why? You probably knew her better than I did," he said. "I left. You stayed."

"She understood."

Danny smiled with a quick, dry quirk of his mouth. "No," he said. "She didn't. But I'm who she raised me to be, so I guess that was her own fault. Something else she wouldn't understand, Jack? Why we're wasting time with the dead when the bastard who did this is still alive."

The anger in his voice was flat and steady, as though it was here for the long haul. It left Jack uneasy, but he could hardly blame Danny for it. He was right to be angry, and this was a waste of time they couldn't spare.

It didn't mean it wasn't important.

"You should stay goodbye," he said.

"I never did before."

Danny headed for the door, but Jack caught him before he got there and pulled Danny into his arms. He cupped the back of Danny's head, curls springy against his palm, and pulled him down into a rough, hungry kiss. For a second. Danny was stiff in his arms, but then he shuddered and leaned into Jack. A wet, salty sob hitched between their lips—Jack would swallow that secret for him—and Danny wrapped his arms around Jack as though he were scared to let go. The edges of his glasses dug into Jack's cheekbones and eyebrow, the awkwardness of it familiar enough to be bittersweet.

Jack broke the kiss and rested his forehead against Danny's. He could feel Danny's breath, damp and ragged against his lips. He opened his mouth to say something, anything, and this time Danny pressed his mouth over Jack's in a hard "shut up" kiss. He touched Jack's cheek for a moment and then pulled away.

"Don't," he said. "Not now."

Jack could have protested that Danny didn't know what he was going to say, but Danny probably knew better than Jack did.

"I'm glad it wasn't you," he said anyhow. "I'm glad you were in my bed instead of here. Kath would be too."

Pain twisted Danny's face into a hard mask. "I could have done something. I could have—"

"Died," Jack finished for him. "Then I'd have killed us all. Instead we'll kill them and get Bron's baby back."

Danny shuddered. The full-body tremor wasn't a human expression. If he'd been in the dog's skin, his hackles would have gone up and his tail down. The same emotion was somehow conveyed without ears or tail to flag what he felt.

"I can't believe that," he said apologetically. "It's too hard. What if we're wrong?"

Jack nodded. "We'll kill Lachlan," he said. "And Rose. After that, we'll see. Say goodbye to Kath, she'll be worried about you."

He clapped Danny on the shoulder and went outside.

Outside, around a bonfire they'd lit to keep the chill of Winter from even *their* bones, the wolves were waiting… what were left of them, the ones that hadn't been murdered or suborned by the prophets. It was maybe two-thirds of the wolves that would have been at Da's heels, and some of them were dogs.

One of them—Jack glanced over the Pack until he found Nick's bony profile under his crest of dark hair—was a bird, and their enemy's next of kin.

"You can trust him," Gregor said from just behind his shoulder.

Jack didn't twitch. The two of them might not be at each other's throats openly anymore, but that didn't mean Jack didn't make it a point to know where his brother's teeth where. To be fair, Gregor would have been insulted otherwise.

"You would say that," Jack said. "You love him."

Out of the corner of his eye, he saw Gregor's smile—a quick, unaffected twitch of joy in the midst of all this. Jack remembered how *clean* it had felt to just hate his twin.

"I do," Gregor said. He still had enough sense to sound bemused by how ridiculous that was. "That doesn't mean I'm blind to him. I'm not you."

Jack snorted. He knew Danny's faults. They were just less major than being a prophet's spawn and a Sannock.

"If it comes down to it, will he put his… beak in her eye?" Jack asked.

It reassured him when Gregor took the time to think about the answer. "I won't let it come to that," Gregor said finally. "Nick doesn't need to live with killing someone he loved, and I have enough reasons to rip that bitch's throat out to justify calling dibs on her death."

Jack didn't know if that was a reassuring answer or not, but it was an answer, and it would have to do.

The wolves still waited. Some had already given in to the itch of the Wild and the moon hunt and pulled their fur on, chest high to the tallest man in the Pack. Their breath steamed between their fangs as they hung their tongues out and panted in anticipation of the run. Others hung on to the human skin that made it easier to nurse a grudge. A wolf understood the necessity behind wiping out a threat to the Pack, but humans were the ones who could enjoy it.

Jack took a deep breath—the anger of the Pack stung his throat like cinnamon, itchy and red—as he stepped forward.

"Tonight the full moon will rise, but for the first time in generations, we have fresh prey to hunt. Selene might be faithless and a fool, but the prophets are worse. They dripped lies in our ears and called it the catechism, they took our young like we were stock bred for slaughter, and they fed us poison meat rather than face a fair fight."

Tea would be more accurate, but it didn't have the same resonance.

The wolves groaned low in their chests, a thick noise that wasn't quite a howl. Not yet.

"No more prophets," Jack said. "If we kill them tonight, we'll howl a new catechism that they have no place in."

One of the wolves threw her head back, black-striped nose to the sky, and howled. It was a sharp and lonely noise, mournful in the way only wolf-song could be. Others scrambled to their feet or shed human skin for brindled fur and growled their support.

"What if we *don't* kill them?" someone asked. It was the strange dog—Kier, the one Ellie knew. Everyone turned in unison to look at him. He took a step back and then steadied himself to give Jack an almost challenging glare. "What then, Numitor?"

"Kier," Ellie said, her voice tight in her throat. She raised her hand and tightened her jaw when he glanced at her, a shorthanded "not now" that Jack recognized. What had she said, last night? *"It isn't easy to love a dog."*

She'd been wrong. It was. Jack couldn't imagine how *not* to love Danny.

"Then they'll have killed us, so what do we care?" Danny said as he stalked out of his childhood home, goodbyes apparently done with. "But I'll be fucked if they have *anything* of mine or my kin for a trophy."

He stalked over to the bonfire. It cast harsh red shadows across the soft planes of his face as he shoved his way through the gathered wolves. They gave way out of surprise that didn't have time to mature into affront. Danny shoved his hand into the flames and grabbed a thick, tarry chunk of wood. It shed a trail of sparks as he dragged it out, enough to singe the fur or clothes of anyone who crowded him, and the end of it flared hot and angry as the cold tried to dim it.

"If the gods want this to be the Prophets' Winter?" Danny yelled as he turned around. The wind picked up, prickly with ice and annoyance, and tried to steal the words out of Danny's mouth. He hunched his shoulders against the shove of it but held his ground. "Then fuck it, I'd rather let Surtr eat the world down to the bones than the prophets enjoy one bite of it."

He drew the torch back and threw it toward his house with a raw, wordless shout. It tumbled end over end, off-balance and not well suited to being a spear. Jack dodged back in case it landed on him and bumped into Gregor as he did the same.

The torch arched neatly through the door that Danny had left ajar. It hit the wooden floor and the little stone cottage ignited with a hungry whoosh of flame, as though it were built of dry tinder and oil instead of brick.

There was stunned silence for a minute, and then Hector shook it off as he took a quick step forward.

"Get buckets—"

"Leave it," Jack interrupted harshly. He glanced at Danny and then turned back to the Pack. He could feel the rightness settle into his bones, finally as certain of something as he'd been of the Wild's favor back in Durham. One way or another, the Pack was done here. "All of it. Take children, the injured, the old—anyone who can't put on fur to fight—and anything you want to keep. They'll go to Lochwinnoch and then south, with or without the rest of us. This? Let it burn."

Chapter Twenty-One—Danny

Old stone groaned like a living thing as it burned, and slate tiles snapped like bones as the flames reached them. Flames wriggled eager, bright fingers through dried-out mortar and tapped at glass windows that warped as they melted in slow motion.

The walls would still be standing when the fire finally guttered out—centuries took more than one disaster to wipe away—but no one would mistake this for safe shelter again.

In the middle of the conflagration, the Old Man's farmhouse squatted resentfully, ice still caked on the roof and walls as though the winter had retreated there for its last stand.

Danny watched it burn from the edge of the lake, flames reflected dim and strange in the dark water, and tried to feel… something. It seemed like he should. He'd never belonged here, but he'd spent more time not fitting in here than he had anywhere else. There was also the fact that his mam's ashes were mixed in with the sparks and smoke that rose, black as an eel, against the storm-white sky.

If there was anything, he didn't have time to feel it. There was a hollow, black pit in his gut that opened when he walked into the slaughterhouse that had been his mam's kitchen, and it ate everything—grief, anger, satisfaction. It flashed through him and then dropped like a stone, just like his heart had done as the door creaked open until it caught on Bron's arm.

He'd known something was wrong. It had dragged him out of the warm, Jack-musky nest of blankets and out into the cold—an itch in his hackles, a ghost of a scent that woke a snarl in the back of his throat, and gut instinct.

Not this.

It was like something popped as he crossed the threshold, a thin film that had blocked the hot salted-penny stink of blood that washed over Danny. He saw his mam first, sprawled on the ground with empty eyes and a ripped-open throat. She hadn't died easily. There was blood on her fingers, bruises on her knuckles. Bron lay curled on her side nearby, in a puddle of wet red blood that spread slow and treacly over the tiles.

The kitchen should have smelled like beeswax and family, his mother and his sister. Instead it just smelled like meat. Danny's knees hit the floor before he realized he was on his way down, and his throat felt raw as an awful, hurt whine clawed out of him.

Then Bron's heart tried to beat—a ragged creak of noise—and all that pain just slid into the hole.

It wouldn't last.

Danny knew that. He'd dealt with enough bereaved students back in Durham—mostly dead pets, sometimes a grandparent, and the occasional visit from grave-faced cops with bad news about closer relatives—to know that. The hollow was to help him cope *right now*. Once this was over, it would collapse in on itself and he'd have to sink or swim with what he had left.

Not yet, though.

Danny dragged his eyes away from the fire and slogged through the snow to where the kids and the old wolves waited. Bron was laid out on a makeshift stretcher, strapped down with sheets twisted into ropes and with blankets piled on top of her. Despite the layers, she trembled hard enough to make her teeth chatter. Her eyes moved restlessly under her bruised lids, and soft whimpers scraped at the back of her throat.

His scrappy, pain-in-the-ass little sister. She'd never needed him for anything, and if they made it out of this, she'd deny she ever had. Danny bent over and kissed her forehead under the stringy tangle of her curls. Her skin was hot and dry under his lips, slick with metal-bitter salt.

"I'll give them a kick in the throat before I kill them, just for you," he promised. Then he looked up at Millie. "If we don't come back, head down the coast to Girvan. We left people there that have no love for the prophets."

Millie scowled. Her arm was still broken, but she had a terrier's heart. It would take more than being on three legs to truly cow her.

"We're part of the Pack too," she said. "If you're going to fight, we should fight with you. It's the Wolf Winter. It's Ragnarok. There aren't any noncombatants anymore."

Danny tucked the blankets in more securely around Bron's shoulders. Her bones felt so *thin* under his fingers, and she seemed so small. It frightened him a little how delicate she was without her horrible personality to buoy her up.

"We'll fight now," he said. "And if we lose, you fight later. Bron will make sure of that. Once she's back on her feet, she'll drag you all up into the Highlands by the scruffs."

Millie didn't quite laugh, but her face softened for a second.

"I'll take care of her," she promised finally, "whether she likes it or not. Are you sure the Sannock shouldn't come with us? He's a doctor. If something happens, if she doesn't heal…."

Danny pushed himself up. He could have corrected Milly about Nick being Sannock, but him being a god wouldn't slice the suspicion out of her voice. It shouldn't either. All the evidence was that Nick was a good man—a moral one, despite his taste in company for his head and his bed—so he'd understand why no one Rose had crossed trusted in that.

"We need him," he said. "He knows where the prophets are holed up. When Bron wakes up, tell her… tell her I love her."

That would piss her off.

Danny gave a last, stiff nod to Millie and then headed over to the waiting hunters. Most of them had pulled their skins on already, dire wolves so massive they tricked the eye into scaling them down. A few of them waited on him.

Danny stripped his—Jack's—sweater off and kicked his unlaced boots off as he walked. Snow crunched between his toes and stabbed cold needles under his toenails and down to his marrow. He shivered as he stopped to push his trousers down and hop out of them.

"That was a good show," Gregor said. "After all those years you didn't believe in gods or prophecy."

"I don't know what I believe in anymore," Danny said. "Except I didn't want to see Rose look at me from my mam's wolf. After that, it was all Jack."

"You don't think you called Surtr down?" Gregor asked. He pointed with his chin toward the fire. "That he's not there, wallowing in the embers? Do you think the Winter and the Wild would let it burn otherwise?"

"It's a fire," Danny said. "That's what it does."

Except…. Danny's fingers still smelled of the potion he'd doused the kitchen in. He knew why the fire had caught there, ignited as the flames hit the sharp, lighter-than-air stink of ethanol. The rest of the houses shouldn't have burned so easily, but they had.

He scrubbed both hands through his hair to drag it back from his face, his fingers unblistered despite the fact he'd reached into the fire.

"They went north when they left," he said. The reminder of what had happened steadied him, and the pit in his chest dropped to his heels like an anchor. "I saw the tracks before I was dragged away."

James, who'd also hung on to his human skin, crossed his arms. "So we follow a dog on the hunt now?" he asked.

Danny shrugged. "Not my fault you can't keep pace with me," he said. "If you don't want to be at my heels, run faster."

"Enough," Jack snapped as he grabbed the nape of Danny's neck in hard fingers. "Don't goad, Danny-dog. Your grief only gets you so much leeway."

James wrinkled his lips back from his teeth, far enough to show gum, and opened his mouth to say something. It was going to be awful; Danny could see that in the greasy satisfaction that floated in James's eyes, and he tensed, ready to respond.

"The same goes for you, James," Jack snapped as he jabbed a finger at the big man. "If you can't bite your fucking tongue, go join the prophets and lick a god's toes."

It looked like James wasn't going to back down. Danny leaned against the leash of Jack's hand on his scruff, almost eager for the fight. Before it could break out, Nick interrupted them sharply.

"You're not following a dog," Nick said. He looked more like a crow now, even when he was human. Danny didn't know if that was new or if exhaustion had just ground Nick down to bird-sharp bones and a beak of a nose. "But you need to chase a bird."

He hunched his shoulders, lifted his arms, and shifted to feathers in the middle of the gesture. His clothes dropped to the snow—Danny, his balls tight and resentful from the cold, envied the ease of that—and the crow slapped the air with wide black wings as it took flight. One of the younger wolves crouched, haunches tight under pale fur as he got ready to spring.

Ellie, ruddy and lean, snapped at the young hunter's nose to get him to flinch and back down.

This bird wasn't prey. Not tonight.

The crow cawed mockery down at them as the wind caught under its wings and tossed it skyward. Its cruciform shadow spread over the snow like an inkblot as it briefly spun on a wing tip and then flew north.

Jack tightened his fingers on Danny's scruff and pulled him over and down. The brush of his mouth, the cold-intense taste of him when he kissed Jack was so familiar it hurt. Danny wanted to wrap Jack around himself, to lose his grief in the hard muscles and warmth of him.

"Behave," Jack chided as he stepped back. "It's not the time."

He was right. Danny let all that want fall into the pit, the emptiness it left easier to navigate, and stepped back to give Jack room as he shed his human skin. The wolf shook itself, all tawny fur and heavy muscle, and snorted impatiently at Danny.

Time to go.

Maybe this time, Danny thought wearily as he took his glasses off and bent down to set them on top of his jeans, he'd just stay in the dog's coat. It had terrified him once, the thought of losing himself to the soft-edged, simpler world of his other shape. Right now it felt like it would be… easy. He pulled the dog up out of his bones before the Wild took the choice from him.

The dog shook itself briskly, nose to tail, to settle its flesh *right* on its bones. It could feel the ache of grief in its chest—a dull pressure that pushed against the keel of its breastbone—and in the pinch of muscles that clamped its tail and pinned its ears.

It could taste Danny's grief on the air, complex with notes of resentment and old, old pain, and the bright, clean red of blood teased at its nose.

Jack bumped against the dog's shoulder, hard enough to stagger the lanky dog and jar it out of its misery.

The pain was in the past. It hurt, but it was already done, like a tail caught in a door or a tooth cracked on bone, and nothing would help it. It wouldn't change if the dog worried at it.

Only Gregor was still in his human skin now. The dog could smell the *lack* on him, the thin edge of a scent that was meant to be layered over musk and fur. But he still smelled like a predator, and the dog grumbled a low-in-the-chest growl at him as Gregor buried his hand in Jack's ruff.

"We don't let her walk away again," Gregor said quietly. His hatred was yellow and bitter, like something stale left under a rock. "She dies or we do."

Jack snarled his agreement with a short roll of noise in his throat and stepped away from Gregor. The sun hadn't set yet, but the moon had already crawled up into the sky. It hung low and faded against the blanched-out horizon.

If the goddess was in it, she'd have a long night ahead of her.

Ahead of them, almost lost in the gray, the bird shrieked impatiently. Jack threw his head back and answered, the hollow, mournful bell of his howl sharp as it pierced the crackle of the fire and the breathing of the wolves.

The other wolves joined in as they scrambled to their feet and jostled eagerly for position, shoulders and hips pushed together. Only Gregor stayed quiet, his jaw clenched against the sound. The dog felt the urge tug at its stomach, but it died to a creak of a groan before it could get past tongue and teeth.

It wasn't in a dog's nature to hold a grudge, but beat one long enough and it would learn.

Gregor was right. Rose and the prophets needed to die tonight, and the dog didn't see any reason to warn her ahead of time.

Jack let the howl trail to silence and took off after the bird's shadow. He forged his way through the snow, the rest of the Pack on his heels. Gregor loped along next to them, the ground-devouring strides of his long legs able to keep pace with the Pack for now.

The dog hung back out of habit. Its place had always been at the back of the Pack, bottom of the pecking order, and last to get the pickings from the kill, even if it could outrun most of the wolves in a pinch, over a short distance at least.

THE BIRD flew, and the wolves followed.

The dog could tell they were on the right track. Tom and Lachlan couldn't afford to linger in the Wild. It took babies, and this one didn't even have a mother's flesh to keep it anchored. They staggered across the countryside in jolts and starts. Every mile or so, Danny would catch the thin, antiseptic scent of amniotic fluid where it had dripped on the snow. Drops of blood stained the snow like gory breadcrumbs, still wet and running despite what had passed since their murder.

The core of Danny that the dog hung on to thought bleakly about curses, but it was more likely to be the way the Wild was twisted. Not as much time had passed for the killers.

Curse or not, it was useful.

Under it all, the stink of Tom's guilt and fear hung in the air in thin gray strands that clung like cobwebs to the snow. The weakness of it made the dog's hackles go up from his ears to the base of his tail, stiff with anger. It was too little, too late. Tom could salt the Highlands from here to John O'Groats, and the dog's mam wouldn't be any less dead.

The spike of emotion hit the dog like a hammer hit a bell. It stumbled briefly over its own feet as dog and Danny jostled for space. The dog caught its balance as one of the other wolves, frost crusted heavily on its fur, turned to snap at him. Jagged white teeth clicked shut just in front of his nose. The dog snarled back. There was a difference between being at the bottom of the pack and being a punching bag. It was a thin, hard-defended line.

It ended the same way it always did. The aggression rippled outward—a growl, a shoulder block hard enough to jar, fur in the snow—and then faded before it reached the high-ranked wolves. They settled down and found a steady pace again.

The Wild faded in and out around them, a lungful of eerily clean air—like it had never known the inside of anything's lungs—and pocks of salt-melt in the snow. Ahead of them the storm brewed like a wall of gray, snow and hail tangled around each other as it hammered the world *thin* to make way for something older.

It was a landscape the dog had run through all his life, but in a month, he doubted he could find a landmark he'd recognize.

Ahead of them, the bird suddenly pitched out of the sky. Dead, the dog assumed at first, but then black wings snapped out and it pulled out of the dive just before it hit a frost-limned thicket of gorse.

A second later something cracked, a harsh pop and echo of noise, and the bird squawked its objection as it banked hard to the side. A handful of feathers, so black they looked like shadows, tore free of its wing and floated to the snow.

"Nick!" Gregor yelled.

He split away from the Pack and broke into a dead run across. The wolves tangled themselves up as they tried to decide if that made him something to follow or something to chase.

The dog had never liked him, but right now it knew they were on the same side. It pushed through the wall of muscle and fur and raced after Gregor with a burst of speed that left the wolves in his wake.

The noise barked again—a gun, the dog realized as it laid ringing ears flat. Gregor had already dodged to the side, and Danny was always faster than people expected a huge, dark wolfhound to be. Something clipped his ear, a sharp pinch, but he'd had worse.

He threw himself into the gorse. Sharp branches scraped at him and plucked at his back, but that was what the dense coat of hair was for. There were tufts of hair left caught on the thorns, but Danny ignored it as he wriggled deeper.

The man sprawled on his stomach in the damp ruins of an old hide, gun propped up on a rock in front of him. An acrid, dry smell leached from his pores and clung to the ragged suit he was wearing.

"Fucking animals," the man spat through split, dry lips as he reared back.

He swung his gun like a club. The barrel of it caught the dog over the head, the metal hot enough to scorch his skin through the thin hair around his ears. It ignored the sting of pain and sank its teeth into the man's arm, deep enough that fabric and down gave way to meat and blood. The man yelped and let go of his gun. He groped down at his belt with his free hand, but it was cold, and he was clumsy.

The dog got his feet braced on the ground and dragged the man out of his makeshift hunter's blind, close enough for Gregor to reach in and grab him by the collar. A blade flashed in the man's hand as he finally got the knife out of his belt. The hooked tip of it opened Gregor's arm from wrist to elbow, his blood spice and metal on the air. Then Gregor twisted it out of the man's hand. Finger bones popped with that distinctive chicken-wing sound, but the man just cursed and spat at Gregor.

Not quite a man, the dog saw, not anymore. His bones were loose under his skin, halfway through a decision of where to set, and his eyes were full of dry, brittle temper, like the townsfolk Rose had turned to her purpose, the parts of them that cared scarred over from the poison she fed them.

Gregor shook the man like a terrier with a rat and then roughly frisked him. He came up with another gun—it was tossed away into the snow—and a cheap flask that the man grabbed for with his broken hand.

"One of Rose's cult," Gregor said with disgust. He dropped the man to the ground and emptied the liquid onto the snow. It bubbled and stained the white flakes with a greasy, iridescent film. "Drunk on god piss."

The man laughed and bared bloody teeth. "You're fucking monsters," he said. "Animals. Beasts."

Gregor shrugged. "We know."

He coldcocked the man and tossed him aside to be sniffed at by the rest of the Pack. Then he reached into the thicket for the gun. The dog laid his ringing ears back and doubted *that* could end well. Gregor slung the weapon over his shoulder and turned to search the sky. The bird dropped out of it, battered by the wind, and landed awkwardly in the snow. A flap, a hop, and its feathers peeled away like shadows as Nick stood up. The pale, dark-haired man wrapped his arms around himself, although he didn't shiver. It was habit—an old scar stitched over his stomach, an untidy cord of knotted tissue.

"Down there," he said as he pointed with his chin. "It's open."

"A trap?"

Nick frowned and cocked his head to the side. His eyes flickered as though he could see more than wolves and snow. "I don't think so," he said. "They're getting ready for something."

There was a pause as Jack and Gregor traded a look with matched green eyes. Then Jack flicked his ear, and Gregor nodded. They led the way down the hill, and the wolves followed. The dog sniffed the man, not sure what he thought he'd smell, and then jogged after the last wolf's tail to catch up.

Ice-crusted nets were hung over the rocks that disguised the entrance to the bunker, heavy and layered to disguise the deeply set metal door. Even half open, the stink of confined human and the agitation of hot, *infected meat* thick in the air, it was hard to see. The wolves milled around outside, wary and nervous, but then slunk in on slow, wary paws.

The dog didn't follow. Something in the air got its attention. It lifted its nose, snorted out snow, and tasted the air. It was nothing, but the ghost of it made the hackles on the dog's neck itch. A nervous growl tickled the dog's throat, and the big wolf that smelled of grief rounded on him with a snarl meant to quell him.

The dog scrambled back, ears flat, but once the wolf's attention was back on Jack, it scrambled to its feet.

It had hunted on its own for years, in narrow streets that smelled of a hundred things on a good night. Maybe it wasn't a wolf, but it could pick out a fox's spoor through curried goat, old piss, and the rainbow dizziness of spilled petrol. Sometimes it knew to trust its nose even if it didn't know why.

Jack was busy with his brother and the bird. The other wolves would wait on them. The dog shuffled slowly backward, snow matted in shaggy fur until it was out of the line of sight. Then it scrambled to its feet and cast about until instinct tugged it forward.

It was off the track they'd followed. The dog glanced back, and it had already lost sight of the rest of the Pack. It didn't matter. Sound carried farther, and it didn't take long to howl.

The ripe green stink of decomposition shimmered around the base of a tree, and the faded scent prints of humans hung like grease stains in the air.

Somewhere in the back of its mind, the dog felt Danny worry, but the humans weren't the dog's problem. They hadn't hurt it.

Not yet.

The dog twitched its ear to shed that thought and plowed through the nonrelevant scents. It could almost catch the cobweb smell it was after—a damp, sharp smell like rusted metal. Like….

The connection clicked into place, and the dog stopped dead in its tracks. It stood frozen ankle-deep in the snow, and a growl rumbled up from its stomach to the back of its throat.

Lachlan.

When it was younger, the dog had good reason to be aware of Lachlan's stink. It made it easier to stay out of his way, especially when he smelled of blood and the sticky satisfaction of someone else's pain.

A quiver trembled through the dog's haunches as it tried to decide what to do. Chase the trail now it had the scent hooked in its nose, or go back and try to convince the wolves to go with it?

Safer to go back. Wolves hunted in a pack for a reason. The dog took a step back but hesitated. They might not believe him. He was a dog. Even a Sannock was more tied to the Wild than him. The dog didn't really understand why that mattered—a nose was a nose—but it did.

Jack might be able to convince them, but… would he?

That wasn't the dog's thought, but it knew that the human side of it understood that sort of thing better. So it forged forward through the snow after the smell of shed blood and Lachlan. The wind picked up as the Wild grew stronger, like a hand on the dog's ruff to urge him forward.

"Please." The word was whined in a strangled, snot-filled voice from over a low rise. The dog flicked its ear as it tried to decide if that was Tom's voice. "I did what I was told. I was a good dog. That's what she wanted. She *said* that if we were good dogs, the gods would keep us."

"She lied." That was definitely Lachlan, his Highlands brogue thicker than normal on his words. "She does that. To you. To me. Worse for you, though, I suppose."

He sounded drunk, but the edges of the word were still crisp. The dog pulled its lips back from its teeth in a silent snarl as it cast around the landscape. There was no cover worth the name, just a few scrubby patches of heather that sagged under the weight of the snow and a scattering of stones. The dog stalked, stiff-legged and slung low, up and around the rise. The steady drone of the wind disguised the soft crunch of his paws on the snow as he climbed. He came up behind the two murderers, barely out of their line of sight.

The baby wasn't there, and it looked like they weren't allies anymore.

Tom lay on the bloody ground, naked and blanched with the cold. His arms and legs lay at unnatural angles, jerked roughly loose from where they'd been moored in the joints, and his fingers and toes looked gray. Stiff. His ribs and chest were deformed, the bones lumpy and misshapen under red-blotched skin.

The dog felt a cold satisfaction that felt alien. It laid its ears flat to its skull and pushed the Danny-feeling back down under the surface. Tom was no threat now, and that was good, but gloating was a human thing.

Down below, Lachlan tilted his head up to the sky. "The bitch…. *Selene*," Lachlan corrected himself self-consciously, "will be in her chariot soon. You'll turn then, like it or not. Why drag this out?"

Tom squirmed on the snow as he tried to push himself back on ruined elbows. He wouldn't have gotten far, but Lachlan bent down to grab his ankle and drag him back. Tom's leg stretched in a way that a human leg wasn't meant to, and he screamed.

Tears dripped down his face. His blind eye was flushed pink with broken blood vessels.

"I did everything she asked," he said. A sob retched out of him. "I helped you kill Kath. I held Bron down. They'd never done owt to me. They'd been kind, but I did for *her*."

"You *hated* them for being kind," Lachlan spat. "And she appreciates your service, but now we need one thing from you."

"Why?" Tom begged, his voice breaking.

"You were the only dog stupid enough to think you'd ever matter," Lachlan said. He booted Tom in the side with a slippery crunch of already damaged bone. The impact rolled Tom onto his side. "And she needs one more skin."

As Tom flopped back onto his side, he saw the dog midslink down the hill. His face twisted with self-hatred, but he still opened his mouth.

"Take him, then." He waved his blistered hand in the dog's direction. "Let me go. I won't tell her."

Once a traitor.

The dog bolted down the hill. Long straps of muscle in its back legs and hips burned with the quick flare of exertion. Snow slipped and stones slid underfoot, but the dog had already shifted his footing before it could lose balance.

It had never won a fight with Lachlan. Lachlan had never *enjoyed* his win, but that had never gotten the dog back on its feet faster. It didn't matter. The past was gone, and the future hadn't happened to it yet. All that mattered was the wind in the dog's ears as it lunged, and the howl that escaped Lachlan as the not-quite-wolf-sized hound slammed into him.

The dog tore at Lachlan's throat, the wolf's blood sickly sweet as it spilled, until its teeth hooked around his collarbone. Then it shook itself like a terrier with an oversized rat.

Bone snapped, and Lachlan howled again. He managed to grab hold of the dog's scruff and toss him toward a nearby rock. The dog hit the stone, felt the shock pop of its ribs as they gave, and then nothing as it slid to the ground.

Its legs didn't want to work. Pain radiated from between its shoulder blades up into its skull.

"Fine," Lachlan snarled. His T-shirt hung in rags where the dog had torn it. Something was wrong until the shreds of cotton, but the dog couldn't tell what. "Have it your way. I've wanted to cut the fucking pride out of you for years."

He reached behind him and pulled a knife out of his waistband. Blood was scabbed along the worn blade, clotted around the handle. The dog could still smell the ash wood that stained the old ritual blade under that. It had been in Kath's kitchen. Danny had seen it.

The dog tried to move again. This time its legs cooperated, or tried to, although they were still numb and clumsy. Pain stitched down its spine to its toes as it scrambled to its feet. Blood—its own? Lachlan's?—splattered from its mouth as it panted.

"I'd rather you were human for this," Lachlan said. "I'd make you beg for all the times you shamed me."

It had been a lot of times. The dog shook its head despite the pain and crouched down. Lachlan was predictable. He always went for the kick to the ribs before he went for the throat.

Blood-smeared teeth flashed in a tight grin as Lachlan lunged forward and slashed the knife across the dog's face. It caught under its lip and ripped up to its ear in an uneven gash. The edge might have caught the dog's eye too on the way through, but it was hard to tell as a welter of blood filled its vision on that side.

It burned with an itch that stitched back from the injury, into its skull. The last time it hurt like this, it had stuck its head into a nettle patch. The dog yelped at the pain and latched on to Lachlan's wrist before he could slice at it again. Its fangs slid between the bones, sawed at the tight hawsers of tendons, and the knife slid from suddenly boneless fingers and dropped into kicked-up, turned-over snow.

Lachlan swore and punched the dog in the side of the head, hard enough that it couldn't see at all for a second. It hung on, jaws locked and growl strangled by its grip, and Lachlan hit it again. He wrenched backward, and the dog let go. Lachlan sprawled back on his ass in the snow and over Tom's legs as the dog screamed and Danny pushed himself to his feet.

He sucked in a ragged breath of cold air and regretted it. The cold pinched at the raw cut on his face sent jabs of pain through exposed teeth. It would heal, Danny reminded himself as he reached up to push the flap of skin back into place with the back of his wrist… eventually.

The dog felt too big under his skin as the Wild crested with the moon on the horizon. Danny could feel his bones creak with the need to change, the first dim warning of the pain that resistance could bring.

He'd done that once—his first month at university, hunched in the corner of his room as his bones turned to hot milk and he felt hair grow on the *inside* of his skin while he tried to stay human. But this time he hoped the Wild would be more tolerant. It had helped him once against the prophets.

"Where's the baby?" Danny asked.

Lachlan propped himself on his elbow. The T-shirt hung by the seam on his shoulder, and Danny could see what had looked wrong about Lachlan's torso. It had been flayed, strips of ginger, freckled flesh peeled off and the holes patched with…. Jack. The scraped-thin rashers of skin were marked with tattooed lines and deep worked dots that Danny remembered from when they were fresh and still sweated ink.

Danny recoiled in unexpected disgust, and Lachlan flushed as he dragged the rags of his shirt back up to cover the patchwork mess he'd been made into.

"Don't look at me like that," Lachlan spat as he scrambled to his feet. "She gave me his rank, his strength. Don't pretend you wouldn't have taken that deal if she'd told you she could make you into a wolf."

"You were already a wolf," Danny said.

"Not enough of one," Lachlan said. "I was never good enough until she came. Then they all bowed, didn't they? Your ma."

"Fuck she did." Danny's mouth was dry, his lips like leather, and he didn't know if it was the pulse of poison under his face or just anger. "And I don't care why you did it, Lachlan. If you wanted to make excuses, you should have done it before you had my sister's blood under your nails."

Lachlan looked at his fingers and shrugged. "That could be anyone's."

"What did you do with the baby?"

"I gave it to her," Lachlan said as he lunged forward. He grabbed for Danny with both clawed hands, and Danny ducked under them and scrambled between Lachlan's legs. He scraped through the snow as he lurched back to his feet. Lachlan spun around and paused at the sight of the knife clutched in Danny's hand. Then he shrugged it off. "That won't help you. Or Gregor's bastard. You know it wouldn't have lived anyhow, right? I could tell that when I pulled it out of your sister. It was made wrong, like that other brat of his."

"That's not what I asked," Danny said.

"Why should I tell you anything?" Hair prickled over Lachlan's chest as the Wild tried to shift him around Jack's stolen skin. Lachlan grimaced and spat into the stained snow. Tom whined and rolled onto his side as he felt the shift pull at him.

Danny feinted forward. Despite his stolen skin and his brave words, Lachlan flinched. At the last second, Danny veered to the side and stooped over Tom's body. He grabbed a handful of tangled, unwashed hair, yanked his head back, and cut his throat.

Bile scalded the back of Danny's throat as hot blood spilled over his fingers, and he had to choke back a retch. It shouldn't have bothered him—no matter how pathetic Tom was right now, he'd helped kill Kath—but it did.

Tom stared at him, face slack with shock as his mind tried to catch up with his body, and then his lips moved jerkily.

"I'm… sorry," he croaked out. A tear slid out of the corner of his eye and dribbled back into his hair. "I just… I wanted…."

There was no pleasure in Tom's death, but Danny didn't care about his regret. He dropped Tom's head back into the snow to let him bleed out and backed away.

"Where you going to get her a dog skin now?" Danny asked.

His voice sounded weird around the hot pressure in his face. The skin felt numb and his skull weirdly soft. He still couldn't see out of that eye. It gave him something to distract him from the dog as it squirmed around in his bones.

Lachlan shrugged. "You," he said. "What? You think I'm not going pull the skin off your bones just 'cause I knew you when we were kids. That just makes it better."

Danny flipped the knife in his hand and pressed the point against his throat. He could feel it scratch the skin as his heart thumped.

"Where are you going to get a skin?" he repeated.

Lachlan laughed. "So you'll kill yourself to stop me killing you? Not much of a threat."

"So you have to go back to your bitch prophet empty-handed?" Danny asked. "Sure. What do I have to lose, Lachlan?"

Confusion creased Lachlan's face, and he rocked uncomfortably on the balls of his feet. He stepped forward, and Danny dug the knife into his skin. Now both sides of his face pulsed unhappily, and he could feel the burn in his blood. He inhaled raggedly through his nose as Lachlan jumped back.

"What's to stop you, then?" Lachlan demanded. "You'd just fucking die to spite me."

Danny grinned at him. It hurt his face, and one side of his mouth didn't want to cooperate.

"I'll have hope," he said, "and I only lie down to die when there's no point in fighting anymore."

"Hope?" Lachlan shuddered, and his face twisted around itself in a moment of unexpected self-loathing. He scratched at his chest and dug his fingers into the raw, tender spans of Jack's skin. "I gave your sister's brat to Rose. She's going to feed it to that abomination she's growing in her stomach. To my son, so he can be strong and worthy."

"Where is she?" Danny asked. His voice cracked with the need to know. "Is she at the bunker?"

"She was," Lachlan said almost absently. "She's done with them, but she's still got to finish him. You'll all show the throat to him then."

Danny lowered the knife from his throat. His hand had started to shake anyhow, his fingers stiff and clumsy. Lachlan relaxed slightly at the sight and smirked.

"Ready to fight, then?" he asked. "One last time?"

"Go fuck yourself," Danny said and threw the knife.

It wasn't a great throw—the knife wobbled end over end in a weak arc—but it was good enough. Danny let the dog out as Lachlan's attention shifted to the blade, and he bolted at the still-two-legged wolf. He dodged at the last second, and Lachlan grabbed at the empty air where he expected the dog to be.

The dog *hurt*, but it ran anyhow. Long legs boosted it through the now-thick snowfall in a brutal gallop that ate up the ground. Each time its paws hit the ground, pain jarred up through its bones to its ears and its blood felt too hot. But it left Lachlan behind, curses tossed after it into the dark.

"Run, then," Lachlan yelled. He sounded afraid. "It's too late for the brat! It's too late for all you fuckers. She won't stop now, and you'll all bend the neck."

Chapter Twenty-Two—Gregor

BLOOD SPLASHED the institutionally gray walls as Gregor used the butt of his stolen gun to hammer at the thick-domed skull of a monster's head until it went limp. The impact jarred up his arm into his shoulder, and there was something viscerally satisfying about it. He had to force himself to stop, sweat itchy on the back of his neck and his mouth dry as he panted raggedly.

The prophet's handmade wolves smelled *wrong* in that way that made Gregor want to scrape them out of existence. They healed efficiently enough that they needed to be.

Sprawled out on the floor in a puddle of its own blood and liquids, the half-made monster twitched as its body tried to string itself back together. Gregor put his boot down on the back of its neck and bent down to grab the gray strings of hair it had left. One sharp yank popped the spine and it went limp. The acrid smell of death seeped out of its pores.

He straightened up and tried not to groan. His leg burned with each step and teased his nose with the sour smell of the wound. More than that, he was *tired*. His muscles ached from the run, from the fight, and his joints felt gritty.

It wasn't new. This was life without a wolf. Like any other pain, it was something to endure and ignore. But he'd already been hurt and sore when they set the Old Man's house on fire, already down to the fumes of what he had left. Now he could feel himself slow down, the strength sapped from his muscles as he fought. The moon hung fat and smug in the sky outside, and his gut ached as the Wild soured and clotted where the wolf should be.

His brother's dog was probably more use in a fight. At least Danny had a lifetime to get used to his limitations. Gregor closed his eyes for long enough to take a deep breath and think about giving up. It would be easy, but the cobweb idea of it shriveled to nothing under the weight of obligation.

And guilt.

He didn't love the baby the fucking prophets had cut out of Bron. It wasn't like his daughter—his first dead child—whose heartbeat he'd listened to through her ma's belly. Gregor had time with her to let his sticky satisfaction at being the first to sire a child turn into something… better. He'd never found it easy. Love. Except with Nick.

Bron's child had doorstepped him. It felt like a trap, the universe's pitfall if Gregor let his heart soften. But it was still *his*, and that was why Rose had sent her curs to cut the wee thing out of its ma's stomach. He owed it to the child and to Bron to take it home.

Gregor spat on the corpse at his feet and limped away from it. His own limitations would have to wait. Today wasn't the day to accept them. He pushed into a loping run and followed the sound of fighting down.

It was always down.

The bunker was a rabbit warren of sunken concrete boxes connected by a plumber's nightmare of pipes and junctions. Scents stuck like oil to the cheap paints that plastered the walls, sound bounced off high ceilings and doubled back on itself, and the open doors had let Winter in. The floors were slippery with a thin rime of frost, and the vents rattled and groaned as they were blocked with ice.

Halfway down the tunnel, Jack was thrown out of a door and bounced off a wall. The huge wolf grunted at impact as it landed on the ground, green eyes unfocused as Jack tried to remember how to breathe. Gregor backed up and leaned against the door frame to wait.

His breath was tight in his throat, like it still needed to pant, but he kept it steady.

The monster shouldered through the doorway, clumsy on thick-knuckled paws. A fat round skull swelled out of a puff of dandelion-white hair that clung to the back of its head and to the ends of its stretched-out, flopped-over hound ears. Its skin was furrowed in thick, scaled creases down the back of its neck and into the grotesque hump of his shoulders. The pads of fat and muscle had been ripped open, and strips of tallow-laced raw meat hung from its back as it swaggered forward.

It was one of the ones that Rose had brought with her, hardened as they dragged it up along the coastline. The frantic elasticity of the first change had faded, and its shape had set like a bone. It made it easier to kill—not easy, but easier—and harder to fight.

Jack staggered to his feet. One ear was torn, folded down against his skull, and blood was crusted around his nose. He dropped his head down, sharp shoulder blades hunch-raised and bloody ruff spiked out, and growled thin and high in his nose.

The monster wheezed out something, the sound half-strangled in the loose fat of its throat, and wrinkled liver-dark lips back like a chimp. It didn't have teeth, but ulcerated gums peeled back from a ridge of serrated chipped bone. Shreds of meat and hair were caught in the gaps and cracks.

It lurched forward, and Gregor raised the stolen gun in both hands and brought it down like a post-hole digger into stony ground. The barrel of the gun wasn't sharpened, but Jack had already split the calloused hide. All Gregor had to do was punch down through raw meat and hawser-thick spine. The monster shrieked and reared back… or tried to. Its forequarters were so thickly overmuscled that the scrawny back end—a drapery of loose, crepey skin hung from wasted thighs—couldn't quite lift it.

Gregor braced a foot against the thing's muscle-larded ribs and wrenched at the gun to twist it in the wound. Vertebrae cracked against the cast metal, and fresh blood welled up dark and red as veins split open.

The monster managed to twist around enough to fix Gregor with a pus-scabbed, milky-blue eye. Its tongue, cut to thin, cured-meat ribbons against the bony ridges on its gums, curled and fluttered.

"… it 'urts," it said mournfully.

"Good," Gregor said as he twisted the gun to drive it deeper.

It was a sham of a thing, repulsive despite its best efforts to find the shape of a wolf in a human's bones. Probably it hadn't volunteered. It just had the bad luck to survive the prophet's bite. Gregor didn't deny that; he just didn't care. Pity was a hobble in a fight. He didn't ask for it from anyone and wouldn't give it away either.

Anger twisted the monster's face up, deep, chafed wrinkles red and clotted with dry white pus, and it flung itself around it in a furious attempt to get hold of Gregor. He grabbed the exposed, bloody blade of its shoulder for balance, the surface rough against his fingertips, and hung on. His booted feet scraped over the floor as he dodged the stamp of the monster's thick, clubbed feet.

Around the swollen bulk of its chest, he could see Jack as his brother harried it to keep its attention. Jack took a chunk out of a forearm turned muscle-bound, bowed front leg and latched on to the end of its muzzle.

The monster rattled out a tea-kettle sound of pain and shook its head violently from side to side. It managed to lift Jack off his feet and flail him about until it smacked him down against the concrete. Jack's paws slid out from under him, and he went down hard. Without him to run interference, the monster turned its attention to Gregor. It twisted around to snap at him, but it couldn't reach.

"Just die," Gregor told it. "Do us all a favor."

Some sort of spite glittered in the thing's milky eye, and it shuffled around until it could slam Gregor into the wall. The bulk of it pinned him like a bug, and he felt his ribs creak as they started to give. His chest was so compressed he could hardly breathe, and what air he could suck in was rank with the reek of the thing. The monster grunted in satisfaction and shifted its weight so it could grind him against the wall.

Pain spread through Gregor like heat. His fingers slipped on the bloody gun, and gray bled through his vision as his focus narrowed down to the pressure in his chest.

A harsh caw snapped his attention back to the world around him, and he looked up as Nick dropped out of the rafters. Wide black wings snapped out, the edges of sleek feathers iridescent, and battered the monster's head as Nick croaked angrily at it. He dug long, thick talons into the creases that furrowed the thing's low brow and jabbed his thick, bone-white beak down viciously. Shreds of flesh peeled off the monster's face, and it forgot about Gregor.

It staggered away from Gregor and ducked to paw blindly at its head. The thick bone spurs that jutted from the backs of its wrists raked down Nick's wings and hooked in. It dragged Nick off its face and pinned him down to the floor. Nick shrieked and squirmed, blood flicked from the ends of his wings as he flapped, and the monster snarled down at him.

Gregor pushed himself off the wall and jumped onto the monster's back. He scrambled up the sweaty mound of it until he could grab a handful of the wiry mane that bristled around the back of the deformed skull. It cut into his fingers and stung like a nettle. The gun jutted out of the thing's back, canted to one side, but Gregor ignored it. He shoved his hand down into the raw wound. It was hot and wet, and the meat moved against Gregor's skin as it tried to heal around him.

He closed his fingers around the monster's spine. The vertebrae were thick as his fist and rough with chips and cracks where he'd battered it with the gun. Between them the spinal cord ran like a twisted root with a firm core under a pustule-caked, spongy layer.

Gregor grabbed it and yanked. It resisted for a moment and then split apart in his fingers. The reek that spilled out as the cord snapped made Gregor retch in disgust. If he thought the monsters couldn't smell any worse, he'd been wrong.

The monster moaned in pain and confusion as its legs went from under it. The huge, bloody bulk of it rolled over onto its side, and its eyes bulged as it choked to death on its own lungs. Before it could, Jack, balanced on three legs, took its throat out.

Nick scrambled back to his feet, flicked his wings to settle his fingers, and preened himself angrily. One wing hung awkwardly and stuck out at odd angles, the feathers broken.

It would heal.

"I didn't need help," Gregor said. The bird gave him a skeptical look out of one black, shiny eye and then swiveled its head to look at him out of the other, as though the view might be different. "And if I did, it took you long enough."

Nick shed his feathers and stood up. He looked unharmed, but the smell of his blood was ripe and sweet. Gregor took his shoulders and turned him around. Bloody red lines raked down his back from his bony shoulders to the curve of his ass.

"I'll heal," Nick said. He twisted his head around to check out the damage. "Even before the bird, I'd have healed."

He shouldn't have to, but Gregor was glad he would. The prophets had left enough scars on Nick. They didn't get to claim any more of him.

Gregor tightened his fingers. "Just be careful," he said. "I like all your bits the way they are."

The bird glanced at him through Nick's eyes, black and wicked. "Even me?"

He didn't fall in love with the carrion god. He fell in love with a sharp-nosed man with restless, gentle hands and a stubborn streak. But without the bird, Nick would have been laid in a cold grave under the Scottish stones.

"I put up with you," he said. Both of them grinned at that.

He stepped back and wiped his hands on his jeans. It didn't make him sleep any better, but at least it didn't feel like *his* stink so much.

"Did you find her?" Gregor asked. He watched Nick's expression settle into unhappy lines. The old tension worried with sharp fingers at the scars on Gregor's spirit. Under his skin the Wild slid uneasily in search of something to do. Nick had enough reasons to hate his grandmother, but reasons weren't always enough?

Nick shook his head. "No sign of her," he said. "The Pack hasn't cleared the whole compound yet, but… it feels too easy for Gran."

Every time Gregor breathed in, his chest ached in a dozen delicate fractures. His hands were red and chafed from contact with the sour innards of the monster. He wouldn't have said "easy," but he knew what Nick meant.

For all her flaws, Rose was a mean old Scottish wolf with a traitor's mind. If she didn't have anyone to torment, she'd make her own life difficult for practice.

"What about prophets?" Jack asked, his voice tight with the effort it took to pull his human skin back on. He crouched next to the dead monster, his forearm braced over his bare knee and his hair slicked to his scalp with blood. "I've seen monsters and madmen, but not one flayed hide."

Nick started to shake his head. He stopped midmotion, and his eyes flickered past Gregor's shoulder. The hair on the back of Gregor's neck prickled, but he knew that if he turned around, there'd be nothing there.

Gunfire rattled from farther down in the bunker, and a woman screamed and spat out profanities mixed in the howl of rage. Wolves snarled and yelped, the sounds distorted as they bounced off the thick walls and high ceilings. The need to move—or sit down and die—twisted at Gregor's guts.

"We don't have time to gossip with shades," he said. "Where's my child?"

The reminder made Nick's jaw tense as he refocused on Gregor. He swallowed and ignored the jab to his sore spot.

"They want to tell you something," Nick said. "They want something from you."

Gregor scowled and stepped away from the dead thing behind him. "From me?" he asked. "They can have anything but you."

"Not you," Nick said. He scratched the back of his neck and corrected himself. "Not *just* you."

"Then what?" Jack asked. He braced one hand on the wall as he pushed himself up. Even with his wolf and the hot pulse of the Wild, he held himself carefully. One leg wasn't quite ready to bear his weight. "What do they want?"

Nick blinked and his eyes shone with the bird's bright wickedness. "Permission."

It was obviously a trap. But—Gregor glanced at Jack and raised an eyebrow—it wasn't as though there were a lot of options. The monsters could be killed, but if they didn't find the prophets, then this was just another waypoint to the next atrocity.

"Fuck it," Jack said. "Tell them to go on. Do it. The Numitor gives his leave."

The flicker of anger on Nick's face caught Gregor off guard for a second. Then it recognized it wasn't Nick's expression.

"They don't need words," Nick said precisely. "They need you to let them back in, the same way you locked them out."

"That was Da."

Nick twitched and glanced irritably at something next to him. This time Gregor could almost see it too—a hit of soft, greasy flesh and dry scoops of old injuries where fillets had been carved from it—but he turned away. If he didn't have to look at the Sannock, he wouldn't. They'd killed Nick once, tried to kill Gregor, and he couldn't even blame them for it, since he saw the charnel house his kind had made of the Sannocks' last hiding place.

The things should still have tried harder at death. Whatever peace Nick had made with them, Gregor didn't share in it.

"They don't… understand the difference," Nick said. "So you're good enough. They want to be free, but the only way is the same way they left the world. Through a wolf. Any wolf."

Jack recoiled.

"The Pack would never agree," he said.

"They don't need to," Gregor said. He shrugged when Jack looked at him. "You're Numitor now. You speak for the Pack. If they don't like your decisions, maybe they shouldn't have been so quick to acclaim you."

Gregor managed to keep his voice steady, but despite everything, the words tasted like bile on his tongue. Acceptance he had—without a wolf he'd never lead the Pack—but that didn't mean he liked it.

"I can't do that," Jack said. He raked his hand through his hair, blood and scraps of skin matted into the curls. "They'd never forgive me. I might be Numitor, but I'd be the first with no wolves at my heels. No."

Nick tilted his head slightly. "If you want your help, then you will."

"We don't," Jack said. He spat on the bloody corpse of the old monster. "The prophets are here somewhere. We've torn down or burned every other lair they had. So we kill their monsters, and if we don't find the prophets, then we wall them up in here to starve. Seal the Wild to them, the same way they did the Sannock."

Nick took a deep breath, and it misted around his lips as he exhaled, as though the chill of winter had abruptly deepened.

"Last chance," he said, voice thick with the crow's rasp. "They won't ask again."

Three times. The old stories had the Sannock obsessed with rituals, with numbers and rules. If they said this was the last chance, it wasn't something they'd revoke.

"Will Danny forgive you?" Gregor interrupted Jack before he could refuse again. He slipped the emotional knife between Jack's ribs to find the tender part of his heart and then twisted. "If you let Rose get away again? After she tortured him and killed his ma? When she gutted his little sister like a fish and left her for him to find? If we don't kill Rose, he will or die trying."

For once Gregor didn't take any pleasure in the flash of frustrated anger that twisted Jack's face. They'd vied their whole lives to be Numitor, to be the one the Pack said was real and not the shadow. If Gregor were Jack, he would have tried to make the same choice.

But Gregor was just a man without a wolf or a child. He didn't have the right to understand his brother's hesitation.

Jack glared at him. "Since when do you care about Danny?' he asked. "Or who I value? If you want the Sannocks' help, Gregor, why don't you bend over for them?"

"I would," Gregor said. That might not be true, but what he said next was. "Except you're the Numitor. You're the one they need. Da never cared who loved him, Jack. Not even with us."

Jack closed his eyes and took a quick, angry breath.

"Do it," he said. "Whatever you need to do. Take whatever you need to take, but you do lasting harm to one of my people? I'll find a way to kill you better than those old wolves did."

For once the cold wind that blasted around them was nothing to do with the Winter. It was stale with old salt and older blood and full of muttered anger and hatred. The intensity of it prickled Gregor's skin with goose bumps and an instinctive fear of what strange thing lurked in the dark. It was all the stronger for the knowledge that, for most people, Gregor was the thing to be afraid of.

The Sannock had their own reasons behind this aid, and it wasn't forgiveness or kindness.

"There's going to be a price," the bird said. It hunched Nick's shoulders and clicked his teeth. "We… regret… that."

Jack grimaced and glanced at Gregor. Whatever he wanted, he seemed to think he'd gotten it. He took a deep breath, clenched his fists at his sides, and ducked his chin in a grim nod.

"Get on with it."

Nick shifted into his feathers, a black bird that looked even bigger in the confines of the tunnel than it did in the world outside. Its wings hammered the air and drops of blood splattered over the walls from broken feathers as the Sannock wind swirled around it. The stirred-up mist of blood and ice chill outlined a spindle-long leg here and a tattered wing there, the planes of almost human faces and things that hadn't even tried.

It turned Gregor's stomach with a sour, inbuilt bile. He started to look away but caught a glimpse of Jack's grim face before he could. If Jack could look—had to look—then so would Gregor.

The bird cawed angrily at the Sannock and snapped at them when they got too close. The pinch of its beak ripped shreds of them loose, but they didn't draw back. With a final, frustrated croak, the bird jabbed its head forward. The pitted white awl of its beak stabbed into Jack's eye with surgical precision.

Jack yelped and staggered back, his hand clapped to his face although it was too late to do any good. Blood and clearish goop dripped between his fingers and ran down over his knuckles.

It took a moment before Gregor could move. He didn't know if it was shock or some sort of Sannock magic that froze him in place. Once he could move, he scrambled to Jack's side and grabbed his arm.

"Let me see," he said.

"Fuck off," Jack hissed through clenched teeth as he tried to double over around the pain.

"Don't be stupid."

Gregor pulled Jack's hand down and grimaced at the gory hole where a green eye should be. It was a small favor, but the bird had been precise. The eye was split and ruined, but Jack's eyelid was intact, and it drooped over the socket when he blinked.

"I guess we don't look the same anymore," Jack said. His grin was bitter and crooked, with only one side of his mouth twisted up. "Finally."

"It'll grow back," Gregor pointed out. "Eventually."

Jack hissed and pressed his hand back to his face. His fingers dug into his brow bone. "It hurts. Why does it hurt so much?"

"More," the bird croaked ominously from where it had landed on the dead monster. Gregor gave it a bleak look, and it fluffed its feathers at him before it stropped its beak clean on the thing's ruff. "Soon."

Gregor jerked Jack's hand out of the way a second time. In the empty pit of his brother's eye, ice spread like hoarfrost and the socket filled with a thin, gray sea fog that clotted like cobwebs. It smelled like Sannock.

Behind his back they shrieked with alien glee, and then the cold weight of them washed over Gregor. He felt—*teeth rip through his flesh and crack his bones, heard a child scream like its world was over, and a red-haired woman with wolf's eyes stirred his cock even as she put a knife to it*—and then just a bone-deep despair that made his legs weak.

In his arms Jack screamed and convulsed, bent back until it seemed impossible his spine could hold. The wind pushed at his face and pried his eyes open so they could all fit. Behind him the bird screamed at them, furious and loud, and Gregor hung on to his brother.

In seconds the Sannock were done and their bleak, old grudge spread through the Wild. Gregor gagged on it, his mouth suddenly glutted with rancid meat, but it couldn't touch him any more than the Wild could. There was no wolf left for them to get their teeth into, just a tender scar over a raw pocket of sour resentment. The Sannock filled him to bursting, until he could feel the ache as they crowded the sockets of his teeth. But they couldn't get hold of him.

They spilled back out of him, into the Wild, and wolves screamed.

Jack was limp in Gregor's arms. It felt strange. He laid Jack down on the ground and pressed a hand to his shoulder in… gratitude? Apology? He didn't know.

"Did you have to?" he asked without looking around. He heard the rustle of the bird's wings as it shrugged and then Nick's answer.

"I don't know," he said. "They thought so. The Sannock and the bird."

Gregor grunted. "They'd know, I suppose."

"The bird wasn't surprised," Nick said. "I think it always knew it would come to this."

"It's a god, Nick," Gregor said. He slapped Jack's face, one side and then the other. "It might love you, but you can't trust it."

Jack's chest hitched as he sucked in a ragged breath of cold air. He pulled away from Gregor and propped himself on his elbow as he puked up thin bile and sticky shreds of goo.

"Would you have ever forgiven me?" he asked as he wiped his mouth on his sleeve when he was done. "For that?"

Gregor squeezed his shoulder. "I never forgave you for being born," he said. "Not the man to ask."

The sounds of agony bounced through the cold, concrete halls. Jack shuddered and used Gregor to scramble to his feet. He wiped under his eye gingerly with the back of his wrist. It mostly just smeared the goo. Nick grimaced at the mess and guiltily disappeared back under his feathers.

"Come on," Jack said. "Let's go see what I've let loose."

CHAPTER TWENTY-THREE—GREGOR

THE BIRD led the way down into long, empty boxes of concrete in short, careful hops that cosseted its injured wing. It had been supplies, from the look of the boxes and packaging, and storage for things that humanity had thought precious.

Gregor stepped over a broken gold frame. Scraps of canvas still hung in the corners, thick with paint, but he couldn't identify what it had been. Even if it had been whole, he'd have probably drawn a blank. Jack, shifted into his wolfskin, followed. The fur around his eye was dark and spiked with blood.

There were the dead too—monsters torn to shreds, deformed faces oddly human in the surprise of death. Two soldiers in Kevlar, armed with rifles, who were propped against each other as their bodies melted and dripped like colored ice.

The farther down they went, the colder it got. Gregor's breath steamed, and he could feel the pressure of the cold in his chest with each breath.

"If you're leading us into a trap," Gregor grumbled at the bird, "you could have killed us up there and saved us the trek."

It gave him a reproachful look over its wing, as though Jack's blood wasn't still caught in the pits on its beak. One last clumsy flight ended with it perched on top of a stack of broken boxes. It twisted its head around to preen its wing, the beak that had just taken out Jack's eye oddly delicate as the bird plucked broken feathers.

The wolves slunk around the corner. Gregor felt what it was like to prey, a chill clutch at his heart and the sour pop of adrenaline in his veins. Next to him Jack flattened his ears and his thready, uneasy growl caught in his throat.

Gregor knew every wolf in the Pack that faced them, but he didn't *recognize* them. Milky films covered their eyes from one corner to the other and matted thick winter coats down to their skin. Their shadows, cast in stark relief by the fluorescent lights, writhed and squirmed in a jittery transformation from wolf to… something else. Thin gray horns sprouted on one shadow, branched like a stag, and another stretched out long, spindly limbs—too many of them for a wolf—before they snapped back to four.

The Sannock in Ellie's skin staggered forward. It wasn't clumsy, but it tried to crawl when the wolf wanted to walk. Gregor could *feel* it through the Wild, like a taut line hooked through his gut. He wouldn't have called the faded, dusty emotion that touched him enjoyment, but the Sannock took satisfaction in their discomfort.

It opened its jaws, and Ellie screamed—a wolf's scream, high and terrible in a way that nothing else was. The Sannock spoke through the noise.

"Once upon a time you couldn't wait to have us in you," he singsonged. The voice was clear but somehow sounded like it came from a long way away. "Chewed us off our own bones you were so. Eager."

"Yeah, well," Gregor said. "Done is done. You told Nick that you'd help us."

Ellie's head ticked to the side to stare at the bird. Her neck popped like knuckles with the force of the movement.

"We did," it said. "Maybe we lied."

"Stories say you can't."

It somehow managed to shrug like a man with a wolf's shoulders. It was a disturbing motion. "Stories lie. That's what they are for. We might have lied to it, but we made a deal with you. Oaths aren't stories. They're true. We can help. We will help. After we get the skins we take tonight."

Jack snarled and took a step forward. Before he could take another, Gregor reached down and hauled him by the scruff.

"Not those skins," Gregor said. "You get out of the wolves."

The Sannock tried to spit but was thwarted by Ellie's muzzle. "We want to live again. To learn to *die*, so we can go. We tolerate your hides for that, but we'd rather linger in the shade forever than live in your hungry flesh. Even if we could bear the shame, there's no room."

"I get my child," Gregor said. "We get Rose's throat. Anything else is yours."

The Sannock smiled. It wasn't a friendly expression, stretched over a wolf's muzzle, but it wasn't meant to be.

"Deal," it said. "May you live to regret it."

Gregor shrugged. "Wolves don't waste time on regret," he said. "If you double-cross us, we'll make sure the Sannock have all the time in the shade to dwell on yours."

The Sannock bobbed its nose in a nod. "Follow."

It turned and ran. The rest of the Pack fell in behind it, almost as smoothly as when the wolves were in charge of their own paws. There was still something alien about how uniform each step was and the perfectly aligned noses.

Jack pulled away from Gregor and watched them go. Then he whined softly under his breath and looked up at Gregor with a worried expression in his last green eye. Gregor knew what he'd noticed—the one face not in the furry crowd.

"He's a dog, not a wolf," Gregor said. "You couldn't hand him over to the Sannock if you wanted. If he were dead, we'd have seen him already. If Rose has him, we get him back."

Jack shuddered from nose to tail, but he had to accept it. There was nothing else they could do.

The Prophets had left monsters to guard their last stand—four gaunt things, bones stretched out like greyhounds and stitched together with heavy, raw lumps of muscle that split their thin skin, and one who looked almost human. Her face was a caul of swollen bone, bloodshot eyes sunken deep and full of rheum, but she still stood up straight, and her hands worked well enough for a gun.

Barely.

The first splatter of gunfire just grazed the leading edge of the Sannock wolves. It scored a raw line across a black wolf's shoulder and took a nick out of his ear. The red wolf next to him was unluckier. They caught a bullet to the leg, and it shattered like a stick. The Sannock didn't care. It ran on splinters and ragged flesh. In eerie silence.

Jack shuddered at the offense of it but threw himself into the fight.

The gaunt monsters took point and tore into the Sannock wolves as the Pack surrounded them. Thin, bony muzzles, the skin peeled back from the jut of raw gums like a glove, snapped at the press of fur and muscle that eddied around them to snatch wolves up and shake them like rats. Clawed paws, fingers braided together and their nails thick and yellow where they poked from the raw beds, tore through shoulders and slapped unlucky wolves to the ground or into the wall.

It didn't even slow the Sannock. They didn't need a moment to shake the ringing from their ears or let the Wild knit their bodies back together. They just picked themselves up and slunk back into the fight with teeth that slowed the monster's healing when they sank down to bone. Infected flesh withered and dried into creased, stained leather.

Jack dodged between the Sannock and harried the gaunt monsters. He took a chunk from one's thigh, meat and gristle torn from the bone, and lunged in to tear at the stretched-out point of an ear when the monster went for a wolf. In the middle of the fight, he looked, somehow, more vivid than the other wolves, as though what had taken up residence in them had faded them down. Gregor grimly stuck to his heels and watched his back. The Sannock might be their allies right now, but they'd hated the wolves for as long as there had *been* a Scottish Pack.

One of the monsters swung its head around. It had eyebrows, thin and black, that arched over the distorted orbits of its eyes. Twisted as the things were, sometimes the most grotesque part was the shreds of who they'd been. Gregor dodged as it swung its head like a hammer. His foot slipped on the gore that splattered the floor, and his knee twisted as he went down. The slip saved him, and he only had to absorb part of the impact. He sucked in a breath and let the disgusted rage wash the pain away as he pulled his knee back to kick the monster in the throat.

It squalled and reared back, throat bulged out like a frog's around the shattered trachea. One of the Sannock leaped for it and hit it in the chest. It staggered backward, and they toppled over, tangled around each other as they scrapped and clawed.

Gregor scrambled to his feet and threw himself back into the fight.

The almost-human monster had backed up to guard the door. She squinted around the bony jut of her own sockets and strafed the room with a volley of bullets, careless of whether they punched through wolves or her own allies. Gregor swore and hit the ground again, his ears ringing. Two wolves caught bullets to the head and dropped like a stone, the mist gone from their eyes. Maybe they could have gotten up again, probably not, but maybe. Instead the monsters tore them apart and spat out the remains.

The Sannock seeped out of the dead, shrugged the corpses off their hollow shoulders like old coats, and drifted back into the fight. They couldn't deal out the same damage, but they sucked the breath from the monsters' mouths and pinched their ears with thin, grave-filthy fingers.

Gregor cursed under his breath—he'd rather the Sannock died and the wolves got up—and got his elbows under him. His chest ached from the hard landing on the ground, and it took him a second to catch his breath. He forced the pain down and scrambled up. If the body count of Jack's deal got too high, then Jack would be useless. To Gregor. To the Pack.

The monster fumbled the gun back up toward her shoulders. Her head was turned toward Jack, his tawny fur easy to pick out from the faded wolves, and the curve of her cheekbones blocked her peripheral vision. Gregor took a breath—his lungs cramped around the chill of it—and darted toward her. He jumped over the Sannock who got in his way and dodged the snake-like strikes of the monsters who saw him pass. Mostly dodged. Blood dripped down his arm from a bloody gash in his shoulder.

One of the monsters loomed up in front of him, dappled gray and liver with raised, wrinkled moles, and screamed at him. One of the disembodied Sannock hung from its throat, fingers worked in deep under the skin, and another had its teeth buried in the thing's loose breasts. Its attention was on Gregor.

He put his head down and made straight for it. At the last second, he went down on the floor—slick enough to take his feet from under him earlier—and skidded between the thing's legs. It nearly knocked itself out on the ground as it tried to chase him between its own ankles. One of the Sannock darted in as it was occupied and tore open the taut skin of its neck.

Gregor rolled to his feet on the other side. The muzzle of the gun was pointed directly at him, the monster's scab-ringed eyes focused on him. Twelve feet of empty ground stretched out between them, and experience told Gregor that he couldn't cover it in time, not on two legs.

He went for it anyhow, with a staggered lunge across the distance. The Wild that stung under his skin might not be able to find what it needed to turn him, but given something to do, it cooled the ache in his joints and flooded him with the quick, endless adrenaline of the moon hunt, when he could run forever, tireless and fast as the wind.

He covered two-thirds of the ground before the monster could react. It still wasn't going to be enough. The monster tightened its finger, and Gregor, his hearing sharpened by the Wild until he could hear the pulse of the thing's blood in its throat, caught the click as something engaged.

The world slowed down. Gregor skinned his lips back in one last frustrated snarl. He could accept death, but it stuck in his throat to fail.

The black bird crashed into the side of the monster's head. Sharp talons scraped on the skull and worked gouges down into the bone, and the thick, carved beak cracked it open like a nut.

Gregor supposed that was what that awl of a thing was meant to do.

A squawk escaped the monster as she jerked the gun up as it fired. A single bullet sang by Gregor's ear, and the rest stitched over the ceiling. Splinters of concrete and dust rained down, and the square box creaked around him.

"Nick," Gregor yelled. "Move."

Black wings curved and the bird pushed off with a croak and a splatter of blood drops. It was well-timed. The bird was just clear as Gregor slammed into the monster. He grabbed the gun, metal hot against his palms, and slammed it up into the monster's face. It staggered backward briefly and then swung him around to slam into the door.

It rang like an untuned bell.

The monster dropped the gun and grabbed Gregor's head. Her fingers wrapped almost all the way around, and it felt like a vise when she squeezed. The sharp tips of her thumbnails dug into Gregor's eyelids like knives. Her mouth, lips shredded by a lamprey excess of teeth, writhed with the effort of speech.

"Mek yo' uglee," she slurred. The scabs around her eyes cracked as she narrowed them. "Mek it stick whatever yo' do."

Pressure throbbed behind Gregor's eyes, a hot pulse in time with his heart. He struggled to focus past the pain and the blood that dripped into his eyes.

Maybe it was enough. The monster wasn't going to shoot another wolf, and that was a victory of sorts. He could give up.

Gregor bared his teeth in a hard snarl of a grin that made his bruised face ache. *Fuck that.* He forced his arms up and grabbed the monster's head, dug his fingers into the hole the bird made, and pulled. Bone creaked and split along the fracture lines the bird had left in the skull. It cracked open like an egg, and blood and clots of hair spilled out around his fingers.

The monster howled like a dog and slammed Gregor's head into the door until his vision grayed out. He couldn't see, but he didn't need to. He thrust his fingers through the thin membrane of scalp and into the wet slop of its brain. The monsters healed quickly, but Gregor pulped the delicate tissue in his fist and pulled it off the stem.

That wasn't something to come back from.

Big hands flexed around Gregor's skull for a heartbeat. Then they went lax. The monster staggered back and pitched over onto the ground. Its brains dripped, wet and sticky, from Gregor's fingers. He shook them off and pushed himself off the door.

The Sannock pulled the last of the gaunt monsters to the ground, and Jack, so matted in blood that the flash of his one green eye was the only thing that broke the monochrome gore, tore its guts open.

Gregor wiped blood out of his eyes and turned around to try the door. His blood was smeared over the metal, but it didn't make any difference. It didn't open. He swore and smacked the heel of his hand against it.

"Can you step into the Wild?" Nick asked. "Come out the other side."

Jack, still in his wolfskin, grunted his opinion of that.

"Not a good idea," Gregor said. "We ask the Wild to let us in, and if it wants, it does. Then we hope it lets us out again, where it wills and when it wills. With how twisted Rose has left it? It might never let us out, or it might drop us in the middle of a wall."

James screamed this time. It was a raw, bloody noise, as though he'd screamed all the time the Sannock had been silent, but the voice that came out was the same.

"Wolves," it said. "All appetite and anger and cur's luck. The Wild bless you, for nothing else ever will. Sannock are old, wise, and we were loved once. Step aside."

Gregor hesitated. It galled on a deep, uneasy level to even abide the Sannock, never mind obey them, but they'd gone this far. He stepped aside.

The Sannock in James padded over to the door on silent paws and reared up onto its back feet. It pressed its nose to the seal and whispered. Gregor tried to listen, but it stuck to his brain like tar. He recoiled before it could coat it all and took a step. The bird landed on his shoulder and clipped him around the ear with a wing as it caught its balance. He reached up and stroked its beak, the hard surface warm and pitted with ogham.

"I thought I disliked them before," he said. "Now I see them in wolves, I realize I'd barely begun."

The bird croaked quietly against his ear. Gregor didn't understand it, but he decided to assume that it agreed with him.

There was a yell of surprise on the other side, and something smacked into the door hard enough to rattle it. Gregor traded a quick glance with Jack. They didn't need to speak. Understanding passed silently between them.

If the Sannock had set a trap, they'd bleed to get the meat out of it.

The door rattled again, and blood seeped out from under it in a thick, dark trickle. Then it pulled open, and a familiar man, scar raw and pink across his forehead, staggered out.

Boyd—the soldier Gregor had left for dead in the snow, now on his feet and on their side. He had a heavy knife in one hand, the curved blade coated with blood, and a desperate look in wild, dry-looking eyes.

"There," Boyd said as he dropped the knife and went down on his knees. "I did what you asked. Keep your side of the bargain. Now."

He sounded desperate, and he smelled like death—not the agitating stink of the monsters, but just death.

"We made a deal, we keep a deal," the Sannock said through James's sobbing wails. Then it snapped gray, brittle-looking teeth at the man. "At the end. Once we're done."

Boyd tried to protest, but the Sannock ignored him. What would he do, after all? Who would he appeal to for justice against them? He sagged to the ground like a discarded toy, his hands slack and palm up on his knees.

The Sannock flowed around him, uncaring, into what had been meant to be a safe room.

A snarling prophet, the skinned corpse he'd pulled on tattered and dry, looked shocked as he saw the Sannock-ridden Pack halfway through his grab for Boyd. It was too late for him to stop. Jack pushed Gregor out of the way and flew at the prophet in a lean, bloody streak of muscle. He hit the prophet in the stomach and knocked him to the ground. They rolled back and forth as they snarled and snapped at each other and the

Sannock went around or over them. The prophet tore at Jack with taloned hands, but the thick, gore-matted coat protected him, and the prophet's wolf split like cheap leather as Jack ripped into him. Jack sank his teeth into the man's throat and snarled as he shook his head.

"No!" Ailsa screamed in frustration as she shoved one of the fever-skinned humans away from her. Liquid that Gregor assumed was the prophets' poison spilled onto the floor from the silver flask she held. Since he'd seen her last, she'd patched her shabbily tailored wolf hide with fresh skin, roughly tanned with piss and still fresh enough to stink. Reddish fur sprouted from the darkened skin in rough patches. Gregor didn't know if Ewan deserved better or not, but he'd peel the skin of Ailsa's back for Nick's sake. "You can't be here yet. We aren't ready. Why won't you just give up and *die*."

Gregor showed her his teeth.

"We're wolves," Gregor told her. The Sannock prowled slowly forward, ears flat and lips curled back to show fangs and gums. One slow step after another. "And the Old Man's sons. We might die, but we don't give up."

The prophets were gathered behind her, around a guttering bonefire. Their hands were thrust into the embers, fingers scorched raw red and swollen with blisters. A handful of soldiers fed the fire with chunks of raw flesh and rolls of salted dog skin that charred and stank as they burned. The rest of the soldiers stood and watched, entranced by the flicker of flames and the black streams of smoke as they rose toward the ceiling.

Gregor glanced around the room as he totted up the scabby hides. Ten prophets. Eleven if Gregor counted the half-dead prophet on the floor, almost strangled by the grip of Jack's jaws around his throat. There should have been more, even accounting for the ones they'd already killed. Maybe some of them had the good sense to turn coat on Rose and run.

She wasn't here, nor was the baby. He could smell it. Under the smoke, the honey sweetness of a newborn cut with salt and copper hung in the air, but it was diffuse—a trace the child had left, but no source.

"Where's the baby?" he asked.

Ailsa laughed raggedly and tossed back a swig of the clear potion. She shuddered and made a bitter face as the taste hit the back of her throat.

"You're too late," she said. "Too late for him. Too late for us. It's time. Kill them."

Gregor braced himself.

The prophets pulled their hands out of the fire, strings of raw tendons strung around the knuckles, and their bodies crackled and popped as their chests thickened and the wolf crawled up over them. Snarls tore out of their dry vocal cords, and then they tore into the humans around them. Clawed fingers hooked into throats and tore them out and grabbed heads to snap the necks with one quick twist.

And the soldiers lined up for the slaughter, faces open and eager as their blood sizzled on the fire.

The Sannock laughed—a wispy sound that carried on the breath of the wolves' screams.

"Too late, too late," they rhymed mockingly. "Everything is too late tonight. Wolves, prophets, and the gods who never came when *we* called. Too late, we'll say."

They surged forward on fast, stolen paws and tore through the prophets and soldiers both. Blood doused the fire, killed the flames, and Gregor and Jack—human and wolf—stood back and watched in silence.

Strange, after everything they'd gone through to get here, but this particular butchery wasn't for them. That was still to come.

CHAPTER TWENTY-FOUR—NICK

THE BIRD could feel Nick's agitation in the back of its brain—a mix of guilt and anger. It hadn't told him what the price would be, not until the eye had slipped wet and slippery down their throat.

It had been the Sannocks' gelt—the blood debt the wolves owed—and not to be bartered down. The bird would admit it hadn't *savored* the bite, but its role had been set with the price to be paid… as had this visceral moment, with blood on concrete and the stink of smoke and charred meat in the air.

Nick would have to wait. It was safer. The bird twisted around to strop its beak against its shoulder to clean off the blood. They weren't done yet.

The Sannock pulled the prophets apart—rags of dry hide pulled away in a shower of scabs and brittle hair and raw flesh peeled away from muscle and bone. They paid for it, but it wasn't in their pain or their blood. Not this time.

As the prophets fell, fought, or tried to flee, what was left of the soldiers realized this wasn't the murder they'd agreed to and tried to rally. The man who'd lusted wetly after Nick in the hospital bed, a pair of broken glasses perched on his nose and mangled arm left to dangle by strings of tendon and skin, threw himself between Ailsa and a Sannock wolf.

It ended as such things always did.

The Sannock wolf took him to the ground and ripped his stomach open. It buried its muzzle in his guts, gray fur stained red as ochre, and tore out handfuls of them. The bird blinked, a sliver of *other* flicked over its eyes so it could see, and it watched the thread-thin snakes milked from Loki's sores spill out of the man along with his stomach. They writhed, translucent and soft, between chunks of half-chewed bread in sticky puddles of bile.

His shredded lungs flapped like ribbons as he tried to inhale to scream, but death took him before he could force the sound out.

The bird boosted itself off its perch and strained its wings to gain some height in the cold, still air. It could feel the press of the ground overhead, the earth's displeasure at the upending of the way of things. Birds didn't fly underground, so it was lucky that it was only almost a bird and flew where it liked.

In the past—someplace so far away that the bird could only remember that it remembered them—there had been other things that came for the dead. Battlefields had been glutted, every death a feeding frenzy as they jockeyed for the heady prize.

Not now. Not *yet*.

Nick shuddered at the correction. The bird ignored him. There was a dead man caught in the air, still tethered to his corpse by a rope of what he'd been and seen and wanted. It wouldn't last long. The snakes had worked their venom in to soften it and peel off shreds, but long enough.

The crow shot through the dead man. Slivers of him caught in fight-ragged feathers—the taste of coffee, a sunrise, the feel of Nick's thigh under his hand—and the bird pinched folds of what was left in its beak.

Murder and suicide were what it concerned itself with, and the soldier who'd show his throat to the prophets before the Sannock tore it out was both. What death had wanted to take, the bird spat back into the corpse.

Even the Wild had rules. Even the gods. To walk in mortal skin, you needed a mortal soul. To die, you needed something that knew death… and the Sannock had neither soul nor mortality.

It tasted Nick's horror for a moment, the flutter of resentment as he realized the Sannock's game, but it was already done. On the ground, the wolf opened its crimson maw and retched the Sannock, a thing half-formed from memory and mist, into the gore. It squirmed down into the raw meat, pulled the folds of liver and intestine over itself, and opened the corpse's eyes. Whatever color they'd been before, now they were cobweb gray with silver-steel pupils.

The wolf staggered away. Greasy drool hung from her lips, and she nearly collapsed as she put her weight on a dislocated back leg. A dry, panicked whine filtered down her nose as the Sannock folded its guts back into its stomach and stood up. Flesh melted, sealed, and reshaped itself into something taller, stranger, and paler. Horns, new-budded and still soft with velvet, tore through the skin of its temples, and it rose up onto its toes as its bones cracked and stretched. Dense, short fur the color of beech bark sprouted on its legs and across its cheekbones. The smell of pine and thick musk sweated out of its skin as he looked around.

He smiled, and it was terrible. Ailsa snarled her defiance in her stolen skin and went for him. The Sannock caught her by the throat. His fingers dug down and the loose skin split under his nails. He ignored the great rents she tore in his chest with her claws. Then he leaned down and opened his mouth as though he were about to whisper into her ragged ear. Instead a stag's guttural bell rang out, a hoarse, deep sound that was full of something essentially awful.

Ailsa convulsed. Her eyes bulged, and her throat worked around the pinch of the Sannock's fingers. He shook her twice and then tore the wolf off her back. The hide tore off her skin with a wet, ripping sound, stitches torn out in long, dripping runs, and she was left pink, greasy, and naked. The Sannock broke her neck, tossed her aside, and belled again. The sound echoed off the walls, cracked the gray paint in flakes and strips, and drove the prophets still on their feet to their knees. Blood seeped out of their ears and matted in dead wolf's fur as they tried to rise under the weight of throat-closing terror.

The Sannock mobbed them before they could recover. Some of the prophets struggled to their feet, grabbed the ridden wolves by the scruff, and threw them aside. Others went down under the mass of the Pack.

The bird spun away on the point of a wing to catch another dead man in its beak. Another Sannock rose and then another, and the prophets fell.

Wolves sprawled on the stained concrete and leaned against the walls. They panted, tongues torn to raw ribbons, and their sides heaved under dull, staring coats. It was no light thing to be ridden by the dead.

Not—the bird tucked its head down to tidy the feathers on its wings—for the living at least.

"Nick."

The bird stretched both its wings out as far as they would go, the muscles tight under its feathers, and then snapped them back into its sides. It folded itself down, tucked into a ball of soft darkness inside itself, and let Nick pull his skin back on.

Nick staggered as being human again caught him by surprise and his body felt long, strange, and naked. Gregor caught his elbow before he could trip over his own feet and steadied him until Nick could do it himself.

"Did you know what they were going to do?" Gregor asked harshly. When Nick didn't answer, Gregor squeezed his shoulder hard enough to hurt to get his attention. "Nick. What *did* they do?"

"The wolves took what belonged to us, belonged to *us* in a way nothing else could. Our skins, our magic, our meat," the horned Sannock answered for Nick. Something horrid lurked under his voice, pinned down by the shape of words. It made Nick shiver with an atavistic dread of the things in the shadows that he'd spent most of his life trying to convince himself were his own imagination. "So we took what the wolves had offered the gods. Empty vessels, empty *enough*."

"And now?" Gregor asked. He pulled Nick back a step to put him behind Gregor's shoulder. "Or did you really expect us to believe this made us even? Our people slaughtered yours, wiped them off the face of the island. I wouldn't rest till the heather grew through our bones."

The horned Sannock showed blunt white teeth. They were meant for an herbivore's mouth, but shreds of skin were caught between them. "You played a shell game with the gods, wolf. They threw themselves at a door your prophets opened and had it slammed in their face. Your death is only when you *start* to pay us back."

In the back of Nick's head, he could feel the bird's disquiet as it clacked its beak on the sour taste of that warning. The gods would not, it knew, look any kinder on them than the wolves. If anything, the opposite would be true, but it was too late for second thoughts.

Or, Nick supposed dryly, first thoughts. The bird's black humor sparked in acknowledgment, but they both admitted there hadn't been much choice in the moment. There hadn't been any choice ever, even if the wolves would never accept him now.

Not that he thought there had been much chance of that to start with. Nick could live with that, as long as it turned out to be worth it. He nudged Gregor.

"The gods can wait," he said and then looked at the Sannock. It was odd to see them so solid and anchored. "The baby can't. Where's my grandmother?"

The Sannock stared at him pensively. "What is that to us? We walk again." He stamped his foot—almost hoof—and the rest of the Sannock in their stolen bodies whistled or laughed as they joined in. They sounded almost drunk, heady on the solidity of it all. "Why should we risk that for you? Why should we court her vengeance when once and twice you've failed to end her?"

It was Nick's turn to tighten his grip on Gregor's shoulder before Gregor could say anything.

"You think she'll let this go?" he asked. The Sannock rolled its eyes. Nick stepped forward. On some level he was aware he was naked, his vulnerable parts bare to the elements. He put that to the back of his head to freak about later. "Rose, my gran, she's never forgiven, forgotten, or let anything rest. If she can't control you, then she'll destroy you whether you help us or not."

The Sannock turned its back. Another—only its gray pebble eyes and bark fingers transformed from its human form—shook its head.

"We don't fear her," it fluted, three voices woven into one. It ignored the horned man's snarl as it bowed its head. "Death has been on our tongue for centuries. But imagine, little carrion crow, what terrible thing we might actually fear. Then fear it too. Your grandmother treads dark water."

Gregor pulled away from Nick. "You killed all the prophets, and you're wearing her human followers like coats. So you're going to tell us. She has my child."

The Sannock looked at Gregor with dead, pebble eyes and shrugged. It had no sympathy and no real understanding of the need. "Breed another, steal another. Babies are birthed every day. Even in the Winter. Surrender this one to the dark water, for the dark water will win the fight."

Gregor grabbed the Sannock by the torn Kevlar vest that was a remnant of the person it used to be. He hauled it toward him while the rest of the Sannock bridled in anger.

"I will, when…."

The scrape of toenails on concrete and the harsh, ragged pant of a run-out animal interrupted Gregor's threat before he could finish it. Nick turned as the big, gray dog skidded into the door frame, bounced off, and staggered into the room. Its ribs pressed against its sides in sharp relief as it panted heavily, clouds of steam around its jaws, and sweat knotted coarse, gray fur.

The side of its face was a bloody, swollen mess, one eye swelled shut and a few too many teeth visible through the torn edges of the wound.

It stood there for a second, legs trembling, and then Danny crawled out from the dog's skin. He sprawled awkwardly on the ground, elbows braced under him and his head hung so dark curls obscured his face.

"I know what Rose wants the baby for," Danny said, voice thick and clumsy in his mangled mouth. He pressed the back of his hand to his cheek, over the gash, as he looked up. "The same thing she took Nick for. To put something else in, only something bigger than a carrion crow."

"Danny," Jack gasped as he shed his wolf. He bolted over to crouch next to Danny, his hand cautious as he touched the bloody cheek. "Danny-dog. What happened? Who did this?"

"Don't call me that," Danny grumbled on autopilot, no real heat behind the words. His eyes flickered over Jack's face, and he winced in sympathy. The brush of his hand mirrored Jack's, light and cautious as it skimmed over Jack's bruised cheekbone. "And I could ask you the same thing."

Jack leaned into the touch as though he were a cat, not a wolf. "It'll heal," he said. "What happened to you, Danny?"

One of the wheezing wolves painfully shed their fur. The woman sprawled back against the wall, legs stretched out in front of her and eyes still wild. Spit crusted in the corner of her mouth as she spat, "You sell us to the prophets, abandon James's boy to the Wild, but what happened to some dog is who you care for?" she asked, contempt in her voice. "Maybe we should have made Gregor Numitor instead. Even gelded, he's more of a wolf."

Ellie propped herself up on shaking legs to aim a disciplinary snap at the woman. Other wolves backed her. Most of them, even, but there was a hesitation before they picked their side.

"What do you mean, the same as me?" Nick asked as he decided to ignore the dispute. He thought Gregor would be a better wolf king than his brother, but that was because he loved Gregor and it didn't really matter right now. He waved a hand at the Sannock. "She gutted these men to make room for the gods or the Sannock, why would she need a baby?"

"She needed Bron's baby. She needed a wolf pup," Danny corrected. He tried to get up, but only managed to leverage himself into a crouch. His legs trembled under him as he put his weight on them, the muscles taut under the skin. "I caught up with Lachlan in the storm, but he'd already handed the baby on to Rose. He told me what she was going to do, although I don't think he really understands it. She did this for the same reason she took Nick as a baby. The same reason she took your sister, Jack."

Nick glanced askance at Gregor, his head tilted curiously, but Gregor looked as confused as him. It was the wolves, a few of them, who put their eyes down and put their noses guiltily between their paws.

"How do you even know about that?" the wolf in her human skin asked. "None of us would have told you. Told anyone, never mind a *dog*."

Danny's lower lip trembled for a moment until he made himself swallow hard. "Kath did," he said. "My mam told me about it, about the Numitor's little girl who came out a dog and how Rose drowned her in the lake."

"Da let that bitch kill my sister?" Gregor asked after a stunned second.

"He wouldn't," Jack protested. "Da backed you when you wouldn't let the prophets take your little girl before she died. He told them to fuck off when they wanted her body after she died. Dog or not, he'd never give his pup to the prophets."

"He didn't," Danny said. He rubbed the back of his hands over his eyes as he tried to focus. "Rose took her, and I think that's when she got the idea—with the baby, and the loch, and the monster that lived there. It didn't work, but that's why she took Nick. That's why she took Bron's baby. Humans? Even once they're hollowed out by the prophets' potion, only have room for little gods and dead things. They're not *made* for it. Wolves are. Rose took Bron's baby because of the *potential*, because of the *room*."

Gregor inhaled sharply and then breathed out a word. "Fenrir," he said, as close to reverent as Nick had ever heard him. It didn't seem like the moment to ask for details. Nick knew the name, but not the details behind it. Gregor didn't notice his confusion as he shook his head in frustration. "That's what Ewan meant, Nick, *who* he meant. If Rose has him on a collar and lead, then the wolves will follow her no matter what a raddled old monster she is. Odin *fuck* us all. Fenrir will lead the wolves into the Winter, and he'll be trained to walk at that bitch's heel."

Silence greeted his announcement. The only sound in the room was the wheeze of the wolves breathing and the drip of blood as it oozed from gutted bodies. The Sannock stood in still silence, not accustomed enough to their new bodies to fidget or move.

"Where is she?" Jack asked. He gripped Danny's shoulder in one hand and squeezed to catch Danny's attention. "Danny, did Lachlan say where Rose was going?"

There was a pause, and then Danny gingerly shook his head. The motion made him flinch. "I couldn't beat him in a fight. If I didn't run, he'd have skinned me for Rose. I didn't expect everyone to be dead already."

"Dead or fucking unhelpful," Gregor said as he gave the Sannock a bitter look. "I always thought you were cowards, hidden in a hole waiting for the slaughter. It looks like I was right."

The horned Sannock opened its mouth and let loose that terrible, hollow bell of noise that reverberated in Nick's bones. Gregor staggered, caught himself, and screamed back, the wolf's howl caught in his throat shrill enough to undercut the Sannock's roar. The horned Sannock snapped his jaw shut and snorted as he grimly lowered his head. The horns on his brow were thicker now, branched in two short nubs.

"I have killed wolves in my first skin. Do you beg to be the first in my second?" he said. "Let the world freeze and end. We will end with it and *rest*."

The other Sannock sighed and repeated the word. It murmured around the room, passed from mouth to mouth like a prayer. It was the first time that Nick hadn't heard them sound bitter or angry.

"No," Nick said. "You won't."

The bird stirred uneasily as it caught the edges of his idea. It dug its claws into him with a quick prick of pain to warn him, but wicked humor made it cluck approvingly as well.

"The little spirit of carrion and battlefields rides you," the Sannock said. He narrowed eyes that were too black, the rim of white eaten by the liquid spill. "The past, spent days and breath, are your preserve. You have no oversight on the future."

"In this I do. We put you in those bodies, and we can put you in others. Every death we will jam you back into a corpse, trim what doesn't fit, and make you walk," Nick said. His voice was dry as dust in his throat, and he'd have felt more confident in his threat if he had clothes. "You never lie down and rest. Not if that baby dies. Help us. You've nothing to lose.

Trust me, my gran won't need any more excuse than what you did here to make you suffer. And you don't want to be on the run from us both."

The Sannock snorted, low and wet like an animal. Nick remembered cloth on his shoulders, like woven shadows, and hissed some of his tension out between his teeth.

"Please."

Gregor made a disgusted noise at the plea.

The Sannock turned slightly as they traded glances, conversation worn down to sketched expressions and twitched fingers by centuries of familiarity. After a moment they came to an agreement, and the horned Sannock turned back to Nick. He smiled, not pleasantly.

"Why lie, little bird?" he asked. "You already know where your great mother has fled. Does the crow have your tongue?"

Everyone looked sharply at Nick, even Gregor, suspicion cracked through those sharp, green eyes.

Nick swallowed the pain of that like a stone, like the bird's bones his gran had pushed down his throat. He started to shake his head, but then he remembered the dead Sannock's coat on his shoulders and the musky stink of the thing on the moors. He could almost taste it, oily and rank on his tongue as he swallowed.

"The Run-Away Man," he said.

Gregor grimaced and looked away impatiently as he scrubbed his hand over his face. "It's not the time for fairy tales." He looked grim, his face tired and pale under the filth and blood. Nick supposed he'd look the same if *he* had a child that his gran somehow got her hands on. She'd never had any kindness in her. Not—Nick remembered the faded affection, cut with fear, on his grandfather's face as Ewan talked about Rose—for as long as he'd known her.

"The wolves and the Wall were fairy tales too, to me," Nick said. "So is the Run-Away Man. I saw him out in the storm with a dead thing on the moors. But… why would Gran have anything to do with him? She was afraid of him, as close as she could get to being afraid."

He could remember the pinch of her fingers—on his ear, just behind his armpit, on the backs of his thighs—as she made him look at the old picture. So he'd always remember what the Run-Away Man looked like and what he was to do if he ever saw him.

Run. Of all the terrible things his gran had conjured in her stories, that was the only one he was to run from.

"That was then. This is the Wolf Winter," Danny pointed out. He made a wry face around his torn cheek as he said the words. "Maybe her position on him has changed, or he… he might have. Your Run-Away Man might not be what he once was."

Danny looked thoughtful as he said that, as though something had occurred to him, but he shook his head when Jack raised a questioning eyebrow at him. He was pale, except for the shiny flush of infection on his cheek, and once Jack nodded at him, he slouched back down into his dog. It flopped onto the ground, stretched out so as much of its skin touched the cold floor as possible, and panted.

"Fine. I don't care who he is, or what he was," Jack said. "Is Rose there? Is that where we'll find her?"

The Sannock shrugged. "If you run." They traded another shorthand conversation in a look. It ended with a nod from a woman, her hair black at the ends and almost translucent at the roots as if she'd run in the wash. "If we help."

"And the cost?" Gregor asked cynically. "Another eye?"

"Peace," the Sannock said. "You take your wolves down over your wall, and you forget we breathe and walk again on this world's dirt."

It would have been an easy "done" from Nick. He'd learned not to love anywhere he lived as a kid, bounced from placement to placement. Where Gregor went, he'd follow.

He expected it to be harder for the wolves, who'd called this their place for centuries.

"Done," Jack and Gregor said in unison, their voices overlapping almost perfectly.

They glanced sharply at each other, and Gregor shrugged his surrender before he stepped back to cede authority to his brother. He took Nick's hand and squeezed it roughly as they waited, cold blood-slick fingers tangled together. It meant something, Nick was too tired to work out what or hold a grudge against that flash of doubt. He leaned against Gregor and slouched down to rest his chin on his shoulder.

"Any wolf that follows me leaves Scotland," Jack said. "Any wolf that doesn't, that's up to you, but my Pack won't avenge them."

A snarl echoed from a few of the wolves in shocked protest. A few of the most recovered pulled their skin on, pale and clammy with the effort of it, and found the words to disagree.

"This is our land!"

"The prophecies said we'd go down over the Wall to reclaim the whole island, not that we'd lose our home."

"We killed them once, we can do it again."

"Should we even try to stop her?" It was James's protest, his voice thick and congested, that silenced the others. He braced himself against the wall as he pulled himself to his feet. Scars, faded but not yet gone, laced his leg where Kath had shredded it, and he looked smaller somehow. The Sannock couldn't touch his bones, but they seemed to have culled some of the bulk from his muscles and the fat from under his skin. "Fenrir rises. Isn't that what we want? Isn't that what we've spent the last centuries here to wait for? So what if it is early? So what if this sackcloth-and-skin bitch does it for us? Once Fenrir is here, we won't need a Numitor anymore. We won't give one green blade of what is ours to these freaks. And what is the life of one child compared to that? How many of us have lost children? How many have had their get sent away if they weren't strong enough, weren't good enough? We've all sacrificed, except the Old Man's sons. Let them bleed for the Pack. Then maybe Fenrir will let them run with us."

As they listened to him speak, a few of the wolves nodded slowly in agreement. Others refused to look at Jack and Gregor, faces turned away and ears flat on those still in their fur.

"Idiots," Gregor said. He cast a scathing look around the room. "You think that Fenrir will be grateful for this? That he'll think a change of chains is as good as a rest? Would you?"

"And we should take your word that Rose is evil?" James spat out. "Maybe all she wants is for us to have the Wolf Winter we were promised. More than you seem to want."

"Go fuck yourself, James," Gregor said. "If you're too scared to face down an old woman, just admit it."

James shoved himself off the wall and took an unsteady step forward, his fists knotted. Before he could go any farther, Danny, back on his paws, shot in front of him. The dog's thick ruff was matted with blood, and the thready nasal growl that squeezed out of him sounded dangerous. He waited until James spat on the floor and loosened his fists. Then the dog backed up cautiously to take up position next to Gregor.

"I'd say the dog was smarter than you, James, but that wouldn't be news," Jack said. He picked a scab of blood out of the corner of his ruined eye and flicked it away. "Do what you want, what you can live with, but since when does a wolf lie to itself? Rose has stolen and murdered our children, maimed our wolves, and defiled our dead. Yet you'll stand here and say she did it for our own good? The Scottish Pack will live or die with my brother and me, because anyone who stays here because they buy that? They aren't wolves. They're just humans with a fur coat."

"Are we to die for the Pack?" Ellie asked. "Or because a dog wants it? Prove you're our Numitor, Jack. Take me as your mate—name any wolf as it—and we'll follow you to Surtr's door. He's a dog. Love him if you want, but he's not pack. Not really."

Jack looked around as wolves nodded and looked at him expectantly for the excuse they needed to do the right thing. They'd just given him the excuse he needed to do the necessary thing, and Gregor waited expectantly for his brother to seal his position as Numitor.

"Danny doesn't make my decisions for me. I lead the Pack," Jack said. Then he spat on the floor. "But he is my mate, my Pack. If you don't like it, then rot down here with the prophets."

He was a fool, Gregor thought with frustration as Jack turned his back on the Pack and stalked over to the Sannock, but it was the first time he'd ever admired his brother. Their da had raised them to put the Pack above everything, and here they both were—idiots in love with the impossible choice.

"I told you it's a deal," Jack said to the horned Sannock. "So let's go. The Sannock and Scottish wolves hunt together for the first and the last time."

Gregor squeezed Nick's hand again and then let go. "I hope you can keep up."

The Sannock tilted his head and gave Gregor an unreadable look. "Not the first."

It raised its hand and flexed its fingers. As it closed them, a spear was already there, ice-caked and thrust headfirst into the ground. The smell of the Wild, air so fresh it felt like it had never seen the inside of someone's lungs, bloomed in the dank concrete slaughterhouse as the Sannock wrenched the spear free.

The blade was chipped obsidian, black and glossy, and the shaft just plain wood. It wasn't ornate or enchanted, just a very old thing that belonged in the Wild.

"You know the way, murder-bird," the Sannock said as he raised the spear. His arm tensed as though there were something heavy caught around the chipped blade. The air *creased* around it and then parted in a long, rippled sheet, and the Wild poured around them. "Lead the way."

This time the change wasn't a choice. Nick and the bird both cried out in pain as the Wild remade them to its design and tossed it into the air. Its scream was a harsh rasp of indignation, and it flapped it wings frantically as it took flight.

Chapter Twenty-Five—Jack

THE EDGE of the bird's wing clipped Jack's cheekbone, the impact of it hard enough to sting. He hadn't realized it was so close, hadn't seen it. He dodged backward to avoid another blow and absently touched his cheek. His eye, where it had been, throbbed with a dull, hot ache spread back into his skull. He could smell his own blood, taste it caught in the back of his throat.

It would heal. If Jack lived long enough.

The carrion god shot up toward the high ceiling, and angry croaks trailed behind him. But it wasn't the smooth, cast concrete of the humans' bunker anymore. Now it was the vaulted roof of a huge cave, strung with stalagmites and limned with streaks of soot and salt, that he swooped around.

The gray bloody walls had ceded the space to rough rock, painted with strong ochre lines half lit by the glow from the bonefire's embers. Blood still stained the uneven floor, but it was old and dried out. The dead were left behind, but the skins the prophets had worn lay spread out on the stone—whole again, lush and clean. Whatever the prophets thought they'd gained from their treachery, the Wild had chosen what belonged to it.

Jack took a deep breath. The air was so fresh that he thought it might never have seen the inside of someone else's lungs before. He could have used it to try and rally his wolves, but there was a bitter knot in his throat that wouldn't give way. Let them do what they wanted. He was done trying to be what they wanted.

The carrion god screeched and swooped down from the ceiling. It skimmed over their heads close enough that Jack could smell the odd sweet-and-salt smell of its feathers as they brushed his head and disappeared through the twisted fracture that was the mouth of the cave.

Jack pulled his wolf up from under his skin and went after the bird as soon as his feet hit the uneven floor of the cave. He squeezed his heavy shoulders through the crack and heard Gregor curse as he got stuck behind Jack's tail. It didn't take long to lose the bird in the narrow, switchback tunnel, but he could feel a tickle of fresh air on his nose, so he followed that.

He scrambled up a bank of shale at the end of it, gravel sharp as it dug under his toes, and out into the frozen, snow-blind maw of a storm. Ice pinched at his nose, and snow crusted in his ears as the wind slammed into him. The raw socket of his eye felt like it had cracked as the cold seeped into his bones.

Even a wolf could shudder at this Winter.

Gregor grabbed a handful of Jack's fur and dragged himself up out of the cave. He tightened his grip as the wind hit him with spiteful force, and he hunched down to brace himself against Jack's shoulder. For the first time in his life he was glad of his brother's company.

"Where's Nick?" Gregor asked. He had to stop and cough, hunched over, his free hand braced against his side as the air got into his lungs. When he was done, he rested his head against Jack's, his confession for Jack's ears only. "If I'm the one who can't keep up, leave me."

Jack growled at him but didn't shrug him off. He could smell blood and exhaustion on Gregor, the stale chemical stink of spent adrenaline. Even without his wolf, Gregor would run until he dropped… but he'd already tapped his reserves. There wasn't much left.

A flick of Jack's ear signaled his agreement as he turned his head away. If Gregor fell behind, Jack would let him… but if they lived, he'd come back. The only people his brother had ever loved were Nick and his dead daughter, so he deserved the chance to at least hold this child.

To rest with them if that was all he could offer.

Danny scrambled out of the cave, ungainly and graceless. His front paws scraped the rock, and Gregor grabbed him by the scruff to drag him the rest of the way out.

The Sannock were next, boneless and graceful as they slid out of the hole. They had dirt in their hair and scrapes on their hands. It didn't make them any less strange, any less *other*. Nothing else followed them out of the cave.

Jack sagged. He'd thought some of the Pack would follow, from the habit of loyalty if nothing else. But they'd had too much asked of them, from his dog to the Sannock. The Wolf Winter was meant to be their triumph, not their undoing. Maybe it was best that Jack wouldn't be remembered in the catechism—king for a day and then packless.

Before he could slide too far into self-pity, the dog bumped against him, all rangy muscle and bony shoulders. It laid its head over Jack's shoulders in reassurance, and Jack remembered he *had* a pack. A bird, a dog, and his brother—but they were his.

"Pick your path, wolf king," the horned Sannock said. "Pick up the thread, never mind the blood, and pull your fate to you."

The bird dipped out of the storm overhead. Its wings were rimed with frost, threads of it spread over black pinions like lacework, and it cracked on its beak as he croaked at them. It turned on one weighted wing, buffeted by the wind, and headed toward the frozen sea of the moors.

The dog lifted his head off Jack and focused on the bird, ears pricked forward as though it were prey. The side of its face was still bloody, half-frozen and raw, but it ignored that as it bolted after the bird. The big gray dog plunged over the lip of the hill and skidded down through the shale and snow, his momentum all that kept him on his feet and aimed at the right one.

"Not going to be shown up by a dog," Gregor said dourly as he pushed himself up straight. He flashed Jack a shadow of his old, challenging smirk. "Last hunt, brother. Let's see who's best."

He followed Danny down the hill, nearly on his ass as he slid down, one misstep away from a fall. His boots kicked deep muddy furrows in the virgin sheet of untouched white. Jack tensed to lunge after him—old habits and older instincts—and then hesitated as he remembered the Sannock. Before he could check on them, they surged past him and ran over Gregor's trail, gleeful as malicious children as they kicked stones and trampled the brittle leaves of frozen heather underfoot.

The Sannock had been tragic and dead, but even in memorial, no one had ever claimed they were nice.

Jack chased after them and growled to himself in annoyance at being last. The wind yanked at his ears and tweaked his tail as he dodged through the Sannock's legs. It buffeted him roughly, a rude shove that banged his shoulder against a rock or rolled the snow away from under his feet.

Overhead the bird pitched and rolled on the wind. Its wings battered the air, wrenched and awkward as it tried to make headway.

Did the Wild agree with the rest of the Pack that they should let Fenrir rise, no matter how? Jack's head ached at the thought, but he roughly pushed it away. He didn't serve the Wild any more than it served him. If it wanted to stop him, it would have to do worse than a breeze.

Maybe it didn't want to. The closer Jack got to the bottom of the hill, the more the push and pull of the Wild felt less angry and more… impatient. It reminded Jack of sleepy mornings and the clip of his da's hand around his ear to hurry him on down to the ferry.

The memory made Jack's heart rattle painfully against his ribs as he sucked in his breath. He let it ache as he reached the bottom of the hill. It felt right to mourn here, even if he couldn't stop to do it.

The bird was already gone, tossed on the storm. It was the unsteady cross of his shadow they chased over the snow. The dog raced ahead on long, rangy legs, just a shadow of lean haunches and tail in the storm. For once, there wasn't any sense of joy in the long stretch of the lean body, just determination. At some point they slid out of the Sannocks' way, into the Wild and back into the world, where the snow was tinged with gray and the air was stale with use.

Jack pushed himself into a dead run and ignored the danger of the uneven ground underfoot. His lungs ached, swollen with the cold, and his muscles were hot and liquid as they stretched and pulled along his bones. The Wild pulsed through his veins, green and sharp as nettles, and stitched him back together—a cracked ankle as his paw plunged into a pothole, the burst blood vessels that spat blood up his throat and onto his tongue—so he could run.

He didn't have to stop. The thought itched through his head that he'd never have to stop, he could just let the Wild have him. A distant howl caught his ear. Twisted on the wind, it almost sounded like one of his wolves. Like home. He could stay here, where it didn't matter if the world ended in blood, fire, and ice. The Wild had existed once and so it always would. The wolf could stay and hunt, chase endless prey whose meat was so clean it was almost candied. Forever.

Jack sucked in a lungful of air. Snow melted on his tongue, and the cold was sharp and seasoned with Danny. Layered under the sweat-and-hair smell of the dog, Jack could taste Danny's clean, familiar smell. If he stayed in the Wild, Danny couldn't stay with him.

That wasn't a choice at all.

Jack powered up a steep hill and caught up with an exhausted Danny at the top. He stumbled to a stop and stared down at the line of prophets and monsters as they struggled into the storm. The wind that was at Jack's tail, under his feet, had shifted to be in their faces. They hunched down and huddled together against the cold as the wind pried at their stolen hides and pinched their noses. Patchwork wolves loped along beside monsters with chill-blistered skins and blackened extremities. Some of the wolves, their fur matted and hides full of rotted holes, were hard to tell from the monsters.

In the middle of the group, Rose stumbled grimly along, her arms folded under her swollen, bloodstained stomach as though it might tear away from her ribs if it slipped. A hunched figure sloped along beside her, wrapped in dog hides tied with dirty lengths of string around wrists and over a barrel chest. The figure staggered in the snow and fell with a thud to the ground. A length of the twine slipped out of Rose's fingers, and she cursed a sharp, foul retort.

The thing on the ground rolled away from her and scrambled onto all fours. It struck out at one of the prophets with a clawed hand—paw?—and tore the woman's stomach out in one wet handful. Blood splattered the snow a shocking red, and the figure shouldered the woman out of the way as he made a dash for freedom.

He ran like a bear, a lumbering shuffle that covered more ground than you'd expect as he charged into the storm. The mishmash of hides tied around him flapped raggedly in the wind as he ran—a flayed leg, a dry bush of a tail, an ear that had always torn loose from its moorings.

Lachlan tackled the man before he could get away, and they crashed into the snow in a tangle of limbs and stolen skins. They snarled as they punched and kicked at each other. The hide-covered man came out on top, with Lachlan pinned to the ground by the shoulders, his thick cable sweater torn to rags as the drool dripped onto his face from the man's snarl. Just before Lachlan lost his nose, Rose grabbed the loose end of the twine from the ground.

She yanked, and the man came to heel.

The roughly tied hides had bagged and torn in the shuffle. Under them, blood smeared the man's body in thick, clotted streaks that had dried into scabs on his thick hair. It didn't quite hide the old blue-black rank marks that curled over his shoulders and circled thick thighs.

Jack took a shocked breath of cold air, and it cramped in his chest. His ribs squeezed in around the weight of recognition as though that might contain the pain. It was Gregor who managed to put it into words.

"It's Da," he said. "What the fuck has she done to the Old Man?"

As if he'd heard them, the Old Man snarled and scraped at the thick, pale leather collar that dug into his throat. His nails tore open old sores and dug new ones into the blotched, irritated skin. Rose yanked on the lead again and then winced. She reached under her coat and pressed her hand to her stomach.

"Look at that," she crooned as she pulled her coat open. Her stomach hung, bruised and stretched until it was ready to tear, in a heavy fold over her hipbones. She rubbed it with her hand as though she were a real mother instead of an old monster who'd slit her own grandson open. Then she dug her finger and thumb down into the loose skin to pinch at whatever was in there and make it squirm. "The baby wants to meet his da."

The Old Man snarled at her. It didn't sound like him. The sound was too deep, too... *big* to come from him. It felt more like something else was behind him and snarled through his mouth.

Lachlan scrambled to his feet. His torso was raw, and great swatches of skin had peeled off to reveal raw meat and muscle underneath. He scraped snow from the nape of his neck and spat at the Old Man.

"We should kill him now," he said. "He's just slowing us down."

Jack tensed and glanced behind him. They had left the Sannock behind, shadows in the snow. It wouldn't take them long to catch up, but it might be too long for Da.

"I wanted you to choose this," Rose said tiredly. Then she kicked the Old Man in the face with a booted foot, hard enough to snap his head back. Jack heard Gregor's low growl. He reached out and grabbed his shoulder to hold him in place. "But you are still a stubborn, stupid bastard, so we'll do it the hard way."

She wrapped the lead around her hand. The knots in it dug into her flesh, and she hauled Da to his feet. He choked on the collar, and it was the dog who snarled—a quiet, angry sound in the back of his throat. Of them all, it was the one who'd spent time on Rose's leash. Jack growled back at it.

"Wait," he said.

"Since when do I obey you?" Gregor growled, although for once, the anger in his voice wasn't for Jack.

The Sannock reached the hill and stepped out of the storm, their hair frosted into elflocks and sharp, unsettling smiles on their mouths. It seemed strange to hear the snow crunch under their feet. The horned Sannock bent his head, and daggers of ice dripped from its antlers like a crown.

"We're too late," it said. "Fenrir cannot be put back to sleep."

"That's why we don't let her wake him," Jack said.

The Sannock's chuckle was a mean squeeze of humor. "Once it's done, it can't be undone. A throat slit can't be sealed back up by regret, and the bitch has none anyhow. She's ready to split, and the end of the world will hasten with what spills out of her."

Jack glanced at Rose's belly. The Sannock might have meant that literally. She'd strapped her belly up with strips of badly cured leather, but blood seeped through in dark, crusted stains. Whatever was in there wouldn't come out peacefully.

"We came this far. I'm not going back without blood in my throat," Jack said. He glanced at Gregor and, for the first time, didn't see his own face. "We get to Rose. That's all that matters."

It wasn't a plan. There was no point. The Sannock evened the odds a bit, but not enough. They might get to Rose, but they wouldn't go home.

Gregor knew that too. He nodded grimly and then looked up, to pick out Nick's dark shape through the dense clouds—the closest to a goodbye they might get.

At least Jack had Danny here, part of him, at least. He pulled the dog into a rough hug and buried his face in its fur as it panted and leaned into him. It licked his face with a wet swipe that drenched his ear.

"You need to take the baby back to Bron," he told the dog. "I need you to promise."

The dog pulled back and leveled a steady look at Jack. There was more humanity in its gaze than there usually was, the complexity of grief and understanding. It nodded and then butted its head under Jack's arm as the dog took control again.

There was no more time. Jack turned to the Sannock. He didn't know them, and he couldn't trust them, but he still had to use them. They were all he had.

"I assume you know how to fuck up wolves without a how-to," he said.

A pale Sannock smiled. Her teeth were nearly translucent, matching her floating hair, and something black and awful wriggled with interest behind her lips.

"Yes," she said without opening her mouth. Her voice was beautiful. "That we can do. I will not even add a tally to your debt."

Jack snorted. "I think we've paid enough."

She gave him a flat look, and the smile slid from her face. Her beautiful voice was full of venom as she said, "Never."

It would have been a better threat if Jack saw any way out. He shrugged the wolf back on, the clarity of it welcome as fur and focus settled over him. The Wild surged around them and the storm with it, snow so thick it was like a curtain, and the dull thud of hailstones as they dented the ground.

Jack ran between them… most of them. He could feel the dull heat of a bruise under his skin and the itch of blood in his ear where one had caught him, but it would pass.

The Sannock caught up with him and then past him. The first prophet they reached died without a sound. His eyes were wide and surprised, the last thing he saw a smiling, gray-toothed woman who tore his throat out with a hook on the way past. His blood spilled out on the ground, and Jack ran through it.

Another prophet fell, but not in silence. He had time to yelp, and the element of surprise was lost. Jack grimaced, lips drawn back from his teeth, as they yelled and cursed in confusion. He lunged at a shadow in the snow and slammed into one of Rose's monsters. It staggered backward, caught off-balance, and Jack sank his teeth into its front leg. The infection-bitter taste of its blood filled his mouth. He bit down to the bone and clamped on until he could feel the muscles strain against their moorings in his jaw. The bone snapped and he shook his head to shred the flesh that held it in place.

The monster howled and toppled over to writhe in the snow as its leg gave way. It would heal, but not in time. Jack dodged the snap of its jaws and ran past it. The baying of the dogs spun around the hill, and the Sannock howled with surprise as they rediscovered pain. Out of the corner of his eye, as Jack got to his feet, he saw Gregor stagger as the prophets harried him.

A harsh caw sounded from above, and the bird dropped down. It hooked its beak into a seam in the prophet's skin and tore away a thick layer of wolf.... Gregor laughed raggedly in satisfaction as the bird swooped away with its prize and the prophet choked back to humanity.

"So you brought your brother after all, Gregor," Rose yelled, her voice cracked and raw. "A shame it's too late. I found another way, and I don't need you anymore. But kill him anyhow. Maybe I'll give you a wolf just to be kind."

Jack curled his lip. He'd spent his life with one eye on his brother for betrayal, and Rose thought he'd be shocked at the idea Gregor couldn't be trusted? That was the baseline of their relationship. He knew this wasn't a trap despite that distrust, because the only thing deeper in Gregor than his mean streak was his pride. Gregor would doubtless do a lot to get his wolf back, to be able to challenge Jack again on equal footing again, but he wouldn't accept help.

All her taunt had done was help him narrow in on her location. Jack followed her voice through the snow.

He didn't even see the blow coming. It caught him on his blind side and slammed him into a low, rough-edged rock. The stone dug into his ribs—he felt the pop before he felt the pain—and knocked the breath out of him. He tried to suck in a breath or struggle to his feet, but he couldn't do either just yet. His ears rang with a sharp, precise note....

Lachlan walked out of the snow. Blood coated his stomach and dripped down his thighs from the raw patches of skin on his stomach.

"Your dog taught me something," Lachlan said as he reached the crowbar over his head. Slick muscle moved visibly under his skin. "What the fuck do I get out of a fair fight?"

He brought the crowbar down. Jack tried to move out of the way, but his body didn't want to cooperate.

Chapter Twenty-Six—Jack

His front leg snapped between the crowbar and the frozen ground. It stitched roughly together, but the crowbar was already back up over Lachlan's shoulder. Jack sucked in a breath—his lungs still tender from the recent thump—and braced himself.

The dog hit Lachlan in the back and knocked him forward. He stumbled over Jack and went face-first onto the stone. The dog snapped and snarled in his ear—what was left of it after it got shredded in the dog's teeth—while Lachlan gagged on his own blood and flailed blindly as he tried to get the dog off him.

Jack scrambled out from under Lachlan's feet and hesitated. He had to get to Rose and stop her. If he didn't, if she got her hooks into Fenrir, then it didn't matter how many of her monsters and traitors they killed. They'd lose.

But it was the dog. It was Danny.

Lachlan swung the crowbar blindly over his shoulder. The hooked end caught the dog on the shoulder and tore a wet, bloody gash through the gray hide. The dog whined at the pain but didn't scramble away. Instead it sank its teeth into Lachlan's shoulder and viciously shook its head as it tried to rip the tendon and bone out of its moorings. Lachlan howled at the pain and dropped the crowbar so he could reach back and grab the dog by the scruff.

It was *Danny*. If anything happened to him, Jack would have already lost.

He shot in and tore Lachlan's hamstrings out with his teeth. The blood that spilled over his tongue tasted… thin and familiar. It tasted like Gregor the times Jack had pinned him down long enough to get his teeth into him, like Jack's own blood as it coated his throat after a punch to the face.

It made him retch in surprise and back off a step.

Lachlan screeched in rage as he dragged the dog off—strips of his shoulder still caught in the dog's jaws—and threw him aside. The dog rolled as he hit the ground and scrambled to his feet, his wiry coat matted with blood and a low, rattling snarl in his throat.

Dogs were useful to the Pack because they were likable. Happy things that enjoyed the collar and didn't upset the human world with reminders of the teeth and hunger that waited in the dark and the trees. They were tame creatures that wagged their tails and grinned happily if they liked you.

But that wasn't the dog that faced Lachlan and made him flinch back against the bloody pile of rocks. This was the dog that humans kept because *it* knew what waited in the dark, the loyal companion that chased off monsters while they slept and had forgotten how to run.

It was the dog that the Wild remembered, and maybe it wasn't so far off what Danny had always been.

Lachlan pressed his hand to his torn neck and inhaled nervously.

"Just a dog," he said, as if he needed to remind himself. He spat at it. "The Wild knew it didn't want you when your ma squeezed you out…."

The dog took a stiff-legged step forward and gave Jack an impatient sidelong glance. It knew what Jack should be doing too.

Even without Danny's shape, Jack could hear his voice in the back of his head, *I can take care of myself. Go.*

Jack didn't want to—he *needed* to believe Danny knew that—but he did it anyhow. He was the Numitor, and he had a duty… at least until what was left of his pack rejected him. After that, he'd find Danny… one way or another.

He snarled at Lachlan with an old, familiar threat in his throat and left them to their fight. Monsters and Sannock stumbled out of the near-whiteout snow around him as they tore at each other, bloodied and muddied and gone again. The ghost hounds blew through on the storm, all wind-sketched ears and bloody maws as they harried anyone they came across. Jack could hear them above him, howls shredded on the wind, as they hunted the bird.

The one person Jack didn't need to look for was Gregor. He might not know where his brother was, but they were both headed in the same direction.

Da found them first. He hit Jack shoulder first out of the storm and bowled him over like a pup, ears over tail in the snow. It was so like the games they'd played years ago that Jack was paralyzed for a second as his brain tried to make sense of it.

If Da remembered the same thing, it didn't give him pause. He wrapped his hands around Jack's long, narrow head and squeezed.

Gregor saved him. Again. He hooked his arm around the Old Man's throat and throttled him until he let go of Jack to deal with the new threat. As he scrambled back to his feet, Jack groggily made a note to himself to tally who owed what and see who the loser was. He didn't want to die in debt to Gregor.

It was stupid, but the old habit of pettiness helped Jack focus. The end of the world might have slipped out of the wolves' control, the man he loved might or might not die at the teeth of a petty bully, and Da wasn't dead but a traitor—all of that was so big that Jack didn't know where to start. A lifetime of scorekeeping with his brother was just an instinct.

Jack ignored the dull ache in his head and joined the fight. He sank his teeth into Da's wrist as Da swung it at Gregor, and he grunted in shock as Da lifted him off his feet. His jaw ached as his weight dangled from it, the hot pulse of his da's blood on his tongue. Except it wasn't Da, not the one Jack knew. There was something… gone, new, different… about his scent and the *idea* of him in the Wild.

There wasn't time to put his paw on it as Da swung Jack around and smacked him against a tree. The coating of ice cracked and gouged into Jack's side. He grunted and lost his grip on Da's arm, but before Da could rally, Gregor slammed into him from the side and kicked Da's knee out from under him with the always surprisingly loud pop of a dislocation as the leg bent entirely the wrong way.

Da howled, wordless and frustrated, and went down to one knee. It wouldn't slow him down for long. His arm was already healed, the thick rents in the muscle stitched back together. His backhanded slap left Gregor sprawled and bloody in the snow.

"Da," Jack said, on his knees in the snow as he forced the wolf down. It didn't want to go, but for once, he didn't listen as he shoved it away. He needed to be human; he needed words. Jack crawled forward and reached out his hand. "Da, it's us. Stop. Let us help you."

The Old Man snarled at him with a broken nightmare of a mouth, his teeth broken and crowded with fangs. His eyes were all black and red rimmed, nearly buried under his heavy brows. His body was scratched with a lattice of scars under the filth, where his body had to leave the seams to move onto fresher injuries.

When Jack tried to reach for him again, Da snapped at him and tore a chunk out of the heel of Jack's hand. A rough collar around his neck pulled tight, and the inked leather dug into his skin as he strained against it.

"He's gone," Rose said. Her voice was unsteady as she limped out of the storm. The end of the leash was in her hand. Her stomach was blue from the cold, and something squirmed inside it, pushed against the thin, overworked skin. "I thought if I cut his wolf out, there'd be room, but it was still too tight. So I cut the man out too, a little bit at a time, to shove all the god in. It still spills out, slops over, and tries to slither back into its corpse. Stubborn bastards, man and god. I thought they'd be a good fit. But no, just to spite me, no."

She rapped her knuckles on the back of the Old Man's head. He cowered.

Jack stared at the collar and back along the leash. His life was lined up in ink-and-salt-darkened skin, strips of leather tied together in tight, stretched-to-unwinding knots. Fenrir was already awake, the Sannock had said, and bound with flesh like his father.

"You're right. It's your skin," Rose said as she jerked the lead to pull Da back to her side. Or whatever wore his skin, anyhow. "I peeled it off Lachlan's bones for this. It would have been better fresh, wet with your meat and blood, but your brother failed me. His regard for you outweighed his love for his wolf."

Gregor laughed harshly as he picked himself up from the roots of a tree.

"He's got nothing to do with this," he said. He glanced down Rose's body, then grimaced uncomfortably as he dragged his eyes away. "You can't give me my wolf, old bitch. It's just some dead thing to hate me and rot on me. I wouldn't be a wolf, just another fucking monster, the same on the outside as you on the inside."

Rose's scarred mouth twisted angrily, and she yanked on her lead. The collar cut into the Old Man's throat, and he reluctantly shuffled backward as she reeled him in. "I would have spared you for my grandson's sake," she said. "But I can find him another wolf. Maybe Lachlan, once his skin grows back. He's not a skilled lover, but he's pathetically grateful."

Gregor curled his lip at her.

"You think we won't kill him because he's our da?" he asked as he edged to the side. "After what you've done to him, it's a mercy."

Jack scrambled to his feet and took the other flank. He shifted to the side to minimize the swathe of ground on his blind side.

Out of the corner of his eye, he saw one of the monsters charge toward them, bone claws dug deep into the frozen ground. It opened its mouth to roar, and a Sannock stapled it shut with a broken stick shoved through its jaw and up into the roof of its mouth. The monster's teeth snapped together on its tongue and punched through the pink muscle. Its eyes bulged out and blood oozed out of the corners as it squealed in shocked pain.

The Sannock dragged it back into the snow, into a shadowy diorama of alien shapes and howls.

"Oh no," Rose said, sickly surprise layered over her voice. "I don't care how this plays out. Betray him, little pups, or die at his teeth. Either will send him back to me."

She hauled back on the lead to pull the Old Man onto his knees. He choked on the bite of the collar and the snarl that wanted to escape his throat. Rose leaned down to press her lips against his ear. "Rip them the fuck apart and bring me their skins. I have a baby to birth."

The lead dropped from her fingers, and she stepped back. She gave them the finger and then stalked away. Two prophets scurried up to her, one of them with blood matted on his arms from clawed fingertips to elbows. Monsters loomed out of the snow after them, frost crusted like scabs on their battle. The prophets took Rose's arms and hurried her away between the monsters, who glowered at the wolves but backed up after their makers.

A snarl ripped from the Old Man's throat as he lunged forward.

"Da," Jack pled as he stepped back. His chest hurt. He didn't know if it was the cold or grief. "Please. I don't want to do this."

Split lips peeled back from broken teeth, and the Old Man lunged for him. Jack scrambled backward and banged into a tree that he'd forgotten he couldn't see on that side. He ducked as the Old Man swung a clumsy, clawed hand at his head. Hooked fingers dug into the bark of the tree and ripped a chunk out of it.

Jack scrambled out of the way, and Gregor grabbed him by the arm to haul him to his feet.

"It's not our da," Gregor said grimly as they backed away. "And you're not much fucking use without teeth, brother."

The back of Jack's neck burned. He reached around and felt splinters dug into the base of his skull. His fingers came away wet and bloody.

"What if she wants us to kill him?" he pointed out. "Maybe it's part of her plan."

Gregor made a sour sound in his throat and pulled away from Jack as the Old Man tore a thick branch off the tree and threw it at them. It arced between them and crashed into the ground in a spray of splinters and snow.

"You think we have a choice," Gregor asked as he shook the bark and ice from his hair. "If we want to get my baby back and put Rose down, we have to go through the Old Man. Better us than one of her monsters."

Jack laughed bitterly. "Keep the killing in the family?"

Gregor shrugged and stooped down to grab a sharp sliver of the broken branch. They both knew that was exactly what they had to do and that Gregor was right. Jack was more use with teeth. His wolf pushed at him in agreement, fur rough against the inside of his skin. It just didn't feel right, not without… saying something.

What, though? That Jack was Numitor despite what his father had decided, and he'd fucked it up for all the reasons the Old Man had banished him? That the Wolf Winter wasn't what any of them had expected. Or just that this wasn't *fair*?

Whatever was left of his da, wherever he was, Jack supposed he knew that.

Jack let the wolf out in an explosion of tawny fur and snarls as he lunged at the Old Man. He ripped chunks out of the Old Man's heavy thighs and dodged the wild swing of heavy-knuckled fists. It didn't always work. A backhand caught Jack under the jaw and snapped it out of the joint with a jolt he felt all the way up into his skull. He staggered backward, and Gregor broke his chunk of branch across the small of the Old Man's back and then jammed a sharp, dagger-sized length of it up and under his ribs.

Pain made the Old Man stagger, his knees suddenly unreliable, and reach back to pluck the splinter out of his kidneys. His fingers closed around the bloody bit of wood as Gregor grabbed his wrist. There was too much muscle to bend it far, but he wrenched it as far as it would go. The joint visibly strained under the skin, tight and swollen, as Gregor threw his weight behind it.

Jack lunged in and ripped at the Old Man's heavy stomach. His teeth tore through skin and yellow fat down to the hard slabs of laid-down muscle. The raw weave of muscle tightened as Jack slashed at it with a physical pressure that he could feel against his teeth. Blood soaked his face, clotted in the thick ruff of hair around his throat. He tore a long strap of muscle from its moorings before the Old Man got a leg up and kicked him away. Jack skidded backward into the snow, his breath tight as his breastbone throbbed. A second later Gregor was sent after him and rolled head over heels. He landed badly on something buried in the snow and felt a bone snap with a loud, definite crack. The pain made Gregor try to squirm away from it, bent like a bow and with a curse caught in the back of his throat.

The Old Man threw his head back and roared in triumph.

Hail hammered down around them, balls of Ping-Pong-sized ice that bounced off rocks and dented trees. It caught Jack on the hips and back, impact dulled by thick fur, and rattled down onto the Old Man. The skin over his eyebrow was split, blood splattered down his face, and bruises showed up red and gray on his shoulders and arms. It didn't seem to bother him any more than the open wound on his stomach, where a bulge of pink intestine was visible through the shredded muscle.

Jack sucked in air—his already bruised lungs tight as the cold hit them—and threw himself forward. He didn't bother to look at Gregor to make sure they were on the same page. Either they were or they weren't, and there was no time to make another plan. Besides, it might not even make a difference.

The Old Man grabbed at him. He closed his fist around Jack's ear and yanked. Jack pulled free and sank his teeth into the thick, muscled forearm. He bore down until he felt his teeth grate against bone, and the Old Man swung him up in the air and then slammed him to the ground. The scattered hail dug into his side and skull. It was cold enough that it was almost comfortable. A heavy foot came down on his tail and jolted him into movement as Gregor tussled with their da over Jack's sprawled body. He dug his fingers into the Old Man's wounds and smashed his nose—again—with a short, brutal headbutt that rattled bone on bone.

Blood splattered them both, and the Old Man snarled as he sank his broken, sharpened teeth into Gregor's shoulder. His jaws worked, muscles thick as ropes under his skin, until Gregor's arm hung limp from shredded meat.

This time Jack took out the big muscle in the back of the Old Man's thigh. It squirmed under his teeth as he viciously shook his head to drag it out of the meat, and he was nearly crushed as the Old Man toppled back onto him.

They struggled on the ground for a moment, the Old Man's hands in Jack's mouth as he tried to yank his jaws to dislocation. Jack howled in pain as he felt the joint click out of true. Before the tendons could snap, Gregor hooked an arm around the Old Man's neck and yanked back until his throat was taut and bared for Jack's teeth.

Flesh tore open and blood spluttered out. The ground was already sodden, the white snow trodden into a mire. The Old Man gagged and dragged himself off Jack to scrape Gregor off against a tree. He lost a hamstring to that distraction.

Jack had seen Nick after a fight. The bird god in his head stitched him back together, quicker than a wolf sometimes, but not immediately. Humanity gave it a skin to walk the world in, but it cut its godhood too, like water in whiskey.

The Old Man had always healed fast, and he did it faster with whatever scraps of Fenrir Rose had shoved in there, but not instantly. All Jack and Gregor had to do was hurt him faster than he could undo it, bleed him until he dropped like a stag on the moors.

Then they could kill him.

Between the two of them, together or in turn, they wore him down bite by bruise. It cost them—and their bones took longer to heal—but they were willing to pay.

Eventually the Old Man staggered to his knees and didn't get up. He doubled over and wheezed like a half-dead horse, and blood and spit sprayed from his lips as he strained for breath. His guts lay in his lap in thick loops, and his bones showed through his skin.

"Do it," Gregor said. He staggered back, arm folded over his chest to clutch his ruined shoulder. When Jack hesitated, Gregor snarled in frustrated desperation. "He said you couldn't be Numitor. Prove him wrong. For fuck's sake, do it before he gets back up."

Jack limped over on three legs. He steeled himself to do what he had to. The Old Man snarled at him, mean as a beaten dog, and crawled away. He dragged himself through the mud of the fight, after Rose.

Before Jack could strike, Lachlan staggered out of the thick curtain of snow. His face was shredded, barely recognizable, and one hand dangled like so much chewed mince from a swollen wrist. He dragged a snarling dog with him under his arm, muzzle clamped shut with his good hand.

"Let him go," he yelled, his eyes swollen and clotted black under torn lids. "Go near him and I'll kill your fucking dog. Maybe I'll skin him, wear him like the prophets do their wolf. Would you like that?"

Jack curled his lip in silent answer. Out of the corner of his eye, he could see the Old Man drag himself farther away, but he couldn't take his eyes away from the strain of the dog's neck. It would only take a little more pressure to snap the bone, sever the spinal column. Like the rabbit that Jack had killed earlier.

"Let him go, Lachlan," Gregor said. "Fuck's sake, Lach, look around. The old bitch has left you to die here."

Lachlan grimaced around the ruin of his face. "She… she's gone to have our baby in peace, safe from you. We're going to rule the world together. Fuck being Numitor. I'll have sired a *god*."

The dog growled, noise strangled by the angle of its neck. Lachlan jerked roughly at its nose and it choked on its own blood, the tender scar on its face torn open again. It scraped the ground with its paws and tried to twist its head free. Jack lost sight of the Old Man as he took two quick steps forward.

"She's dried up like an old bit of jerky, you idiot," Gregor spat. "She's got a bitch's skin on that makes you sniff after her like she's in heat, but whatever she's going to pull out of that gut of hers isn't going to be a baby."

Lachlan gagged on his own laugh. "You're wrong," he said. "I saw her put it in."

Jack forgot about Danny as he realized what that meant. He dropped his head and whined in disgust at the image. It took a second for Gregor to catch up with him, but when he did, he roared in angry grief and went for Lachlan. Fear made a brief, understandable appearance on Lachlan's ruined face as his fingers tightened around the dog's nose. Before Lachlan could do anything, Jack got in Gregor's way and shouldered him back with a snarl.

If it would have done them any good, if it would have gotten the baby back, then maybe Jack would have sacrificed Danny. He knew it was what Danny would have wanted. So maybe, but not for nothing.

"The dog's already dead," Gregor spat as he tried to shove Jack out of the way. "Even Lachlan isn't going to fuck that up."

Overhead the bird's caw was a sharp, insistent sound that made Lachlan flinch and cast a quick, nervous glance at nothing. At most, at a shadow.

"Shut up. Shut up," he muttered as he shifted away. He dug his fingers into the dog's nose until his nails broke the skin. "I didn't do it. Leave me be. Bother them!"

He backhanded the hair with his ruined hand. Outlined by snow and blood, Jack saw a sketch of a girl. The brief glimpse of her profile was dark as loch water, and her expression was mean and pinched with anger.

Then the bloody snow drifted away and the faint lines of her were gone. Jack was left with the idea that she looked familiar, although he couldn't place her. Lachlan still could, or at least he knew she was there.

Someone groaned—a harsh, raw splutter of grief. Jack looked at Gregor first and then over at the Old Man. He'd stopped his slow crawl through the snow and stared at the space the girl had been, his battered face twisted with ugly intensity. It was bleak and angry, but for the first time, it was Da and not some angry beast that glowered out of those dark eyes.

"Da," Gregor said as he recognized it too.

The Old Man didn't look at either of them. His bloodshot eyes were focused on Lachlan, who shuddered and stepped away from the weight of that banked rage. The dog squirmed in his grip and kicked him. His nails raised welts on Lachlan's legs.

"I'll kill the dog!" Lachlan yelled, but his voice cracked, and he jerked his head away from something at his cheek. "I killed its ma, didn't I?"

The Old Man growled and dragged himself to his feet. He staggered as though something hooked into his shoulders was trying to pull him back.

"Not. Again," he ground out through his ruined teeth. "You won't. Betray us. Again."

Something gave at that idea—a wolf-god's centuries-old resentment toward his traitors, maybe—and the Old Man roared forward. Lachlan dropped the dog, who splayed out awkwardly as his paws hit the ground, and pulled a stained knife from the back of his jeans.

He sliced the Old Man's throat open down to the bone and then jammed the knife hilt-deep in his gut, through the torn muscle, and into the soft organs. His elbow pumped as he jabbed the knife in again and again.

The Old Man got his hands around Lachlan's throat, but he didn't squeeze. His battered fingers twitched weakly, and then he grunted softly as though it surprised him. He fell backward into the snow and cupped his hands over the ruin of his stomach.

No one moved. Lachlan looked more shocked than any of them, almost guilty as he stumbled back with his bloody hands held in front of him. The dog nudged the Old Man's fingers with its nose and then scrambled to its feet to snarl at Lachlan.

A newborn squalled, the sound drawn out like taffy by the wind, and the Old Man died.

Jack held his breath and waited, but that was it. He'd been wrong, he thought dully. The Wild didn't ring with Da's passing. He was gone, and there was meat where he'd been. Jack was truly the Numitor now. He could feel it in his bones.

Chapter Twenty-Seven—Danny

THE DOG felt sick and sorry for itself as it snarled at Lachlan. It hurt from its nose to its paws, the Old Man smelled like a dead thing—and that was wrong—and the stink of blood and screams from the fight made it flinch under its skin.

It wanted to run, but it stayed. For Jack, for Bron's pup.

Loyalty the dog could understand. The rest of this it would leave for Danny to make sense of.

Lachlan grinned at them, his teeth bloody in a face that hadn't worked out how to put itself back together.

"It's done," he said. "You're too late, Jack. Fenrir is born again in blood and in death. And I killed the Old Man. You all treated me like shit, like a dog, but I'm the one who put him down!"

The dog snarled and lunged for Lachlan. He flinched back in surprise from bared teeth and then jumped away from the chill touch of something the dog couldn't see. It was *there*. The dog knew that in the hackles over its shoulders, and so did Lachlan. They just couldn't see it. Lachlan spat at it and laughed as he staggered into the storm.

"You should have showed throat when you had the chance," he yelled over the howl of the storm. "Maybe Bron will. She was still alive when I left her. I should fix that."

The dog snarled furiously and charged after him. Jack shoulder-checked it off course, and Gregor grabbed it by the scruff of its neck and hauled it up onto its back legs.

"Leave him," Gregor snapped. "Lachlan doesn't matter anymore. We need to get to Rose, before she kills another fucking child. Bron's child. Mine."

The dog showed its teeth to Lachlan, so he knew, and backed, stiff-legged, away from him. It whined sadly as it passed the Old Man. Danny's feelings for the Numitor were complicated, but the dog's world had always been simpler. It could just do what Danny couldn't easily do—mourn.

Somewhere in the storm, the wind caught the threads of the child's thin, weak cry and tossed it to them. It caught at Danny's instincts with the knowledge that this was his kin, his sister's pup.

"Follow Rose," he said. "You're fast enough to catch her. We'll be behind you."

The dog didn't want to do it, but Gregor was right. It could run better than it could fight.

It gave Jack one quick, longing look and then took off after the not-dead Fenrir.

The cold was a two-edged sword as it ran. It numbed raw wounds but stiffened bones, dredged up the dregs of its last reserves, and pushed itself to go faster. It stumbled over a dead Sannock in the snow, human flesh torn apart to reveal lichen and stick bones underneath. The Sannock parts were already half dust, brittle and crumbling as the Wild fastidiously picked them out of the world. That meant something to Danny too, and the urgency of his thoughts was a distraction.

Something bad was going to happen. The dog could see the knots of Danny's thoughts as it pieced together, but it couldn't chase the trail down to the *why*. That didn't matter. It knew what mattered.

Bron's pup. Jack. Distance from the slaughter behind it.

The dog shook its head in annoyance. It would give Danny his skin back if what he thought was so important. Otherwise that part of it needed to let the dog be until this was done.

It didn't help. Danny's worry picked nervously at the edges of the dog's mind no matter how it tried to ignore it. On the snow ahead of it, a gray shadow, distorted by the wind and the dim moonlight, kept pace with him.

The reek of the place hit the dog's nose before it saw it—a low cairn stacked up on a hill, ringed by scrubby trees and gorse. Dead dogs flapped from trees like flags, flayed paws staked to the frozen trunks. The hackles on the back of the dog's neck stood on end as it felt something brush in and around it. Cold, not-there noses sniffed at its wounds, and teeth clicked silently—but he still knew—next to its ear. The dog swallowed the whine in its throat, clamped its tail between its legs, and sidled closer.

Rose lay on top of the stones. Her scrawny legs were spread, another hide laid over her thighs and groin. It was filthy with blood. The few prophets she had left gathered around and chanted guttural prayers as they rubbed grease over her stomach and up along her scarred thighs.

Under the draped hide the baby squalled, and Rose braced both hands on her swollen stomach and pushed down.

Fresh blood spilled into the stone, and the baby slipped after it, into the greasy hands of a prophet. Bron's pup, small, blind, and red as a skinned rabbit as the prophet passed it to Rose. She laid it on her breast, and it squalled as it turned its screwed-up face away from the slack nipple presented.

Something else squirmed and wriggled in her stomach. It didn't need any encouragement to find its way out as it clawed at the thin membrane that wrapped around it. Rose grimaced at the pain and clutched the baby to her chest. She thrust her hand into her old stomach and hauled out a wet, unfinished thing that was all bones and spider limbs. It opened its mouth and croaked a tea-kettle hiss through razor-sharp teeth.

She gave it a hard shake and tossed the thing at one of the prophets. With Bron's baby clutched in one arm, she scrambled up onto her feet.

The dog… *needed*… to understand the stale-penny stink of Danny's panic in its throat. It knew it was about the pup, and it had promised. *They'd* promised Bron. Kath.

If the Wild didn't like it, the Wild could fuck off.

Danny tumbled face-first into the snow. He scrambled to his feet and regretted it. The dog hurt but it didn't *think* about it, but Danny could feel the damage and work out how long it would take to heal… if it healed. He was a dog, not a wolf. With him, some things just patched back together good enough.

"It never works," Danny muttered to himself as he scraped snow from his eyes. "I was wrong. *New* isn't enough. *Wolf* isn't enough. It killed Nick, getting the bird stuffed in him."

The realization was still all knots and threads in his brain. He knew he had to stop Rose, but he hadn't picked it apart to understand it yet. Or why he'd thought he'd do better—naked and half-blind in the storm—than the dog would. He staggered toward the hill anyhow, slowed down by the thick drifts that the dog had sailed over.

He remembered the taste of dead sheep on his tongue and the long nights he'd spent out with Hector during lambing season. Wolves were useless for that. The sheep would rather run off a cliff than come to a wolf's hand, so the dogs were always recruited. Sometimes lambs died or the sheep died giving birth, but there was a trick to get a bereaved sheep to accept an orphan lamb.

Just skin her dead lamb and dress the live one in it. The sheep would never know any better.

Wolves were smarter than sheep, smarter than the dog. Fenrir wasn't like Jack, though. He'd never been human, never learned how to lie or trick. Rose had dressed Lachlan in Jack's skin to fuck him, so she'd smell like the skin Fenrir wore. Then she'd skinned it back off the moron to make a leash for the wolf. Now she'd taken the Old Man's grandson, his blood and his bone to….

Danny cursed to himself and forced himself to run faster. He'd left Jack and Gregor behind, caught in the middle of a slaughter, and there wasn't time to wait for them to catch up. He'd promised to bring the baby home, but someone else would have to do that. If Danny didn't stop this, all they'd bring home was a corpse.

Probably.

Some wild flash of humor sparked through Danny's brain as he thought about how stupid he'd look if he was wrong. It probably wouldn't be for long, but it would be impressive.

Danny didn't bother to fight the prophets. He just flung himself between them and ignored the yank of urgent hands on his arms and the fingers in his hair. Rose's scarred face twisted in contempt when she saw him—there was a horrid, impossible beauty knit into that scarred corpse mask, but the thought of his mam's corpse dulled Danny's reaction to it—and she raised her hand to push him away.

He stooped to grab a rock that had rolled away from the cairn. It was round and smooth in his palm, and he straightened up to swing it in one smooth motion. It crushed her fingers and snapped her wrist at a weird angle. She swore at him for the indignity, and he caught her on the jaw on the backswing. It broke with a dramatic pop and knocked her backward onto the altar.

Danny dropped the rock, grabbed the baby from her loosened grip, and backed away. It didn't cry, but he soothed it anyhow as he looked around for a way out.

"The dog," Rose said, her voice slurred. She poked her jaw back into place with her fingers. "I should have expected it. Loyal as a cur and just as dumb."

Fear stuck in Danny's throat like nettles, and a bleak, awful fury backed up behind it. It felt like an allergic reaction, a physical response to the scarred old prophet that made Danny feel like he was about to throw up or have a heart attack. He wanted to run away. He wanted to peel her apart like a present in musical chairs, just tear off the stolen layers until all that was left was the bitter old bag whose voice he heard when Nick talked about his childhood.

"You killed my mother."

Rose's scarred lips twitched in a sour smile. "She killed me."

"If my mam had killed you, you'd be dead," Danny said flatly. One of the prophets grabbed for him, and he dodged away from the swollen hand. He knew the face under the dead wolf, the too-small eyes and too-wide mouth of a girl he'd grown up with. She'd never been particularly nice, but he wondered what she'd done that the Old Man had sent her for a prophet. He growled at her and backed away. "I won't let you have my sister's baby."

Rose leaned forward. Her stomach squelched as it folded around her knee. She tilted her head, and her eyes glittered. It was a look that sourly reminded Danny of Nick. "Are you sure that's him? Is that the *right* baby?"

Danny glanced down. It had been too early for the baby to come, and it had spent hours sweltered in Rose's curse-foul guts. Yellow-gray crud coated the pale, bluish body like grease, and it had a jellyfish translucency to it. Danny could practically see its heartbeat through its skin. The wean wouldn't win any prizes, but it was a baby.

The other—

He glanced at what the prophet held roughly by the back of the neck. It looked the same, the rough edges of inhumanity rubbed down from instinct. Danny fumbled the baby he did have as he tried to convince himself that Rose hadn't exchanged babies in the minute it had taken him to reach her.

She hadn't.

She couldn't.

It was possible.

Danny glanced down at the little thing in his arms and tried to see something of Bron in it. When he couldn't—his little sister had always been bonny, no matter what a goblin she could be—he tightened his grip on it anyhow. Whatever it was, it was new and soft and had no idea why anyone wouldn't love it. It moved weakly against his chest.

Dogs weren't that bright either, after all, and a puppy didn't even need to smell like them for them to take it in. It didn't even need to be the same species.

"Go fuck yourself," Danny said harshly. It was satisfying to finally get to spit it the words in her face after days spent in Girvan stuffed unwillingly into his fur. His throat ached with the memory of the too-tight collar. "Maybe I can't stop you, but I'll kill him myself before I let you touch him."

"Liar," Rose mouthed at him. Then she glanced past Danny into the darkness of the storm and raised her voice. "Do you hear him? He's going to kill your son, my love. You'll be trapped again, because of some dog that doesn't know its place."

The reek washed over Danny. He retched, the sting of bile in his throat better than the greasy glue of sweet infection and old musk that filled his nose and stuck to his teeth. Danny tightened his grip on the baby and turned around. The shadow under the trees got its feet under it and rose, stiff and unsteady, onto its paws. Wolves were always bigger than people imagined, and the Scottish wolves bigger still. Jack and Gregor were dire wolves the size of ponies, so big that humans just didn't believe their eyes when they saw them.

The wolf that lowered its scabbed muzzle to sniff the air was the size of a Clydesdale. Its eyes were raw pits scabbed with ice and blood, and its lips were stitched with old, white scars.

It made a passable Fenrir, although Danny balked at the idea it was the real one. He didn't think he could deal with that, but this was just some old thing from the Wild. A long-dead wolf who—like the thing in the loch—had forgotten the actual boundaries of his body.

Danny had spent his whole life dealing with things bigger and meaner than him.

"It's not a child," he said as he backed away. "She made a changeling, some empty thing she stitched together from skin and old bones, a baby she dug up from some hole in the ground."

Fenrir snorted, his breath visible as it steamed in the cold air. It stank too, like sour milk and morning breath. The baby whimpered, and Fenrir turned his blind head toward it. He twitched a torn ear. Danny scrambled backward. He caught a glimpse of a prophet out of the corner of his eye and twisted to face the man. The baby's neck felt very small as he closed his hand around it.

"Get away from me, or I'll do it," he threatened desperately. "I'll kill him rather than let you have him."

He tried to sound like he meant it. He tried to mean it. His mam would have meant it. She'd have killed any of them before she let Rose use them. Danny just hoped that when he didn't do it, his sister would forgive him one day.

For a second, he thought he heard her voice—the shrill rasp of a howl that was never as piercing as she wanted no matter how she practiced—on the wind. It wasn't her. If Bron had come up from the loch, she'd have shamed the world into coming with her, but Danny thought maybe she would understand if he was weak.

The prophet spat at him, but he must have thought Danny sounded convincing enough. The scabby-hided man backed away a step.

Fenrir slammed into Danny from the side and knocked him flying. Stones and old sticks scraped at Danny's back and hips as he rolled. He tried to hunch around the baby to protect it from the impact. He slammed into an old tree, and the frozen paw of a dead dog draped over his shoulder. Out of the corner of his eye, he saw something in the snow—the outline of a fat Labrador in frost and leaves. It bristled at the wolf as it came closer, ears flat as it snarled and snapped. Fenrir swiped a paw through it when it got too close, and the wind pulled it apart.

There was no time to panic or hurt. Danny got his feet under him and shoved himself up. The baby sniffled, so at least it was alive. Fenrir heard it too, and his scarred lips wrinkled back from yellow, ax-sharp teeth as he growled.

"You were in the Old Man," Danny said. His back was pressed against the tree so hard that he could feel the bark. The reminder made Fenrir pause. "He knew me, he trusted *me*. Not the old hag."

Fenrir hesitated, and the growl died away in his throat. It was hard to read his face. He was a wolf, but the scars and his torn-out eyes twisted his expressions out of true. Rose swung her legs off the altar. Her stomach lay open, unzipped like a carrier bag, and she stuffed it with one of the dog hides to fill it up.

"The Old Man didn't want you," she said viciously. "No one's ever *wanted* you, wolf, no one but me. Now you're going to turn on me? Betray me? *Me*?! When I made you a home from my own womb? When I *bled* for you?"

Fenrir flinched like a beaten dog at the accusation. He pinned his ears flat and struck at Danny. His teeth were so close that they were all Danny could see, and then the black bird dropped out of the storm and slammed into the side of Fenrir's head.

Broad black wings battered at Fenrir's face while a carved white beak tore at the wolf's ears and cheeks. Gobbets of flesh were pecked out and discarded as blood filled the carved line in the bird's beak.

"Nick!" Rose howled in fury as she stood up. "You ungrateful little bastard!"

It would have been a good time to strike, but Danny didn't think he could muster much of a fight. So he grabbed the pale gold hide from the tree and yanked it off the spikes. The wind caught it and then it settled around the shape of a dog.

The Lab gave itself a shake to settle in, woofed happily, and threw itself at Fenrir with all the fury of a genial but very heavy dog pushed too far. Rose screamed at it, but the Wild slid away from her words. It was just an old woman's rage.

No matter how the Wild bent to meet the wolves' needs, at the end of the day, it had its own vision of how the world should be, an idea that it had stitched through onto the real world as the Winter spread white and old over the country.

The Wild thought dogs should run in packs, not answer to a wolf.

Danny could feel the thread that the Wild pierced through him—the old Lab's sorrow at her death and the memory of a pup fat and content against her belly. She wouldn't let this wolf have the squalling thing in Danny's arms.

"The skins," Danny yelled. He lunged past another prophet and yanked a collie's spotted fur off a gorse. The wind plucked it out of his hands, and he felt the collie's furious determination to see off a predator it understood, gene deep, would prey on its flock. "Get them loose."

The bird took half of Fenrir's ear with it as it pushed off his skull. It raked a prophet's face down to the bone with its talons and ripped a red, glossy setter skin off the nails that pinned it to an old fence post. It took off in the wrong direction, corrected itself in a tangle of legs and kicked-up snow, and dashed back into the fight with mad glee and unpredictable speed.

A spaniel. A shepherd. A dachshund that decided, in death, that it was finally the size it always believed it was—mongrels that had been pampered pets and ones that had been nearly as feral as wolves.

The prophets had killed a lot of dogs on their way here, and Rose hadn't entertained the idea that someone would cut their leashes. Free of whatever spells the prophets had chained them with, the dogs darted between Fenrir's feet and snapped at his tail. The monsters lumbered around in circles as the dogs, just hide and wind, disappeared into the storm.

Danny wrenched a curly-furred skin off an old rowan. Whatever dog it belonged to was already gone. The skin dangled limply from his fingers.

He turned, and Lachlan grabbed him by the throat. His face had healed, but not quite right. A drooping eyelid half obscured his glare as he slammed Danny back into the tree.

"Give me the baby," he snarled.

Danny kneed him in the balls. The man really never learned. Although to be fair, he knew how to take a punch. Lachlan hunched over as Danny's bony knee crushed his balls, but he didn't loosen his grip. His thumb crushed Danny's windpipe until the blood pulsed in Danny's ears and behind his eyes.

"You can fuck every wolf you meet," Lachlan said as he straightened back up. "It wouldn't change shit. You're still just a fucking dog."

The dachshund, badger-sized and hefty, tore Lachlan's calves open with icicle teeth. Its ears, half skin and half sheer fuck-off attitude, flapped as it locked on and shook its whole body. Lachlan swore as he threw Danny aside and turned to kick furiously at the snarling hound.

"Get the baby, you idiot," Rose yelled. "He matters more than your pride or your hamstrings."

Lachlan turned on her. His neck was red, the muscles in his scarred shoulders bunched as he stood in front of her. "You said you loved me! You promised me *everything*, and all I got was fucked."

Rose slapped him out of the way. The almost absentminded backhand laid Lachlan out in the snow.

"I lied." She stalked past him. "You don't matter at all."

Danny scrambled backward away from her. His shoulder had popped out of the socket when he hit the ground, and there wasn't time to push it back in. He glanced down at the baby. It looked cold, snow caught in its scant strands of hair, but when he pinched its leg, it screwed up its face and mewled weakly.

"I'm going to try," he promised it.

The dogs harried Rose as she stalked toward Danny. They snapped at her heels and nipped at her close-stitched hides, but they couldn't stop her. And the more dogs came after her, the fewer there were to distract Fenrir.

Danny cursed himself for a dog, because Lachlan was right. He'd gotten in over his head, made promises he couldn't keep, and now he was going to die.

Him and the baby.

Then Bron, just so she could come to find him and kick his ass.

"Give me the fucking baby," Rose snarled. She kicked Danny in the chest as he tried to get up and pushed him down into the snow. "Fucking Kathleen. Dog or bitch, all her whelps are a pain in my ass. I'm going to change *everything*, I'm going to rewrite the world, and all quail before murdering one child. I would kill them *all*, and when I'm a god, people will call it my tithe."

The bird dropped out of the sky and shed its feathers. Nick stepped forward. "Gran," he said, his hands held out. "Don't. Just stop. Maybe everyone is against you because you're wrong."

She sneered at him. "If your ma begging me not to kill her, the pup I squeezed between my own legs, didn't work, do you really think I care about this mongrel?"

Her heel dug into Danny's chest as she leaned down to pull the baby roughly out of his arms. Nick cursed her and grabbed for feathers again as he took off. He shot skyward as he cawed his anger in a rough, furious voice.

Danny cursed him for a coward as Rose straightened up with the baby in her arms. It clenched its fist and puled its displeasure. She ignored the thin little whimper as she spread her hand over its chest. Fur sprouted between her knuckles and crawled toward her wrist. Her fingernails thickened and darkened, blood at the quick, into claws that she dug into the baby's chest.

"For your mother's sake," she said, as blood dripped onto Danny's chest. "I won't make you watch."

The baby cried harder, shrill and breathy, as Rose squeezed it like a fruit.

Danny dragged in a wheezy breath through the pressure on his chest. There was one thing Rose was right about. He was his mother's son, and Kath had taught him one thing. If you can hurt them, do it.

He craned his head forward, pain all the way down between his shoulder blades, and sank his teeth into Rose's shin. His teeth were blunt and human, but that just meant he had to bite down harder.

Rose jumped in surprise and staggered backward. She caught herself, and her mouth twisted in mean satisfaction as she made an abrupt gesture at a prophet.

"Fine," she said. "If you want to watch, then you'll watch."

Torn hides littered the top of the hill. The dogs still snarled and tore at the monsters, but there were fewer of them. Fenrir snapped them up from the ground and shook the spirits out of their skins.

A prophet dragged Danny to his feet and hauled him over to watch as Rose laid the baby out on the old stone altar next to its fetch. She held her hand and someone put a wolf's fang in it. The tooth was longer than her hand, cracked and yellow, and she pressed the point of it to the baby's breastbone.

"I hope you burn," Danny said as he struggled against the hands holding him. "Burn like Surtr's candle, for years."

Rose snorted and dragged the fang down. "I'll bend him over too," she said. "After this, I'm done being ruled."

The Sannock blew in with the storm, bloody and light-footed, and the wolves came behind. Jack and Gregor were at the head of the Pack, but just behind them was a sleek, small wolf with sharp ears and rage-bristled fur.

Bron.

Danny sagged as his muscles turned to lead and exhaustion ached in his bones. It didn't matter. He still wanted to laugh. His sister was alive, and she'd brought the laggard wolves with her. If they told Bron to her face that they should help Rose, after the old bitch had gutted her and stolen her child, Danny would have paid to see that.

Rose wouldn't get to kill the baby, now. Danny could stop fighting.

Chapter Twenty-Eight—Gregor

Dead dogs didn't know their place. They snapped at Gregor's heels and jostled his shoulder for position in the fight. He growled and shoved through them. The bird shot overhead, close enough that Gregor felt wings skim his hair, and dive-bombed his bloody, scarred grandmother. It raked at her face and dragged talons over her skull, strings of coarse gray hair caught in the sharp, black hooks. She ducked twice and then grabbed Nick out of the air by a wing.

"You had your chance," she said as she drove the bloody tooth into the bird's throat. Feathers fluffed around the white spike as the bird strangled on its own voice. "I *had* a grandson."

She tossed the bird aside. It landed in a lump of ruffled, unruly feathers and flapped spasmodically as it tried to catch itself. All it managed to do was shovel snow over itself.

Gregor tasted his own heart, but he couldn't leave the fight yet. His son lay on the stone, bloody and blue, and for the first time, Gregor realized what it was like to love two things at once.

It hurt. He wasn't a fan.

Bron snarled as she raced by him, her ears pinned flat to her skull and teeth bared. She'd caught up with him in the snow, with what was left of the Pack shamed and silent at her heels. Only Ellie and James had refused to come to their senses, lost somewhere out there in the Wild or the Winter.

They'd live or they'd die. Gregor flicked a thin bone knife he'd taken from one of the fallen Sannock and opened a prophet from groin to collarbone. The wolf peeled back to expose slack, fish-belly skin, and Bron knocked the man down to rip his guts out through the hole. Two of the half-seen dogs piled in, teeth set in his ankles and wrists as they held him down.

Gregor leaped over them and raced for the altar. Out of the corner of his eye, he saw the tawny blur of his brother as he arrowed across the hill toward Fenrir. Frustration scraped at the inside of Gregor's skin at the unfairness of it, but he ignored the pulse of bile and spite in his gut. He couldn't fight Fenrir, not for long enough to be useful, and they weren't here for his pride.

He ducked around a monster, not quite quick enough to avoid a blow that numbed his already torn shoulder, and left the dogs to distract it behind him. Rose sneered at him and wiped the bloody fang on her breast before she lifted it, ready to bring it down onto the baby's chest. Bron screamed, a human sound in a wolf's throat, as Rose tightened her grip. Behind her, Danny sagged down so the prophet had to hold him up, and he swung up both legs to kick Rose in the back. She lurched forward, stomach split open against the carved edge of the altar, and screeched with absolute, unreasonable fury.

That was Danny-dog for you, Gregor thought with a flash of almost affection. He might not be a wolf, but he had never known when to quit. Gregor fully expected that, if it came to it, Danny would spit in Odin's only eye just to make a point.

Rose clutched her stomach closed with one hand as she pushed herself up off the stone. She swung around and grabbed Danny's face with her free hand. The raw meat that Lachlan had left of his face earlier split open as she squeezed.

"Your mother should have drowned you, the Old Man should have killed you, and Job should have torn out your throat," she snarled as she lifted him up. "But I am surrounded by incompetents and have to do everything myself."

Her hand tightened, knuckles white through leathery skin, and Danny's eyes bulged at the pain. He moaned, but the sound was muffled against her palm.

Gregor vaulted up onto the altar. Two babies lay on it, identical except for the blood, and he hesitated for a breath in surprise.

The smell of heather and blood was the first thing he'd smelled and the glimmer of the moon above the first thing he'd seen. That he should have been alone and that he wasn't—that was the first thing he'd known. The first irritant awareness of "the other" that would stay inside him, like grit that never made a pearl, for the rest of his life.

For the first time, Gregor wondered what his father had thought when he'd seen them, whether they'd been a curse or a blessing. He'd loved them well enough, but they were doomed to be at odds.

These two would be lucky enough to live that long, he supposed. He shelved the next question for later—how he felt—as he reached around and slit Rose's throat in one sure, practiced slash. He twisted the blade as it reached her ear and dragged it down, to be sure he got the big vein.

Blood gouted out of the wound and dripped from her stomach. Gregor pulled the knife back and punched it neatly into the base of her neck. He felt the blade snick through bone and the thick, grainy length of her spinal column. He yanked it back out and a pink, greasy-looking liquid seeped out and ran down her back.

Rose choked on her own blood, her voice garbled as it drowned in her throat. She went down on her knees and then pitched over onto her side. Her eyes, wild and white-rimmed, rolled as she tried to scrape back control. She clenched her jaw, the muscles bunched and rock hard under her skin, as she tried to move. All that happened was her little finger scraped the snow.

"No," she slurred out with a mouthful of blood. "No. I'm… a god."

Gregor jumped smoothly down off the altar and knelt next to her. He gently smoothed her hair back from her face. His fingers crazed over the scars, thick as cord and rougher, where she'd stitched herself back together. Whatever enchantment had been in the skin she'd stolen from the Sannock reached into his gut and squeezed it frantically with *lust/love/want/need.*

Everything wanted to live, even spells and skin.

Gregor let the itch of distraction sink down into the pit of his brain and set the point of the knife against her temple. The prophet shoved Danny aside and took a step forward. Then he changed his mind and fled into the darkness and the snow instead.

"This is for Nick," Gregor said as he braced her head on the other side with his free hand. "This is for his ma, your daughter. Maybe she'll rest now."

He slid the knife through into her brain and watched the fever fade from her eyes.

Dead she was still—unreasonably—compelling. The sort of corpse that got itself laid out in a glass coffin for passersby to grieve the loss, even though a small, cold part of Gregor could see she was all scars, wrinkles, and overstretched grafts.

Beautiful or ugly, it didn't matter. She wasn't Nick.

Gregor left the knife in Rose's brain—just in case—as he got up.

"You okay?" he asked Danny. When he got a nod, he waved his hand at the altar. "Take care of them. Please?"

Danny grimaced. "I haven't done great so far," he said bitterly as he levered himself up onto his knees. "If I were a wolf—"

"You're alive. They're alive," Gregor said flatly. "Dog or wolf, that's good enough for me."

He left Danny to mind the babies and looked around the fight for the black ball of the bird where it had fallen. Feathers were scattered in a wide circle in the snow. The bird lay in the middle of them, too black to be real and afloat on a red puddle of its own blood and ice.

The wolves had driven Fenrir back into a thin copse of frozen trees and had him at bay. His hide hung in dry, matted strips from his bones and blood coated his muzzle. They didn't need another wolf, and they definitely didn't need Gregor. He pushed through the scrapping prophets and dogs to get to the bird and scoop it up out of the slush. The head dangled, slack as an eel, and its wings draped over his hands. He could feel its warmth against his fingers and the slow stutter of its heart. It was still bleeding, slick and hot as it filled his palms. The feathers were so soft as he folded the bird's wings in and lifted it up to his chest.

"You don't get to die," Gregor told it roughly. "Not again. We won, Nick. It's all down but—"

"Gregor!" Danny yelled. "Watch out!"

The blow hit his back hard enough to knock the breath out of him. Gregor tried to force a breath into his lungs, but they wouldn't expand. He could feel them, slack and unresponsive behind his ribs. Then he felt snow, cold and wet, against his knees and realized his legs had gone from under him.

There was something cold and hard in his gut. He could feel his body shift around it. When he looked down, a frost-sheathed branch, shreds of skin caught on jagged spurs of ice, thrust out of his stomach. He touched it gingerly with his fingertips and jostled pain out of the wound to bleed through his body.

"That's for Rose," Lachlan's familiar voice scraped in his ear, rough fingers twisted into Gregor's hair. He dragged the makeshift weapon out slowly. "That's for every time you ignored me, every time your fucking brother picked that dog first. Now fuck off and die at last."

Lachlan shoved Gregor down into the snow and stalked past him toward Fenrir. He held his arms out like the statue of Jesus that Gregor vaguely remembered from assembly in the primary school Da had dragged him to.

"Take me!" Lachlan yelled. He dragged the broken branch, smeared with Gregor's blood, over his stomach to roughly carve it open. "Fenrir! Eat my wolf, wear my skin. Make me a god!"

He raked his stomach again, deep enough to make him grunt. Fenrir looked toward him, ears pricked with interest. Jack snarled and went for his throat and tore at the loose flap of skin. His teeth ripped deeply, but it didn't make much impact on Fenrir. The great wolf shook himself and slapped the heavy, tawny wolf away as though he were a terrier. He doggedly plowed through the wolves, ignoring their teeth and attempts to drag him down.

"I have been loyal," Lachlan said as he dropped the branch. "I did *everything* she asked. I deserve this. You *owe* me my reward."

Gregor hunched over the bird and rested his forehead against the thick breast feathers. His lungs still didn't want to work properly so he couldn't take a deep breath, but he inhaled what he could of the familiar dusty sweet scent. Nick had always smelled like that, even before the bird.

"I didn't see him," Danny apologized in his ear, a hand under his elbow. "Can you get up?"

"Probably," Gregor said. He straightened up and scowled at Danny. "I told you to stay with the babies."

Danny nodded. "Then Lachlan stabbed you in the back. They're safe. Bron has them."

Gregor glanced over at the altar. The small, black wolf glared at him with amber eyes as she stood over the two infants, her ears flat and head so low it was even with her shoulders. He gave her a slight inclination of his head and grabbed Danny's shoulder to lean on it.

"I asked you," he said as he stooped down to lay the bird on the chest of one of the dead monsters. "You will, won't you? They might as well be yours. Bron's your sister. Me and Jack are basically the same person. What difference is there?"

Danny grimaced. "They're *not* mine?" he said. "No matter how many problems it would solve for your pack."

"Your pack too," Gregor said. "Jack said. Come on, then."

Fenrir had reached Lachlan, who trembled and bled in front of him. Wolves hung off the dark, neglected hide like ticks as they bit and tore to try and bring him down. Jack picked himself from where he'd landed and loped back in to tear at Fenrir's back leg. The huge wolf ignored them all as he lowered his head and exhaled into Lachlan's face.

Piss ran down Lachlan's leg and stained the snow as he inhaled. His skin flushed over his muscles as though he were about to cook from the inside, and he trembled as power filled him.

"You keep Lachlan busy," Gregor said.

Danny snorted. "I've never won a fight with him."

"You still always got what you wanted," Gregor said. "And what you want is to keep him busy. Can you do it?"

"I guess I have to," Danny said grimly. "What are you going to do, Gregor?"

Gregor grinned. It felt tight and awful on his mouth. "Whatever the fuck I have to."

He gave Danny a shove toward Lachlan and broke into a jog toward Fenrir. His stomach ached with each step. It wouldn't have killed him—even now—but his body already had a bullet hole in his chest to stitch back together and tendons to stitch in his shoulder so he could use it.

There wasn't much left.

"Tell Nick this doesn't get him off the hook," he said, just in case one of the dead had an ear out. "He doesn't get to die yet."

Danny tackled Lachlan hard and sent them both flying into the snow. They landed against the roots of a tree, and Danny hammered his fist down into Lachlan's dazed face. His knuckles split as he broke Lachlan's nose and resplit his lips, the aim as much damage as possible before Lachlan recovered. Or Danny collapsed from exhaustion.

A monster, face half-covered with lichen that worked long fingers into its ears and up its nose, staggered into Gregor's path. He ducked under the clumsy swipe of its maul-like paw, and a dog—the skin of a great black hound draped over bones of snow and wind—slammed into the monster with a whistling, windy snarl and sank its teeth into its jowls.

A wolf went flying as Fenrir shook them off. He pinned Jack to the ground with one huge paw and snarled into his bloody, one-eyed face.

Gregor reached for the Wild. He had a full hunt's worth of it curdled under his skin, and letting it out made his bones rattle with it and his skull ache. The back of his face burned with the pressure as it ripped him apart in search of his wolf.

Maybe, he thought dully, this was for the best. He didn't know how the prophets lived with this every full moon as the Wild chewed their scars open and rubbed their faces in what it couldn't find.

This once he could bear it. He glanced around, hopeful for a last glimpse of Nick or a black wing against the sky. Nothing. Gregor supposed he shouldn't be surprised. The world had spent years not giving him what he wanted. Why change now?

Gregor took a deep breath, the cold like splinters in his lung, and threw himself forward. He slammed into Fenrir's shoulder, the full weight of his stocky frame barely enough to make the wolf grunt, grabbed a greasy, knotted hank of fur, and dragged him out of the world and into the Wild. Dragged them both.

Virgin snow crunched underfoot as Fenrir staggered at the sudden shift. He snarled and twisted around to snap at Gregor with sharp, jagged teeth. Gregor punched him on the nose and dragged himself in close enough to sink his teeth into the wound Jack had opened in Fenrir's neck. The meat was dry, mealy with age, and the jelly of thick blood that coated Gregor's tongue tasted like rotting apples and nails.

Gregor steeled himself against the urge to retch and swallowed the mouthful he'd torn free. It curdled as it hit his stomach, something so wrong his whole body wanted to puke it out, and Fenrir dragged them back into the World.

Danny was crouched in the snow, blood on his back and his arms, with the dead dogs clustered close around him. They snarled at Lachlan—whose eyes were wild and black with stolen power—as he stalked across the snow. Jack tore at a monster's throat with desperation as he tried to squirm free of its grip in time to reach his lover.

"Nice try," Gregor said as he reached up to grab Fenrir's ear, twist, and yank them back into the Wild.

Again.

Again.

Danny as he spat blood into the snow.

The oddly shaped bundles of branches that memorialized the fallen Sannock in the Wild, lashed together with strips of human sinew and stacked for a fire that might never come.

A glimpse of Nick, one hand cupped over the wound pierced between his ribs, as he dragged a bloody prophet out from under Bron's feet.

Again.

Again.

The thin, weak mewl of Gregor's son on the wind, the gray-blue stain of the cold on newborn skin as it squirmed.

The dead hounds at the horned Sannock's heels as they loped after Lachlan. The damned wolf, gray and choking on blood from his own lungs as he ran, and the wild bay of the new hunters on the wind.

Again.

Again.

It was Fenrir who gave up. His sides, ribs prominent through his staring coat, heaved, and his breath smoked from between his jagged, flesh-picked teeth. A long red tongue hung from his mouth, and his anger pushed at Gregor like the tide.

"You don't need a body to walk the world. Not you," Gregor said. He rested his forehead against Fenrir's. The stink of old meat and sweat wasn't as sweet as Nick's scent, but it mingled with it in Gregor's lungs. "You just want one, lonely old wolf. So take me."

Fenrir tried to recoil in confusion, but Gregor didn't let him go. He could taste the infection the prophets had left in his spirit when they cut his wolf out, the rot-hollowed cyst it had left.

Why?

The voice was the howl of the wind between trees, the gargle of blood in a throat as fangs bore down. Gregor stepped back and stared at Fenrir. He could feel the blood in his stomach, the ache in his chest as his heart slowed and struggled.

"Because you won't fuck off otherwise," Gregor said. "And you can't have my son."

Fenrir stared at him with blind, ruined eyes and waited. If Gregor hadn't been dying, he might have won that contest.

"Because it's the last thing I can do for them. The Pack has Jack, Jack will have my son, and my son will have them all to take care of him."

That only left Nick. Gregor didn't have a generous enough spirit to hope Nick would forget him or be better off without him. He'd survive, though. After this, Jack would feel guilty enough to take care of him.

But that wasn't enough for Fenrir. He waited, slabber thick on his jowls as he panted.

Finally, Gregor tipped his head back to look at the ice-blue sky and admitted bitterly, "I miss it," he said. "I was never made to be human."

Done.

Gregor set himself and waited. That had been Rose's mistake. She'd tried to stuff a god into a human skin and then pull the flaps back together, when there was obviously more room the other way around.

He felt Fenrir's teeth as they tore into him. The pain cracked his bones as the hot red darkness swallowed him down.

EPILOGUE

"ONLY ONE of them's real," Bron said. She braced her arms on her knees and watched with wary eyes as the babies rolled on the floor. "The other's just something Rose made."

Danny sat cross-legged on the floor. The Pack's old home was charred bricks and stones now, his grief burned down into the dirt. They had taken over the empty streets of Lochwinnoch while they licked their wounds and got ready to go down over the Wall.

"Do you think it knows that?" Danny asked. He picked up a blond, green-eyed baby and grinned at it. The baby scowled like Danny had embarrassed him, and tried to grab his glasses. "If they don't know, how can we?"

Bron snorted at him. "Maybe if *someone* had kept better track of them, we wouldn't need to wonder," she said. "How hard is it to keep two babies apart, Danny?"

He put the baby down and rubbed his jaw. He traced the scar that ran up to his eye, a rope of thick wax that might melt one day. It might not.

"I had a lot on my mind," he said. Then he chewed his lower lip, sighed, and asked, "If we knew… would you stay, Bron?"

She looked up from the twin blond babies and gave Danny a surprised look. Her eyebrows twitched toward her forehead.

"Fuck off, Danny," she said. "As long as it thinks it's real, who am I to burst its bubble? I was never going to stay, although I expected Mam to be the one who'd raise him. There's a whole world out there, Danny. You got to see it, why wouldn't I want to?"

Danny shrugged. "You always seemed happy here, I guess. Everyone knew I wanted to leave."

"I was," Bron said. She stood up and grabbed his old backpack from the chair. It dangled from her hand as she shrugged at Danny. "You don't have to be running from something to want to go somewhere else."

"Did you read that in a fortune cookie?" Danny asked as he unfolded himself from the ground.

"You know I don't read," Bron said. "It's bad for your eyes, and one of us being blind is bad enough."

They hugged tightly, desperately for a moment. Danny pressed his scarred face to her curls and swallowed hard.

"You know I love you, right?" he said.

Bron tightened her grip on him, dug her fingers into the muscles of his back, and then shoved him away with a snort.

"You've spent too much time with humans," she said. "You've gotten soft. Softer. We're family. I don't need to love you, just kill anyone who ever hurts you."

Danny leaned in quickly and dropped a kiss on her forehead. "I love you anyhow."

"Ugh." Bron wiped her forehead ostentatiously with the back of her hand. Then she threw herself back into a hug and squeezed him tight enough to make him grunt. "Just try not to do anything stupid now I won't be here to take care of you, okay? I'm leaving you with my kid and the other one. Don't let me down."

"I'll try not to," Danny said. "Mam would—"

Bron shook her head firmly and stepped back. She held up a hand to silence Danny and stepped back.

"No. Not yet," she said. Then she took a deep breath and changed the topic. "Are you sure Jack is okay with taking the kids? Him and Gregor—"

She trailed off with a shrug, a lifetime of enmity and one bright, shining moment of sacrifice too complicated to put into words.

"It's the last thing I do to piss him off," Jack answered for himself as he prowled in from the kitchen. He was shirtless, an old pair of jeans dragged up over his hips, and had a brace of scrawny pheasants dangling from his fingers. He'd been looking for Greer, the little boy still lost in the Wild, but that didn't stop him getting lunch too. "And thank him, which would also piss him off. He died to save us from what Rose or Lachlan would have made of Fenrir. The least I can do is feed his children."

"*One* of them is his," Bron corrected.

Jack shrugged as he dangled the pheasants over the babies. They crowed and groped with pudgy fingers at the brightly colored tail feathers. At the same moment, they shifted to puppies, fat and round and floppy-eared, and hopped on stumpy legs for a mouthful of down.

"They won't know that," he said. A grim expression narrowed his eye as he watched them, the other still empty and scarred. There was always a price, and the Wild didn't indulge regret. "Not until they have to."

He hung the pheasants from the fire and grabbed the pups by the scruff of their necks to pick them up. One got passed off to Danny, and they headed out into the street to see Bron off. It was still Winter, the Wolf Winter, whatever that meant now they knew the prophets had lied. Snow crunched underfoot and the cold had broken the streets and worked fissures into the walls. A black crackling storm brewed up in the mountains.

"What about the bird?" Bron asked. "Gregor's mate. Maybe he should have a say in what happens to them?"

She tapped one of the pups on the nose. It wriggled and bit her finger with needle-sharp teeth.

"No," Jack said flatly.

"No one's seen Nick, or the bird, since the fight," Danny said more diplomatically. "Without Gregor, maybe there was just nothing here for him. He's not a wolf or a dog. The only reason he came up here with us was to be with Gregor."

"He's not missed." Jack ignored Danny's scowl. "If he comes back, he's welcome for Gregor's sake. But we don't need any more reminders of Rose around here."

At the mention of her, he absently touched the scarred edge of his eye.

Bron shrugged. "He helped get my kid back," she said. "Whatever else he was, I'll always be grateful for that."

She stared at the two puppies and then shook her head.

"My kids," she corrected herself. "What the hell. People will be impressed I threw twins, as long as they don't ask too many questions."

She didn't hug Danny again, but she gripped his hand tightly.

"Be careful," he told her.

"Be happy," she said. Then she gave Jack a sharp, fierce grin. "Maybe I'll find Greer before you do. Be a hero."

Jack tilted his head back to aim his eye toward the horizon.

"I hope you do," he said. "I saw him a few days ago, but he's lost himself to the Wild. I don't think he knew me."

Bron hitched the bag up on her shoulder and headed out of town. She didn't have a coat with her, but wolves didn't care about the cold.

FENRIR RESTED his chin on his paws and let the window out of the Wild seal itself.

His chest ached with a knot of new human emotions that refused to wait their turn. Relief, a bright, pure pop of love, grief, fear—they demanded to be felt all at once and immediately. He stood up and stretched to give himself something to do, snow matted in the hair under his armpits and stomach.

The broken, dead thing that had crawled off the altar was gone. A wolf didn't think about what he'd been, or what he could be. It was the human who provided that anchor—the perspective to consider change. Now his fur was thick and ruddy, warmed by the pale, distant sun, and his bones fit under his skin again. Last time he'd looked in the stream before he took a drink, his eyes were bright green, the color of new grass.

He didn't remember what color they'd been before he was chained to wait for Winter. It was possible he never knew.

Fenrir shook himself and pulled the old, consuming hunger up from the pit of his gut. It made him ache too, but it was familiar, and it drowned out everything else. He'd hunt. He'd glut himself. He'd—

A sharp pain in his tail made him jump and spin around in a tight circle. He wrinkled his lips back from his teeth and let a warning growl trickle out of him, but there was nothing there. His ears flattened, and he looked around suspiciously.

The pinch made him jump again and spin around like a dog chasing its tail. Anger wasn't new. Fenrir had *basted* in anger during his long wait, but the sting of offended pride *was* new.

He grumbled at the empty snow and waited, his head half turned to watch the stretch of rocky hill out of the corner of his eye. There had been a pup he'd seen in the snow, lanky legs and more ears than it knew what to do with. It had scavenged his kill, and he'd turned a blind eye for… some reason the wolf couldn't pinpoint. Maybe that had been a mistake. A shadow flickered in the edge of his vision, and he spun around as the cheeky bastard pinched his tail. He snarled and snapped at the interloper.

The bird hopped backward, and then it was a man who danced away from Fenrir's teeth. A long black coat swirled around his legs as he skipped to the side. The man was tall and bony, with a crest of dark hair and a face that had more angles than seemed necessary. He had a wide, mischievous smile, and he was beautiful—so beautiful it hurt—and *here*.

"Nick," Fenrir said as he pulled his skin out from under the wolf. He hadn't done it before, but it was easy now he needed to do it. The human he'd been—was, part of—glared at the man in the dark coat. "You asshole. We didn't know what happened to you."

"And I knew what happened to you?" Nick asked, eyebrows raised. "They all think you're dead."

Fenrir scratched the back of his neck. He wanted… he *wanted.* The memory of Nick under him, salt-sweat flesh and sweet kisses caught in his gut like a stone. He'd never had that. The body the prophet had forced him into had fucked her, but it hadn't felt like the memory did. It hadn't mattered, every breath, every featherlight touch of clever fingers hadn't been something to store away and remember.

Yet….

"I am," he said. A glance down at himself showed long, tawny limbs and lean hips that were simultaneously new and familiar. His body and one he'd never worked before. "He is."

"Me too."

Nick jumped down off the rock and walked into Fenrir's arms. He cupped Fenrir's face in both hands, his touch gentle like the lean jaw and stubble was something precious, and leaned close enough to not quite kiss him.

"I found you," he said. "And I won't leave again."

Whatever shred of good intentions Fenrir had scraped together blew away like mist. He dragged Nick closer, until their bodies pressed together, and kissed him with desperate, hopeless hunger. He'd known he missed Nick—it had felt like an essential trait of the man he'd been—but it was only now he realized how deep that crack had run.

It felt like… everything.

He broke the kiss and rested his forehead against Nick's.

"I love the way you act like that's a choice," he growled as he pushed Nick down into the snow. The zippers and buttons of his clothes briefly confused him, but then his fingers remembered how they worked. Nick laughed under him and kissed his throat, his shoulder, and scraped sharp teeth over his collarbone in a bite. "You won't leave me again."

TA MOORE is a Northern Irish writer of romantic suspense, urban fantasy, and contemporary romance novels. A childhood in a rural seaside town fostered a suspicious nature, a love of mystery, and a streak of black humour a mile wide. As her grandmother always said, "She'd laugh at a bad thing, that one," mind you, that was the pot calling the kettle black. TA studied history, Irish mythology, and English at University, mostly because she has always loved a good story. She has worked as a journalist, a finance manager, and in the arts sectors before she finally gave in to a lifelong desire to write.

Coffee, Doc Marten boots, and good friends are the essential things in life. Spiders, mayo, and heels are to be avoided.

Website: www.nevertobetold.co.uk
Facebook: www.facebook.com/TA.Moores
Twitter: @tammy_moore

TA MOORE
DOG DAYS

A Wolf Winter Novel

The world ends not with a bang, but with a downpour. Tornadoes spin through the heart of London, New York cooks in a heat wave that melts tarmac, and Russia freezes under an ever-thickening layer of permafrost. People rally at first—organizing aid drops and evacuating populations—but the weather is only getting worse.

In Durham, mild-mannered academic Danny Fennick has battened down to sit out the storm. He grew up in the Scottish Highlands, so he's seen harsh winters before. Besides, he has an advantage. He's a werewolf. Or, to be precise, a weredog. Less impressive, but still useful.

Except the other werewolves don't believe this is any ordinary winter, and they're coming down over the Wall to mark their new territory. Including Danny's ex, Jack—the Crown Prince Pup of the Numitor's pack—and the prince's brother, who wants to kill him.

A wolf winter isn't white. It's red as blood.

TA MOORE
STONE THE CROWS

Sequel to *Dog Days*
A Wolf Winter Novel

When the Winter arrives, the Wolves will come down over the walls and eat little boys in their beds.

Doctor Nicholas Blake might still be afraid of the dark, but the monsters his grandmother tormented him with as a child aren't real.

Or so he thought…until the sea freezes, the country grinds to a halt under the snow, and he finds a half-dead man bleeding out while a dead woman watches. Now his nightmares impinge on his waking life, and the only one who knows what's going on is his unexpected patient.

For Gregor it's simple. The treacherous prophets mutilated him and stole his brother Jack, and he's going to kill them for it. Without his wolf, it might be difficult, but he'll be damned if anyone else gets to kill Jack—even if he has to enlist the help of his distractingly attractive, but very human, doctor.

Except maybe the prophets want something worse than death, and maybe Nick is less human than Gregor believes. As the dead gather and the old stories come true, the two men will need each other if they're going to rescue Jack and stop the prophets' plan to loose something more terrible than the wolf winter.

www.ingramcontent.com/pod-product-compliance
Lightning Source LLC
Chambersburg PA
CBHW050035030726
47506CB00001B/276
* 9 7 8 1 6 4 4 0 5 7 1 9 3 *